THE DUTCH SHOE MYSTERY

ELLERY QUEEN

Introduction by
OTTO PENZLER

**AMERICAN
MYSTERY
CLASSICS**

Penzler Publishers
New York

Published in 2019 by Penzler Publishers
58 Warren Street, New York, NY 10007
penzlerpublishers.com

Distributed by W. W. Norton

Cover image: Andy Ross
Cover design: Mauricio Diaz

Paperback ISBN 9781613161272
Hardcover ISBN 9781613161265
eBook ISBN 9781453289426

Library of Congress Control Number: 2018963377

Printed in the United States of America

9 8 7 6 5 4 3 2 1

THE DUTCH SHOE MYSTERY

ELLERY QUEEN was a pen name created and shared by two cousins, Frederic Dannay (1905-1982) and Manfred B. Lee (1905-1971), as well as the name of their most famous detective. Born in Brooklyn, they spent forty-two years writing the greatest puzzle mysteries of their time, gaining the duo a reputation as the foremost American authors of the Golden Age "fair play" mystery.

Although eventually famous on television and radio, Queen's first appearance came in 1928 when the cousins won a mystery-writing contest with the book that would eventually be published as *The Roman Hat Mystery*. Besides co-writing the Queen novels, Dannay founded *Ellery Queen's Mystery Magazine*, one of the most influential crime publications of all time. Although Dannay outlived his cousin by nine years, he retired the fictional Queen upon Lee's death.

OTTO PENZLER, the creator of American Mystery Classics, is also the founder of the Mysterious Press (1975), a literary crime imprint now associated with Grove/Atlantic; MysteriousPress.com (2011), an electronic-book publishing company; and New York City's Mysterious Bookshop (1979). He has won a Raven, the Ellery Queen Award, two Edgars (for the *Encyclopedia of Mystery and Detection*, 1977, and *The Lineup*, 2010), and lifetime achievement awards from NoirCon and *The Strand Magazine*. He has edited more than 70 anthologies and written extensively about mystery fiction.

THE DUTCH SHOE
MYSTERY

INTRODUCTION

OFTEN CALLED the Golden Age of the detective novel, the years between the two World Wars produced some of the most iconic names in the history of mystery. In England, the names Agatha Christie and Dorothy L. Sayers continue to resonate to the present day. In America, there is one name that towers above the rest, and that is Ellery Queen.

That famous name was the brainchild of two Brooklyn-born cousins, Frederic Dannay (born Daniel Nathan, he changed his name to Frederic as a tribute to Chopin, with Dannay merely a combination of the first two syllables of his birth name) and Manfred B. Lee (born Emanuel Lepofsky). They wanted a simple nom de plume and had the brilliant stroke of inspiration to employ Ellery Queen both as their byline and as the name of their protagonist, reckoning that readers might forget one or the other but not both.

Dannay was a copywriter and art director for an advertising agency while Lee was writing publicity and advertising material for a motion picture company when they were attracted by a $7,500 prize offered by *McClure's* magazine in 1928; they were twenty-three years old.

They were informed that their submission, *The Roman Hat Mystery*, had won the contest but, before the book could be published or the prize money handed over, *McClure's* went bankrupt. Its assets were assumed by *Smart Set* magazine, which gave the prize to a different novel that it thought would have greater appeal to women. Frederick A. Stokes decided to publish *The Roman Hat Mystery* anyway, thus beginning one of the most successful mystery series in the history of the genre. Almost immediately, the cousins' plan to brand the author and character under the same name paid off, and the Ellery Queen name gained an iconic status.

Although Dannay and Lee were lifelong collaborators on their novels and short stories, they had very different personalities and frequently disagreed, often vehemently, in what Lee once described as "a marriage made in hell." Dannay was a quiet, scholarly introvert, noted as a perfectionist. Lee was impulsive and assertive, given to explosiveness and earthy language. They remained steadfast in their refusal to divulge their working methodology, claiming that over their many years together they had tried every possible combination of their skills and talent to produce the best work they could. However, upon close examination of their letters and conversations with their friends and family, it eventually became clear that, in almost all instances, it was Dannay who created the extraordinary plots and Lee who brought them to life.

Each resented the other's ability, with Dannay once writing that he was aware that Lee regarded him as nothing more than "a clever contriver." Dannay's ingenious plots, fiendishly detailed with strict adherence to the notion of playing fair with readers, remain unrivaled by any American mystery author. Yet he did not have the literary skill to make characters plausible, settings visual, or dialogue resonant. Lee, on the other hand, with his dreams of writing important fiction, had no ability to invent stories, although he could improve his cousin's creations to make the characters come to life and the plots suspenseful and compelling.

The combined skills of the collaborators produced the memorable Ellery Queen figure, though in the early books he was clearly based on the best-selling Philo Vance character created by S.S. Van Dine. The Vance books had taken the country by storm in the 1920s so it was no great leap of imagination for Dannay and Lee to model their detective after him. In all candor, both Vance and the early Queen character were insufferable, showing off their supercilious attitude and pedantry at every possible opportunity.

When Queen makes his debut in *The Roman Hat Mystery*, he is ostensibly an author, though he spends precious little time working at his career. He appears to have unlimited time to collect books and help his father, Inspector Richard Queen, solve cases. Although close to his father, the arrogant young man is often condescending to him as he loves to show off his erudition. As the series progresses (and as the appetite for Philo Vance diminished), Ellery becomes a far more realistic and likable character.

One characteristic of the Queen novels is an opening situation in which a murder is committed that appears so confounding that it may be insoluble. If it weren't, the police would handle it and not have to bring Ellery Queen to the scene to help them figure out what happened, how it was achieved, and who did it.

In *The Dutch Shoe Mystery*, the third book in the series, the richest, most famous, and possibly most eccentric woman in America, Abby Doorn, suddenly goes into diabetic coma, falls down a flight of stairs, lands on her abdomen, and ruptures her gall bladder. She awaits surgery in the hospital she founded, where an operation will be performed by the head of surgery, a doctor who owes his career to the generosity of Doorn.

The surgery is scheduled in the main operating theater with

numerous hospital staff, family members, friends (and enemies), and Ellery Queen on hand to watch the procedure. When everyone is settled in their seats, the noted surgeon calls for the patient to be wheeled out. He lifts the sheet and finds Abby Doorn strangled to death with a piece of picture wire.

As would be expected, Queen leaps into the mystery and uncovers clues that he shares with the reader: a pair of hospital shoes, one with a broken shoelace that has been repaired with surgical tape; a file cabinet that does not appear to be in exactly the right position; and other seemingly insignificant facts that have been observed and lead to certain deductions.

There will be an "Interlude" in which Queen summarizes the major elements of the case and, nearing the conclusion, a "Challenge to the Reader," which is a trademark of the Ellery Queen mysteries. Here, he advises the reader that all the information needed to solve the mystery have been presented and, "by the exercise of strict logic and irrefutable deductions from given data, it should be simple for the reader to name at this point the murderer." It is not, of course, at all simple, but a daring challenge in which the detective (that is to say, the author) has pitted his own cleverness against that of the reader.

"Ellery Queen *is* the American detective story," as Anthony Boucher, the mystery reviewer for the *New York Times*, wrote, and it would be impossible for any reasonable person to disagree.

The tantalizing puzzles created by the Ellery Queen writing team are irresistible to anyone who enjoys fair-play detective stories, no matter how outre or impossible they may seem. We selected *The Chinese Orange Mystery* for the American Mystery Classics series because it features one of the most extraordinary scenes in the history of mystery fiction, and are following it with

The Dutch Shoe Mystery, which some readers have called his masterpiece of observation and deduction.

We are confident that you will agree that these have been the right choices—although there are other Queen novels tempting us. After you have read one or two, you will understand why the London *Times* wrote that "Ellery Queen is the logical successor to Sherlock Holmes."

The American Mystery Classics series plans to bring back into print the greatest authors and books of the Golden Age of the detective novel. Please look at the back of the book to see other distinguished crime novels included in the line.

—OTTO PENZLER

FOREWORD

THE DUTCH SHOE MYSTERY (a whimsicality of title which will explain itself in the course of reading) is the third adventure of the questing Queens to be presented to the public. And for the third time I find myself delegated to perform the task of introduction. It seems that my labored articulation as oracle of the previous Ellery Queen novels discouraged neither Ellery's publisher nor that omnipotent gentleman himself. Ellery avers gravely that this is my reward for engineering the publication of his fictionized memoirs. I suspect from his tone that he meant "reward" to be synonymous with "punishment"!

There is little I can say about the Queens, even as a privileged friend, that the reading public does not know or has not guessed from hints dropped here and there in Opus 1* and Opus 2.** Under their real names (one secret they demand be kept) Queen *père* and Queen *fils* were integral, I might even say major, cogs in the wheel of New York City's police machinery. Particularly during the second and third decades of the century. Their memory flourishes fresh and green among certain ex-officials of the metropolis; it is tangibly preserved in case records at Centre Street and in the

* *The Roman Hat Mystery*

** *The French Powder Mystery*

crime mementoes housed in their old 87th Street apartment, now a private museum maintained by a sentimental few who have excellent reason to be grateful.

As for contemporary history, it may be dismissed with this: the entire Queen *ménage*, comprising old Inspector Richard, Ellery, his wife, their infant son and gypsy Djuna, is still immersed in the peace of the Italian hills, to all practical purpose retired from the manhunting scene. . . .

I remember clearly the gasp of horror, the babble of conjecture that rippled outward from New York, spreading through the civilized world, when it was learned that Abigail Doorn, the mighty, had been murdered like any poor defenseless devil. She was of course a figure of international stature—an eccentric whose least financial operation, whose quietest benefaction, whose most ordinary family affair were automatically front-page news. Distinctly a "press personality," she was one of perhaps two dozen in the past decade who, struggle or protest as they might, could not escape the all-seeing eye of the journalistic and consequently the lay world.

Ellery's pertinacity in resolving the strange and perplexing circumstances which accompanied Abigail Doorn's death, his masterly manipulation of the many people involved—some famous, some wealthy, some merely notorious—and his astonishing revelations at the last, added considerably to the prestige of the old Inspector and privately, needless to say, magnified Ellery's reputation as adviser extraordinary to the Police Department.

Please bear in mind that the story about which *The Dutch Shoe Mystery* revolves is in essence truth, although from policy names have been altered and for fictional purposes certain details revised.

In this puzzling chase Ellery indisputably reaches the full

blossom of his mental prowess. Not even the maze of the Monte Field investigation or the remarkable complexity of the French murder case demanded more of that amazing intellect. I firmly believe that no keener deductive mind has ever, in fact or fiction, probed the murky depths of criminal psychology or unraveled the twisted skeins of criminal deception. I wish you pleasure in the reading!

—J. J. McC.

CHARACTERS

ABIGAIL DOORN . . . . a millionairess

HULDA DOORN . . . . an heiress

HENDRIK DOORN . . . . an *ovis ebenus*

SARAH FULLER . . . . a companion

DR. FRANCIS JANNEY . . . . a Head Surgeon

DR. LUCIUS DUNNING . . . . a diagnostician

EDITH DUNNING . . . . a sociologist

DR. FLORENCE PENNINI . . . . an obstetrician

DR. JOHN MINCHEN . . . . a Medical Director

DR. ARTHUR LESLIE . . . . a surgeon

DR. ROBERT GOLD . . . . an interne

DR. EDWARD BYERS . . . . an anæsthetist

LUCILLE PRICE . . . . a trained nurse

GRACE OBERMANN . . . . a trained nurse

MORITZ KNEISEL .... a "genius"

JAMES PARADISE .... a superintendent

ISAAC COBB .... a "special"

PHILIP MOREHOUSE .... an attorney

MICHAEL CUDAHY .... a racketeer

THOMAS SWANSON .... a mystery

LITTLE WILLIE, JOE GECKO, SNAPPER .... a bodyguard

BRISTOL .... a butler

PETE HARPER .... a newspaperman

HENRY SAMPSON .... a District Attorney

TIMOTHY CRONIN .... an assistant D. A.

DR. SAMUEL PROUTY .... a Medical Examiner

THOMAS VELIE .... a Detective-Sergeant

LIEUTENANT RITCHIE .... a District Detective

FLINT, RITTER, PIGGOTT, HESSE,
JOHNSON .... a detective squad

INSPECTOR RICHARD QUEEN .... a policeman

ELLERY QUEEN .... an analyst

CONTENTS

PART I

TALE OF TWO SHOES

OPERATION. 3

AGITATION 16

VISITATION. 18

REVELATION. 24

STRANGULATION 30

EXAMINATION 34

IMPERSONATION 42

CORROBORATION 52

IMPLICATION 62

MANIFESTATION 71

INTERROGATION 79

EXPERIMENTATION 111

ADMINISTRATION 121

ADORATION 127

COMPLICATION 128

ALIENATION 143

MYSTIFICATION 150

CONDENSATION 154

Interlude

PART II

DISAPPEARANCE OF A CABINET

DESTINATION 187

CAPITULATION 194

DUPLICATION 203

ENUMERATION 211

TRIPLICATION ? ? ? 217

REEXAMINATION 230

SIMPLIFICATION 241

EQUATION 244

Challenge to the Reader

PART III

DISCOVERY OF A DOCUMENT

CLARIFICATION 253

ARGUMENTATION 260

TERMINATION 265

EXPLANATION 272

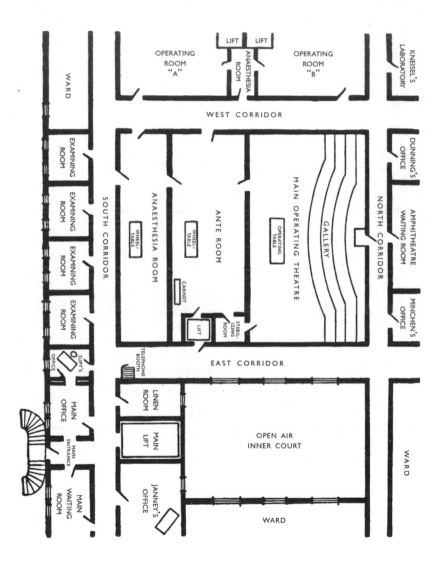

WARD

EXAMINING ROOM

EXAMINING ROOM

EXAMINING ROOM

EXAMINING ROOM

SOUTH CORRIDOR

OFFICE

SUPT'S OFFICE

MAIN OFFICE

MAIN ENTRANCE

MAIN WAITING ROOM

OPERATING ROOM "A"

LIFT   LIFT

ANAESTHESIA ROOM

OPERATING ROOM "B"

KNEISEL'S LABORATORY

WEST CORRIDOR

ANAESTHESIA ROOM

WHEEL-TABLE

ANTE ROOM

WHEEL-TABLE

CABINET

LIFT

STERIL-IZING ROOM

MAIN OPERATING THEATRE

OPERATING TABLE

GALLERY

NORTH CORRIDOR

DUNNING'S OFFICE

AMPHITHEATRE WAITING ROOM

MINCHEN'S OFFICE

EAST CORRIDOR

TELEPHONE BOOTH

LINEN ROOM

MAIN LIFT

JANNEY'S OFFICE

OPEN AIR INNER COURT

WARD

WARD

PART I

TALE OF TWO SHOES

"There are only two detectives for whom I have felt, in my own capacity as hunter-of-men, any deeply underlying sympathy . . . transcending racial idiosyncrasies and overleaping barriers of space and time. . . . These two, strangely enough, present the weird contrast of unreality, of fantasm and fact. One has achieved luminous fame between the boards of books; the other as kin to a veritable policeman. . . . I refer, of course, to those imperishables—Mr. Sherlock Holmes of Baker Street, London, and Mr. Ellery Queen of West 87th Street, New York City."

—from *30 Years on the Trail*
—by DR. MAX PEJCHAR*

*Ed. Note: Viennese police-consultant

1

OPERATION

INSPECTOR RICHARD Queen's *alter ego,* which was in startling contrast with his ordinarily spry and practical old manner, often prompted him to utter didactic remarks on the general subject of criminology. These professorial dicta were habitually addressed to his son and partner-in-crime-detection, Ellery Queen, in moments when they browsed before their living-room fire, alone except for the slippery shadow of Djuna, the wraith-like gypsy lad who served their domestic needs.

"The first five minutes are the most important," the old man would say severely, "remember that." It was his favorite theme. "The first five minutes can save you a heap of trouble."

And Ellery, reared from boyhood on a diet of detectival advice, would grunt and suck his pipe and stare into the fire, wondering how often a detective was fortunate enough to be on the scene of a crime within three hundred seconds of its commission.

Here he would put his doubt into words, and the old man would nod sadly and agree—yes, it wasn't very often that such luck came one's way. By the time the investigator reached the scene the trail was cold, very cold. Then one did what one could to atone for the unsympathetic tardiness of fate. Djuna, hand me my snuff! . . .

Ellery Queen was no more the fatalist than he was the determinist, or pragmatist, or realist. His sole compromise with *isms* and *ologies* was an implicit belief in the gospel of the intellect, which has assumed many names and many endings through the history of thought. Here he swung wide of the fundamental professionalism of Inspector Queen. He despised the institution of police informers as beneath the dignity of original thinking; he pooh-poohed police methods of detection with their clumsy limitations—the limitations of any rule-plagued organization. "I'm one with Kant at least to this extent," he liked to say, "that pure reason is the highest good of the human hodge-podge. For what one mind can conceive another mind can fathom . . ."

This was his philosophy in its simplest terms. He was very near to abandoning his faith during the investigation of Abigail Doorn's murder. Perhaps for the first time in his sharply uncompromising intellectual career, doubt assailed him. Not doubt of his philosophy, which had proved itself many times over in former cases, but doubt of his mental capacity to unravel what another mind had conceived. Of course he was an egoist—"bobbing my head vigorously with Descartes and Fichte," he used to remark . . . but for once in the extraordinary labyrinth of events surrounding the Doorn case he had overlooked fate, that troublesome trespasser on the private property of self-determination.

Crime was on his mind that raw blue Monday morning in January, 192-, as he strode down a quiet street in the East Sixties. Heavy black ulster bundled about him, fedora pulled low over his forehead shading the cold gleam of his *pince-nez* glasses, stick cracking against the frosty pavement, he made for a low-slung group of buildings clustered solidly on the next block.

This was an unusually vexing problem. Something *must* have occurred between the moment of death and *rigor mortis*. . . . His eyes were tranquil but the skin of his smooth brown cheek tightened and his stick struck the concrete with force.

He crossed the street and made rapidly for the main entrance to the largest building of the group. Looming before him were the red granite steps of an immense curving stairway which rose from two distinct points of the pavement to meet on a stone platform above. Carved in stone over a huge iron-bolted double door appeared the legend:

THE DUTCH MEMORIAL HOSPITAL

He ran up the steps and, panting a little from his exertions, heaved on one of the big doors. He was looking into a serene, high-ceilinged vestibule. The floor was of white marble, the walls heavily coated with dull enamel. To his left was an open door displaying a white plaque marked: OFFICE. To his right was a door similarly marked: WAITING ROOM. Directly ahead, beyond the vestibule, he could see through a glass swinging door the grillwork of a large elevator, in the entrance to which sat an old man in spotless white.

A burly, hard-jawed, red-faced man similarly dressed in white trousers and jacket, but wearing a black-visored cap, stepped out of the Office as Ellery paused to look around.

"Visitin' hours from two t' three," he said gruffly. "Can't see nobody in the Horspit'l till then, mister."

"Eh?" Ellery plunged his gloved hands deeper into his pockets. "I want to see Dr. Minchen. Quickly."

The attendant rasped his jaw. "Dr. Minchen, is it? D'ya have an appointment with th' Doctor?"

"Oh, he'll see me. I said quickly, please." He fumbled in his pocket, brought out a piece of silver. "Now get him, won't you? I'm in the devil of a hurry."

"Can't take tips, sir," said the attendant regretfully. "And I'll tell th' Doctor who—?"

Ellery blinked his eyes, smiled, put the coin away. "Ellery Queen. No tips, eh? What's your name? Charon?"

The man looked dubious. "No, sir. Isaac Cobb, sir. 'Special.'" He indicated a nickel badge on his coat, shuffled off.

Ellery stepped into the Waiting Room and sat down. The room was empty. He wrinkled his nose unconsciously. A faint odor of disinfectant pinched the sensitive membrane of his nostrils. The ferrule of his stick tapped nervously on the tiled floor.

A tall athletic man in white burst into the room. "Ellery Queen, by thunder!" Ellery rose swiftly; they shook hands with warmth. "What on earth brings you down here? Still snooping around?"

"The customary thing, John. A case," murmured Ellery. "Don't like hospitals as a rule. They depress me. But I need some information—"

"Only too glad to be of service." Dr. Minchen spoke incisively; he had very keen blue eyes and a quick smile. Grasping Ellery's elbow he steered him through the door. "But we can't talk here, old man. Come into my office. I can always find time for a chat with you. Must be months since I've seen you. . . ."

They passed through the glass door and turned to the left, entering a long gleaming corridor lined on both sides with closed doors. The odor of disinfectant grew stronger.

"Shades of Aesculapius!" gasped Ellery. "Doesn't this awful

smell affect you at all? I should think you'd choke after a day in here."

Dr. Minchen chuckled. They turned at the end of the corridor and strode along another at right angles to the one they had just traversed. "You get used to it. And it's better to inhale the stink of lysol, bichloride of mercury and alcohol than the insidious mess of bacteria floating about. . . . How's the Inspector?"

"Middling." Ellery's eyes clouded. "A stubborn little case just now—I've got everything but one detail. . . . If it's what I think . . ."

Again they turned a corner, proceeding down a third hall parallel to the first through which they had passed. To their right, along the entire length of the corridor, there was blank wall broken only at one spot by a solid-looking door labeled: AMPHITHEATER GALLERY. To their left they passed in succession a door marked: DR. LUCIUS DUNNING, CHIEF INTERNIST; a little farther on another door inscribed: WAITING ROOM; and finally a third door at which Ellery's companion halted, smiling. The door was lettered: DR. JOHN MINCHEN, MEDICAL DIRECTOR.

It was a large, sparsely furnished room dominated by a desk. Several cabinets with metallic instruments gleaming on glass shelves stood against the walls. There were four chairs, a low wide bookcase filled with heavy volumes, a number of steel filing-cases.

"Sit down, take your coat off and let's have it," said Minchen. He flung himself into the swivel-chair behind the desk, leaned backward, placed his square-fingered hard hands behind his head.

"Just one question," muttered Ellery, throwing his ulster over a chair and striding across the room. He leaned forward over the desk, stared earnestly at Minchen. "Are there any circumstances which will alter the length of time in which *rigor mortis* usually sets in?"

"Yes. What did the patient die of?"

"Gunshot . . ."

"Age?"

"I should judge about forty-five."

"Pathology? I mean—any disease? Diabetes, for example?"

"Not to my knowledge."

Minchen rocked gently in his chair. Ellery retreated, sat down, groped for a cigarette.

"Here—have some of mine," said Minchen. . . . "Well, I'll tell you, Ellery. *Rigor mortis* is tricky, and generally I should like to examine the body before making a decision. I asked about diabetes particularly because a person over forty affected by an excess saccharine condition in the blood will almost inevitably stiffen up after a violent death in about ten minutes—"

"Ten minutes? Good God!" Ellery stared at Minchen, the cigarette drooping from his thin firm lips. "Ten minutes," he repeated to himself softly. "Diabetes. . . . John, let me use your 'phone!"

"Help yourself." Minchen waved, relaxed in his chair. Ellery snapped a number, spoke to two people, made connection with the Medical Examiner's office. "Prouty? Ellery Queen. . . . Did the autopsy on Jiminez show traces of sugar in the blood? . . . What? Chronic diabetic condition, eh? I'll be damned!"

He replaced the receiver slowly, drew a long breath, grinned. The lines of strain had vanished from his face.

"All's well that ends ill, John. You've rendered yeoman service this morning. One call more, and I'm through."

He telephoned Police Headquarters. "Inspector Queen . . . Dad? It's O'Rourke . . . Positive. The broken leg. . . . Yes. Broken after death, but within ten minutes. . . . Right! . . . And so am I."

"Don't go, Ellery," said Minchen genially. "I've a bit of time on my hands and I haven't seen you for ages."

They sat back in their chairs, smoking. Ellery wore a singularly peaceful expression.

"Stay here all day, if you want me to." He laughed. "You've just provided the straw that broke a stubborn camel's back. . . . After all, I mustn't be too harsh with myself. Not having studied the mysteries of the Galenic profession, I couldn't possibly have known about diabetes."

"Oh, we're not a total loss," said Minchen. "As a matter of fact, I had diabetes on my mind. Just about the most important personage in the Hospital—chronic case of *diabetes mellitus*—had a bad accident this morning on the premises. Nasty fall from the top of a flight of stairs. Rupture of the gall bladder and Janney's getting ready to operate immediately."

"Too bad. Who is your first citizen?"

"Abby Doorn." Minchen looked grave. "She's over seventy, and although she's well preserved for her age the diabetic condition makes the operation for rupture fairly serious. The only compensating feature of the whole business is that she is in a coma, and anæsthesia won't be necessary. We've all been expecting the old lady to go under the knife for mildly chronic appendicitis next month, but I know that Janney won't touch the appendix this morning—just not to complicate her condition. It's not so serious as I'm probably making it sound. If the patient weren't Mrs. Doorn, Janney would consider the case interesting but nothing more." He consulted his wrist watch. "Operation's at 10:45—it's almost 10:00 now—how would you like to witness Janney's work?"

"Well . . ."

"He's a marvel, you know. Best surgeon in the East. And Head Surgeon of the Dutch Memorial, partly because of Mrs. Doorn's friendship and of course through his genius with the knife. Why not stay? Janney will pull her through—he's operating in the Amphitheater across the corridor. Janney says she'll be all right and when he says so, you can bank on it."

"I suppose I'm in for it," said Ellery ruefully. "To tell the truth, I've never witnessed a surgical operation. Think I'll have the horrors? I'm afraid I'm a wee bit squeamish, John. . . ." They laughed. "Millionaire, philanthropist, social dowager, financial power—damn the mortality of the flesh!"

"It hits us all," mused Minchen, stretching his legs comfortably under the desk. "Yes, Abigail Doorn. . . . I suppose you know she founded this Hospital, Ellery? Her idea, her money—really her institution. . . . We were all shocked, I can tell you. Janney more than the rest of us—she's been fairy godmother to him practically all his life—sent him through Johns Hopkins—Vienna—the Sorbonne—just about made him what he is to-day. Naturally he insisted on operating, and naturally he'll do the job. No finer nerves in the business."

"How did it happen?" asked Ellery curiously.

"Fate, I guess. . . . You see, Monday mornings she always comes down here to inspect the Charity Wards—her pet idea—and as she was about to walk down a flight of steps on the third floor she went into a diabetic coma, fell down the stairs and landed on her abdomen. . . . Luckily Janney was here. Examined her at once, and even from a superficial examination saw that the gall bladder had been ruptured by the fall—abdomen swollen, bloated. . . . Well, there was only one thing to do. Janney began to give her the insulin-glucose emergency treatment. . . ."

"What caused the coma?"

"We've discovered it was negligence on the part of Mrs. Doorn's companion, Sarah Fuller—middle-aged woman who has been with Abby for years, runs the house, keeps her company. You see, Abby's condition called for an insulin injection three times a day. Janney's always insisted on doing it himself, although in most cases of this sort even the patient may inject the insulin. Last night Janney was kept by a very important case, and as he usually did when he couldn't run over to the Doorn house, he 'phoned for Hulda, Abby's daughter. But Hulda wasn't home, and he left word with this Fuller woman to tell Hulda when she got in to administer the insulin. Fuller woman forgot or something. Abby is generally careless about it—the result was the dose wasn't given last night. Hulda slept late this morning, never knowing of Janney's message, and again this morning Abby didn't get her injection. And on top of it ate a hearty breakfast. The breakfast finished the job. Sugar content in her blood quickly overbalanced the insulin, and coma inevitably followed. As luck would have it, it struck her at the top of a flight of stairs. And there you are."

"Sad!" murmured Ellery. "I suppose everybody's been notified? There'll be a sweet family party here, I'll wager."

"Not in the operating-room, there won't," said Minchen grimly. "The whole kit and boodle of 'em will be in the Waiting Room next door. Family's barred from the theater, don't you know that? Well! How'd you like to take a little walk around? Love to show you the place. If I do say so, it's a model of hospitalization."

"With you, John."

They left Minchen's office and walked down the North Corridor the way they had come. Minchen pointed out the door to the Amphitheater Gallery, from which they would later view the operation; and the door to the Waiting Room. "Some of the Doorn crowd are probably in there now," commented Minchen. "Can't have 'em wandering around. . . . Two auxiliary operating-rooms off the West Corridor," he went on as they rounded the corner. "We're pretty busy at all times—have one of the largest surgical staffs in the East. . . . Across the corridor, on the left here, is the main operating-room—called the Amphitheater—which has two special rooms, an Anteroom and an Anæsthesia Room. As you can see, there's a door to the Anteroom off this corridor—the West—and another entrance, to the Anæsthesia Room, around the corner in the South Corridor. . . . Amphitheater's where the big operations take place; it's also used for demonstration purposes to the internes and nurses. Of course, we have other operating-rooms upstairs."

The Hospital was strangely quiet. Occasionally a white-garbed figure flitted through the long halls. Noise seemed to have been entirely eliminated; doors swung on heavily oiled hinges and made no sound when they slipped shut. A soft diffused light bathed the interior of the building; and except for the chemical odor the air was singularly pure.

"By the way," said Ellery suddenly, as they sauntered into the South Corridor, "I believe you said before that Mrs. Doorn wouldn't be given anæsthetic for the operation. Is that only because she is in a coma? I've been under the impression that anæsthesia is administered in all surgical cases."

"Fair question," admitted Minchen. "And it's true that in most cases—virtually all cases—anæsthesia is used. But diabetics are funny people. You know—or rather I suppose you don't know—that any surgical operation is dangerous to a chronic diabetic. Even minor surgery may be fatal. Had a case just the other day—patient came into the dispensary with a festered toe—some poor devil. The doctor in charge—well, it's just one of those unforeseeable accidents of dispensary routine. The toe was cleaned, the patient went home. Next morning he was found dead. *Post mortem* examination showed the man to be full of sugar. Probably never knew it himself. . . .

"What I started out to say was that cutting is holy hell on diabetics. When an operation is absolutely necessary a buildup process is instituted—which accomplishes over a comparatively short period the task of temporarily restoring a normal sugar content in the patient's blood. And even while the operation is being performed alternate injections of insulin and glucose are given without let-up to *keep* the sugar content normal. They'll have to do that with Abby Doorn. She's being injected now with these insulin-glucose treatments; taking blood-tests right along to check up on the diminution of sugar milligrams. This emergency treatment takes about an hour and a half, perhaps two hours. Generally the treatment is stretched over a month or so; too rapid building up may affect the liver. But we have no choice with Abby Doorn; that gall bladder rupture can't be neglected, even for half a day."

"Yes, but how about the anæsthetic?" objected Ellery. "Would that make the operation even riskier? Is that why you're relying on the comatose condition to pull her through the shock?"

"Exactly. Riskier and more complicated. We must take what the gods provide." Minchen paused with his hand on the knob of a door lettered: EXAMINING ROOM. "Of course, an anæsthetist will be standing beside the operating-table prepared to administer without a second's delay should Abby pop out of the coma. . . . Come in here, Ellery; I want to show you how a modern hospital does things."

He pushed the door open and waved Ellery into the room. Ellery noticed that a small panel on the wall illuminated by a tiny electric bulb flashed on as the door opened to announce that the Examining Room was now occupied. He paused appreciatively on the threshold.

"Neat, eh?" grinned Minchen.

"What's that thingamajig over there?"

"Fluoroscope. There's one in every Examining Room. Of

course, there's the stock examining-table, small sterilizing-machine, drug cabinet, instrument racks. . . . You can see for yourself."

"The instrument," said Ellery didactically, "is an invention of man to mock his Creator. Heavens, aren't five fingers sufficient?" They laughed together. "I'd stifle in here. Doesn't anybody ever throw things around?"

"Not while John Quintus Minchen is boss," grinned the physician. "Actually, we make a fetish of orderliness. Take minor supplies, for instance. All kept in these drawers—" he flipped his hand at a large white cabinet in one corner, "and quite out of sight or knowledge of meddling patients or visitors. Everybody in the Hospital who *has* to, knows just where to get supplies. Makes things confoundedly simple."

He pulled open a large metal drawer at the bottom of the cabinet. Ellery bent over and stared down at a bewildering display of assorted bandages. Another drawer contained absorbent cotton and tissue; another medicated cotton; another adhesive tapes.

"System," murmured Ellery. "Your subordinates get demerit marks for dirty linen and untied shoelaces, don't they?"

Minchen chuckled. "You're not so far off at that. Standing rule of the Hospital makes it mandatory to dress in Hospital uniform, which for men is white canvas shoes, white duck trousers and coat; and for women white linen throughout. Even the 'special' outside—well, you remember he wore white, too. The elevator men, mopmen, kitchen help, clerical force—everybody wears the standardized uniform from the moment he sets foot on the Hospital premises until he leaves."

"My head's absolutely a-buzz," groaned Ellery. "Let me out of here."

As they emerged once more into the South Corridor, they

caught sight of a tall young man dressed in a brown greatcoat, hat in hand, hurrying toward them. He looked their way, hesitated, then turned suddenly into the East Corridor at his right and disappeared.

Minchen's frank face fell. "Forgot Abigail the Mighty," he muttered. "There goes her attorney now—Philip Morehouse. Bright young coot. Devotes all his time to Abby's interests."

"He's heard the news, I gather," remarked Ellery. "Is he interested so personally in Mrs. Doorn?"

"I should say in Mrs. Doorn's lovely young daughter," replied Minchen dryly. "He and Hulda have hit it off quite famously. Looks like a romance to me. And from all accounts Abby, in her grand lady-of-the-manor fashion, smiles on the affair. . . . Well! I suppose the clans are gathering. . . . Hullo! There's the old master himself. Just out of 'A' operating-room. . . . Hi there, Doctor!"

2

AGITATION

THE MAN in the brown greatcoat ran up to the closed door of the Waiting Room in the North Corridor and rapped sharply. There was no sound from beyond the door. He tried the knob, pushed. . . .

"Phil!"

"Hulda! Darling. . . ."

A tall young woman, her eyes red with tears, flew into his arms. He cradled her head on his shoulder, murmuring wordless incoherent sympathy.

They were alone in the vast bare room. Long benches squatted stiffly along the walls. Over one was thrown a beaver coat.

Philip Morehouse gently raised the girl's head, tipped her chin upward, looked into her eyes.

"It's nothing, Hulda—she'll be all right," he said huskily. "Don't cry, dear, I—please!"

She blinked, made a convulsive effort to smile at him. "I'll— oh, Phil, I'm so glad you've come . . . sitting here all alone . . . waiting, waiting. . . ."

"I know." He looked around with a slight frown. "Where are

the others? What the devil are they thinking of to leave you alone in this room?"

"Oh, I don't know. . . . Sarah, Uncle Hendrik—they're about somewhere. . . ."

She groped for his hand, snuggled against his breast. After a long moment they walked to a bench and sat down. Hulda Doorn stared wide-eyed at the floor. The young man fumbled desperately for words, but none came.

About them, silent and huge, lay the Hospital, humming with the work of life. But in the room there was no sound, no footfall, no cheerful voice. Only white dull walls. . . .

"Oh, Phil, I'm afraid, I'm afraid!"

3
VISITATION

A SMALL, QUEERLY shaped man had walked into the South Corridor, heading toward Minchen and Ellery. Ellery received an instant impression of personality, even while the man's features could not be clearly distinguished. Perhaps this feeling arose from the peculiarly stiff manner in which he held his head, and the pronounced limp with which he walked. That there was something wrong with his left leg was apparent from the manner in which he put his weight on the right. "Probably muscular paralysis of some sort," muttered Ellery to himself as he watched the little doctor approach.

The newcomer was dressed in full surgical regalia—a white gown under which protruded the bottoms of white duck trousers and the tips of white canvas shoes. The gown was stained with chemicals; on one sleeve was a long bloody smudge. On his head perched a white surgical cap, turned up at the corners; he was fumbling with the string of his face-gag as he limped toward the two waiting men.

"Ah there, Minchen! We did it. Perforated appendix. Managed to avoid peritonitis. Dirty job. . . . How's Abigail? Seen her? What's the milligram content at last report? Who's this?" He spoke with gatling-gun rapidity, his bright little eyes never still, darting from Minchen to Ellery.

"Dr. Janney, meet Mr. Queen. Particularly old friend," said Minchen hastily. "Ellery Queen, the writer."

"Hardly," said Ellery. "This is a pleasure, doctor."

"Pleasure's all mine, all mine," snapped the surgeon. "Any friend of Minchen's is welcome here. . . . Well, John—got to rest up now. Worried about Abigail. Thank God for her pumper. Bad rupture. How about those intravenous injections?"

"Coming along splendidly," replied Minchen. "They pulled her down from 180 to 135 when I last heard, a little before 10:00. Ought to be ready as scheduled. She's probably in the Anteroom now."

"Good! She'll be hopping around again in no time."

Ellery smiled apologetically. "Pardon my ignorance, gentlemen, but just what is meant by your cabalistic reference to '180 to 135'? Blood pressure?"

"Good God, no!" shouted Dr. Janney. "180 milligrams of sugar to 100 c.c. of blood. We're pulling it down. Can't operate until we get to normal—110, 120. Oh, you're not a medical man. Excuse me."

"I'm overwhelmed," said Ellery.

Minchen cleared his throat. "I suppose our plans for tonight on the book are shot, with Mrs. Doorn so badly off?"

Dr. Janney rubbed his jaw. His eyes continued to dart between Ellery and the Medical Director. They made Ellery distinctly uncomfortable.

"Of course!" Janney turned unexpectedly toward Ellery, placing his small rubber-sheathed hand on Minchen's shoulder. "You're a writer, aren't you? Well—" he chuckled, showed tobacco-stained teeth in a weird grin, "you're looking at another writer, here, young man. Johnny Minchen. Smart as a whip. Helping me profoundly with a book we're doing together. Something quite revolutionary. And I've picked the best co-author in the profession. Know what *Congenital Allergy* is, Queen? Didn't think you would. Make a big stir in the medical world. We've proved something the bone-setting business has been messing about for years. . . ."

"Well, John!" Ellery smiled in amusement "You didn't tell me—"

"Pardon me," said Dr. Janney abruptly, swinging on his right heel. "Well, Cobb, what is it?"

The white-garbed doorman had shuffled shyly up to the three men, and now stood uncomfortably in the background trying to attract the attention of the little surgeon. He took his cap off.

"Man outside wants t' see ye, Dr. Janney," he said hastily. "Says he's got an appointm't. Sorry to bother ye, Doctor—"

"He's a liar," barked Dr. Janney. "You know I can't see anybody, Cobb. How many times must I tell you not to bother me about these things? Where's Miss Price? You know she takes care of all that truck for me. Go on now—beat it. Can't see him. Too busy."

He turned his back on the doorman. The scarlet of Cobb's face deepened. Nevertheless, he did not move away.

"But I—she—he says . . ."

"You must have forgotten, Doctor," interposed Minchen. "Miss Price has been copying the *Congenital Allergy* manuscript all morning, and she's with Mrs. Doorn now, by your own order. . . ."

"Shucks! That's right, too," muttered Dr. Janney. "But I won't see that man, Cobb, I—"

Mutely, the doorman lifted his huge hand and thrust a white card toward the surgeon, handling it as if it were a precious document.

Janney snatched at it "Who's this? Swanson—Swanson. . . . Oh!" The tone of his voice changed instantly. His bright little eyes clouded as he froze to immobility. Then he lifted his gown and tucked the card into a pocket of his coat. With the same deft motion he whipped a watch from his underclothes. "10:29," he mumbled. Surprisingly, with that effortless ease which marked all his manual movements, he replaced the watch and smoothed down his gown. "All right Cobb!" he said clearly. "Lead the way. Where is he? . . . See you later, John. 'Bye, Queen."

As suddenly as he had appeared, he swung about and limped off in the wake of Cobb, who seemed anxious to depart. Minchen and Ellery stared down the corridor after them for a long moment. Both men turned away just as Janney and the doorman were passing the elevator opposite the main entrance.

"Janney's office is down there," said Minchen, shrugging. "Queer sort of cuss, isn't he, Ellery? But as great as they come. . . . Let's go back to my office. There's still a good quarter of an hour before the operation."

They turned the corner and walked with leisurely steps up the West Corridor.

"Reminds me of a bird, somehow," said Ellery thoughtfully. "They way he holds his head, keeps darting those avian eyes of his about. . . . Interesting little fellow. About fifty, isn't he?"

"Thereabouts. . . . Interesting in more ways than one, Ellery." Minchen spoke boyishly. "There's one medical man who's really devoted his life to his profession. He's spared neither himself nor his personal fortune. I've never known him to refuse a case on grounds of a small fee. In fact he's done scores of jobs for which he never saw a cent, and didn't expect to. . . . Don't get him wrong, Ellery; you've just met a genuine personage."

"If what you said about his relationship with Mrs. Doorn is true," commented Ellery, smiling, "I don't suppose Dr. Janney has much to worry about financially."

Minchen stared. "Why, how did you—? Well, of course," he chuckled sheepishly, "it's probably evident. Yes, Janney is due for a whacking big legacy on Abby's departure from this world. Everybody knows that. He's been quite like a son to her. . . . And here we are."

They had reached Minchen's office. Minchen telephoned briefly, seemed satisfied with what he heard.

"They have Abby in the Anteroom already," he stated, putting down the instrument. "They got her blood sugar down to 110 milligrams—it's a question of minutes now. Well, I'll be glad when it's over."

Ellery shivered slightly. Minchen pretended not to notice. Over cigarettes, they sat in silence; an indefinable gloom hovered between them.

With an effort Ellery shrugged his shoulders and exhaled a cloud of smoke. "About this co-authorship, John," he said lightly. "I never suspected that you'd succumb to the writing bug. What's it all about?"

"Oh, that" Minchen laughed. "Most of the work is bound up with actual case histories, proving a theory which both Janney and I hold in common; and it is possible to predict the predisposition to specific ailments of embryos by careful analysis of congenital influences. Complicated?"

"Overwhelmingly scientific, professor," murmured Ellery.

"How about letting me peep at the manuscript? I might be able to give you a few pointers in a literary way."

Minchen flushed. "Thunder! Can't do that, old son," he said awkwardly. "Janney'd have my life. As a matter of fact, both the manuscript and the case records we are using in the book are kept absolutely private; Janney guards 'em as jealousy as his life. Why, the old man recently cashiered an interne who had the unhappy impulse to root around in Janney's filing-cabinet—merely out of academic curiosity, I suppose. . . . Sorry, Ellery. The only people who can see those records are Janney, myself and Miss Price, Janney's assistant—she's a trained nurse—and she does only the routine clerical work."

"All right, all right!" grinned Ellery, closing his eyes. "I surrender. I just wanted to *help* you, you blamed old codger. . . . Of course you remember your *Iliad*? 'Light is the task when many share the toil.' If you spurn my assistance. . . ."

They laughed together.

4

REVELATION

ELLERY QUEEN, dilettante of criminology, had no stomach for blood. Raised on stories of crime, fed with tales of murder, in daily contact with desperadoes and manhunters, he nevertheless endured the sight of maltreated flesh with difficulty. His position as son of a policeman; his association with brutality and warped minds; his own literary dabblings in the mire of criminal psychology—these had not inured him to the reeking evidences of man's inhumanity to man. On the scene of a slaughter his eyes were keen, his judgment swift, but always his heart was sick. . . .

He had never attended a surgical operation. Dead bodies he had seen galore; mangled corpses in morgues, fished out of rivers and the sea, huddled on railroad tracks, lying still in the streets after gang-fights—of death at its unprettiest he had bitter and plentiful knowledge. But chilled steel biting into warm flesh, cutting through live tissue, severing veins through which red blood spurted—the thought nauseated him.

It was with a sensation of mingled dread and excitement, then, that he took his seat in the gallery of the Dutch Memorial Hospital Amphitheater, eyes glued on the scene of calm noiseless activity being enacted twenty feet away in the orchestra of the theater. Dr. Minchen lolled in a chair by his side, quick blue eyes missing nothing of the preparations for the operation. . . . A whisper of conversation came dimly to their ears from a group of people seated about them in the gallery. Directly in the center was a handful of white-garbed men and women—internes and nurses gathered to watch the professional handiwork of the surgeon. They were very still. Behind Ellery and Dr. Minchen sat a man, also in hospital regalia, and a fragile-looking young woman in white who whispered intermittently in his ear. The man was Dr. Lucius Dunning, Chief Internist; the girl his daughter, attached to the Social Service Department of the institution. Dr. Dunning was grey, with a startling seamed face from which mild brown eyes peered. The girl was fair and unhandsome. There was an appreciable tic in one eyelid.

The gallery rose from the floor of the theater, separated from the orchestra by a high impassable barrier of white wood. The rows of seats ascended steeply toward the rear—much as in the balcony of a theater for the drama. At the rear wall was a door, opening outward on a circular staircase which led to the floor below and gave directly on the North Corridor.*

The sound of footsteps now became audible, the door swung open, and Philip Morehouse stepped nervously into the gallery, his eyes roving. His brown overcoat and hat had disappeared. Spying the Medical Director, he ran down the stepped ramp and bent over to whisper into Minchen's ear.

Minchen nodded gravely, turned to Ellery. "Meet Mr. Morehouse, Ellery—Mr. Queen." He waved his fingers. "Mrs. Doorn's attorney." The two men shook hands; Ellery smiled mechanically, turned back to watch the orchestra.

Philip Morehouse was a lean man with steady eyes and a stub-

*See map on page xiv

born jaw. "Hulda, Fuller, Hendrik Doorn—they're downstairs now in the Waiting Room. Can't they possibly be present during the operation, Doctor?" he whispered urgently. Minchen shook his head. He indicated the seat next to him. Morehouse frowned, but sank into the chair and instantly became absorbed in the movements of the nurses below.

An old man in white shuffled up the steps, peered into the gallery, caught the eye of an interne, nodded violently, and at once disappeared. The click of the lock in the door held a note of finality. For an instant the old man could be heard rustling about behind the door; then even the sound of his movements died.

The orchestra of the Amphitheater had settled down now to a hushed expectancy. Ellery thought it very like the moment in a legitimate theater just before the rise of the curtain, when the audience holds its breath and absolute quiet descends on the house. . . . Under a triple brace of electric globes of immense size, emitting a cold, steady and brilliant light, stood an operating-table. It was denuded, pitiless in its lack of color. Near it was a table stacked with bandage, antiseptic cotton, small bottles of drugs. A glass-covered case of shining, wicked-looking steel instruments was being watched over by an interne, who kept sterilizing them in a compact little machine at his right hand. At one side of the room two white-gowned surgical assistants—men—stood over porcelain bowls carefully washing their hands in a bluish fluid. One imperiously reached for a towel handed him by a nurse; he dried his hands quickly and on the instant bathed them once more, this time in a watery-looking fluid.

"Bichloride of mercury solution, then alcohol," whispered Minchen to Ellery.

Immediately upon drying his hands of the alcohol, the assistant surgeon held them out while a nurse removed a pair of rubber gloves from a sterilizing machine and smoothed them onto the doctor's hands. A similar procedure was followed with the other surgeon.

Suddenly the door at the left of the room opened and the slight, limping figure of Dr. Janney appeared. He looked around with one of his bird-like glances, then limped rapidly over to a wash-bowl. He slipped out of his gown and a nurse skilfully dressed him in a freshly sterilized gown. While the surgeon bent over the bowl, rinsing his hands thoroughly in the blue bichloride solution, another adjusted a fresh white cap on his head, carefully tucking in his greyish hair.

Dr. Janney spoke without looking up. "The patient," he said brusquely. Two assistant nurses quickly opened the door leading to the Anteroom. "The patient; Miss Price!" one said. They disappeared into the room, emerging a moment later pushing a long, white rubber-shod wheel-table on which lay a quiet figure covered with a sheet. The patient's head was thrown far back; it was ghastly, bluish-white. The sheet was tucked around the neck. The eyes were closed. A third figure entered the operating-room from the Anteroom—another nurse. She stood quietly in a corner, waiting.

The patient was lifted from the wheel-table and deposited on the operating-table. The wheel-table was instantly removed to the Anteroom by the third nurse. She closed the door carefully, disappearing from sight. A gowned and gagged figure took his place close by the operating-table, fussing with a small taboret on which were various instruments and cones.

"The anæsthetist," muttered Minchen; "they've got to keep one handy in case Abby comes out of the coma during the operation."

The two assisting surgeons approached the operating-table from opposite sides. The sheet was whipped off the patient, dis-carded; a peculiarly-cut garment was immediately substituted. Dr. Janney, now gloved, gowned and capped, was standing patiently at one side while a substitute nurse adjusted a gag about his mouth and nose.

Minchen leaned forward in the chair, a curiously intent look in his eyes. His gaze was riveted on the body of the patient. He muttered to Ellery in a queerly tense tone.

"Something wrong, Ellery; something wrong!"

Ellery answered without turning his head. "Is it the stiffness?" he whispered. "I noticed that. A diabetic. . . ."

The two assisting surgeons were bending over the operating-table. One lifted an arm, let it fall. It was rigid and unbending. The other touched an eyelid, peered at the eyeball. They looked at each other.

"Dr. Janney!" said one of them insistently, straightening up.

The surgeon wheeled, stared. "What's the matter?" He brushed aside a nurse; limped forward rapidly. In a flash he had covered the distance, bent over the inert body. He tore the garment from the table, felt at the old woman's neck. Ellery saw his back stiffen as if he had been struck.

Without raising his head Dr. Janney uttered two words: "Adrenalin. Pulmotor." As if by magic the two surgical assistants, the two nurses, the two substituting nurses leaped into activity. The words were hardly dead before a large slender cylinder was carried over and several figures grew busy about the table. A nurse handed Dr. Janney a small glistening object; he forced open the mouth of the patient, held the object before it. He then intently examined its surface—it was a metal mirror. He threw it aside with a muffled curse, reached with one prehensile arm for a hypodermic ready in the hand of a nurse. He bared the torso of the old woman, plunged the needle into her body directly over the heart Already the pulmotor was in operation, forcing oxygen into her lungs. . . .

In the gallery the nurses and internes, Dr. Dunning, his daughter, Philip Morehouse, Dr. Minchen, Ellery sat on the edge of their seats, motionless. There was no sound in the Amphitheater except the sucking of the pulmotor.

In fifteen minutes, exactly at 11:05—Ellery mechanically consulted his watch—Dr. Janney straightened from his crouched position above the patient, turned around and crooked his forefinger furiously toward Dr. Minchen. Without a word the Medical Director left his seat, ran up the steps toward the door at the rear and disappeared. A moment later he had burst through the theater-door on the West Corridor and run up to the operating-table. Janney stepped back, pointed mutely at the neck of the old woman.

Minchen's face whitened. . . . Like Janney, he too stepped back and turned; and this time the crooked finger beckoned Ellery, who sat like stone where Minchen had left him.

Ellery rose. His eyebrows went up. His lips formed one soundless word, which Minchen caught. Dr. Minchen nodded. The word was:

"Murder?"

5

STRANGULATION

ELLERY NO longer felt the qualms of temperament which had assailed him while viewing the preparations for an assault on mortal flesh. Life was now extinct, he felt sure, although as he opened the door of the theater from the West Corridor the surgeons and nurses still worked over the body. One who had lived was dead; and dead of violence. And deaths of violence were commonplace to a writer of mystery stories, an unofficial investigator of crime, and the son of a police Inspector.

Unhurriedly he approached the nucleus of swirling activity. Janney looked up, frowned. "Have to stay out, Queen." He turned back to the table, Ellery already forgotten.

Minchen interposed. "Dr. Janney."

"Well?"

Minchen spoke eagerly. "Queen is practically a member of the Police Department, Doctor. He's the son of Inspector Queen, and he's helped solve a lot of murder mysteries. Perhaps he'd—"

"Oh." Janney's smoldering little eyes twisted toward Ellery. "That's different. Take charge, Queen. Anything you want. I'm busy."

Ellery immediately turned to face the gallery. Every one had stood up. Dr. Dunning and his daughter were already hurrying up the steps toward the rear exit

"Just a moment." His voice rang crystal-clear in the amphitheater. "You will oblige me by remaining in the gallery—every one, please—until the police arrive and give permission to leave."

"Preposterous! Police? What for?" Dr. Dunning turned, his face white with strain. The girl placed her hand on his arm.

Ellery did not raise his voice. "Mrs. Doorn has been murdered, Doctor." Dr. Dunning, speechless, took his daughter's arm; they groped their way down to the fore portion of the gallery; no one spoke.

Ellery turned to Minchen, spoke insistently in a low voice. "Do this at once, John. . . ."

"Whatever you say."

"See that every door of the Hospital is *immediately* closed and guarded. Have some one with intelligence discover, if possible, who has left the premises within the past half-hour. Patients, staff—everybody and anybody. That's important. Telephone my father at Police Headquarters. Get in touch with the local precinct and tell them what's happened. Understood?"

Minchen hurried away.

Ellery stepped forward, stood slightly aside. He watched the smooth efficient movements of the doctors working over the old woman. But, he could see at a glance that there was no hope of restoring life. The founder of the Hospital, millionairess, benefactress of countless charities, social leader, manipulator of fortunes, was beyond human aid.

He asked quietly of Janney's lowered head, "Any hope?"

"None whatever. This is utterly useless. She's gone—was dead a half-hour ago. *Rigor mortis* had already set in when she was brought into this room." Janney's muffled voice was as impersonal as if he had been discussing a Potter's Field cadaver.

"What killed her?"

Janney straightened; he ripped the gag from his face. He did not reply to Ellery at once. Instead he motioned to his two assistants, shook his head significantly. The doctors removed the pulmotor apparatus in silence. A nurse, stony-faced, lifted the sheet to conceal the aged flesh. . . .

Ellery restrained a start when Janney turned to him. The surgeon's lips were trembling. His face was grey.

"She's been—strangled," he said thickly. "God."

He turned away, reached beneath his gown with shaking fingers and brought out a cigarette.

Ellery bent over the corpse. Around the old woman's neck was a deep, thin bloody line. On a small table nearby lay a short length of ordinary picture-wire, stained with blood. Without touching it, Ellery examined it and noted that it bent in two places, as if the wire had been tied in a knot.

Abigail Doorn's skin was dead-white, with a faint bluish tinge, and peculiarly puffy. The lips were tightly pressed together, the eyes deep-sunken. The body was stiff, unnatural. . . .

The corridor-door opened and Minchen reappeared.

"Everything taken care of, Ellery," he croaked. "I put James Paradise, our Superintendent, on the job of checking up arrivals and departures; we'll have a report soon. Called your father; he's on his way with his staff. The precinct is sending a few men—"

A bluecoat stamped into the theater, looked around, made for Ellery.

"Hullo, Mr. Queen. Just got me flash from the precinct. Takin' charge?" he rumbled.

"Yes. Stand by, won't you?"

Ellery glanced about the Amphitheater. The occupants of the gallery had not moved. Dr. Dunning sat sunk in thought His daughter looked faint, sick . . . In the orchestra Dr. Janney had walked to the farther wall and stood facing it, smoking. The nurses, the assistants wandered aimlessly.

"Let's get out of here," said Ellery suddenly, to Minchen. "Where can we go?"

"Shall I—?"

"Notify Mrs. Doorn's relatives outside of what's happened?" finished Ellery abruptly. "No. Not yet. We have plenty of time. In here?"

"Yes."

Ellery and Minchen approached the door. Ellery turned, his hand on the knob.

"Dr. Janney."

The surgeon turned slowly, took a limping step forward, stopped.

"Well?" His voice was harsh, again emotionless.

"I should appreciate your not leaving this room, Doctor. I want to talk with you—soon."

Dr. Janney stared, seemed about to speak. But he clamped his lips firmly together, wheeled and limped back to his wall.

6

EXAMINATION

THE ANTEROOM to the Amphitheater was almost square except for one corner, where it was cut off by a small cubicle. On the same wall stood a compartment, the door of which bore the words:

AMPHITHEATER LIFT
(For Operating-Room Use Only)

For the rest, there were a few of the familiar cabinets, shining with enamel and glass, a washbowl, a wheel-table and one white metal chair.

Minchen paused at the door from the theater, and commandeered the use of several chairs. These were brought in by nurses and the door closed.

Ellery stood still in the center of the room and surveyed this unpromising domain.

"Scarcely a plethora of clews, eh, Minchen?" he said with a grimace. "This, I take it, is the room in which Mrs. Doorn was kept before being taken into the theater?"

"That's right," replied Minchen gloomily. "Was brought in here about a quarter after ten, I think. She was certainly alive then, if that's what you're driving at."

"There are a few elementary problems to solve, old man," murmured Ellery, "besides the question of whether she was alive when they brought her into this room. By the way, how can you be sure? She was in a coma, wasn't she? Seems perfectly possible that she might have been done in *before*."

"Janney ought to have an idea about that," Minchen muttered. "He examined her pretty thoroughly in the theater while they were applying the oxygen and adrenalin."

"Let's get Dr. Janney in here."

Dr. Minchen went to the door. "Dr. Janney," he called in a low voice. Ellery heard the slow, limping footsteps of the surgeon approach, lag, then resume with a sudden vigor. Dr. Janney stamped into the Anteroom, regarded Ellery challengingly.

"Well, sir!"

Ellery bowed. "Be seated, Doctor. We may as well be comfortable. . . ." They sat down. Minchen prowled back and forth before the door to the theater.

Ellery smoothed his right palm on his knee, regarded his shoetop lovingly. Suddenly he looked up. "I think, Doctor, it would be best for us to begin in the most incipient place—to wit, the beginning. Please relate to me the incidents of this morning in relation to Mrs. Doorn. I have an avid ear for detail. Would you mind—?"

The surgeon snorted. "Good God, man, do you want me to give you a case history now? I've things to do—arrangements to make—patients to see!"

"Nevertheless, Doctor," smiled Ellery, "as you must know very well, there's nothing quite so important in a murder investigation as the apprehension of the murderer. Perhaps you're not familiar with the New Testament? So few scientists are! 'Gather up the fragments that remain, that nothing be lost.' I mean to gather up the fragments. I believe you possess some of them. Well, sir!"

Janney stared fixedly at Ellery's cheerful lips. He darted one of his quick, keen glances at Minchen from the corner of his eye.

"I see I'm in for it. What precisely do you want me to tell you?"

"A small order. Everything."

Dr. Janney crossed his legs, lit a cigarette with steady fingers. "At 8:15 this morning I was summoned from my first inspection in the Surgical Ward to the foot of the main stairway of the third floor. There I found Mrs. Doorn, where she had just been picked up. She had fallen from the head of the stairs and ruptured her gall-bladder as a result of the impact to her abdomen as she landed. Preliminary examination indicated that she had been seized by a typical diabetic coma while in the act of descending, and naturally, becoming unconscious, lost command of her muscular action."

"Very good," murmured Ellery. "You had her immediately removed, I suppose?"

"Of course!" barked the surgeon. "Had her taken to one of the private rooms on the third floor, undressed at once, and put to bed. Rupture was bad. Absolutely demanded immediate surgical attention. But the diabetic complication forced us to lower the sugar content by the dangerous but essential insulin-glucose treatments. The coma was lucky—only bit of good fortune in the whole business. Anæsthesia would have added to the risk. . . . As it was, we worked her sugar down to normal by these intravenous injections, and by the time I was through with a rush case in Operating Room 'A' the patient was already in the Anteroom, waiting."

Ellery said swiftly, "Are you prepared to say, Doctor, that Mrs. Doorn was alive when she was wheeled into the Anteroom?"

The surgeon's jaws clamped together. "I'm prepared to say

nothing of the kind, Queen—not from personal experience. Patient was under the care of Dr. Leslie, an associate, while I operated in 'A.' Better ask Leslie. . . . From the condition of the body, though, I should say she'd been dead no longer than twenty minutes, possibly a few minutes less, when we discovered the wire around her neck."

"I see. . . . Dr. Leslie, eh?" Ellery stared thoughtfully at the rubber-tiled floor. "John, old man, would you mind calling Dr. Leslie, if he's available? It's all right, Dr. Janney?"

"Oh, yes. Of course, of course." Janney waved his white muscular hand negligently. Minchen left the room by the Amphitheater door, returning promptly with a white-garbed surgeon in tow—one of the men who had aided Dr. Janney.

"Dr. Leslie?"

"Arthur Leslie, that's right," said the surgeon. He nodded to Janney, who sat morosely in his chair puffing at his cigarette. "What's this—an inquisition?"

"Of a sort. . . ." Ellery leaned forward. "Dr. Leslie, were you with Mrs. Doorn from the time Dr. Janney left her to attend his other operation until the time Mrs. Doorn was wheeled into the Amphitheater?"

"Not at all." Leslie looked interrogatively at Minchen. "Am I suspected of murder, John? . . . No, old man, I wasn't with her all the time. Left her in this Anteroom under the care of Miss Price."

"Oh, I see! But you were with her every minute of the time before she was brought here?"

"Now you're talking. That's right."

Ellery tapped his finger lightly on his knee. "Are you prepared to swear, Dr. Leslie, that Mrs. Doorn was alive when you left this room?"

The surgeon's eyebrows went up quizzically. "Don't know how valid my oath is, but—yes. I examined her before leaving this room. Heart was certainly pumping. She was alive, brother."

"Well, well! We're getting somewhere at last," murmured Ellery. "Limits the time nicely, and corroborates Dr. Janney's estimate about the approximate time of death. That will be all, Doctor."

Leslie smiled, turned on his heel. "Oh, by the way, Doctor," Ellery drawled. "At exactly what time was the patient brought into this room?"

"Ask me a harder one. 10:20. Wheeled right from her room on the third floor to the lift over there"—he pointed across the room to the door marked AMPHITHEATER LIFT—"and carried directly from the lift into this room. Lift's used only to convey patients to and from operations in the Amphitheater, you know. To make the report minutely correct, Miss Price and Miss Clayton accompanied me downstairs, after which Miss Price was left to watch the patient while I went into the theater to get things ready and Miss Clayton departed for other duties. Miss Price is Dr. Janney's assistant, you know."

"She's been helping Dr. Janney with Mrs. Doorn for several years," interposed Minchen.

"Is that all?" demanded Dr. Leslie.

"Quite. Will you ask Miss Price and Miss Clayton to step in here, please?"

"Right!" Leslie departed, whistling cheerfully.

Janney stirred. "Look here, Queen, surely you don't need me any more. Let me get out of here."

Ellery rose, flexed his biceps. "Sorry, Doctor—we've still a use for you. . . . Ah, come in!"

Minchen opened the door wide to admit two young women in regulation white uniform.

Ellery bowed gallantly, looked from one to the other. "Miss Price—Miss Clayton?"

One of the nurses—a tall, fair girl with roguish dimples—said quickly, "Oh, I'm Clayton, sir. *This* is Miss Price. Isn't it *dreadful?* We—"

"Undoubtedly." Ellery stepped back, indicated two chairs. Janney had not risen. He sat glaring savagely at his left leg. "Won't you sit down? . . . Now, Miss Clayton, I understand that you and Miss Price brought Mrs. Doorn down on a wheel-table from the third floor some time ago, in company with Dr. Leslie. Is that correct?"

"Yes, sir. Then Dr. Leslie went into the Amphitheater and I had to get back to Ward G—that's off the third floor—and Miss Price remained here," replied the tall nurse.

"Right, Miss Price?"

"Yes, sir." The second nurse was a medium-sized brunette with fresh rosy skin and clear eyes.

"Excellent! Ellery beamed. "Miss Price, can you recall what happened while you were in this room alone with Mrs. Doorn?"

"Oh, perfectly."

Ellery shot a quick glance toward the other occupants of the room. Janney still sat glowering; to judge from the expression on his face, he was absorbed in dour reflections. Minchen leaned against the door, intently listening. Miss Clayton was watching Ellery with a sort of frank fascination. Miss Price sat quietly, hands folded in her lap.

Ellery leaned forward. *"Miss Price, who entered this room after Dr. Leslie and Miss Clayton left?"*

The extraordinary earnestness of his tone seemed to befuddle the nurse. She hesitated. "Why— no one but Dr. Janney, sir."

"Hey?" roared Dr. Janney. He had leaped to his feet so suddenly that Miss Clayton uttered a stifled scream. "Why, Lucille, you must be mad! Do you mean to sit there and say to my face that I came into this room before the operation?"

"Why, Dr. Janney," said the girl faintly. Her face had whitened. "I—I saw you."

The surgeon stared at his assistant, his long simian arms dangling ludicrously to his knees. Ellery looked at Janney, at Miss Price, at Minchen—and clucked tenderly beneath his breath. When he spoke his voice was soft, a little vibrant.

"You may go now, Miss Clayton."

The fair nurse opened her eyes widely. "Oh, but—"

"If you please."

She left the room reluctantly, casting a longing glance back over her shoulder as Minchen closed the door behind her.

"Now!" Ellery removed his *pince-nez* eyeglasses; he began with a gentle circular motion to polish them. "We seem to have reached a slight point of disagreement. You say, Doctor, that you *weren't* in this room before the operation?"

Janney glared. "Of course I say so! It's the most ridiculous nonsense! Why, you yourself talked to me about 10:30 in the corridor just after I'd been operating for twenty minutes, and I don't doubt saw me leave with Cobb the doorman to go toward the Waiting Room. How could I have been in this room? Lucille, you're absolutely mistaken!"

"Just a moment, Doctor," interposed Ellery. "Miss Price, at what time did Dr. Janney enter? Can you recall?"

The nurse's fingers were nervously plucking at her starched gown. "Why—I don't remember exactly—about 10:30—perhaps a few minutes later. Doctor, I'm—"

"And how do you know it was Dr. Janney, Miss Price?"

She laughed, nervously. "Why, naturally I thought—I just rec-
ognized him—I took it for granted it was Dr. Janney. . . ."

"Ah! You took it for granted?" said Ellery. He took a swift step
forward. "Why, didn't you see his face? Surely, if you had seen his
face you'd have known *positively.*"

"Certainly!" interrupted Janney. "You've known me long
enough, Lucille. I can't understand—" Beneath his irritation he
seemed bewildered. Minchen looked on in stupefaction.

"Oh, you—he wore gown, cap and gag," stammered the girl,
"so I could only see the eyes—but—well, he *limped,* sir, and he
was about the same height, and—you see, that's what I mean by
taking it for granted. You never quite know *why.*"

Janney stared at her. "By God, some one's been impersonating
me!" he cried. "That's it! I'm damn easy to impersonate . . . game
leg . . . gag . . . Queen, some one—some one . . ."

7

IMPERSONATION

ELLERY PLACED a restraining hand on the little surgeon's quivering arm. "Take it easy, Doctor. Sit down, sit down. We'll get to the bottom of this only too quickly. . . . Well. Come in!"

There had been a short knock on the door. It opened now to admit a giant of a man in street clothes. He had tremendous shoulders, light eyes, a rock-ribbed face.

"Velie!" exclaimed Ellery. "Dad here already?"

The newcomer under thick brows examined Janney, Minchen, the nurse. . . . "No, Mr. Queen. On his way. Men from the local precinct and detectives from District Headquarters are here. Want to come in. I suppose you don't want—" He glanced significantly at Ellery's audience.

"No, no, Velie," said Ellery quickly. "Keep those fellows busy outside. Don't let any of 'em in here until I give the word. Let me know the instant dad arrives."

"Okay." The giant retreated silently, and as silently closed the door behind him.

Ellery addressed the nurse again. "Now, Miss Price, you must be as exact as if your life depended upon accuracy. Tell me just what happened in here all the time from the moment Dr. Leslie and Miss Clayton left you alone with Mrs. Doorn until she was wheeled into the theater next door."

The nurse moistened her lips and cast a shy, nervous glance at the surgeon, who had subsided into his chair and was watching her with dull eyes.

"I—well . . ." she laughed forcedly. "It's so simple, really—Mr. Queen, is it? . . . Dr. Leslie and Miss Clayton left directly after we brought Mrs. Doorn down here from the third floor room. There was nothing for me to do. The doctor had taken another look at the patient and everything was apparently all right. . . . Of course you know that no anæsthesia was used?" Ellery nodded. "That meant that it wasn't necessary for an anæsthetist to be present with me, nor for me to watch the patient's pulse continually. She was in a coma and ready for the operation. . . ."

"Yes, yes," said Ellery impatiently, "we know that, Miss Price. Please get on to your visitor."

The nurse flushed. "Yes, sir. . . . The man I—I thought was Dr. Janney came into the Anteroom about ten or fifteen minutes after Dr. Leslie, and Miss Clayton left. He—"

"Through which door did he enter?" demanded Ellery.

"This one." The nurse pointed to the door leading to the Anæsthesia Room.

Ellery turned swiftly to Dr. Minchen. "John, who was in the Anæsthesia Room this morning? Was it being used?"

Minchen looked blank. Miss Price volunteered, "There was a patient being anæsthetized there, Mr. Queen. I think Miss Obermann and Dr. Byers were there. . . ."

"Very well."

"This man who came in limping, with surgical clothing on, closed the door—"

"Quickly?"

"Yes, sir. He immediately closed the door behind him and approached the wheel-table over there on which Mrs. Doorn was lying. He bent over her, then looked up and sort of absent-mindedly made a washing motion with his hands."

"Mum, eh?"

"Oh, yes, sir; he didn't say a word—just rubbed his hands together. Of course I understood immediately what he wanted. It's a very familiar, well, gesture with Dr. Janney. It signified he wanted to disinfect his hands—probably because he meant to give the patient a last examination before the operation. So I went into the Sterilizing Room there"—she pointed to the cubicle at the northeast corner of the room—"and prepared a bichloride of mercury solution and an alcohol wash. I—"

Ellery looked pleased. "How long, do you judge, were you in the Sterilizing Room?"

The nurse hesitated. "Oh, it was three minutes or so. I can't recall exactly. . . . I came back into the Anteroom and placed the disinfectants on the washbowl there. Dr. Janney—I mean the man, whoever he was—rinsed his hands quickly—"

"More quickly than usual?"

"Yes, I noticed that, Mr. Queen," she replied, keeping her head averted from the surgeon, who leaned his elbow on his knee and stared steadily at her. "Then he dried his hands on a surgical towel I had ready and waved the bowls away. As I was taking them back into the Sterilizing Room I noticed that he went back to the wheel-table and again leaned over the patient. When I returned he was just straightening up, patting the sheet back into place."

"Very clear, Miss Price," said Ellery. "A few questions, if you please. . . . When you stood near him as he disinfected himself, did you notice his hands?"

She knit her brows. "Why—not particularly. You see, I wasn't suspicious about anything and naturally took all his actions as a matter of course."

"Too bad you didn't notice his hands," murmured Ellery. "I have great faith in the character of hands. . . . Miss Price, tell me this. How long were you gone the second time—when you restored your materials to the Sterilizing Room?"

"Not more than a minute. I just poured out the bichloride and alcohol solutions, rinsed the basins, and came out again."

"How soon after you returned did this man leave?"

"Oh, immediately!"

"Through the same door by which he entered—the Anæsthesia Room door?"

"Yes, sir."

"I see. . . ." Ellery took a short turn about the room, tapping his *pince-nez* thoughtfully against his chin. "From what you say, Miss Price, there seems to have been an astonishing dearth of conversation. Didn't your mysterious visitor say anything at all during the entire proceedings—a word, just one all-important word?"

The nurse looked faintly surprised. Her clear eyes stared into space. "Do you know, Mr. Queen—why, he never opened his mouth all the time he was here!"

"Scarcely amazing," said Ellery dryly. "Ingenious, the whole thing. . . . Didn't you say anything either, Miss Price? Didn't you greet him when he entered the room?"

"No, I didn't greet him, sir," she said quickly, "but I did call out to him while I was in the Sterilizing Room the first time."

"Exactly what did you say?"

"Nothing terribly important, Mr. Queen. I know Dr. Janney's nature quite well—he's a little impatient some times." A smile hovered about her lips. It faded quickly as the surgeon grunted. "I—I called out: 'I'll have it ready in a moment, Dr. Janney!'"

"You actually called him 'Dr. Janney,' eh?" Ellery looked quizzically at the surgeon. "A perfect get-up, I should say, Doctor." Janney muttered, "Evidently, evidently!" Ellery turned to the nurse again. "Miss Price, is there anything else you remember? Have you covered absolutely everything that occurred while this man was in the room?"

She looked thoughtful. "Well—if I recall correctly, something else did happen. But it wasn't very important, Mr. Queen," she added apologetically, turning her eyes upward to his.

"I'm considered a good judge of unimportant things, Miss Price," smiled Ellery. "What was it?"

"Why, while I was in the Sterilizing Room the first time, I heard a door in the Anteroom open and a man's voice say, after the slightest hesitation, 'Oh, pardon me!' and then the door swung back. At least I heard the sound of a door again."

"Which door?" demanded Ellery.

"I'm sorry, sir, but I really don't know. You just can't make out direction of sounds like that; at least I can't. And of course I was out of sight."

"Well, then! Did you recognize the voice?"

Her fingers twisted nervously in her lap. "I'm afraid I'm not much help, Mr. Queen. It sounded sort of familiar, I suppose, but I wasn't particularly interested, really, and I don't know who it might have been."

The surgeon got wearily to his feet, looked in despair at Minchen. "God, what stuff and nonsense!" he growled. "It's the baldest kind of frame-up. John, you don't believe that I was implicated in this business, do you?"

Minchen ran his finger under the collar of his gown. "Dr. Janney, I don't—can't believe it. I don't know what to think."

The nurse rose swiftly, approached the surgeon, put her hand appealingly on his arm. "Dr. Janney, please—I didn't mean to get you in wrong—of course it wasn't you—Mr. Queen understands that. . . ."

"Well, well!" chuckled Ellery. "A tableau! Come, now, let's not be melodramatic about this matter. Please sit down, sir. And you, too, Miss Price."

They seated themselves, a trifle stiffly. "Did anything strike you as unusual, or out-of-the-way, during the time this—well, let's call him 'impostor' temporarily—this impostor was in the room?"

"At the time, no. Of course, now I can see that his not talking, and the disinfectant business, and all that—I can see now that it was funny."

"What happened after our precious impostor left?"

"Why, nothing. I took it that the doctor had just examined the patient to see that nothing had gone wrong. So I just sat down on the chair and waited. Nobody else came in and nothing really happened until the operating-room staff came in from the theater to wheel the patient away. And then I followed them into the theater."

"Didn't you look at Mrs. Doorn during all this time?"

"I didn't go over to feel her pulse or examine her closely, if that's what you mean, Mr. Queen." She sighed. "Of course I glanced at her now and then, but I knew she was in a coma—her face was very pale—but then, too, the doctor had examined her—well, you see . . ."

"I see. I quite see," said Ellery gravely.

"Anyway, my orders had been not to disturb the patient unless something unexpected happened, or seemed to be wrong. . . ."

"Yes, of course! One thing more, Miss Price. Did you notice on which foot the impostor placed his weight? You remember you said he limped?"

Her body drooped wearily in the chair. "It was his left foot that seemed to be the weak one. He put all his weight on the right—just like Dr. Janney. But then—"

"Yes," said Ellery, "but then any one who wanted to do a thorough job of impersonation would be careful about that. . . . That's all, Miss Price. You've been very helpful. You may go into the theater now."

She said, "Thank you," in a low voice, looked earnestly at Dr. Janney, smiled to Dr. Minchen, and departed through the door to the Amphitheater.

There was a little silence after Minchen softly shut the door. The Medical Director coughed, hesitated, then sank into the chair the nurse had left. Ellery put his foot on another chair, leaning his elbow on his knee and playing with his glasses. Janney fidgeted, took out a cigarette, crushed it between his hard white fingers. . . . Suddenly he leaped to his feet.

"Now, look here, Queen," he shouted, "this thing's gone far enough, don't you think? You know damn well I wasn't there. Why, it could have been any murdering scoundrel familiar with me and the Hospital! Everybody knows I limp. Everybody knows I'm wearing surgical clothes three-quarters of the time I'm here. It's as plain as a pregnancy! God!" He shook his head like a shaggy dog.

"Yes, it looks remarkably like an imposition on your good nature, Doctor," said Ellery mildly, peering at Janney. "But you can't get away from it—the man's clever."

"I'll give him credit for that, all right," grumbled the surgeon. "Fooled Miss Price—she's been with me for years now. Probably fooled a couple of others in the Anæsthesia Room. . . . Well, Queen, what are you going to do with me?" Minchen stirred uncomfortably.

Ellery's eyebrows shot up. "Do?" He chuckled. "My *métier*, Doctor, is dialectic. I'm an avatar of Socrates. I ask questions. . . . So I'm going to ask you—and I know you'll be truthful—where were you, Doctor, and what were you doing during the time this droll bit of play-acting was taking place?"

Janney straightened, sniffed. "Why, you know where I was. You heard Cobb's piece. You saw me go off with the man to see my visitor. Good God, man, that's infantile."

"I'm singularly ingenuous this morning, Doctor. . . . How long did you speak with your visitor? And where? These are some of the things, Doctor. . . ."

Janney grunted. "Luckily, I looked at my watch just as I was leaving you. If you recall, it was 10:29. And my watch is accurate—has to be. . . . Went back with Cobb, met my caller in the Waiting Room, and took him to my office, which is just across the corridor next to the main lift. That's all, I think."

"Hardly, Doctor. . . . How long were you in your office with your visitor?"

"Until 10:40. Zero hour was approaching, and I had to cut the interview short. Still had to get ready—get into fresh surgical clothes—be disinfected. . . . So my visitor left and I went directly to the Amphitheater."

"Entering from the West Corridor door, as I saw you," murmured Ellery. "Check. . . . Did you escort your visitor to the main entrance? Did you see him out?"

"Naturally." The surgeon grew restless again. "Now see here, Queen, after all—You're questioning me as if I were the criminal." Again the dynamic little surgeon had worked himself into a rage. His voice rose shrilly; livid veins stood out on his gnarled neck.

Ellery approached Janney with a pleasant smile. "And by the way, Doctor, who was your visitor? Of course, since you've been so frank with me about everything else, you won't mind telling me this?"

"I—" Janney's rage ebbed from his face slowly. He grew quite pale. With a sudden gesture he stood straight, clicked his heels together, moistened his lips with the tip of his tongue. . . .

A peremptory knock on the Amphitheater door sounded like thunder in the Anteroom. Ellery swung about instantly. "Come!"

The door opened and a small, slim man dressed in dark grey, white-haired and white-mustached, smiled in at them. Behind him stood a group of formidable-looking men.

"Well, dad," said Ellery. He hurried forward. Their hands clasped and they looked earnestly at each other. Ellery shook his head the merest trifle. "You come in a most dramatic moment. It's the most fascinating mess you've ever tackled, sir. Come on in!"

He stepped aside. Inspector Richard Queen advanced with springy steps, motioning the men behind to follow. He shot one quick comprehensive glance around the room, nodded affably to Dr. Janney and Dr. Minchen, hopped forward again.

"In, boys, inside," he chirped. "There's work to do. Ellery—on the job? Solved it yet? Thomas, come in and shut that door! And these gentlemen? Ah, doctors! A great profession. . . . No, Ritchie, you'll find nothing in this room. I take it the poor old lady was lying here when she was done in? Shocking, shocking!"

He looked around, chattering incessantly, his keen little eyes missing nothing.

Ellery introduced the two doctors. Both bowed without speaking. The detectives with the Inspector had spread about the room. One poked the wheel-table curiously; it slid a few inches on the rubber floor.

"District detectives?" asked Ellery with a grimace.

"Ritchie's gang like to be in on everything," chuckled the old man. "Don't let 'em bother you. . . . Come over to that corner, sir, and let's hear the worst. I gather it's something of a puzzle."

"You gather correctly," replied Ellery with a grim smile. They moved quietly away, by themselves, and Ellery in an undertone gave his father a résumé of the morning's events, including the testimony that had been given. The old man nodded often. As Ellery's recital drew to a close, the Inspector's face grew graver. He shook his head.

"Worse and worse," he groaned. "But that's the life of a policeman. For every hundred open-and-shut cases there's one that requires a mind trained in a dozen universities. Including the university of crime. . . . There are a few things to be done at once."

The Inspector turned back to his staff, approached the tall, hard-jawed detective-sergeant named Velie.

"What did 'Doc' Prouty say, Thomas?" he demanded. . . . "No, sit still, Dr. Minchen; I'll be prancing around. . . . Well?"

"Medical Examiner kept him on something," boomed Velie in his deep bass. "Be here later."

"Good enough. Well, gentlemen . . ."

He grasped Velie's lapel, opened his mouth to speak. Ellery paid scant attention to the Inspector; out of the corner of his eye he was watching Dr. Janney, who had retreated to the wall and stood quietly regarding his shoe-tips.

With an unmistakable air of relief.

8

CORROBORATION

THE INSPECTOR was talking paternally to Velie, who towered above him.

"Now, you've got some things to do, Thomas," said the old man. "First thing is to run down this feller Paradise—that his name, Dr. Minchen?—he's superintendent of the Hospital, Thomas—and get his report on people who came in and people who went out this morning. I understand Paradise was put on the job immediately after the murder was discovered. Find out what he's done. Second thing—check up the guards at all exits and entrances and substitute our own men. Third thing—send in this Dr. Byers and Miss Obermann on your way out. Scoot, Thomas!"

As Velie opened the Amphitheater door, a number of bluecoats became visible, wandering slowly about the operating-room. Ellery caught a brief flash of the gallery; Philip Morehouse was on his feet, protesting violently about something. He was in the grip of a burly policeman. To the side, Dr. Dunning and his daughter sat in what seemed to be stupefied silence.

Ellery exclaimed sharply, "Heavens, dad, the relatives!" He turned to Minchen. "John, there's a dirty job for you. Will you go back to that Waiting Room—here's an idea; take young Morehouse with you; he's evidently in trouble up there—and inform Hendrik Doorn and Hulda Doorn, Miss Fuller and whoever else is there. . . . Just a moment, John." He conversed in low tones with the Inspector. The old man nodded and motioned to a detective.

"Here, Ritchie, you're aching for something to do. Let's see the District acquit itself," said the Inspector. "Go over to that Waiting Room with Dr. Minchen and take charge. Keep 'em all in there— Doctor, you'll probably need help; shouldn't wonder if there'd be fainting and things there; might get a few nurses to help. Don't let one of them go until I give permission, Ritchie."

Ritchie, a black-jowled individual with a sullen air, made some indistinct reply and followed Minchen surlily from the room. Through the open door Ellery saw Minchen gesture upward toward Morehouse, who ceased struggling and bounded up to the gallery exit.

The door swung shut. Almost immediately it opened again to admit a white-clad physician and a nurse.

"Ah—Dr. Byers?" cried the Inspector. "Come in, come in! Glad you could come so soon. Not taking you or this charming young lady away from your work? No? Well, well! . . . Dr. Byers," he snapped suddenly, "were you in that Anæsthesia Room next door this morning?"

"Certainly."

"Under what circumstances?"

"I was administering anæsthesia to a patient with the aid of Miss Obermann here. She's my regular assistant."

"Was any one besides you, Miss Obermann and your patient in the room?"

"No."

"At what time were you attending to this duty?"

"We used the room from 10:25, when we took it over, until

about 10:45. The patient was an appendectomy, scheduled to be operated on by Dr. Jonas, who was a little late. Had to wait for both 'A' and 'B' operating-rooms to be vacated—we're busy to-day."

"Hmm." The Inspector smiled pleasantly. "And, Doctor, did any one enter the Anæsthesia Room while you occupied it?"

"No—that is," added the physician hastily, "no stranger. Dr. Janney passed through about 10:30, I should say, perhaps a min-ute or two after, going into the Anteroom; and about ten minutes later came out again. Ten minutes or a little less."

"You, too," muttered Dr. Janney, flashing a venomous glance at Dr. Byers.

"Eh? I beg your pardon—?" stammered Dr. Byers. The nurse at his side looked astonished.

The Inspector came forward a little, speaking hurriedly. "Ah—never mind that now, Dr. Byers. Dr. Janney is not feeling well—a little upset—naturally, naturally! . . . Now, sir, you would be will-ing to make a sworn statement, I suppose, that the man you saw pass in and out of that room this morning was Dr. Janney?"

The doctor shifted restlessly, hesitating. "You put it pretty bluntly, sir. . . . No, I wouldn't make a sworn statement. After all," he said, brightening up, "I didn't see his face. He wore a surgical gag, gown, and the rest. Quite covered—oh, yes!"

"Indeed!" commented the Inspector. "So you wouldn't swear to it. Yet a moment ago you seemed very sure it was Dr. Janney. Why?"

"Well . . ." again Dr. Byers hesitated, "of course there was the limp that we have grown so accustomed to. . . ."

"Ha! The limp! Go on."

"And then too, subconsciously, I suppose, I more or less anticipated the presence of Dr. Janney, since I knew that his next surgical case was in the Anteroom—we were upset about it—Mrs. Doorn, you know . . . and, well—I just thought so, that's all."

"And you, Miss Obermann," the Inspector turned swiftly to the nurse, taking her by surprise—"did *you* assume it was Dr. Janney?"

"Yes—yes, sir," she stammered, flushing. "For the—the same reasons as Dr. Byers."

"Hmm!" grunted the Inspector. He took a turn about the room. Janney was staring unwinkingly at the floor. "Tell me Doctor," continued the old man, "did your patient see Dr. Janney enter and leave? Was he conscious during this time?"

"I think," faltered the physician, "that he might have seen Dr.—Dr. Janney come in, because the cone had not yet been applied and his table faced the door. But he was under ether when Dr. Janney reappeared, and couldn't have seen, of course."

"And who is this patient?"

A fleeting grin appeared on the lips of Dr. Byers. "I imagine he's quite well known to you, Inspector Queen. Michael Cudahy."

"Who? What! 'Big Mike'!" The exclamations flew about the room. Every detective there had jerked about in surprise. The Inspector's eyes narrowed.

He turned abruptly to one of his staff. "I thought you told me Michael Cudahy went to Chicago, Ritter," he snapped. "You certainly get the fanciest ideas!" He wheeled on Dr. Byers. "Where's 'Big Mike' now?" he demanded. "What room? I want to see that guerrilla!"

"He's in a private room—32—on the third floor, Inspector," replied the physician. "But it won't do you any good to see him. He's dead to the world, sir—they've just carted him out of the operating-room 'B.' Jonas operated. Your man caught me just as Jonas finished. He's in his room now, but he won't be out of the ether for a good couple of hours."

"Johnson!" said the Inspector grimly. A small drab-looking man stepped forward. "Make a note to remind me to grill 'Big Mike.' Under ether, hey? That's a new one."

"Dr. Byers." Ellery's voice came quietly. "While you were working in the Anæsthesia Room, it is barely possible that you overheard some conversation emanating from here. Do you recall? Or you, Miss Obermann?"

Doctor and nurse regarded each other for a long moment. Dr. Byers looked frankly at Ellery. "Now, that's funny," he said. "It just happens that we overheard Miss Price call out to Dr. Janney that she would be ready in a moment, or something like that; and I remember remarking to Miss Obermann that the old ma—I mean Dr. Janney must be unusually cross to-day, because he didn't even answer."

"Ah! Then you mean you overheard no statement or question of any kind from Dr. Janney during the entire course of his visit to this room?" asked Ellery quickly.

"Not a syllable," said Dr. Byers. Miss Obermann nodded in agreement.

"Do you remember hearing a door open and close in here and a voice say, 'Pardon me!'?"

"I don't believe I do."

"You, Miss Obermann?"

"No, sir."

Ellery whispered into the Inspector's ear. The Inspector sucked his lip, nodded, motioned imperiously to a Swedish-looking detective of solid build. "Hesse!" The man slouched near. "Get this straight now, won't you? Go out into the operating-room and ask the doctors and internes if any one of them poked his head in here between 10:30 and 10:45. And bring him back."

While Hesse departed on his errand the Inspector dismissed Dr. Byers and the nurse. Janney watched them go with gloomy eyes. Ellery conversed with his father until the door reopened to admit a young dark-haired man of Semitic cast, dressed like the others in white Hospital regalia. Hesse herded him into the room.

"Dr. Gold," said Hesse briefly. "He was the one."

"Yes," said the young interne at once, addressing himself to the diminutive Inspector, "I stuck my head in through that door—" he pointed to the door leading to the West Corridor—"about 10:35, I should say, looking for Dr. Dunning to ask about a diagnosis. Of course I immediately saw it wasn't Dr. Dunning—saw it just as I opened the door—so I excused myself without going in and went away."

Ellery leaned forward. "Dr. Gold, how far did you open the door?"

"Oh, just about a foot or so—enough to get my head in. Why?"

"Well," smiled Ellery, "why not? At any rate, whom did you see?"

"Some doctor—don't know who it was."

"How did you know it wasn't Dunning?"

"Why, Dr. Dunning is tall and thin, and this man was rather short and stocky—cut of the shoulders was different—I don't know—simply wasn't Dr. Dunning."

Ellery polished his *pince-nez* vigorously. "And how was this doctor standing—tell me what you saw when you opened the door."

"His back was to me, and he was slightly bent over the wheel-table. His body concealed whatever was on the table."

"His hands?"

"I couldn't see them."

"Was he the only person in the room?"

"Only one I could see. Of course, the patient must have been on the table; but as for any one else, I can't say."

The Inspector cut in gently. "You said, 'Oh pardon me!', didn't you?"

"Yes, sir!"

"And what did the man reply?"

"Why, nothing. Didn't even turn around, although I saw his shoulders sort of twitch when I spoke. Anyway, I stepped back, closed the door and went away. The whole business didn't take more than ten seconds."

Ellery approached Dr. Gold, tapped him on the shoulder. "One thing more. Might this man have been—Dr. Janney?"

The young interne drawled, "Oh-h, I suppose so. But it might have been a dozen others, too, from what I saw. . . . Anything wrong, Doctor?" He twisted his head to stare at the surgeon, who did not reply. "Well, I guess I'll be going if that's all. . . ."

The Inspector cheerily waved him out

"Get Cobb—the doorman." Hesse sauntered out.

"Good God," said Janney quite tonelessly. No one paid the slightest attention.

The door opened to admit Hesse and Isaac Cobb, the crimson-faced 'special.' His cap was jauntily set on his head and he looked around expansively, as if he felt a kinship with these men of the police.

The Inspector wasted no words. "Cobb, stop me if I say something that isn't so. . . . You approached Dr. Janney while Mr. Queen and Dr. Minchen were talking with him in the corridor. You told him that a man wanted to see him. He refused at first, but when you handed him the man's card—bearing the name 'Swanson'—

he changed his mind and followed you down the corridor toward the Waiting Room. What happened then?"

"The Doctor says 'Hello' t' this man," replied Cobb in a conversational tone, "an' then they went out of the Waiting Room, turned t' the right—ye know Dr. Janney's office is that way—an' they went into the Doctor's office. An' they closed the door—I mean the Doctor. So I went back t' my station in the vestibule an' I stood there all th' rest of the time until Dr. Minchen came along an' said . . ."

"One moment, one moment!" said the Inspector testily. "Granted that you didn't leave your post for a moment. Suppose—" he glanced at Dr. Janney, who was hunched up in his corner, suddenly tense, alert—"suppose Dr. Janney or his visitor had decided to leave Dr. Janney's office to go toward the, let us say, operating-rooms, could he have passed without your seeing him?"

The doorman scratched his head. "Sure! I guess so. I don't always face the inside. Sometimes I open th' door and look out into th' street."

"*Did* you look out into the street this morning?"

"Well—sure! I guess so."

Ellery interrupted. "You say Dr. Minchen came along and told you to lock the door. How long before this did Dr. Janney's visitor—this man Swanson—leave the building? By the way, he left the building, didn't he?"

"Oh, sure!" Cobb grinned broadly. "Even gave me—I mean wanted to give me a quarter. But I wouldn't take it—against the regulations. . . . Yes, I'd say this feller passed out into th' street about ten minutes or so before Dr. Minchen gave me the order."

"Did any one else," continued Ellery, "go out of that front door between the time Swanson left and the time you locked the door?"

"Nary a soul."

Ellery confronted Dr. Janney, who immediately straightened and looked off into space. "There's a little matter, Doctor," Ellery began softly, "that we haven't had time to settle. You recall, don't you? I believe you were about to tell me who your visitor was when the Inspector came in and . . . ." He broke off with a tightening of his lips as the door banged open and Sergeant Velie stalked in, flanked by two detectives.

"Ah, well," said Ellery with a slight smile, "we seem doomed to defer the fatal question. . . . Carry on, sire. Messer Velie seems bursting with information."

"Well, Thomas?" demanded the Inspector.

"No one left the Hospital since 10:15 except Dr. Janney's visitor. Cobb told us about this Swanson a few minutes ago outside," Velie growled. "Got a list of some people who came into the building during that time, but we've checked 'em over and they're all accounted for. Got 'em all in the building too—we haven't let any one go out."

The Inspector beamed. "Excellent, Thomas, excellent! There you are, Ellery," he exclaimed, turning to his son, "the Queen luck for you. Our murderer's still in the building. Can't get away!"

"Probably doesn't want to," said Ellery dryly. "I shouldn't be too hopeful about *that*. . . . And, dad—"

"Well?" said the Inspector, suddenly glum. Janney looked up with a peculiar gleam in his eye.

"A persistent idea has been buzzing about in my conk," said Ellery dreamily. "Let's assume, for the sake of argument and—" he bowed toward the surgeon—"and I should hope for the sake of Dr. Janney, that the gentleman who perpetrated this plot was not Dr. Janney but a rank and nervy impostor."

"Now you're talking sense," growled Janney.

"And let us go further in our supposition," continued Ellery, rocking on his toes and gazing at the ceiling, "by assuming that our slippery criminal, having a dark but valid reason for putting as much distance as possible between himself and the clothes which he wore, divested himself of these figuratively bloody garments and hid them somewhere. . . . Now we know that he hasn't left the building. Is it too much to hope that by assiduously scouring the premises . . ."

"Ritter!" barked the Inspector. "You heard Mr. Queen? Take Johnson and Hesse and start!"

"I heartily detest," grinned Ellery, "introducing a literary allusion at such a solemn moment—but Longfellow seems to have anticipated me. Remember? 'Till all that it foresees it finds. . . .' And I sincerely pray you *find*, Ritter—if only for Dr. Janney's peace of mind!"

9

IMPLICATION

"AND AGAIN," said Ellery, bowing deferentially to Dr. Janney as the door closed on the three detectives, "we return to the fountain-head of knowledge. Doctor . . . precisely who was your visitor?"

Inspector Queen moved chairward. In walking across the room he trod softly, as if he were afraid of breaking a spell. Ellery stood in utter stillness—even the practical, unimaginative men circulating slowly about the room sensed something of the drama in his lightly worded question.

Dr. Janney did not reply at once. He puckered his lip and frowned, as if within himself he was debating some abstruse problem known to him alone. And when he spoke his brow was untroubled.

He said simply, "You're making a fuss, Queen, about a very small matter. My visitor was a friend. . . ."

"A friend by the name of Swanson."

"Exactly. He happens to be strapped financially, and he called upon me for a personal loan."

"Very laudable, very!" murmured Ellery. "He needed money,

and he asked you for some. . . . Nothing mysterious about that, I agree!" . . . He smiled again. "Of course you gave it to him?"

The surgeon stiffened. "Yes—my personal check for fifty dollars."

Ellery laughed outright, inoffensively. "Hardly an embarrassing touch, Doctor! You were lucky at that. . . . By the way, what is your friend's full name?"

He paused carelessly, as if his question were the most natural one in the world. Inspector Queen, keeping his eyes on Janney, explored his pocket and brought out a brown old snuff-box. Midway between the box and his nostrils, his hand stopped—waiting. . . .

Janney's rejoinder was curt. "I prefer not to tell you!" Inspector Queen's hand continued its journey, performed its function and returned. He sniffed and rose, stepping forward with a mild look of inquiry on his placid features.

But Ellery forestalled him. He said in even tones, "That is exactly what I wanted to know, Doctor. . . . This chap Swanson must be very dear to you indeed to merit such heroic shielding. He is an old friend, of course?"

"Oh, no!" said Janney quickly.

"No?" Ellery's eyebrows went up. "Scarcely consistent with your attitude, Dr. Janney. . . ." He stepped up to the little surgeon, loomed over him. "Answer one question, Doctor, and you silence me forever. . . ."

"I don't see what you're driving at," muttered Janney, retreating a step.

"Nevertheless," said Ellery softly, "answer . . . Why, if this man Swanson is not a particularly close friend, did you give him fifteen minutes of your precious time this morning, while your benefactress lay desperately ill, unconscious, awaiting the unique skill of your hand and knife? . . . And take all the time you want in answering."

He turned on his heel even while Janney, a steadily growing light of rebellion in his eyes, said coldly, "I have nothing to say that can have any bearing on your investigation."

Ellery sauntered to the chair his father had vacated, sat down and waved his hand, as if to say, "Your witness."

The old man's smile, if anything, grew gentler. He paced up and down before Janney, followed by the surgeon's defiant little eyes.

"Needless to say, Dr. Janney," began the Inspector politely, "we cannot accept your stand in this matter. You see that, of course. . . ." It was a challenge. "Perhaps you'll honor me by giving straight replies, without subterfuge." Janney said nothing. "Very well, let me begin. . . . What happened between you and Swanson in the fifteen minutes you were together in your office?"

"I'm really not being stubborn," said Dr. Janney with a startling change of manner. He looked tired, sought the back of a chair for support "Swanson came to see me, as I told you, to borrow fifty dollars, which he needed urgently and could not get elsewhere at the moment. I refused at first. He began to explain the circumstances. They were such that common decency demanded I accede to his request. I gave him my check, we talked about his affairs, he left. That's all."

"A most reasonable statement, Doctor," replied the Inspector gravely. "However, if this is all as innocent as you make it out to be, why won't you give us the man's name—his address? You must realize that we have certain routine inquiries to pursue, that your friend's testimony is necessary to support your own. Give us the information we're lacking, and there's an end of it!"

Janney wagged his shaggy head heavily. "I'm sorry, Inspector. . . . Perhaps I should explain that my friend is an unfortunate, a victim of circumstances—sensitive nature and excellent breeding. Any notoriety particularly at this time would be bad in its effect on him. And he simply couldn't have had anything to do with the murder of Mrs. Doorn." His voice rose slightly, became shrill. "By God, why do you insist?"

Ellery scrubbed his *pince-nez* glasses thoughtfully, his eyes never leaving the face of Dr. Janney.

"I suppose it's useless for me to ask you to describe Swanson?" demanded the Inspector. The smile had left his face.

Janney clamped his lips together.

"Very well, then!" snapped the old man. "You realize that without Swanson's testimony to bolster yours your position becomes downright dangerous, Dr. Janney?"

"I have nothing to say."

"I shall give you exactly one more chance, Dr. Janney." The Inspector's voice was deadly now with cold rage; his lips trembled slightly. "Give me Swanson's visiting card."

There was a short stifling silence. "Eh?" growled Janney.

"The card, the card!" cried the Inspector impatiently—"the card with Swanson's name on it, which the doorman handed you while you talked in the corridor with Dr. Minchen and Mr. Queen. Where is it?"

Janney raised haggard eyes to the old man. "I haven't got it"

"Where is it!"

Janney remained still as the grave.

The Inspector whirled instantly to Velie, who stood aloof and glowering in the corner. "Search him!"

The surgeon gasped, retreated to the wall, glaring about him with a hunted, animal look. Ellery half-rose in his chair, but sank back as Velie crowded the little man to a corner and said, impersonally, "Will you hand it over or do I have to take it from you?"

"By God!" gasped Janney, livid with rage, "you touch me and—and I'll . . ." His voice trailed off from sheer impotence.

Velie swept his huge arm about the fragile figure of the surgeon, gathered him in as easily as if Janney had been a child. Beyond one frantic shudder of his frame, the surgeon did not resist. The rage fled from his face, drained out of his eyes. . . .

"Nothing." Velie stepped back to his corner.

Inspector Queen gazed earnestly at the little man, with a sort of unwilling admiration. He spoke without turning his head, spoke almost casually. "Search Dr. Janney's office, Thomas."

Velie lumbered out of the room, taking a detective with him. . . .

Ellery was frowning. He unrolled his lean length from the chair. He spoke in low tones to the Inspector. The old man waggled his head doubtfully.

"Dr. Janney." Ellery's voice was low. The surgeon stood limply against the wall, staring at the floor. His face was dark with blood and he breathed in heavy, uneven pants. "Dr. Janney, I'm frightfully sorry this occurred. You gave us no choice. . . . We are trying, really trying, to see your point of view. . . . Doctor, hasn't it struck you that if Swanson, whom you mask so valiantly, is as good a friend of yours as you are of his he will *want* to step forward and substantiate your story? No matter how unfortunate he is. . . . Don't you see?"

"I'm sorry. . . ." Janney spoke in so hoarse a tone that Ellery cocked his head sharply to catch the words. But defiance had fled. The doctor seemed utterly spent.

"I see." Ellery was grave. "Then there is only one thing more to ask. I can see no way of forcing you to reply. . . . Dr. Janney, did either you or Swanson leave your office even for a moment, between the time you entered and the time you said good-by to each other?"

"No." And Janney raised his head to look full into Ellery's eyes.

"Thank you." Ellery stepped back and sat down again. He brought out a cigarette and lighted it, puffing thoughtfully.

Inspector Queen sent a detective off with a curt command. A moment later the man returned with Isaac Cobb. The doorman entered confidently, his red face shining.

"Cobb," began the Inspector without preliminary, "you said before that you saw Dr. Janney's visitor both when he entered the Hospital and left it. Describe him to me."

"Oh, sure!" Cobb beamed. "I never forget a face, sir. . . . Yes, sir. This feller was just about middlin' in height, sort of blond, I'd say, clean-shaved, and he was rigged out in kind of dark clothes. Wore a black overcoat anyway."

"Did you get the idea," put in Ellery instantly, "that he was well off, Cobb—I mean from the way he dressed?"

"Cripes no!" The doorman was emphatic, shaking his head vigorously. "Looked down at th' heel, I'd say. . . . Yeah, an' he must have been—oh, I'd say thirty-four, five or somewhere thereabouts."

"How long have you been here, Cobb?" asked Ellery.

"Mighty nigh onto ten years."

The Inspector said coolly, "And have you ever seen this man Swanson before, Cobb?"

The doorman did not reply at once. "We-e-ell," he said finally, "seems t'me he looked kinda familiar but—I dunno."

"Mmm!" Inspector Queen took a pinch of snuff. "Cobb," he wheezed as the snuff flew up his nostrils, "what was this man's first name? You know it!" he added sharply, slapping, his snuff-box away into his pocket "You brought Dr. Janney his card!"

The doorman looked frightened. "Why, I—I dunno. I didn't look at it—just handed it over t' Dr. Janney."

"Cobb, my dear fellow," interposed Ellery lazily, "this is remarkable! You don't accept honorariums, and you aren't inquisitive. It simply baffles me!"

"You mean to tell me," demanded the Inspector threateningly, "that when this man gave you his card, you walked all the way down the corridor to find Dr. Janney and didn't even look at it once?"

"I—no—no, sir." Cobb was frankly scared.

"Rubbish!" muttered the Inspector, turning his back. "The man's a fool. Get out, Cobb!"

Mutely, Cobb slunk away. Sergeant Velie, who had slipped into the room while Cobb was being questioned, came quietly forward.

"Well, Thomas." The Inspector was clearly not sanguine of his sergeant's report. He looked at Velie almost grumpily. Ellery stole a glance at Dr. Janney. The surgeon seemed unconcerned, wrapped in thought

"Wasn't there."

"Ha!" The Inspector stalked slowly to Dr. Janney. "What did you do with that card? Answer me!" he thundered.

Janney spoke wearily. "I burned it," he said.

"Very well!" growled the Inspector. "Thomas!"

"Right."

"Start the wheels moving. I want this man Swanson at headquarters by tonight. Medium height, fair, dark clothes, shabby, about thirty-five, and in poor circumstances. Get busy!"

Ellery sighed. "Velie." The detective halted on his way to the door. "Just a moment. . . ." Ellery turned to Dr. Janney. "Doctor, have you any objection to showing me your check-book?"

Janney jerked convulsively; anger mounted to his eyes once more. But when he spoke it was with the same deadly fatigue. "Not at all." He brought out a folded check-book from his hip-pocket, handed it without another word to Ellery.

Ellery turned rapidly to the first leaf on which a check appeared. To the left was a memorandum-page. The last notation read: CASH.

"Ah!" Ellery smiled, returned the book to Janney, who, without moving a muscle of his face restored it to his pocket. "Velie, get that check. Your first stop might be the Bank of the Netherlands. Then the clearing-house. The check-number is 1186, made out to Cash for fifty dollars, dated to-day, on Dr. Janney's personal account. You'll have Swanson's signature, at any rate."

"One thing more!" Ellery's voice rang out like a bell. "When you examined Dr. Janney's office, did you look in his personal address-book for a 'Swanson'?"

A wintry smile flickered over Velie's lips. "Sure did. And nothing doing. Nobody by that name. Wasn't listed on a personal telephone list under the glass top of the doctor's desk, either. That all?"

"Quite."

"Look here." The Inspector stalked over to Janney. "There's no necessity for you to be standing, Doctor," he said in a kinder tone. "Why don't you sit down. . . ." The surgeon looked up in dull surprise. "For," continued the old man grimly, "we'll be here for some time yet. . . ."

Janney sank into a chair. There was silence until a tattoo on the West Corridor door brought a detective across the room to open it.

Detective Ritter burst into the Anteroom, bearing a large shapeless white bundle under his arm. Behind him, more sedately, came Johnson and Hesse, both grinning.

Inspector Queen lunged forward. Ellery rose, took an eager step. Janney's head was sunk on his breast; he seemed asleep.

"What's this?" cried the Inspector, snatching at the bundle.

"The duds, Chief!" shouted Ritter. "We found the murderin' crook's duds!"

Inspector Queen spread the contents of the bundle on the wheel-table from which Abigail Doorn's lifeless body had been taken. "At last we've something to go on," he muttered. He looked up quickly at Ellery, glee in his eyes.

Ellery bent over the table, prodded the bundle with his long white finger. "More fuel, more fire!" he murmured, and glanced slyly at the chair in which Dr. Janney was now sitting alertly, craning his neck to see what was on the table.

"What are you mumbling about?" demanded the Inspector, busy prodding the clothes.

"Ashes," said Ellery enigmatically.

10

MANIFESTATION

THEY CROWDED around the wheel-table, heads cocked over and watched Inspector Queen separate the various articles composing the bundle.

Dr. Janney made an impatient gesture. He half-rose, sank back into his chair, raised himself again. Then curiosity, it seemed, mastered him. He sidled toward the table, peered over the shoulders of two detectives.

The Inspector lifted a long white garment and held its spotless length high. "Hmm. Surgical gown, eh?" His grey brows bunched suddenly; he shot a droll sidewise look at Janney. "This yours, Doctor?"

Janney muttered, "How can I tell?" Nevertheless he wedged himself between the two detectives and fingered the gown. Ellery murmured, "Would it fit you, I wonder?" and the Inspector raised the garment before Janney. It reached to the surgeon's ankles. "Not mine," said Janney, distinctly, "Too long."

The gown was crumpled but unsoiled. It had apparently been freshly laundered.

"It's not new," said Ellery. "Look at those frayed hems."

"The laundry mark. . . ." The Inspector twisted the garment

about suddenly; his fingers sought the inner side of the neckpiece, at the back. Two little punctures testified mutely to the rape of the gown's laundry mark.

The old man tossed the gown aside.

He picked up a small, biblike linen article with strings at the upper corners. Like the long garment, it was crumpled and un-soiled; it, too, showed unmistakable signs of previous use.

"Might be anybody's," volunteered Janney, defensively.

It was a surgeon's gag.

The next article was a surgeon's cap; it elicited nothing tangible. Not new, unsoiled, plentifully wrinkled. . . . Ellery took it from his father's hand and turned it inside out. Adjusting his *pince-nez* carefully, he brought the headpiece close to his eyes and probed with a fingernail in the minute crevices of the surrounding hems.

With a diffident shrug he replaced the cap on the table. He merely said, "Extremely fortunate for the murderer."

"You mean—no hair?" demanded Janney quickly.

"Something like that. How alert you are, Doctor. . . ." Ellery leaned forward to examine the fourth article which Inspector Queen had picked up. The old man held it up to the light. It was a pair of stiffly-starched white duck trousers.

"Here! What's this?" cried the Inspector. He threw the trousers onto the table, pointed an eager forefinger at the thighs of the garment. On both legs, two inches above the slightly baggy knee, was a broad pleat.

Ellery unaccountably appeared pleased. He removed a silver pencil from his vest-pocket and delicately lifted the sharp edge of one of the pleats. The pencil caught on something. They bent lower and saw that several basting-stitches had been taken in the thighs to hold down the pleats. The stitches were of coarse white thread, and widely separated. On the under side of the trousers similar stitches appeared.

"Evidently our impromptu tailor," murmured Ellery, "intended his sewing as a purely temporary measure. You see," he said airily, "basting was sufficient unto the moment. . . ."

"Thomas!" The Inspector looked about quickly.

Velie loomed at the other end of the table.

"Think you could trace this cotton?"

"Not a chance."

"Take a stab at it."

Velie produced a pen-knife and cut off a two-inch length of thread from the pleat of the right leg. He stowed it away in a glassine envelope as carefully as if it were a hair from the murderer's head.

"Let's take a look at this on you, Doctor." The Inspector did not smile. "No, I don't mean actually on your legs; up against 'em will do." Janney silently took the trousers and held them up before him, fitting the waistline to his belt. The cuffs fell exactly to his shoetops.

"And with those pleats let out," ruminated Ellery aloud, "since the pleats take in about four inches of the material. . . . What's your height, Doctor?"

"Five-five." The surgeon tossed the trousers back to Inspector Queen.

Ellery shrugged. "Not that it signifies anything," he said, "but the original owner of these trousers is—or was—five feet nine inches tall. But—" he smiled frostily, "that's hardly a clew. They might have been stolen from any one of the hundreds of hospitals in the City, or from any one of the thousands of physicians, or . . ."

He stopped short. Inspector Queen had swept aside gown, gag, cap and trousers, and now reverently revealed a pair of white canvas shoes—low-cut oxfords. The old man's hand shot forward. . . .

"One moment!" rapped Ellery. "Before you pick them up and handle them, dad. . . ."

He eyed the shoes in speculative silence. "Ritter." The detective mumbled in reply. "Did you touch these shoes before you brought them in here?"

"Nope. Just picked up the bundle the way I found it. Felt the shoes inside, in the middle."

Ellery stooped again and applied his silver pencil. This time he stirred the tip of the white lace on the right shoe.

"*Alors*—that's more like it!" he said, straightening up. "A clew at last." He whispered into his father's ear. The old man nodded doubtfully.

On the shoelace at the third set of eyelets there was a half-inch strip of adhesive tape. Its outer surface was perfectly clean. A curious depression in the center of the tape's width attracted the Inspector. He looked up inquiringly at Ellery.

"Lace broke, I'll bet a cookie," muttered the Inspector, "and that dent there is where the two broken ends come together. They don't fit exactly."

"Hardly the nucleus of the point," murmured Ellery. "The tape—the tape! It's uncommonly dazzling."

Dr. Janney stared. "Rot!" he said in a loud clear voice. "Don't see it at all, and I'm accustomed to interpreting phenomena. . . . Somebody's merely used adhesive to mend a broken lace. Only thing I'm interested in is the size. Any one can see that's a smaller shoe than the one I wear."

"Perhaps. No, don't touch it!" cried Ellery, as Janney reached forward to grasp one of the shoes. The surgeon shrugged, looked about pleadingly. Then he trudged back to the farther side of the room and sat down, where he waited with stoic eyes.

Ellery raised a tiny corner of the adhesive, felt the underside briefly with the tip of his forefinger. "Well, Doctor," he called out, "with apologies to you, your skill and your profession, I'm going to supersede you and perform a surgical operation myself. Velie, let's have your pen-knife."

He pried the two ends of the strip of tape apart. One edge was curiously jagged. Grasping a corner, he pulled; the adhesive came away with ease. "Still moist," he said with elation in his voice. "Confirmation—confirmation! Have you noticed, dad—" he hurried on, motioning to Velie "—an envelope, old man!—that it was applied in quite obvious haste? The one edge didn't even adhere to its brother-surface, and this is powerful stuff." He deposited the strip of tape in another glassine envelope, which he immediately tucked into the breast-pocket of his coat.

Stooping over the table once more, he pulled on the frayed end of the upper piece of string—it was still in the shoe—and exercising meticulous care not to waste even a quarter-inch, he tied the broken ends together. To do this, he found it necessary to draw in so much of the tip-end that a bare inch of the white lace remained hanging from the topmost eyelet.

"It doesn't require a necromancer," he smiled, turning to the Inspector, "to see that if the broken ends had been tied together at the break, not enough would have remained to lace the shoe. Consequently—the adhesive, for which we may thank some nameless but divinely-cast shoelace manufacturer."

"But Ellery," protested the Inspector, "what of it? Can't say that I see much to be gay about."

"Believe me, sir, my levity was never in more proper order."

Ellery grinned. "Very well, since you've asked for it.—Suppose your shoelace broke at any given time—let's say a particularly awkward moment—and you found that by knotting the torn ends you had so shortened the lace that it was impossible to tie your shoe. What would *you* do?"

"Oh!" The Inspector tugged at his grey mustache. "Well, I guess I'd make shift with something else, just as the murderer did. But even then—"

"That is so sufficient," said Ellery didactically, "that I *am* beginning to feel the gnawing pangs of interest. . . ."

Detective Piggott coughed with the obvious purpose of attracting attention. Inspector Queen turned impatiently.

"Well?"

Piggott reddened. "Somethin' I sort of noticed," he said shyly. "Where the devil's the tongues of these here shoes?"

Ellery chuckled explosively. Piggott regarded him with hurt suspicion. But Ellery took off his *pince-nez* and began to scrub at them. "Piggott, you deserve a substantial increase in salary."

"Eh? What's that?" The Inspector seemed vaguely displeased. "Poking fun at me?"

Ellery pulled a face. "Now, look here," he said. "Aside from the lace, the—I might call it the Astounding Mystery of the Missing Tongues—becomes a positively integral part of this investigation. Where are they? When I was examining the shoe before, I discovered—this!"

He grasped the shoe swiftly and poked his finger beneath the laces, far into the forward portion of the vamp, near the toe box. With an effort he scraped at something, and in a moment had pulled out the hidden tongue.

"Here it is," he said. "And it's significant that it was pressed, tight and smooth, against the upper wall of the toe box. . . . And, unless a most promising little theory has gone a-begging. . . ."

He explored the recesses of the left shoe. Its tongue was also plastered upward and out of sight.

"That's a queer one," muttered Inspector Queen. "You're sure now, Ritter, that you didn't monkey with these shoes?"

"Johnson'll tell you," replied Ritter in an aggrieved tone.

Ellery looked keenly from the Inspector to Ritter; but it was the keenness of introspection. He turned away from the table, head bowed in thought.

"You might be careful of those shoes," he said absently, striding up and down the Anteroom. He halted. "Dr. Janney."

The surgeon closed his eyes. "Well."

"What size shoe do you wear?"

Janney instinctively stole a downward glance at his canvas shoes—apparently exact duplicates of the shoes on the table. "Guess I'm lucky," he drawled. He rose suddenly, like a Jack-in-the-box. "Still hot on the scent?" he snarled, thrusting his face close to Ellery's and glaring into his eyes. "Well, Queen, you're off your trail this time. I wear size 6 ½."

"Rather small at that," reflected Ellery. . . . "But you see, these shoes are only size 6!"

"Size 6 it is," interrupted the Inspector. "But—"

"Hush!" smiled Ellery. "You can't know how satisfied I feel to find that the murderer wore these shoes—as they are. . . . And my satisfaction has little, Doctor, to do with you. . . . Ritter, where did you find these clothes?"

"Lyin' on the floor of the telephone booth at the corner of the South and East Corridors."

"So!" Ellery pulled at his lip, frowning for a long moment. "Dr.

Janney, you saw the strip of adhesive I took from this shoe. Is it the same brand as the tape used here?"

"Certainly. What of it? It's the brand used by practically every hospital in the City."

"I can't say I'm drooping with disappointment," said Ellery. "It was too much to expect that. . . . Of course, Doctor, none of these articles is yours?"

Janney spread his hands. "Oh, what the devil good will it do me to say yes or no? They don't look it. But I'll have to check over my locker to make sure."

"Cap and gag might be yours, eh?"

"Might be anybody's!" Janney tore at the tight neckband of his gown. "You saw the gown was too long. As for the trousers—just a clumsy disguise. And I'm certain the shoes aren't mine."

"I'm not so sure about that," said the Inspector belligerently. "At least we've no proof they aren't."

"Oh, but we have, dad," said Ellery in his gentlest voice. "Look here."

He turned both shoes over and pointed to the heels. They were of black rubber. The shoes showed signs of long usage and the heels had been rubbed smooth by the friction of walking. On the right shoe the heel was considerably worn down on the right side. On the left shoe the heel was similarly worn down on the left side. Putting the shoes close together, Ellery pointed to the heels.

"You'll observe," he drawled, "that each heel has been rubbed away to approximately the same depth. . . ."

The Inspector's glance strayed floorward, to the little surgeon's left foot. Janney's weight rested on the other.

"Dr. Janney," continued Ellery, "is quite right. These shoes are not his!"

11

INTERROGATION

DR. JOHN Minchen's orderly soul received blow after blow during the hectic morning of Abigail Doorn's death. His Hospital was disorganized. His internes were stewing about the corridors, smoking in flagrant violation of the rules and discussing the murder in lively professional conversation. The feminine contingent seemed to feel that the tragedy suspended all regulations; they giggled and chattered among themselves until the senior nurses, scandalized, herded them back to their wards and private rooms.

The main floor was crowded with detectives and policemen. Minchen, scowling, weaved his way through the groups which dotted the corridors until he came to the door leading into the Anteroom. He rapped and was admitted by a tobacco-chewing detective.

In a quick glance he encompassed the tableau—Janney, his face pale and set, standing as if at bay in the center of the room; Inspector Queen confronting him, lines of perplexity and irritation on his smooth old face; Ellery Queen leaning against the wheel-table, fingering a white canvas shoe; plain-clothesmen scattered about, silent and watchful.

He coughed. The Inspector pivoted on his heel and walked

across the room to the table. A little color came into Janney's cheeks; his body sagged like an empty sack into a chair.

Ellery smiled. "Yes, John?"

"Sorry to interrupt." Minchen was nervous. "But things have taken a slightly serious turn in the Waiting Room and I thought—"

"Miss Doorn?" asked Ellery quickly.

"Yes. She's on the verge of collapse. Really ought to be taken home. Do you think you could possibly—?"

Ellery and the Inspector conferred in low tones. The Inspector looked anxious. "Dr. Minchen, is it really your opinion that the young lady needs . . ." He chopped his thought abruptly. "Who is her closest kin?"

"Mr. Doorn—Hendrik Doorn. He's her uncle—Abigail Doorn's only brother. I would also suggest that a woman accompany her—perhaps Miss Fuller. . . ."

"Mrs. Doorn's companion?" said Ellery slowly. "No, I think not. Not just yet. . . . John, are Miss Doorn and Miss Dunning chums?"

"Fairly well acquainted."

"It's quite a problem." Ellery gnawed at a fingernail. Minchen stared at him, as if he could not understand the exact nature of this "problem."

Inspector Queen interposed impatiently, "Oh, after all, son. . . . She can't very well remain here, in the Hospital. If she's feeling so badly—poor child!—her place is at home. Let her go, now, and let's get on."

"Very well." The frown did not leave Ellery's forehead. He patted Minchen's shoulder absently. "Have Miss Dunning accompany Miss Doorn and Mr. Doorn. But before they go—Yes, that's best. Johnson, get Mr. Doorn and Miss Dunning in here for a moment. I shan't keep them long. I suppose, John, there's a nurse with Miss Doorn?"

"Certainly. And young Morehouse is with her, too."

"And Sarah Fuller?" demanded Ellery.

"Yes."

"Johnson. While you're about it take Miss Fuller up to the gallery of the Amphitheater and see that she's kept there until we call for her."

The drab-looking detective quickly left the room.

A white-coated young interne slipped past the man at the corridor-door and, looking around timidly, approached Dr. Janney.

"Here!" roared the Inspector. "Where do you think you're going, young man?"

Velie sauntered slowly to the side of the interne, who wilted perceptibly. The surgeon rose.

"Oh, it's all right," he droned in a tired voice. "What do you want, Pearson?"

The young man gulped. "Dr. Hawthorne's just called, Doctor, about that angina consultation. He said to get a move on. . . ."

Janney clapped his hand to his forehead. "Rats!" he exclaimed. "Forgot all about it! Slipped my mind completely.—Look here, Queen, you'll have to let me go. Serious matter. Rare case. Ludwig's angina. Terrific mortality rate. . . ."

Inspector Queen looked at Ellery, who waved his hand negligently. "We're certainly not privileged to retard the miraculous processes of healing, Doctor. If you must, you must. *Au revoir!*"

Dr. Janney was already at the door, pushing the young interne before him. He paused, hand at the knob, and looked back with a brown-toothed and strangely-refreshed grin. "Took a death to get me in here, and a near-death to get me out. . . . 'Bye!"

"Not so fast, Dr. Janney." The Inspector stood quite still. "You are not to leave town under any circumstances!"

"Good God!" groaned the surgeon, popping back into the room. "That's impossible. I've got a medical convention in Chicago this week and I planned to skip out tomorrow. Why, Abby herself wouldn't have wanted—"

"I said," repeated the old man distinctly, "that you are not to leave the City. And I meant it. Convention or no convention. Otherwise—"

"Oh, for God's sake!" screamed the surgeon, and he ran out of the room, slamming the door behind him.

Velie crossed the Anteroom in three strides, pulling the burly figure of Detective Ritter with him. "After him, you!" he growled. "And don't let him out of your sight, or I'll fan your tail!"

Ritter grinned and lumbered into the corridor, disappearing in Janney's wake.

Ellery was saying with amusement, "Our surgical friend's fondness for calling upon his Creator doesn't jibe at all with his professional agnosticism, d'ye know? . . ." when Johnson opened the door from the Amphitheater and stepped aside to allow Edith Dunning and a short man of tremendous girth to precede him.

Inspector Queen hopped forward. "Miss Dunning? Mr. Doorn? Come in, come in! We shan't keep you a moment!"

Edith Dunning, her fair hair disheveled, her eyes red-rimmed and cold, stopped short on the threshold. "Make it snappy." She spoke in a remarkably metallic voice. "Hulda's in bad shape and we've got to get her home."

Hendrik Doorn shuffled two paces into the room. The Inspector eyed him amiably, and not without astonishment. Doorn's abdomen bulged in fold after fold of fat flesh; he seemed to ooze forward rather than walk; his gelatinous belly quivered with each step in a gross rhythm. His face shone moon-like and greasy; it was mottled with tiny pink spots, condensed into a broad reddish bulb at the tip of his nose. He was completely bald, with an unhealthy white skull which reflected the light of the room.

"Yess," he said, and his voice was no less remarkable than his appearance. It was pitched high, yet it had a curiously grating, rusty quality. "Yess," he squeaked, "Hulda needts her bedt. What iss this foolish bother? We know nothings."

"A moment, just a moment," said the Inspector soothingly. "Please come in. We must have that door closed. Sit down, sit down!"

Edith Dunning's narrow eyes never left the Inspector's face. Stiffly, like a machine, she sat down in a chair which Johnson held out for her and folded her hands angularly in her lap. Hendrik Doorn waddled to another chair and sank, groaning, into it. His gross buttocks hung limply over the sides.

The Inspector took a generous pinch of snuff and promptly sneezed. "Now, sir," he began politely, "one question and you'll be on your way. . . . Have you any idea who might have had cause to murder your sister?"

The fat man mopped his cheeks with a silk handkerchief. His little black eyes shifted from the Inspector's face to the floor and back again. "I—*Gott!* This iss a terrible business for uss all. Who knows? Abigail wass a funny womans—a wery funny womans. . . ."

"Look here." Inspector Queen was sharp. "You must know something about her private life—enemies, whatnot. Can't you suggest a possible line of inquiry—?"

Doorn kept wiping his face with short heavy swoops of his arm. His porcine little eyes roved, were never still. He seemed inwardly to be debating something with himself. "Well—" he said at last, weakly, "there iss somethings. . . . Budt nodt here!" He heaved himself out of the chair. "Nodt here!"

"Ah, then you do know something," said the Inspector softly. "Very interesting, I'm sure. Out with it now, Mr. Doorn—out with it, or we shan't let you go!"

The girl sitting beside the fat man stirred impatiently. "Oh, for the love of Pete, mister, let's get out of here. . . ."

The door-knob rattled violently and the door was kicked open. They all turned to see Morehouse stagger in, supporting a tall young woman whose eyes were closed and whose head was bent forward, rolling a little. A nurse held tightly to her on the other side.

The young lawyer's face was crimson with anger. His eyes spat fire as the Inspector and Ellery sprang forward to help carry the girl into the Anteroom.

"Dear, dear!" muttered the Inspector in an agitated voice. "So this is Miss Doorn, eh? We were just—"

"Yes, you were just—Junk!" roared Morehouse. "And it's about time. What is this—the Spanish Inquisition? I demand permission to take Miss Doorn home! . . . Outrage! Criminal! Oh, get out of the way, will you!"

He shoved Ellery roughly to one side as they half-lifted the unconscious girl into a chair. Morehouse stood stiff-legged over her, fanning her face with his hand, spluttering incoherently. The nurse pushed him impersonally away and applied a vial to the girl's nostrils. Edith Dunning had risen; she was bent over Hulda, slapping the girl's cheeks.

"Hulda!" she called irritably. "Hulda! Don't be a little fool. Come out of it!"

The girl's eyes fluttered open; she shrank back from the vial.

She looked blankly at Edith Dunning; then she turned her head slightly and saw Morehouse.

"Oh, Phil! She's—she's . . ." She got no further. Her voice blurred with sobs; she stretched her arms blindly toward Morehouse and began to cry. The nurse, Edith Dunning, Ellery stepped back; Morehouse's face had magically softened; he leaned over Hulda, talking rapidly to her in a whisper.

The Inspector blew his nose. Hendrik Doorn, who still stood before his chair and had merely glanced at the girl while she was being attended, quivered all over his immense body.

"Let uss be going," he squeaked. "The girl—"

Ellery confronted him swiftly. "Mr. Doorn, what were you going to say? You know some one with a grudge? A desire for vengeance?"

Doorn quavered, "I had rather nodt say. I am in danger of my life. I. . . ."

"Oho!" murmured the Inspector, stepping to Ellery's side. "A hush story, hey? Somebody's threatening, Doorn?"

Doorn's lip trembled. "I will nodt speak in this place. This afternoon—maybe. At my house. Now—no."

Ellery and Inspector Queen exchanged glances, and Ellery retreated. The Inspector smiled agreeably at Doorn and said: "Very well. This afternoon at your house. . . . And you'd better be there, old boy. Thomas!" The giant grunted. "You'd do well to send some one along with Mr. Doorn, Miss Doorn and Miss Dunning—just to take care of them."

"I'm going along," cried Morehouse suddenly, spinning around. "And I don't need any of your damned snooping detectives, either. . . . Miss Dunning, grab hold of Hulda!"

"Oh, but you're not, Mr. Morehouse," said the Inspector in

his mildest voice. "You're going to stay a while. We need you." Morehouse glared; their glances clashed. Then the lawyer looked around at the ring of grim faces. He shrugged, helped the weeping girl to her feet, walked with her to the corridor door. Her hand clung to his until Hendrik Doorn and Edith Dunning, followed by a detective, reached the door. There was a furtive handclasp, the girl squared her shoulders, and Morehouse was left alone at the door to watch the little company go slowly down the hall.

There was silence as he closed the door and turned back to face them.

"Well," he said bitterly, "here I am. Now what do you want with me? Please don't keep me—too long."

They took chairs as several of the remaining district and local detectives, on a sign from the Inspector, marched out of the Anteroom. Velie put his gargantuan back against the corridor door and folded his arms. . . .

"Mr. Morehouse." The Inspector settled himself comfortably and clasped his tiny hands in his lap. Ellery lit a cigarette and inhaled deeply. He became absorbed in the glowing tip.

"Mr. Morehouse. You've been Mrs. Doorn's attorney for a long time?"

"A number of years," sighed Morehouse. "My father handled her affairs before me. Sort of family client, the old lady was."

"You know her private as well as her legal affairs?"

"Intimately."

"What was the relationship between Mrs. Doorn and her brother Hendrik? Did they get along? Tell me everything you know about the man."

Morehouse made a *moué* of distaste. "You'd be getting an earful, Inspector. . . . Of course, you must realize that some of the things I'm going to say are purely opinions—as a friend of the family I've naturally observed and heard things. . . ."

"Go on."

"Hendrik? An eighteen-carat parasite. He's never done a lick of work in his life. Perhaps that's why he's so abominably fat. . . . He's not only a blood-sucking leech, but an expensive one to maintain. I know, because I've seen some bills. And the little playmate has all sorts of pleasant vices. Gambling, women—the usual thing."

"Women?" Ellery closed his eyes and smiled dreamily. "I can't quite believe it."

"You don't know some women," replied Morehouse grimly. "He's been Broadway's roly-poly sugar-daddy to so many women he probably doesn't remember them all himself. It hasn't reached the papers much—Abigail saw to that. . . . You'd think he might live fairly comfortably with the allowance of twenty-five thousand a year Abigail provided for him. But not Hendrik! He's perpetually broke."

"Hasn't he any money in his own right?" asked the Inspector.

"Not a red cent. You see, Abigail has made every penny of her enormous fortune by her own wits. The family originally was poorer than the public knows. But she had a genius for finance. . . . interesting woman, Abby. It's a damned shame."

"Legal trouble? Shady deals? Anything underhanded?" demanded the old man. "Seems likely he'd have to pay hush money to some of those Jezebels of his."

Morehouse hesitated. "Well . . . I can't say."

The Inspector smiled. "Hmm. . . . And the relationship between Hendrik and Mrs. Doorn?"

"Lukewarm. Abby wasn't anybody's fool. She knew what was going on. She put up with it because she had a fierce pride of family and wouldn't allow the world to talk about any one with the name of Doorn. Occasionally she put her foot down, and there would be a row. . . ."

"How about Mrs. Doorn and Hulda?"

"Oh, the most affectionate relationship!" said Morehouse at once. "Hulda was Abigail's pride and joy. There wasn't anything in Abby's possession that Hulda couldn't have by a mere word. But Hulda has always been pretty conservative in her tastes—certainly she doesn't live up to her position as one of the world's richest heiresses. Quiet, modest—but you saw her. She's a—"

"Oh, beyond a doubt!" said the Inspector hastily. "And does Hulda Doorn realize her uncle's reputation?"

"I imagine so. But it hurts her terribly, I suppose, and she's never spoken of it, even to—" he paused—"even to me."

"Tell me," asked Ellery, "how old is the young lady?"

"Hulda? Oh, nineteen or twenty."

Ellery twisted his neck toward Dr. Minchen, who had been sitting quietly in a far corner of the room, observing everything and saying nothing. "John!"

The physician started. "My turn now?" he asked with a wry smile.

"Hardly. I was just going to comment that we seem to have struck one of those not infrequent gynecological phenomena you pill-peddlers are always talking about. Didn't you tell me this morning in one of our pre-garrotte chats that Abigail was over seventy?"

"Why, yes. But what do you mean? Gynecology refers to the diseases of women, and the old lady wasn't—"

Ellery flicked a finger nonchalantly. "Well, surely," he murmured, "pregnancy past a certain age might have a pathological root? . . . Mrs. Doorn must have been," he said, "a most remarkable woman in more ways than one. . . . By the way, what about the late Mr. Doorn? I mean—Abigail Doorn's spouse? When did he shuffle off the mortal coil? I don't keep in touch with the society editors, you know."

"About fifteen years ago," put in Morehouse. He continued heatedly, "Now see here, Queen, what did you mean by your nasty insinuation that—?"

"My dear Morehouse," smiled Ellery, "it *is* a bit odd, isn't it, that astonishing difference in age between mother and daughter? You can scarcely blame me for politely raising my eyebrows."

Morehouse looked disturbed. The Inspector broke in, "Here! We're getting nowhere. I want to hear things about this Fuller woman in the gallery outside. . . . What was her official position in the Doorn household? I'm not clear on the point."

"Abby's companion—she's been with her for a quarter of a century, more or less. *And* a queer character, too. Crotchety, domineering, a religious fanatic, and I'm certain heartily disliked by the rest of the house—I mean the servants. . . . As for Sarah and Abby, you wouldn't think they'd been together for so many years. They were always quarreling."

"Quarreling, hey?" growled the Inspector. "What about?"

Morehouse shrugged. "Nobody seems to know. Just bickering, I guess. I know Abby has often said to me in a fit of pique that she was going to 'let that woman go,' but somehow she never did. Matter of habit, I suppose."

"And the servants?"

"The usual batch. Bristol the butler, a housekeeper, a tribe of maids—nothing of interest for you there, I'm sure."

"We seem to have arrived," murmured Ellery, crossing his legs and sighing, "at that dreadful stage in every murder investigation when it becomes necessary to ask questions about the—God save us!—the will. . . . Get out your best brand of Will Talk, Morehouse. Let's have it."

"I'm afraid," retorted Morehouse, "it's all duller than usual. Not a thing sinister or mysterious. All absolutely aboveboard and regular. No bequests to long-lost relatives in Africa, or any of that brand of tripe. . . .

"The bulk of the estate goes to Hulda. Hendrik is provided for in a very liberal trust-fund—better than he deserves, the old belly-shaker!—which will keep him in ducats for the rest of his life provided he doesn't try to drain the annual liquor supply of New York.

"Sarah comes in for a neat inheritance—Sarah Fuller, that is—a heavy cash bequest and an assured income for life—more than she can possibly use. The servants, of course, receive generous legacies. The Hospital is provided for by a whopping big fund which guarantees its continued existence for many years. It's a paying proposition, anyway."

"Seems quite in order," muttered the Inspector.

"Well, that's what I told you." Morehouse fidgeted in his chair. "Let's get this over with, gentlemen.—You might be surprised to hear that Dr. Janney comes into the picture twice."

"Eh?" The Inspector bolted upright. "What's that?"

"Two distinct bequests. One is personal. Janney was Abby's protégé almost from the time he took his first shave. The other is for the maintenance of a fund which would allow Janney and Kneisel to continue some research they're jointly working on."

"Here, here!" demanded the Inspector, "hold on. Who's Kneisel? First time I've heard his name mentioned."

Dr. Minchen hitched his chair forward. "I can tell you about him, Inspector. Moritz Kneisel is a scientist—Austrian, I think—who is working with Dr. Janney on a revolutionary idea. Something in the line of metals. He has a laboratory on this floor specially put in for him by Janney—where he keeps busy day and night. Regular mole, that fellow."

"What sort of research is it, precisely?" asked Ellery.

Minchen looked uncomfortable. "I don't think any one knows exactly except Kneisel and Janney. They keep quite mum about it. The laboratory's the joke of the Hospital. No one's ever been inside its four walls except the two of 'em. It has a massive safe-lock door, reënforced walls, and no windows. There are only two keys in existence for the inner door, and you have to know the combination of the outer one to reach it. Kneisel and Janney possess the keys, of course. Janney has absolutely forbidden entry into the laboratory."

"Mystery upon mystery," murmured Ellery. "We're becoming medieval, by gad!"

The Inspector jerked his head at Morehouse. "You know anything more about this?"

"Nothing about the work itself—but I think you'll find a little item of mine interesting. Rather recent development, in fact. . . ."

"Just a moment." The Inspector beckoned to Velie. "Send somebody to get this fellow Kneisel. We'll want to talk to him. Keep him out in the theater until I call. . . ." Velie spoke to some one in the corridor. "Now Mr. Morehouse, you were going to say—?"

Morehouse replied dryly, "I think you'll find it interesting. . . . You see, despite Abby's grand old heart and wise old head, she was still a woman. Mighty changeable, Inspector. . . . And so I wasn't particularly surprised when, two weeks ago, she told me to draw up a new will!"

"By the *Pentateuch!*" moaned Ellery, "this case is simply over-run with technicalities. First it's anatomy, then it's metallurgy, now it's law. . . ."

"Don't get the idea there was anything wrong with the first will!" interrupted Morehouse hastily. "She'd merely had a change of mind about a certain bequest. . . ."

"Janney's, I suppose?" asked Ellery.

Morehouse gave him a startled glance. "Yes, Janney's. Oh, not Abby's personal bequest to him, but the one providing the working fund for the Janney-Kneisel researches. She wanted that clause stricken out entirely. It wouldn't have necessarily de-manded a new will, but there were additional bequests to ser-vants and a few charities and things, since the first will was two years old."

Ellery was sitting up quite straight "And the new will was drawn up?"

"Oh yes. Executed preliminarily—but not signed," replied Morehouse with a grimace. "This coma business, and now the murder, intervened. You see, if only I'd known she'd be taken this way! But of course none of us had the slightest warning. In fact, I was intending to present the will for Abby's signature to-morrow. Now it's too late. The first will remains in force."

"This will have to be looked into," grumbled the Inspector. "Wills always cause trouble in a homicide. . . . Did the old lady sink a lot of money into Janney's metallic ventures?"

"Sink is right," retorted Morehouse. "I'm inclined to think we could all live very comfortably indeed on the money Abby turned over to Janney for those mysterious experiments of his."

"You said," put in Ellery, "that no one except the surgeon and Kneisel knows the nature of the research. Didn't Mrs. Doorn know? It doesn't seem possible, with the old lady reputed so astute in business affairs, that she would finance a project without knowing pretty much everything about it first."

"There's a fault in every strong structure," said Morehouse sententiously. "Abby's weakness was Janney. She hung on his words. I'll give the devil his due and say that, to my knowledge, Janney has never abused her devotion. She certainly didn't know much about this project in its scientific details, anyway. You know, Janney and Kneisel have been working away at this thing, whatever it is, for two and a half years."

"Whew!" Ellery grinned. "*Drachmas* to doughnuts the old lady wasn't as weak as you make her out. Wasn't it because they were taking too long that she wanted to omit the fund from the second will?"

Morehouse raised his eyebrows. "Smart guess, Queen. That's exactly the point. They promised to complete the work in six months originally, and it's dragged out to five times that. Although she was still as crazy about Janney as ever, she said—these are her exact words—'I'm through subsidizing such a tenuous and experimental undertaking. Money's tight these days.'"

The Inspector rose suddenly. "Thank you, Mr. Morehouse. I don't think there's anything else. Get along."

Morehouse leaped from his chair, like a cramped prisoner unexpectedly released from his bonds. "Thanks! I'm on my way to the Doorns," he called over his shoulder. He stopped at the door and grinned boyishly. "And don't bother to tell me to keep in town, Inspector. I'm used to that sort of thing."

And he was gone.

Dr. Minchen whispered to Ellery, bowed to the Inspector, and slipped out.

A commotion in the corridor turned Velie sharply about. He opened the door and wagged his huge head.

"D.A.!" he exclaimed. The Inspector trotted across the room. Ellery rose, fingering his *pince-nez.* . . .

Three men walked into the room.

District Attorney Henry Sampson was a sturdy, powerfully built man, still youthful; at his side was his assistant, a thin, eager man of middle age with violent red hair, Timothy Cronin; and behind them sauntered a slouch-hatted, cigar-smoking old man with shrewd, wandering eyes. His hat was pushed back on his forehead and a ragged thatch of white hair straggled over one eye.

Velie grasped the white-haired man by the coat-sleeve as he strolled across the threshold. "Here you, Pete," he growled, "where you going? How'd you get in?"

"Aw, be yourself, Velie." The white-haired man shook off the sergeant's great fist. "Can't you see I'm here as a representative of the American press by the personal invitation of the District Attorney? Hey—lay off! . . . H'lo there, Inspector. How's every little murder? Ellery Queen, you old son-of-a-gun! It *must* be hot if you're on it. Find the dastardly dastard yet?"

"Be quiet, Pete," said Sampson. "Hello, Q. What's doing? I don't mind telling you we're in one hell of a mess." He sat down and threw his hat on the wheel-table, looking about the room curiously. The red-haired man pumped hands with Ellery and the Inspector. The newspaperman slouched to a chair and sank into it with a sigh of satisfaction.

"It's complicated, Henry," said the Inspector quietly. "No light yet. Mrs. Doorn was strangled while she was unconscious and waiting to be operated on; somebody seems to have impersonated the operating surgeon; nobody can identify the impostor; and we're generally up a tree. It's been a bad morning."

"You won't be able to cover up this case, Q.," said the District

Attorney with a harassed frown. "Whoever did the job picked on just about the most prominent figure in New York City. The newspaper boys are howling their heads off outside—we've got half the local precinct keeping 'em off the premises—Pete Harper here being the privileged character, God help me!—and I received a call from the Governor a half-hour ago. You can imagine what he said. It's big, Q., big! What's behind it—personal revenge, a maniac, money?"

"I wish I knew. . . . Look here, Henry," sighed the Inspector, "we'll have to make an official statement to the press, and, by cripes, there's nothing to say. You, Pete," he went on grimly, turning to the white-haired man, "you're here by sufferance. One breach of faith on your part and I'll have your hide. Don't print anything the other boys don't get. Otherwise you can't sit in. Understand?"

"I'm 'way ahead of you, Inspector," grinned the reporter.

"And Henry. Here's the situation up to the present." He rapidly recounted the events, discoveries and perplexities of the morning to the District Attorney, in an undertone. When the Inspector had concluded his recital he called for pen and paper, and in a short time, with the aid of the District Attorney, had drafted a statement for the reporters milling about outside the Hospital. A nurse was conscripted to make typewritten copies, which Sampson signed; whereupon Velie sent a man to distribute them.

Inspector Queen went to the door of the Amphitheater and bawled a name. Almost immediately the tall, angular figure of Dr. Lucius Dunning crossed the threshold. The physician was flushed; his eyes smoldered; the seams on his face writhed.

"So you've decided to call me at last!" he rasped. His grey head jerked from side to side as he challenged them all, impartially, with stabbing glances. "I suppose you think I've nothing better to do than to sit outside like an old woman or a twenty-year-old boy and await your pleasure! Well, let me tell you once for all, sir—" he stalked up to the Inspector and brandished this thin fist above the old man's head, "this outrage is going to mean something to you!"

"Now, really, Dr. Dunning," said the Inspector meekly, as he slipped under the physician's uplifted arm and shut the door.

"Restrain yourself, Dr. Dunning!" interrupted District Attorney Sampson in his sharpest courtroom manner. "The investigation is in the most capable hands in New York. If you've nothing to conceal, you've nothing to fear. And," he added with asperity, "any complaints you may have should be addressed to me. I'm the District Attorney of this County!"

Dunning jammed his hands into his white coat-pockets. "I don't care a hoot if you're the President of the United States," he snarled. "You're keeping me from my work. There's a bad case of gastric ulcer that I *must* follow up immediately. Your men outside prevented me five times from leaving the theater. Why, it's criminal! I've got to see that patient!"

"Sit down, Doctor," said Ellery with a soothing smile. "The longer you protest, the longer you'll be here. Just a few questions, and the gastric ulcer is yours. . . ."

Dunning glared about like an angry tomcat, struggled with his tongue for a long moment, and finally snapped his lips shut and flung his lean length into a chair.

"You can question me from to-day until to-morrow," he said defiantly, folding his arms across his bony chest, "but you'll merely be wasting your time. I know nothing. You'll get nothing from me that can possibly help you."

"Surely that's a matter of opinion, Doctor?"

"Oh, come, come!" interrupted the Inspector. "Less of this

bickering. Let's hear your little story, Doctor. I want a strict account of your movements this morning."

"Is that all?" muttered Dunning bitterly. His tongue flicked out over his nervous lips. "I arrived at the Hospital at 9:00, and saw patients in my office until about 10:00. From 10:00 until the time of the operation I remained in my office checking over case-records. There were some histories and prescriptions. A few moments before 10:45 I went across the North Corridor to the rear of the Amphitheater, mounted to the gallery, met my daughter there, and—"

"That's quite enough. Any visitors after 10:00?"

"No." Dunning paused. "That is, no one but Miss Fuller—Mrs. Doorn's companion. She stopped in for a few moments to inquire about Mrs. Doorn's condition."

"How well," asked Ellery, bending forward in his chair and clasping his hands between his knees, "did you know Mrs. Doorn, Doctor?"

"Not—intimately," replied Dunning. "Of course, I've been on the staff here ever since the founding of the Hospital, and I naturally came to know Mrs. Doorn in my official capacity. I'm on the Board of Directors along with Dr. Janney, Dr. Minchen and the others. . . ."

District Attorney Sampson leveled his forefinger at the physician. "Let's be frank with each other," he said. "You know Mrs. Doorn's position as a world figure, I might say, and you know what a furor will be raised when the world learns that she has been murdered. For one thing, the reverberations will certainly be heard in the stock market. The sooner this case is solved and forgotten, the better off everybody will be. . . . Just what do you think about the entire affair?"

Dr. Dunning got slowly to his feet, began to walk up and

down, up and down. As he walked he cracked his knuckles. Ellery winced, crouched in his chair.

"You were about to say . . ." he murmured in almost unpleasant accents.

"What?" Dunning appeared confused. "No, no. I know nothing at all. It's a complete mystery to me. . . ."

"Amazing, how all-pervasive this mystery seems to be," snapped Ellery. He eyed Dunning with a species of curious disgust. "That's quite all, Doctor."

Dunning strode out of the room without another word.

Ellery sprang to his feet and began to prowl. "By the Minotaur!" he cried. "All this is leading us nowhere. Who else is waiting outside? Kneisel, Sarah Fuller? Let's get this over with. There's work to be done. . . ."

Pete Harper stretched his legs luxuriously and chuckled. "Headline," he said. "'Noted Sleuth Gets Cramp in Belly; Bad Circulation Affects Temper. . . .'"

"Hey, you," growled Velie, "shut up."

Ellery smiled. "You're right, Pete. It's got me. . . . Shoot, Dad. Out with the next victim!"

But the next victim was destined to bide his time in continued patience. For from the West Corridor came the broken sounds of a violent altercation, and the door crashed open to admit Lieutenant Ritchie and a trio of odd-looking men being prodded forward by three bluecoats.

"What's this?" demanded the Inspector, starting up. "Well, well, well," he said equably, his wand straying to his snuffbox. "If it isn't Joe Gecko, Little Willie and Snapper! Ritchie, where in time did you pick 'em up?"

The policemen pushed the three captives into the room. Joe Gecko was a lean, cadaverous individual with burning eyes and a preternaturally cartilaginous nose. Snapper was his direct anti-type—small and cherubic, with rosy checks and full wet lips. Little Willie was the most sinister-appearing of the three: his bald, triangular head was covered with noxious brown-flecked skin; he was huge and bulky and flabby, but his nervous movements and uneasy eyes belied the promise of strength in his powerful frame; he looked dull, even stupid, but there was something loathsome and terrifying in his very stupidity.

"Pompey, Julius and Crassus," murmured Ellery to Cronin. "Or perhaps it's the Second Triumvirate of Mark Antony, Octavius and Lepidus. Where have I seen them before?"

"Probably in the line-up," grinned Cronin.

The Inspector confronted the captives with a frown. "Well, Joe," he said peremptorily, "what's the racket this time? Sticking up hospitals? Where'd you find 'em, Ritchie?"

Ritchie looked pleased with himself. "Skulking around upstairs—328—a private room."

"Big Mike's room!" exclaimed the Inspector. "So you're playing nurse to Big Mike now, hey? I thought you guerrillas were running with Ikey Bloom's mob. Changed your luck, eh? Spit it out, boys—what's the dirt?"

The three gunmen looked at each other uneasily. Little Willie uttered a hoarse, shy chuckle. Joe Gecko screwed up his eyes and slid back tensely on his heels. But it was Snapper, rosy and smiling, who replied.

"Jeeze, give us a break, Inspector," he said, and the lisp in his mincing voice did not seem strange. "You got nuttin' on us. We wuz on'y waitin' for th' boss. They been takin' out his guts or somepin."

"Sure, sure!" replied the Inspector affably. "You've been holding his hand and telling him bedtime stories."

"Naw, he's a reg'lar," said Snapper seriously. "We been hangin' around his room upstairs. Y'know how it is—th' boss layin' there an' there's a lotta guys don't like'm, sorta. . . ."

Inspector Queen snapped at Ritchie, "Did you frisk them?"

Little Willie shuffled his gigantic feet spasmodically and began to edge toward the door. Gecko hissed, "Snap outa it!" and grabbed the big man's arm. The policemen closed in and Velie grinned expectantly.

Ritchie said, "Three little gats, Inspector," with satisfaction.

The old man laughed merrily. "Caught at last! And by the good old Sullivan Law. Snapper, I'm surprised at you. . . . All right, Ritchie. They're your meat. Take 'em out and book 'em on the gun-toting charge. . . . Just a second. Snapper, what time did you men get here?"

The little gangster mumbled, "We wuz here all mornin', Inspector. Just watchin'. Jeeze. . . ."

Gecko snarled, "I tola you, Snap'. . . . !"

"I suppose you don't know anything about the murder of Mrs. Doorn here this morning, boys?"

"A bump-off!"

They stiffened. Little Willie's mouth began to quiver, it seemed extraordinarily as if he were about to cry. Their eyes curled toward the door and their hands made jerky movements. But they remained mute.

"Oh, all right," said the Inspector indifferently. "Take 'em away, Ritchie."

The district detective followed the policemen and the shambling gunmen with alacrity. Velie shut the door after them with the light of a vague disappointment in his eyes.

"Well," said Ellery wearily, "we're still awaiting the no doubt slavering presence of Miss Sarah Fuller. She's been sitting out there for three hours. . . . She'll need a hospital when she's through, and I need nourishment. Dad, how about sending out for sandwiches and coffee? I'm famished. . . ."

Inspector Queen gnawed his mustache. "Didn't realize the time. . . . How's it strike you, Henry? Have lunch?"

"Well, I'm in favor of it," announced Pete Harper suddenly. "This sort of work gets you hungry. Is it on the City?"

"All right, Pete," retorted the Inspector, "I'm glad to hear it. And, City or no City, you're elected. There's a cafeteria on the next block."

When Harper was gone, Velie ushered in a middle-aged woman dressed in black who held her head so rigidly and whose eyes were so fiercely intent that District Attorney Sampson muttered in an undertone to Cronin and Velie himself hitched more closely to her.

Ellery gave her no more than a passing glance as she entered. He saw through the open door a group of internes gathered about the operating-table on which the dead body of Abigail Doorn still lay, entirely covered by a sheet.

He stepped into the Amphitheater, gesturing to his father.

The Amphitheater was quiet now; it gave a queer impression of disorganization, of indecision. Nurses and internes strolled about, talking in broadly gay voices, deliberately ignoring the bluecoats and plainclothesmen who stood about, placidly watch- ful. And beneath all the talk there was a little note of hysteria that crept quietly along and then, suddenly, leaped out of a conversa- tion, to be followed at once by a painful silence.

Except for the men grouped about the operating-table, no one looked at the outlined body of the dead woman.

Ellery stepped to the table. In the slight hush that followed his appearance he made a brief remark to which several of the young doctors nodded assent. He immediately returned to the Anteroom, closing the door softly behind him.

Sarah Fuller stood somberly in the middle of the room. Her thin, blue-veined hands were clenched at her sides. She stared with hard-pressed stony lips at the Inspector.

Ellery stepped to his father's side. "Miss Fuller!" he said abruptly.

Her agate-like, faded blue eyes shifted to his face. A bitter smile twitched the corners of her mouth. "Another," she said. The District Attorney cursed beneath his breath. There was something weird about this woman. Her voice was hard and cold and tight, like her face. "What do you want with me, all of you men?"

"Sit down, please," said the Inspector fretfully. He shoved a chair toward her; she hesitated, sniffed, and sat down like a stick.

"Miss Fuller," said the Inspector at once, "you've been with Mrs. Doorn for twenty-five years, haven't you?"

"Twenty-one come May."

"And you and she didn't get along, did you?"

Ellery noted with a faint sensation of surprise that the woman had a pronounced Adam's apple which jerked up and down with the vibrations of her speech. She said coldly, "No."

"Why?"

"She was a miser and an infidel. Out of heart proceedeth covetousness. She was a tyrant. The tender mercies of the wicked are cruel. To the world she was the voice of virtue. To her dependents and retainers she was the breath of evil. Sufficient unto the day . . ."

This remarkable speech was accompanied by the most matter-of-fact tone. Inspector Queen and Ellery exchanged glances. Velie grunted and the detectives nodded their heads significantly. The Inspector threw up his hands and sat down, leaving the field to Ellery.

He smiled gently. "Madame, you believe in God?"

She raised her eyes to his. "The Lord is my Shepherd."

"Nevertheless," replied Ellery, "we should prefer less apocalyptic answers. You speak the God's truth at all times?"

"I am the way, the truth, and the life."

"A noble sentiment. Very well, Miss Fuller. Who killed Mrs. Doorn?"

"When will ye be wise?"

Ellery's eyes glittered. "Scarcely a reply upon which to base an arrest. Do you know, or don't you?"

"The deed—No."

"Thank you." His lips quivered with inward amusement. "And did you or did you not quarrel with Abigail Doorn habitually?"

The woman in black did not stir nor change her set expression. "I did."

"Why?"

"I have told you. She was evil."

"But we have been given to understand that Mrs. Doorn was a good woman. You've attempted to make her out a Gorgon. You say she was miserly and tyrannical. How? Household affairs? Little things or big things? Please answer clearly."

"We did not get along."

"Answer the question."

Her fingers were tightly intertwined. "We hated each other deeply."

"Ha!" The Inspector jumped from his chair. "Now we're getting it, and in twentieth century language. Couldn't stand the sight of each other, eh? Scrapped like wildcats. Well then"—he accused her with his finger—"why in tunket did you stay together for twenty-one years?"

Her voice grew animated. "Charity beareth all things. . . . I was the beggar, she the lonely queen. The habit grows. We were linked by ties as strong as blood."

Ellery regarded her with puzzled brows. Inspector Queen's face went blank; he shrugged his shoulders and looked eloquently at the District Attorney. Velie's lips framed the word, "Nuts."

In the silence, the door scraped open and several internes wheeled in the operating-table bearing the body of Abigail Doorn. At the Inspector's furious look Ellery smiled warningly; he stood back, watching Sarah Fuller's face.

A peculiar change had come over the woman. She rose, hand clutching her thin, narrow bosom. Two bright pinkish spots appeared magically in her cheeks; she looked steadily, almost curiously, at the dead face of her mistress, pitilessly uncovered to the neck.

A young doctor pointed apologetically to the blue, bloated face. "Sorry," he said. "Cyanosis. Always pretty ugly. But you said I should un—"

"Please!" Ellery waved him away with acerbity; he was intent on Sarah Fuller's movements. Slowly she approached the table; slowly she examined the stiff outlines of the dead body. When her eyes had traveled the entire length of the corpse and had reached the head, she paused in horrible triumph.

"The soul that sinneth, it shall die," she cried. "In prosperity the destroyer shall come!" Her voice rose to a shriek. "Abigail, I warned you! I warned you, Abigail! The wages of sin . . ."

Ellery chanted deliberately, "Know that I am the Lord that smiteth. . . ."

At the sound of his cool, insistent voice she turned furiously; her eyes shot fire. "Fools make a mock at sin!" she screamed. Her voice fell. "I have seen what I came to see," she continued more quietly, in a repressed, exultant tone. Already she seemed to have forgotten her hot words. She breathed deeply, raising her thin chest. "Now I can go."

"Oh, no, you can't," retorted the Inspector. "Sit down, Miss Fuller. You're going to be here for some time yet." She seemed deaf. An exalted expression crept over the harsh lines of her face. "Oh, for God's sake!" shouted the Inspector, "stop acting and come down to earth! Here—" He ran across the room and gripped her arm roughly, shaking her. The peaceful, remote look did not leave her. "You're not in church now—snap out of it!"

She permitted the Inspector to lead her to the chair, but absently, as if he and all his cohorts could do nothing to harm her. She did not again glance at the dead woman. Ellery, who was watching thoughtfully, signaled to the internes.

Hastily, in open relief, the white-garmented attendants wheeled the table to the elevator-shaft at the right side of the Anteroom, opened the door, and disappeared into the elevator. Ellery could see, beyond the grilled car, another door which apparently led to the East Corridor. The door closed and the slight sound of the moving vehicle came through the thin shaft-wall as the elevator descended slowly to the morgue room in the basement.

The Inspector muttered to Ellery, "Here, son, there's nothing to be got out of her. She's a lunatic. To my mind, we'd do better to follow up by questioning others about her. What do you think?"

Ellery glanced at the woman, who sat stiffly in the chair, eyes far away. "If nothing else," he said grimly, "she's a fine psychiatric object-lesson. I think I'll have another go at her and see her reaction. . . . Miss Fuller!"

Her rapt eyes turned to him, blankly.

"Who might have desired to kill Mrs. Doorn?"

She shivered; the film began to fade from her eyes. "I—don't—know."

"Where were you this morning?"

"At home, first. Some person telephoned. There was an accident, they said. . . . God of vengeance!" Her face flamed; when she continued it was more lucidly, in a flatter tone. "Hulda and I came to this place. We waited for the operation."

"You were with Miss Doorn all the time?"

"Yes. No."

"Which is it?"

"No. I left Hulda in that Waiting Room across the hall. I was nervous. I walked about. Nobody stopped me. I walked, and walked, and then"—a cunning look crept into her eyes—"then I came back to Hulda."

"And you didn't speak with any one?"

She looked up slowly. "I sought information. I looked for a doctor. Dr. Janney. Dr. Dunning. The young Dr. Minchen. I found only Dr. Dunning, in his office. He reassured me, and I went away."

Ellery murmured, "Check!" and began to stride up and down before her. He seemed to be revolving something in his mind. Sarah Fuller sat stolidly and waited.

When he spoke, it was with a crackle of menace in his voice. He whirled upon her. "Why didn't you transmit Dr. Janney's telephone message last night to Miss Doorn about administering the insulin injection?"

"I was ill myself yesterday. I was in bed most of the day. The message came and I took it. But by the time Hulda returned I was asleep."

"Why didn't you tell her in the morning?"

"I forgot."

Ellery leaned over her, stared into her eyes. "You realize, don't you, that by your unfortunate lapse of memory, you are morally responsible for Mrs. Doorn's death?"

"Why—what—?"

"If you had given Miss Doorn Dr. Janney's message, she would have administered the insulin to Mrs. Doorn, Mrs. Doorn would not have fallen into the coma this morning, and consequently would not have been placed on an operating-table to lie at the mercy of a murderer. Well?"

Her glance did not waver. "His will be done. . . ."

Ellery straightened, murmured, "You quote Scripture nicely. . . . Miss Fuller, *why was Mrs. Doorn afraid of you?*"

She drew in her breath sharply. Then she smiled an odd smile, compressed her lips and sank back against the chair. There was something eerie in her bitter old face. And her eyes were still hard and icy and, somehow, unearthly.

Ellery retreated. "Dismissed!"

She rose, arranged her garments with a shy movement and, without a glance or a word, floated from the room. At a sign from the Inspector the detective named Hesse followed. The Inspector took a short and irritable turn about the room. Ellery mused deeply where he stood.

A black-jowled man in a rakish derby hat strolled into the Anteroom, past Velie. He was chewing a dead, foul-smelling cigar. He tossed a black physician's bag onto the wheel-table and stood rocking on his heels, surveying the gloomy little group quizzically.

"Hi there!" he said at last, spitting a piece of tobacco on the tiled floor. "Don't I get any attention? Where's the funeral?"

"Oh, hello, Doc." The Inspector absently shook hands. "Ellery, say hello to Prouty." Ellery dutifully nodded. "The body is in the morgue now, Doc," said the old man. "They've just carted it down into the basement."

"Well, I'll be on my way, then," said Prouty. He strode to the elevator-door. "This it?" Velie pressed a button and they heard the elevator grind upward. "By the way, Inspector," said Prouty, opening the door, "the Medical Examiner may come into this thing himself. Doesn't seem to trust his assistant." He chuckled. "So old Abby's got it at last, eh? Well, she's not the first, and she won't be the last. Keep smiling!" He disappeared into the car and the elevator again clanked its way to the floor below.

Sampson rose and stretched hugely. "A-a-ah!" He yawned, scratched, his fine head. "I'm absolutely stumped, Q." The Inspector nodded dolefully. "And that crazy old loon simply muddled things worse than ever. . . ." Sampson looked shrewdly at Ellery. "What do you make of it, son?"

"Precious little." Ellery fished a cigarette from his capacious side-pocket and fingered it tenderly. He looked up. "Oh, I've managed to deduce a few things—interesting things at that." He grinned. "There's the faintest glimmer of light away down deep in my consciousness, but I'd scarcely call it a complete and satisfactory solution. The clothes, you know . . ."

"Aside from a few obvious facts . . ." began the District Attorney.

"Oh, they're not *obvious*," said Ellery gravely. "Those shoes, for example—most illuminating."

Red-headed Timothy Cronin snorted. "And what do you get out of them? I must be thick. I can't see a darned thing."

"Well," said the District Attorney tentatively, "the person who originally owned them was a good few inches taller than Dr. Janney. . . ."

"Ellery commented on that before you came. And a fat lot of good it does us," said the Inspector dryly. "We'll send out a general alarm for the theft of the clothing, but I can tell you right now it will be like looking for the needle in the haystack. . . . Attend to that, will you, Thomas?" He turned to the giant. "And start with this Hospital; we might get a break right here."

Velie discussed details with Johnson and Flint, and they departed. "Not much there," boomed the sergeant "But if there is a trail, the boys will get it."

Ellery was smoking, inhaling deeply. "That woman . . ." he murmured. "The religious mania is significant. Something has unbalanced her. A very real hatred existed between her and the dead woman. Motive? Cause?" He shrugged. "She's most fascinating. And if her blessed Jehovah is with us, we'll cry 'Selah!' at the proper time, no doubt."

"This man Janney," began Sampson, stroking his jaw, "darned if we haven't enough, Q., to—"

Whatever the District Attorney meant to say was lost in the hubbub of Harper's return to the Anteroom. He kicked the corridor door open and made a triumphant entrance, bearing a huge paper bag in his arms.

"The white-haired boy returns with FOOD!" he shouted. "Dig in, fellers. You too, Velie—you old Colossus. Doubt if we've enough to fill *your* craw . . . Here's coffee, and sweet ham, and pickles and cream cheese and Christ knows what else. . . ."

They munched sandwiches and sipped coffee in silence. Harper eyed them keenly and said nothing further. It was only when the elevator-door reopened and Dr. Prouty, looking gloomy, emerged that they again began to talk.

"Well, Doc?" Sampson paused in the act of biting into a ham sandwich.

"Strangled, all right." Prouty dropped his bag and unceremoniously helped himself from the stack of sandwiches on the wheel-table. His teeth clicked fiercely on the bread and he sighed. "Hell," he mumbled, between mouthfuls, "that was an easy kill.

One twist of the wire and the poor old lady was through. Snuffed out like a candle. . . . This Janney guy. Quite a surgeon." He peered at the Inspector shrewdly. "Too bad he didn't get the chance to operate. Bad rupture of the gall bladder. Diabetic, too, I gathered. . . . No; the original verdict was quite correct. Autopsy's almost unnecessary. Hypo marks all over her arm. Stringy muscles. Must have had quite a job with the intravenous injections this morning. . . ."

He chattered on. The conversation became general. Speculations and conjectures swirled about Ellery Queen as he ate. He tilted his chair against a wall and gazed at the ceiling, his lean jaws masticating powerfully.

The Inspector daintily wiped his mouth with a handkerchief. "Well," he grumbled, "there's darned little left except this man Kneisel. Suppose he's outside, burning up like the rest of 'em. All right with you, son?"

Ellery waved his hand vaguely. But suddenly his eyes narrowed and his chair-legs banged on the floor. "There's an idea," he said. Then he chuckled. "Stupid of me to overlook that!" His auditors looked blankly at each other. Ellery got to his feet excitedly. "Now that you mention it, let's have a look-see at our friend the Austrian scientist. You know, this mysterious Paracelsus of ours may prove interesting. . . . Always charmed by alchemists, anyway. And there's a faint voice—the voice of one crying in the wilderness . . ." he smiled "—to quote the triply blessed authority of Luke, John and patriarchal Isaiah. . . ."

He ran to the Amphitheater door.

"Kneisel! Is Dr. Kneisel in here?" he cried.

12

EXPERIMENTATION

DR. PROUTY brushed a few vagrant crumbs from his lap, rose, inserted his forefinger into the ample orifice of his mouth, probed delicately for a remnant of his sandwich, discovered it, spat it forth in triumph, and finally picked up his black bag.

"Be goin'," he announced. "G'bye." He tramped through the corridor door, whistling tunelessly as he searched his pocket for a cigar.

Unsmiling, Ellery Queen stepped back into the Anteroom to allow Moritz Kneisel to enter from the Amphitheater.

In Inspector Queen's instantly formed although unspoken judgment, Moritz Kneisel joined that classification of human subjects to which the old man referred simply as "a card." Individually, the characteristics of the scientist were not startling; it was only when they were viewed as links in a single personality that they gave that impression of *grotesquerie*. That he was small, that he was swarthy and dark and Central European-looking, that he wore a frayed and tatterdemalion little black beard, that his eyes were as deep and soft as a woman's—these things were common enough. Yet, by some alchemy of nature, they blended to make Moritz Kneisel quite the most unusual character the

Queens had yet encountered in their investigation of Abigail Doorn's murder.

His fingers were bleached, brown-spotted, blotched with chemical stains and burns. The tip of his left index-finger was crushed-looking and raw. His professional gown appeared as if it had withstood a chemical deluge; it was literally covered with ragged color-splotches which in many spots had eaten away the linen. Even the cuffs of his white duck trousers and the tips of his canvas shoes were splattered.

Ellery, regarding him out of half-closed eyes, meaningly put the door to and pointed to a chair.

"Sit down, Dr. Kneisel."

The scientist obeyed in complete silence. He radiated an aura of self-absorption that was disconcerting. He did not meet the impersonal stares of Inspector Queen, the District Attorney, Cronin, Velie; and it was remarkable that they understood at once the cause of his aloofness. He was not afraid, or wary, or evasive; he was simply deaf and blind to his surroundings.

He sat in a world of his own, a queer little figure out of a pseudo-scientific tale of lofty adventure among the stars.

Ellery took his stand solidly before Kneisel, boring him through and through with his eyes. After a strained interval the scientist seemed to sense the force of Ellery's scrutiny; his eyes lifted and cleared.

"I am so sorry," he said in a clipped, precise English that carried in its accents the merest suggestion of an alien tongue. "You want to question me, of course. I have just heard outside that Mrs. Doorn has been strangled."

Ellery relaxed and sat down. "So late, Doctor? Mrs. Doorn has been dead for hours."

Kneisel slapped the back of his neck absently. "I am something of a recluse here. In my laboratory there is a separate world. The scientific spirit. . . ."

"Well," said Ellery conversationally, crossing his legs, "I've always maintained that science is another form of Nihilism. . . . You don't seem overcome by shock at the news, Doctor."

Kneisel's soft eyes became suffused with a queer surprise. "My dear sir!" he protested. "Death is hardly a cause for emotion in the scientist. I am interested in the fatality, naturally, but not to the point of sentimentality. After all—" He shrugged, and a whimsical smile appeared on his lips. "We're above the bourgeois attitude toward death, aren't we? '*Requiescat in pace*,' and all that sort of thing. I should much rather quote the Spaniard's cynical epigram—'She is good and honored who is dead and buried.'"

Ellery's brows rose instantly, much as the tail of a setter jerks to the horizontal in the perfect point. An animated humor, a light of anticipation, leaped into his eyes.

He said warmly, "I salute your erudition, Dr. Kneisel. You know, when the Coachman, Death, takes on his new and unwilling passenger, he sometimes discharges another in order to balance the load. . . . I refer, of course, to the vulgar institution of *post-mortem* bequests. There was something interesting about Abigail Doorn's first will, Doctor. . . ."

"May I complement your quotation with another?—'He who waits for a dead man's shoes is in danger of going barefoot.' That," he said, "is, curiously enough, from the Danish."

Kneisel replied in a grave and pleasant voice, "And from the French, too, I believe. A great many aphorisms have common roots."

Ellery laughed happily; he nodded with open admiration. "I didn't know that," he said. "I shall make a point of checking up on you. Now—" The Inspector chuckled.

"You no doubt wish to know," said Kneisel with the utmost urbanity, "where and how I spent my morning. . . ."

"If you will."

"I arrived at the Hospital at 7:00 A.M., my usual hour," explained Kneisel, folding his hands peacefully in his lap. "I went to my laboratory after changing into these clothes in the general dress-rooms in the basement.

"The laboratory is on this floor, diagonally across the corridor from the northwest corner of the Amphitheater. But I am sure you already know this. . . ."

"*Mais certainement!*" murmured Ellery.

"I locked myself in and I was there until your man summoned me some time ago. I proceeded at once to the theater, according to your request, and there discovered for the first time that Mrs. Doorn had been murdered during the morning."

He paused, holding himself uncannily still. Ellery's glittering watchfulness did not waver.

When Kneisel continued, it was with serene emphasis. "No one disturbed me this morning. To phrase it differently, I was alone in my laboratory without interruption from a few moments after 7:00 until a short time ago. Without interruption—and without witnesses. Not even Dr. Janney appeared in my work-shop, probably because of Mrs. Doorn's accident and his other work which accumulated as a result of it. And Dr. Janney invariably visits the laboratory every morning. . . . I believe," he concluded thoughtfully, "that is all."

Ellery continued to transfix him with his stare. Inspector Queen, watching them both unwinkingly, was forced to make the grudging inner admission that, despite Ellery's outward *savoir faire*, he had never appeared more discomposed.

The old man scowled loyally. He began to feel the stirrings of a vague but tempestuous anger.

Ellery smiled. "Perfect, Dr. Kneisel. And since you seem to know exactly what I intend to question you about, suppose you answer my next query without my asking it at all!"

Kneisel stroked his frumpy beard speculatively. "Not such a difficult problem, Mr.—Queen, I think? . . . You would like to know the nature of the research Dr. Janney and I have been conducting. Am I right?"

"You are."

"The advantages of a scientific mental training are innumerable, you see," commented Kneisel, good-humoredly. Facing each other and smiling with evident pleasure, the two men seemed like old friends. . . . "Very well. Dr. Janney and I have for two and a half years—but no; it will be two years and seven months next Friday—been working on the development of a metallic alloy."

Ellery replied with perfect gravity, "Your intellectual clairvoyance, Doctor, has not been sufficiently *clair*—if I may commit the sin of solecism in a highly modified form. . . . I want to know much more than that. I want to know what the exact nature of this alloy is. I want to know how much money has been expended in experiment. I want to know something of your background, and something of the circumstances under which you and Dr. Janney formed this heroic scientific coalition. I want to know why Mrs. Doorn decided to discontinue her contributions toward the furtherance of your work. . . ." He paused, twisted his mouth wryly. "I also want to know who killed Mrs. Doorn, but that, I suppose . . ."

"Oh, it is not a futile question, sir—not at all," replied Kneisel with a faint smile. "My scientific training has taught me that all the analyst really requires for the solution of a problem is, first, the painstaking assembly of all the phenomena; second, exhaustive patience; and third, the ability to comprehend the whole problem with a fresh and unbiased imagination. . . . But that is not answering your questions.

"The exact nature of our alloy? I fear," he said courteously, "that I must refuse to divulge it. In the first place, knowledge of this phenomena in the array of facts would not help you to a solution of the crime. In the second place, our work is a secret between Dr. Janney and me alone. . . . I can say this, however: when we have completed our task to our satisfaction, we will have produced an alloy which will wipe steel off the face of the earth!"

In silence the District Attorney and his assistant exchanged glances, then turned back to regard the bearded little scientist with newly appraising eyes.

Ellery chuckled. "I won't press you," he said. "If you can replace steel commercially with a cheaper and superior alloy, you and Dr. Janney will become millionaires over night."

"Exactly. That is the reason for the strongly built laboratory, the reënforced walls, the safe-doors, and all of the rest of our extraordinary precautions against curiosity or theft. I might say," Kneisel continued with a trace of pride, "that our finished product will be considerably lighter, more tensile, more malleable, more durable and just as strong, besides being appreciably less expensive to manufacture."

"You haven't by any chance stumbled on the Philosophers' Stone, have you?" murmured Ellery, with a perfect gravity.

Kneisel's veiled gaze sharpened. "Do I look like a charlatan, Mr. Queen?" he asked simply. "Certainly Dr. Janney's open faith in me and cooperation with me is a guarantee of my scientific integrity.

"I tell you," and his voice rose slightly, "that we have perfected the building-material of the future! It will revolutionize the science of aeronautics. It will solve one of the big problems confronting the astrophysicists—an incredibly light metal building-material with the strength of steel. Man will bridge space, conquer the solar system. This alloy will be utilized in everything from pins and fountain-pens to super-skyscrapers. . . . And," he concluded, "it is almost an accomplished fact."

There was a little silence. The words themselves seemed, in retrospect, utterly extravagant. And yet something in the sober matter-of-fact air of the little savant made them poignant possibilities.

Ellery seemed less impressed than the others. "I should heartily dislike placing myself in the same category with those myopic scoffers who martyrized Galileo and sneered at Pasteur, but as one analyst to another—I should like to be shown. Or words to that effect . . . The cost so far, Dr. Kneisel?"

"I do not know exactly, although I believe it is well over eighty thousand dollars. Dr. Janney attends to the finances."

"Naïve little experiment," murmured Ellery. "So simple. . . . Well, sir, chromium, nickel, aluminum, carbon, molybdenum—surely these ores can't possibly total such a huge sum unless you order the stuff by the carload. No, Doctor, you'll have to enlighten me further."

Kneisel permitted himself a discreet smile. "I see you are not unfamiliar with the experimental ores. You might have mentioned molybdenite, wulfenite, scheelite, molybdite and a few others from which the essential molybdenum is extracted. But I shan't even admit that I am using molybdenum. I have tackled the problem from an entirely unorthodox angle. . . .

"As to cost, however, you have overlooked some essential items. I refer to the installation of the laboratory, and the purchase of apparatus. Have you any idea of the cost of a special ventilation system, of smelting furnaces, of refining equipment—of turbines, electrolytic apparatus, cathode tubes and the like?"

"My apologies. I'm the veriest layman. Your background, Doctor?"

"Munich in Germany, the Sorbonne in France, M.I.T. in the States. Special laboratory and research work under Jublik of Vienna and the elder Charcot in Paris. Three years at the United States Bureau of Standards in the Department of Metallurgy, after I had obtained my American citizenship. Five years with one of the largest steel-manufacturing companies on the American continent. Interspersed with independent researches during which the idea I am now working on slowly germinated."

"How did you and Janney meet?"

"We were brought together by a scientific colleague who was slightly in my confidence. I was poor. I required the aid of a man who could secure finances for my experiments as well as assist me in the technical end. And above all a man whom I could trust. . . . Dr. Janney met all my requirements. He became enthusiastic. The rest you can infer."

Ellery stirred lightly. "Why did Mrs. Doorn decide to stop financing your project?"

A thin white vertical line appeared between Kneisel's eyes. "She was tired. Two weeks ago she summoned Dr. Janney and me to her home. The six months' duration of our experiments, which we had originally promised, had stretched to two and a half years and we were still not finished. She had lost interest, she said. In perfect amiability she informed us of this, and nothing we could say would move her to change her decision.

"We left dispiritedly. There was still some money left. We decided to discontinue only when our money was used up, and until then work as if nothing had happened, without stint. In the mean-time Dr. Janney would attempt to raise funds elsewhere."

District Attorney Sampson cleared his throat with a brisk rasp. "When she told you this, did she also tell you that her lawyer was drawing up a new will?"

"Yes."

Inspector Queen tapped the scientist's knee. "To your knowl-edge, *was* this new will drawn up and signed?"

Kneisel shrugged. "I do not know. I sincerely hope not. It will simplify matters if the first will is still in force."

Ellery said softly, "And aren't you curious to know whether the second will was signed?"

"I never allow mundane considerations to interfere with my work." Kneisel stroked his beard calmly. "I am something of a phi-losopher as well as a metallurgist. What will be, will be."

Ellery unslung his length from the chair and got wearily to his feet. "You're too good to be true, Doctor, really." He ran his hand through his hair and stared down at Kneisel.

"Thank you, Mr. Queen."

"And yet I feel that you're not quite so unemotional as you pre-tend to be. For example!" Ellery loomed over the little man, rest-ing his hand familiarly on the back of the chair. "I feel sure that, if a cardiometer were to be attached to your scientific carcass at this moment, Doctor, it would register an accelerated pulse-per-cussion at the following statement: Abigail Doorn was murdered *before* she could sign the second will. . . ."

"On the contrary, Mr. Queen." Kneisel's white teeth glistened in his swarthy face. "I am not at all surprised, since both your method and your motive are so obvious. In fact, I feel morally certain that the innuendo is unworthy of your intellect. . . . Is that all, sir?"

Ellery straightened suddenly. "No. Are you aware of the fact that Dr. Janney is slated for a personal slice of Mrs. Doorn's estate?"

"Perfectly."

"Then you may go."

Kneisel slipped out of his chair and bowed to Ellery with continental grace. He turned to salute the Inspector, the District Attorney, Cronin and Velie, then imperturbably walked out of the Anteroom.

"And there," groaned Ellery, sinking into the vacated chair, "but for the grace of God goes Ellery Queen . . . who, incidentally, confesses to having met his match."

"Oh, tosh!" The Inspector sneezed on a pinch of snuff and irritably jumped up. "The man's a human test-tube."

"He's a fish," grunted Sampson.

Harper, the newspaperman, had been huddled in a chair at a far corner of the room, his hat pulled low over his eyes. Not once during the examination of Dr. Kneisel had he uttered a sound or shifted his gaze from the face of the scientist.

Now he rose and sauntered across the room. Ellery looked up and they regarded each other in silence.

"Well, old boy," said Harper finally, "I think you've got a hot tip. You don't mind my mixing metaphors?" He grinned. "A hot tip on a human iceberg."

"I'm inclined to agree with you, Pete." Ellery smiled wanly as he stretched his legs. "Evidently you haven't glossed over the scientific fact that eight-ninths of most icebergs are completely submerged. . . ."

13

ADMINISTRATION

SERGEANT VELIE's bulky arm rested against the door-jamb as he conversed earnestly with an invisible henchman in the corridor.

Ellery Queen was sitting in a sort of concentrative stupor, communing, from the dark expression on his face, with bitter and unfruitful thoughts.

Huddled together, arms about each other, Inspector Queen, the District Attorney and Timothy Cronin were engaged in a summary discussion of the complex features of the case.

Only Pete Harper, head drooped on his breast, feet entwined about the rungs of his chair, seemed entirely at peace with himself and the world.

This was the vacuous and still-life scene upon which a corps of police photographers and fingerprint experts noisily intruded a few moments later.

The room suddenly filled with officials.

Sampson and Cronin took their overcoats and hats from the chair on which they had been loosely thrown, and stood aside.

The chief photographer muttered some excuse about "another job" and without further conversation the men from headquarters went to work.

They invaded the Amphitheater as well as the Anteroom and Anæsthesia Room; they thronged about the operating-table; two men used the Anteroom lift to descend into the basement for a series of photographs of the dead woman and her wound. Blue-white flashes and muffled explosions punctuated the bedlam all through the main floor of the Hospital. The acrid odor of flash-light powder mingled with the sharp medicinal odor of the halls and rooms in an overpowering stench.

Ellery, chained by his thoughts, Prometheus-like, to the Caucasus of his chair, sat in the vortex of the confusion, barely conscious of sights, sounds and smells. . . .

The Inspector sent a bluecoat off with a word, and almost immediately the officer returned with a youngish, sandy-haired man of serious mien.

"Here he is, Chief."

"You're James Paradise, Superintendent of the Hospital?" demanded the Inspector.

The white-garbed man nodded, gulping. His eyes were liquid, giving him a dreamy, tearful look. The tip of his nose was unnaturally bulbous, the nostrils angular and almost without normal convolutions. He had huge red ears.

The elfin face was not unprepossessing. The man seemed too simple to be insincere, too frightened to be untruthful.

"M-m-my wife . . ." he began to stutter. He was deathly pale, except for the flaming shells of his ears.

"Hey? What's that?" growled the Inspector.

The Superintendent managed a sickly grin. "My wife Charlotte," he whispered. "She's always having visions. She *told* me this morning that she'd had a warning during the night—an inner voice—that said, plain as fate, 'There's going to be trouble to-day!' Isn't that funny? We—"

"Very funny, certainly." The Inspector looked annoyed. "See here, Paradise, you helped us a lot this morning and you don't seem as dumb as you look. We're busy and I want quick answers to quick questions.

"Your private office is directly opposite the East Corridor, isn't it?"

"Yes, sir."

"Were you in your office all morning?"

"Yes, sir. I'm busiest mornings. I didn't leave my desk until Dr. Minchen came running—"

"I know. I understand that your chair and desk face your office door obliquely. Was the door open at any time during the morning?"

"Well—half-open."

"Can you see—did you see—the telephone-booth through the half-open door?"

"No, sir."

"Too bad, too bad," muttered the Inspector. He bit his mustache vexatiously. "Well, then—did a doctor pass your line of vision between 10:30 and 10:45?"

Paradise scratched the bulb of his nose reflectively. "I—don't—know. I was so busy. . . ." His eyes filled with tears. The Inspector retreated in embarrassment, "And doctors keep passing up and down the corridors all day. . . ."

"Oh, very well. Don't cry, man, for heaven's sake!" The old man turned away. "Thomas! All the doors manned? Everything all right so far—no attempts to break out?"

"Nothing stirring, Inspector. And the boys are on their toes," rumbled the giant. He glowered at the shrinking figure of the Superintendent.

Inspector Queen beckoned imperiously to Paradise. "I want

you to keep your eyes open," he snapped. "Work right along with my men: The Hospital will be under guard continuously until we discover the murderer of Mrs. Doorn. Give us your complete cooperation and I'll see you won't suffer for it. Understand?"

"Y-y-yes, but—" Paradise's ears flamed dangerously. "I-I I've never had a murder in my Hospital yet, Inspector. . . . I hope you—your men will not disrupt my organization—"

"Nothing of the kind. Beat it now!" The Inspector slapped Paradise's quaking back, not without friendliness, and shoved him toward the door. "Off with you!"

The Superintendent disappeared.

"I'll be with you in a moment, Henry," said the Inspector. Sampson nodded patiently. "Now, Thomas," went on the old man to Sergeant Velie, "you're to put the finishing-touches on things down here. I want the theater and this room and the Anæsthesia Room next door guarded. No one is to be allowed inside; no one at all.

"And while you're at it, you might try to trace the back-trail of the murderer from the Anæsthesia Room down the corridor, and see if you can't find some one who saw him. He probably kept up that limp business all the way down, wherever he went.

"And then I want you to take the names and addresses of every one—nurses, doctors, internes, outsiders, and all the rest. And one thing more . . ."

Sampson put in quickly, "The histories, Q.?"

"Yes. Listen, Thomas. Put a squad of men to work going over the private history of every person, without exception, that we've encountered so far. Just a check-up, that's all. Kneisel, Janney, Sarah Fuller, doctors, nurses—everybody you have any record of. Don't bother to give me a long report unless you run across something unusual. What I'm interested in is facts which don't corroborate or are missing from the testimony already given."

"Sure thing. Guards, murderer's getaway, names and addresses, morgue stuff. I got you," replied Velie, scribbling in his notebook. "By the way, Inspector, Big Mike is still under the influence of ether. Won't be able to talk for hours yet. Some of the boys are watching upstairs."

"Fine, fine! On the job, Thomas." The Inspector ran through the Amphitheater door, barked rapid instructions to detectives and policemen, and returned at once.

"All set, Henry." He reached for his coat.

"Dismissing them?" The District Attorney sighed and jammed his hat over his ears. Harper and Cronin moved toward the door.

"Might as well. We've done all we can down here for the present. Let's . . . Ellery—wake up!"

His father's voice penetrated dimly into the fog of Ellery's thoughts. Not once had he looked up or lost his frown during the swirling activity of the preceding few minutes. Now he raised his head and saw the Inspector, Sampson, Cronin and Harper ready to leave.

"Oh. . . . All the garbage incinerated?" He stretched mightily. The wrinkles vanished from his forehead.

"Yes, come on, Ellery. We're going to the Doorn place to clean up," said the old man testily. "Don't dawdle, son—there's too much to be done."

"Where's my coat? Here, somebody—my things are in Dr. Minchen's office." He rose to his full height. A policeman was dispatched on the errand.

Ellery did not speak again until the heavy black ulster was on his back. He tucked his stick under one arm and twisted the brim of his hat thoughtfully between his long fingers.

"Do you know," he murmured, as they left the Anteroom and watched a bluecoat set his back against the door, "Abigail Doorn should have emulated the Emperor Adrian. Remember what he had inscribed on his tomb?" As they passed out of the Anæsthesia Room another man took his stand at the door. "'A multitude of physicians have destroyed me. . . .'"

The Inspector froze in his tracks. "Ellery! You don't mean—"

Ellery's stick described a short arc and struck the marble floor resoundingly. "Oh, it's not an accusation," he said gently. "It's an epitaph."

14

ADORATION

"Phil. . . ."

"I'm sorry, Hulda. When I came here an hour ago from the Hospital, you were resting, Bristol said, and I knew Edith Dunning was with you, and Hendrik. . . . I didn't want to disturb you. And I had to go. Some business at the office—very urgent business. . . . But now I'm here, Hulda, and—Hulda—"

"I'm so tired."

"I know, dear, I know. Hulda—how can I say it?—Hulda, I . . ."

"Phil. Please."

"I don't know what to say, or how to say it. Dearest. That means something, doesn't it? Darling. You know how I feel. Toward you. But the world—the newspapers—you know too what they'd say if you—if we . . ."

"Phil! Do you think that would make any difference to me?"

"They'd say I was marrying Abby Doorn's millions!"

"I don't want to discuss marriage. Oh, how can you even *think* . . ."

"But, Hulda. *Hulda!* Oh, darling. I'm a beast to make you cry. . . ."

15

COMPLICATION

THE POLICE car rolled to the curb and stopped before the massive iron gates of the Doorn estate. Mansion and grounds covered the entire Fifth Avenue frontage between two streets in the Sixties. A high stone wall, weather-beaten and moss-grown, surrounded the house and gardens like an old granite cloak. It concealed the lower floors of the structure nestled deeply beyond the lawns.

One might, by stopping his ears to the automotive sounds of the flanking avenues, imagine himself in an old-world realm of châteaus and parks, of marble garden figures, stone benches and winding walks.

Across the street lay Central Park. Up Fifth Avenue the white dome and severe walls of the Metropolitan Museum gleamed. Beyond the bare branches of the park's trees, in the crystal air, the tiny turrets and box-like façades of Central Park West could be seen, small and delicate as toys.

Inspector Queen, District Attorney Sampson and Ellery Queen left three smoking detectives in the police car and tramped unhurriedly through the gates, along the stone approach, toiling up the steep ramp. It led to a portico, a classical structure supported by fluted marble columns.

A lanky old man in livery opened the outer door. Inspector Queen brushed him aside and found himself in a vaulted room of vast dimensions. "Mr. Doorn," he said with a snarl. "And don't stop to ask me questions."

The butler opened his mouth to protest, hesitated. "But who shall I say is—?"

"Inspector Queen. Mr. Queen. District Attorney Sampson."

"Yes, sir! . . . If you'll step this way, gentlemen." They followed him through rich rooms, tapestried halls. He stopped at a double-door, pushed them apart.

"If you will please wait with the other gentleman. . . ." He bowed and slowly walked off in the direction from which they had come.

"The other gentleman, hey?" muttered the Inspector. "Who—why, Harper!"

They stared across the brown somber room to a corner, where Pete Harper, ensconced in the leathery depths of a club-chair, grinned up at them.

"Say," demanded the Inspector, "I thought you said you were going back to your paper. Trying to steal a march on us?"

"Fortunes of war, Inspector." The old reporter waved gayly. "Tried to see Hendrik the playboy, but couldn't—so I waited for you. Sit down, fellers."

Ellery wandered thoughtfully about, examining the library. On all the walls, from floor to the lofty old-fashioned ceiling, were books—thousands of them. Reverently he ran his eye over some titles. The reverence banished and a peculiar smile appeared on his face as he plucked one volume from its shelf. It was a heavy, richly bound tome in golden calfskin. He flipped its pages experimentally. The sheets fell together, in sections.

"Well," he commented dryly, "we, seem to have encountered

another secret vice of our millionaires. Lovely books with neither fathers nor mothers."

"What do you mean?" asked Sampson, who was following with curiosity.

"Here's a copy of Voltaire in a perfectly magnificent format, specially designed, specially printed, specially bound—and specially unread. Poor Arouet! The leaves aren't even cut. I'll wager ninety-eight per cent of these volumes haven't been referred to since they were purchased."

The Inspector had sunk, groaning, into a Morris chair. "I wish that fat old fool . . ."

The fat old fool was genie to the wish: he appeared suddenly between the double-door in the bulky flesh, a wide nervous smile creasing his cheeks.

"Wery nice!" he squeaked. "Gladt to see you, gentlemans. Sidt down, sidt down!"

He oozed forward, like a seal.

The District Attorney obeyed slowly, regarding Abigail Doorn's brother with a scowl of disgust. Ellery paid not the least attention to their host; he kept wandering about the room, looking at the books.

Hendrik Doorn collapsed on a broad divan and folded his fat hands moistly together. His smile vanished as he caught sight of the sprawling figure of Harper across the room.

"Iss that the reporter?" he shrilled. "I will nodt speak before a reporter, Inspector. *Raus,* you!"

"*Raus* yourself," said Harper. He continued soothingly, "Now, keep your shirt on, Mr. Doorn. I'm not here as a newspaperman—am I, Mr. Sampson? The District Attorney will tell you, Mr. Doorn. I'm just helping along with the case. Friendly, sort of."

"Harper's all right, Mr. Doorn," said the District Attorney sharply. "You can speak as freely before him as before us."*

"Well . . ." Doorn eyed the reporter askance. "And he wouldn't prindt anythings I say nodt to?"

"Who—me?" Harper looked scandalized. "Listen, Mr. Doorn, you're insulting me. I'm the original clam."

"You told us at the Hospital," interrupted the Inspector, "about a story. You hinted it was as much as your life is worth to breathe a word about it. Well, sir?"

Doorn settled himself with painful fussiness on the protesting divan. He said carefully, not looking up, "Budt first you gentlemans must promise me somethings." He lowered his voice. "Secrecy!" He regarded them quickly, in turn, like an arch-conspirator.

Inspector Queen closed his eyes. He dipped his fingers into the old brown snuff-box which was his constant companion. He seemed to have lost his ill-temper. "Are you making us a proposition?" he murmured. "A pact with the police, eh? Well, Mr. Doorn," he opened his eyes and sat erect suddenly, "you'll tell us that story and you'll do it without bargains, too."

Doorn wagged his bald head cunningly. "Ah, budt no," he said in his thin falsetto. "You cannodt intimidate me, *Mynheer Inspektor.* You promise, I speak. Otherwise—no."

"I'll tell you what," said the Inspector suddenly. "You're evidently afraid for your hide, Mr. Doorn. Suppose we assure you that, if you need protection, we'll give it to you."

---

* In the whole history of reporter-police relations there has never been a more interesting chapter than that written by Peter Harper. To credit the unique privileges he enjoyed, it is essential to understand that the police never found him an abuser of confidences. In addition, he had been instrumental "in tracking down through his independent efforts several notorious criminals sought by the police. He may be remembered for his inspired journalistic efforts in the nation-wide hunt for Chicago Jack Murphy, in the Barnaby-Ross revelations, and in the case that has come to be known throughout the world as the "Mimic Murders."—The Editor

"You will give me police, detectives?" demanded Doorn eagerly.

"If your safety demands it, yes."

"Wery well." Doorn leaned forward, began to whisper rapidly. "I am in debt to—to a bloodt-sucker. For years I have been borrowing money from him. Large sums!"

"Here, here!" put in Inspector Queen. "This requires a little explaining. I've been given to understand that you have a tidy little income."

The fat man brushed the remark aside with a ponderous wave of his hand. "Nothings. Nothings. I play at cardts, horses. I am—what you call—a spordtsman. My luck has been badt—wery badt. So! This man—he lendts me the money. Then he says, 'I want back my money.' And I cannodt pay. I talk, and he lendts me more. I give I.O.U's. How much—*Gott!* One hundred and ten thousands of dollars, gentlemans!"

Sampson whistled. Harper's eyes flamed. The Inspector's expression grew grim. "What security did you offer?" he asked. "After all, Mr. Doorn, you are not independently wealthy, as all the world knows."

Doorn's eyes narrowed. "Securidty? The besdt in the worldt!" He smirked all over his fat face. "My sister's fordtune!"

"Do you mean," demanded Sampson, "that Mrs. Doorn endorsed your I.O.U's, okayed your notes?"

"Oh, no!" He gasped audibly. "Budt as the brother of Abigail Doorn, I wass naturally known as the heir to greadt wealth. My sister knew nothings of this affair."

"Isn't that interesting," murmured the Inspector. "Shylock loans you the money knowing that when Abby Doorn died you'd come into most of the fortune. A pretty arrangement, Mr. Doorn!"

Doorn's lips hung loose and wet. He looked frightened.

"Well, well!" exclaimed the Inspector. "What's the point of all this? Let's have it!"

"The poindt iss this. . . ." Doorn's jowls sagged as his body inclined toward them. "When the years passed and Abigail did nodt die, and consequently I could nodt repay—he said she must be killed!"

He stopped dramatically. The Inspector and Sampson looked at each other. Ellery had paused in the act of opening a little book; he stared at Doorn.

"Now that's a story, isn't it?" muttered Inspector Queen. "Who is this money-lender? Banker? Broker?"

Doorn blanched. He peered out of his piggish eyes at all corners of the room, uneasily. It was apparent that his trepidation was very real. When he spoke, it was in a heavy whisper.

"Michael Cudtahy. . . ."

"Big Mike!" the Inspector and Sampson exclaimed together. The old man leaped to his feet and began to trot up and down the thick-piled rug. "Big Mike, by juniper! And in the Hospital, too. . . ."

"Mr. Cudahy," said Ellery in cool accents, "has the perfect alibi, dad. At the instant Abigail Doorn was having her throat constricted, he was being put to sleep by a doctor and two nurses." He turned back to the book-shelves.

"Sure he'd have an alibi," chuckled Harper suddenly. "That guy is an eel. Smooth—smooth!"

"Oh, it couldn't have been Cudahy," muttered the Inspector.

"But it could have been one of his three strong-arm boys," put in the District Attorney animatedly.

The Inspector said nothing. He looked dissatisfied. "I don't see it," he mumbled. "This crime is too refined, too polished. Not direct enough for Little Willie, Snapper, or Joe Gecko."

"Yes, but with Cudahy's brain directing it . . ." argued Sampson.

"Now, now," said Ellery from his corner. "Don't be hasty, any of you gentlemen. Old Publius Syrus knew what he was talking about when he said: 'We ought to weigh well what we can only once decide.' You can't afford to make a mistake in calling the turn, dad."

The fat man seemed singularly pleased at the stir he had created. Although his eyes were carefully screwed up in scores of tiny crinkles, he was smirking. "At first Cudtahy said I should do it. Budt," virtuously, "it wass an infamous suggestion. I threatened to go to the police. What? I said. My flesh and blood. . . . He laughed and said *he* midght do it. I said, 'You are nodt serious, Mike?' He said, 'That iss my business. Budt you are to keep your mouth shudt, you understand?' What could I do? He—he would have killed me. . . ."

"When did this conversation take place?" demanded Queen.

"Last September."

"Has Cudahy ever discussed it since?"

"No."

"When did you last see him?"

"Three weeks ago. . . . There iss little else." Doorn was perspiring unpleasantly; his little eyes, unsettled, roved from face to face. "When I saw this morning that my sister she wass dead, murdered—what else could I think budt that Cudtahy . . . You see? Now I will have to—I mean I will be able to pay my debt to him. That iss what he wants."

Sampson shook his head worriedly. "Cudahy's mouthpiece would riddle your story to bits, Mr. Doorn. Have you any witnesses to his threat? I thought not. No, I'm afraid we have nothing on which to hold Big Mike. Of course, we can keep our fingers on his three thugs, but not for long unless definite evidence against them is found."

"They'll try to spring 'em to-day," said the Inspector grimly. "But those boys will stay in our hands. I'll promise you that, Henry. . . . Only, it doesn't ring true. Snapper's the only one of the three who is small enough to have impersonated Janney, and somehow . . ."

"I tell you this story," interposed Doorn in an eager squeak, "because of my sister." His brow darkened. "Vengeance! The murderer will pay the penalty!" He sat erect, like a fattened rooster.

Harper placed the tips of his tobacco-stained fingers together and tapped them against each other in silent applause; Ellery caught the movement and smiled.

Sampson said, "It seems to me, Mr. Doorn, that you have very little to fear from Cudahy or his mob."

"You think so?"

"I'm positive. You're worth much more to Cudahy alive than dead. If something happened to you, he wouldn't stand a chance of collecting—not Cudahy, on I.O.U.'s. No, sir! His best bet is to let you alone, have the estate settled, and then bully you into paying him what you borrowed."

"I suppose," queried the Inspector sardonically, "you're paying regular rates of interest?"

Doorn groaned. "Fifteen per cent. . . ." There was silence as he swabbed the perspiration from his face. "You won'dt tell?" His jowls quivered ludicrously.

"Usury. . . ." The Inspector mused. "We'll treat your story confidentially, Mr. Doorn, I can promise you that. And you'll have ample protection from Cudahy."

"Thank you, thank you!"

"Now, suppose you give us an account of your own movements this morning?" ventured the Inspector casually.

"My movements?" Doorn stared with goggle-eyes. "Budt surely you don't . . . Ha! So. It iss a matter of form, no? I heard by the telephone of my sister's fall. The Hospital called. I wass still in bedt. Hulda and Sarah left before me. I arrived at the Hospital aboudt 10:00 o'clock. I wass trying to findt Dr. Janney. Budt I could nodt, and aboudt five minutes before the operation I came to the Waidting Room where wass Hulda and young Morehouse, the lawyer."

"Just wandered about, eh?" The Inspector looked glum. He gnawed his mustache. Ellery, striding into the group, smiled down at Hendrik Doorn.

"Mrs. Doorn," he said, "was a widow. How is it, then, that she was known as 'Mrs. Doorn'? Isn't the family name Doorn? Or did she marry a distant cousin of the same name?"

"Wery goodt," piped the fat man. "You see, Mr. Queen, Abigail married Charles Van der Donk, budt when he died she took back her maiden name and added the 'Mrs.' for her dignity. She was very proud of the Doorn name."

"I can substantiate that," put in Harper lazily, "because I took a quick look at the back-files before I dashed down to the Hospital this morning."

"Oh, I don't doubt it in the least." Ellery polished his glasses with vigor. "I was just curious. And how about your obligations to Michael Cudahy, Mr. Doorn? You mentioned cards, horses. How about the larger and more exciting game? The ladies, to be literal."

"*Hein?*" Doorn's face once more assumed a glistening aspect as the perspiration beaded it. "Why—ah—"

"*Attention!*" said Ellery sharply. "Answer my question, Mr. Doorn. Are there any women on your list to whom you *still* owe money? Note that I am the perfect gentleman and omit mentioning the reason."

Doorn licked his blubbery lips. "No. I—I am all paid up."

"Danken sie!"

The Inspector was regarding his son keenly. Ellery's head jerked the merest bit. The Inspector rose and, with the utmost casualness, put his hand on Doorn's huge soft arm.

"I think that will be enough for the present, Mr. Doorn. Thanks, and don't worry about Cudahy." Doorn struggled to his feet, wiping his face. "By the way, we should like to see Miss Hulda for a moment. On the way up, will you—"

"Yes. Yes. Goodt-by."

Doorn waddled quickly out of the room.

They looked at each other. Inspector Queen located a telephone on a desk and called Police Headquarters. It was while he conversed with a deputy inspector that Ellery murmured, apropos of nothing, "Did it strike you that friend Doorn, the living Colossus of Rhodes, has upset the dictates of his own slimy nature by spilling his story?"

"Sure it has," drawled Harper. "The cush."

"You mean if Cudahy were convicted of Abigail Doorn's murder he wouldn't . . ." Sampson knit his brows.

"Exactly," said Ellery. "The mammoth wouldn't have to pay back what he owes. Perhaps that accounts for his anxiety to cast suspicion on Cudahy. . . ."

And then Hulda Doorn entered the library leaning on Philip Morehouse's arm.

With a glum and watchful young Morehouse hovering about her, Hulda Doorn soon revealed that behind the thick old walls of the rococo Doorn chambers a bitter feud had grown up. She revealed it only after the combined cross-questions of the Inspector and the District Attorney made excuses and subterfuge no longer possible.

Morehouse stood behind her, his crisp features dark with irritation.

Abigail Doorn and Sarah Fuller . . . two old women, snapping at each other behind closed doors, wrangling like fishwives over no one knew what. Hulda did not know. For weeks the two women, septuagenarian and spinster faded prematurely by an obsession, would live side by side without speaking to each other. For months they would confer only on essentials, and then in monosyllables. For years they had not had a kind word for each other. And yet weeks and months and years passed and Sarah Fuller remained in the service of Abigail Doorn.

"Was there ever any question of Mrs. Doorn discharging her?"

The girl shook her head mechanically. "Oh, mother would be angry and sometimes say she was through with Sarah, but we all knew it was just talk. . . . I used to ask mother why she and Sarah didn't get along. She—she used to look strange and say it was just my fancy, and that a woman in her position couldn't very well be intimate with even a high grade of servant. But that—that wasn't like mother either. I—"

"I told you about all this," snapped Morehouse. "Why do you torture—"

They paid, no attention to him. . . . Domestic quarrels, ventured Hulda finally. Surely it could have been nothing more serious. Otherwise why—

The Inspector suddenly dropped the matter.

Questioned as to her movements of the morning, Hulda corroborated Sarah Fuller's recital in the Anteroom of the Hospital.

"You say," pursued the Inspector, "that Miss Fuller left you in the Waiting Room and wandered off somewhere, and that Mr. Morehouse came to you there shortly after Miss Fuller left. . . . Was Mr. Morehouse with you all the time from then until he left to witness the operation?"

Hulda pursed her lips thoughtfully. "Yes. Oh, except for about ten minutes or so, I think. I asked Philip if he would please find Dr. Janney and bring back some word to me about mother. Sarah had gone and not returned. Philip came back later saying he couldn't find the doctor. Isn't that so, Phil? I—I'm not very clear about—about . . ."

Morehouse said quickly, "Yes. Yes. Of course."

"And at what time, Miss Doorn," asked the Inspector delicately, "did Mr. Morehouse return to you?"

"Oh, I don't remember. What time was it, Phil?"

Morehouse bit his lip. "I should say—it must have been 10:40, because I left you again almost immediately to go to the Amphitheater gallery, and the operation—the operation was begun in a very short while."

"I see." The Inspector rose. "I believe that's all."

Ellery said smoothly, "Is Miss Dunning in the house, Miss Doorn? I should like to speak with her."

"She's gone." Hulda closed her eyes wearily; her soft lips looked parched, fevered. "She was so sweet, coming here with me. But she had to go back to the Hospital. She has charge of the Social Service Department there, you know."

"By the way, Miss Doorn." The District Attorney was smiling. "I'm sure you will want to give the police every possible assistance. . . . It will be necessary to examine Mrs. Doorn's private papers for a possible clew."

The girl nodded; a spasm of horror twitched her white features. "Yes. Yes; I just—can't believe . . ."

Morehouse said angrily, "There's nothing in the house here that can help you. I have all her business papers and those things. Why don't you leave. . . ."

Morehouse bent over Hulda. She looked up at him.

They left the room together, quickly.

The old butler was summoned. He had a wooden face but extraordinarily bright little eyes.

"Your name is Bristol?" said the Inspector briskly.

"Yes, sir. Harry Bristol."

"You realize that I expect you to tell the exact truth?"

The man blinked. "Oh, yes, sir!"

"Very well, then." The Inspector tapped Bristol's quiet livery with a punctuating forefinger. "Mrs. Doorn and Sarah Fuller quarreled frequently?"

"I—well, sir . . ."

"Didn't they?"

"Well . . . Yes, sir."

"What about?"

A helpless look crept into the man's eyes. "I don't know, sir. They were always arguing. We heard them sometimes. But we never knew the reason. Just—they were just unpleasant to each other."

"And you're sure no one belowstairs knew why?"

"No, sir. They were always careful, it seemed to me, not to quarrel before the help, sir. Always in Mrs. Doorn's rooms, or in Miss Fuller's."

"How long have you been serving here?"

"Twelve years, sir."

"That's all."

Bristol bowed and walked sedately out of the library.

They rose.

"How about this Fuller woman again, Inspector?" said Harper. "Seems to me she might be put on the grill."

Ellery shook his head violently. "Let her alone. She won't run away. Pete, I'm surprised at you. We're not dealing with a thug or a normal citizen. She's a mental case."

They left the house.

Ellery inhaled deeply of the fresh cold January air. He was accompanied by Harper. The Inspector and Sampson preceded them at a crisper pace, striding toward the Fifth Avenue gate.

"What do you think Pete?"

The reporter grinned. "Hooey, the whole set-up," he said. "Can't see any real lead. Everybody had a chance to pull the trick and a lot of 'em had motive."

"Anything else?"

"If I were the Inspector," continued Harper, kicking a pebble out of the path, "I'd dig in a little and follow the Wall Street angle. Old Abby ruined many and many a budding Rockefeller. Maybe some one in the Hospital this morning had a revenge-financial motive. . . ."

Ellery smiled. "Dad's not exactly a novice at this game, Pete. He has that line out already. . . . You might be interested in knowing that I've already made certain eliminations. . . ."

"Eliminations!" Harper halted. "Say, look here, old man, give me a break, will you? What is it, this Fuller-Doorn business?"

Ellery shook his head. The smile vanished; his face clouded over. "There's something strange there. Two old viragoes following Napoleon's advice. 'People should wash their linen in private.' It's unnatural, Pete."

"You think there's a deep underlying secret, huh?"

"I'm sure of it. It's perfectly apparent that this Fuller woman shares it, and that somehow it's shameful. . . . By heaven, it worries me!"

The four men climbed into the police car. It sped away, leaving its former occupants, three detectives, on the sidewalk. They sauntered through the gate and up the walk.

At the same instant Philip Morehouse emerged from the front door, looked about with peculiar caution, and stopped dead as he caught sight of the approaching trio of plain-clothesmen.

Then he buttoned his overcoat tightly up to his chin and ran down the steps. He brushed by the detectives with a muttered apology and hurried toward the gate. They stared after him.

Morehouse reached the pavement, hesitated, then struck out with long strides to the left, in the downtown direction. He did not look back.

The three detectives parted at the portico. One doubled on his tracks and slouched after Morehouse. The second disappeared into a patch of shrubbery near the main house. The third clambered up the steps and knocked thunderously on the front door.

16

ALIENATION

DISTRICT ATTORNEY Sampson urged speed; he was overdue at his office. Harper was dropped off on the West Side to dash for a telephone. The police car screamed on its way through the dense midafternoon traffic.

In the lurching vehicle Inspector Queen glumly counted off on his fingers the details which he must supervise when he reached the big stone building on Centre Street. . . . The search for Janney's mysterious visitor; the investigation of the impostor's clothes in an endeavor to trace their real ownership; the hunt for the hardware or department store which had sold the strangling picture-wire; the gathering into a smoother fabric of the dark dangling threads.

"Most of 'em hopeless," shouted the old man above the roar of the motor and the shriek of the siren.

The car stopped briefly at the curb outside the Dutch Memorial Hospital to deposit Ellery on the sidewalk; it immediately picked up speed and disappeared in the downtown traffic.

For the second time that day Ellery Queen found himself mounting the steps of the Hospital, and for the second time alone.

Isaac Cobb was on duty in the vestibule, talking with a police-man. Opposite the main elevator Ellery found Dr. Minchen.

He glanced up the corridors. At the entrance to the Anæsthe-sia Room stood the detective who had been left there an hour be-fore. Bluecoats sat chatting in the main Waiting Room. Three men lugging bulky photographic equipment tramped in his direction from a corridor to the right.

Ellery and Dr. Minchen strolled to the left and turned into the East Corridor. They passed the telephone booth in which the dis-carded clothing had been found. The booth was sealed with tape. Several feet farther up the corridor, to the left as they proceeded toward the North Corridor, there was a closed door.

Ellery halted. "This is the outer door to that Anteroom lift, isn't it, John?"

"Yes. There's a double door here," replied Minchen dreari-ly. "The lift can be entered either through the corridor here or through the Anteroom. The corridor door is used when the pa-tient to be operated comes from a ward on this floor. Eliminates having to cart 'em all the way round into the South Corridor."

"Smart," commented Ellery. "Like everything else around here. And I see our good Sergeant has had the door taped up."

A moment later, in Minchen's office, Ellery said abruptly, "Tell me a little about Janney's relations with the rest of the staff. I'm anxious to discover how people here regard him."

"Janney? He's not an easy man to get along with, of course. But then he's given healthy respect because of his position and reputation in surgery. It makes a difference, Ellery."

"You would say," demanded Ellery, "that Janney has no ene-mies in the Hospital?"

"Enemies? Hardly. Unless there's a personal undercurrent

outside my ken." Minchen pursed his lips thoughtfully. "Come to think of it, there's one individual in the place who's been rather at dagger-points with the old man. . . ."

"Really! Who?"

"Dr. Pennini. Head—or rather former Head of the Obstetrical Department."

"Why 'former'? Is Pennini leaving—resigned?"

"Oh, no. There was a change in administration recently and Dr. Pennini was demoted to Assistant Head. Janney was, nominally at least, put in charge of the Obstetrical Department."

"But why?"

Minchen grimaced. "No fault of Dr. Pennini's. Just another manifestation of the deceased's affection for Janney."

A shadow crossed Ellery's face. "I see. Dagger-points, eh? Just a case of petty professional jealousy. Well . . ."

"Not petty, Ellery. You don't know Dr. Pennini, or you wouldn't say that. Latin blood, fiery, the vengeful type, she's certainly far from—"

"What's that?"

Minchen seemed surprised. "I said she was the vengeful type. Why?"

Ellery lit a cigarette with elaborate ceremony. "Naturally. Stupid of me. You didn't mention . . . I'd like to see this Dr. Pennini of yours, John."

"Of course." Minchen telephoned. "Dr. Pennini? John Minchen speaking. Glad I found you so easily. You usually gad about so. . . . Can you come to my office for just a moment, Doctor? . . . No, nothing, nothing important. An introduction, a few questions . . . Yes. Please."

Ellery regarded his fingernails until there was a knock on the door. Both men rose and Minchen said clearly, "Come!" The door opened to admit a stocky, white-garbed woman of nervous movements.

"Dr. Pennini, allow me to present Mr. Ellery Queen. Mr. Queen is helping with the investigation of Mrs. Doorn's murder, you know."

"Indeed." Her voice was rich, throaty, almost masculine. Motioning imperiously toward their chairs, she sat down.

She was a striking woman. Her skin was olivaceous; the faintest smudge of hair appeared above her upper lip. Keen black eyes flashed in a regular-featured face. Her jet hair, set off at one side by a thick white streak, was parted severely in the center of her scalp. Her age was elusive; she might have been thirty-five or fifty.

"I understand, Doctor," began Ellery in his mildest voice, "that you have been with the Dutch Memorial Hospital for a good many years."

"Very true. Let me have a cigarette." She looked amused.

Ellery offered his gold-chased case, gravely held a match to the tip of the cigarette. She puffed deeply and relaxed, eying him with open curiosity. "You know," he said, "we're up against a stone wall in this investigation of Mrs. Doorn's murder. The thing seems utterly inexplicable. I'm just asking questions of anybody and everybody. . . . How well did you know Mrs. Doorn?"

"Why?" Dr. Pennini's black eyes twinkled. "Do you suspect me of her murder?"

"My dear Doctor . . ."

"You listen to me, Mr. Ellery Queen." She set her full red lips firmly. "I didn't know Mrs. Doorn well. I know nothing of her murder. You're wasting your time if you think I do. Now does that satisfy you?"

"How could it?" murmured Ellery ruefully. Nevertheless his

eyes narrowed. "And I shouldn't jump at conclusions so. The reason I asked you how well you knew Mrs. Doorn is this—if you did know her well you might be in a position to name possible enemies. Can you?"

"I'm sorry. I cannot."

"Dr. Pennini, let's stop fencing. I am going to be very frank." He closed his eyes and rested his neck on the back of his chair. "Did you or did you not"—he snapped bolt upright and fixed her with his eyes—"utter threats at Mrs. Doorn in the presence of witnesses?"

She stared at him too amazed, from her look of astonishment, to be angry. Minchen put up a protesting hand and muttered something apologetic; he was regarding Ellery with the utmost consternation.

"Did you?" Ellery's tone was flat, stern. "In this very building?"

"Utterly preposterous." She laughed without amusement, throwing her head back defiantly. "Who told you that cock-and-bull story? I couldn't possibly have threatened the old lady. I hardly knew her. I never made remarks about her or any one. That is, I—" She stopped suddenly in confusion, flashed a look at Dr. Minchen.

"That is . . . what?" prompted Ellery. He had lost his severity and was smiling.

"Well—you see—I did make derogatory remarks about *Dr. Janney* some time ago," she explained stiffly, "but they weren't threats, and they certainly weren't directed against Mrs. Doorn. I can't see, anyway—"

"Good!" Ellery beamed. "It was Dr. Janney, not Mrs. Doorn. Very well, Dr. Pennini. What have you against Janney?"

"Nothing terribly personal. I suppose you've heard"—she

glanced sidewise at Dr. Minchen once more; he flushed and avoided her eyes—"that I was demoted through the interference of Mrs. Doorn from the position of Head of the Obstetrical Department. I was naturally resentful, and I am still resentful. I feel that it was Dr. Janney's propaganda in the ear of the old lady which was responsible. In the heat of the moment I suppose I said some nasty things, and Dr. Minchen and a few others heard me. But what all this has to do with—"

"Very natural, very natural," said Ellery sympathetically. "I quite understand." She sniffed. "Now, Doctor, a little routine matter. . . . Please account to me for your movements in the Hospital this morning."

"My dear sir," she returned coldly, "you're so obvious! I've nothing at all to conceal. I had an early confinement this morning, operating at eight o'clock. Twins, if it interests you. Caesarian, and one died. Mother will probably go soon, too. . . . I had breakfast and then made my regular rounds in the Maternity Ward. Dr. Janney, you know," she said with sarcasm, "doesn't bother with routine. His title is purely honorary. I visited about thirty-five patients and an army of squealing brats. I was on the go most of the morning."

"And you weren't in one place long enough to provide you with an alibi."

"If I had needed an alibi I might have been careful to provide myself with one," she retorted.

"Not in a certain eventuality," murmured Ellery. "Did you leave the building at all up to noon?"

"No."

"So helpful, Doctor. . . . And you can't offer a plausible explanation of this hideous business?"

"No again."

THE DUTCH SHOE MYSTERY · 149

"You're positive?"

"If I could, I should."

"I'll bear that in mind." Ellery rose. "Thank you."

Dr. Minchen got to his feet awkwardly and they stood silently until the door slammed shut behind the woman. Minchen sank back into his swivel-chair and grinned feebly. "Quite a woman, isn't she?"

"Quite!" Ellery lit another cigarette. "By the way, John, do you know if Edith Dunning is in the Hospital? I haven't talked with her since she left this morning to take Hulda Doorn home."

"See in a moment." Minchen busied himself with his telephone. "She isn't in. Went out on a Service call not long ago."

"It doesn't matter now." Ellery inhaled hugely. "Interesting woman. . . ." He expelled a nimbus of smoke. "Come to think of it, John—Euripides wasn't so far wrong when he said, 'I hate a learned woman.' And don't think, either, that the Grecian remark was so unallied to that classic statement of Byron's. . . ."*

"In heaven's name," groaned Minchen, "of which one are you talking—Miss Dunning or Dr. Pennini?"

"That doesn't matter either." Ellery reached for his coat, sighing.

---

* The allusion becomes intelligible when it is understood to which quotation Mr. Queen was referring. We asked Mr. J. J. McC. to clear up this point, which he was able to do only with difficulty. He discovered it to spring from a little-known quotation, "I hate a *dumpy* woman." Undoubtedly Mr. Queen referred to Dr. Pennini. She was both "learned" and "dumpy," to judge from his own description.—The Editor

17

MYSTIFICATION

THE PECULIAR relationship between Inspector Queen and his son—comradely rather than paternal-filial—was never more marked than at meal-times. The hour of sustenance, whether breakfast or dinner, was a period of jest, of reminiscence, of lively and good-natured chaffing. With young Djuna serving, the fire crackling, the wind howling through the canyons of West 87th Street and rattling the window panes, the Queens-at-home-of-a-wintry-evening was a spectacle famed in story and song throughout the vestries of the Police Department.[*]

But the tradition was shattered on the evening of the January day on which Abigail Doorn went to her reward.

Here was neither laughter nor peace. Ellery sat absorbed in thought and wrapped in gloom, cigarette smoldering above a half-empty coffee-cup. The Inspector shivered and wheezed as he sat hunched in his great armchair before the fire; his teeth chattered despite an armor of three old dressing-gowns. Djuna, ever

---

[*] Detective stories should concern themselves with relevancies. No description of the more or less well-known Queen domicile on West 87th Street is furnished here for the good and sufficient reason that it was fully described in an adventure post-dating *The Dutch Shoe Mystery* in time, but antedating it in appearance as a novel. I refer to *The Roman Hat Mystery* (Frederick A. Stokes Company, '29).—Author's Note

the interpreter of moods, removed the dinner-dishes in a silence inhumanly complete.

The first real search had failed ignobly. Swanson, the wraith, was still at large. Sergeant Velie's myrmidons had failed to find the faintest trace of him, despite a thorough canvass of all the Swansons in the borough directories. Headquarters was in an uproar, the Inspector tied to his chambers by a suddenly developed coryza. Preliminary reports from the detectives scouring hospitals and other institutions brought no word about the original source of the surgical clothing found in the telephone booth. The quest for the establishment which sold the picture-wire seemed hopeless, and chemical analysis of the wire revealed nothing. A scrutiny of Abigail Doorn's financial rivals had as yet borne no fruit. The murdered woman's private papers were as innocent, it seemed, as a child's primary notebook. And, to complicate matters further, District Attorney Sampson had just telephoned to transmit the news of two hurried conferences with the Mayor and another long-distance call from the Governor at Albany. City and State officials were harried, anxious, clamorous for police action. The newspapermen hounded headquarters, besieged the closely guarded scene of the crime.

It was this state of affairs which had the Inspector, helpless in his chair, half hysterical with impotent rage. Ellery persisted in maintaining silence, sunk in a sea of speculation. . . .

Djuna leaped out of his kitchen at the shrill *br-r-ring* of the telephone bell. "For you, Dad Queen."

The old man hurried across the room, shaking with ague and licking his parched lips. "Hello. Who? Thomas? Well. . . ." His voice sharpened, became eager. "Oh. Oh. WHAT? Oh, good glory. Hold the wire a moment."

His face was parchment-ivory as he turned to Ellery. "The

rottenest luck, son. It's happened. Janney has given Ritter the slip!"

Ellery got to his feet, startled. "Stupid!" he muttered. "Find out more about it, dad."

"Hello! Hello!" Inspector Queen wheezed viciously into the mouthpiece. "Thomas. You tell Ritter for me that he has some tall explaining to do or back he goes on a beat. . . . No news on Swanson yet, eh? . . . . Well, you'll have to work all night. . . . WHAT? Good for Hesse. . . . Yes, I know. He was backstairs in the house this afternoon while we were there. . . . All right, Thomas. Have Ritter go back to Janney's hotel and stay there. . . . He'd better!"

"What's up?" demanded Ellery as the old man trundled back to his chair and warmed his hands at the fire.

"Plenty. Janney lives at the Tareyton, on Madison Avenue. Ritter tailed him all day. He hung about watching the place and at 5:30 Janney came out in a hurry, took a cab at the door, which headed north. Ritter got a bad break, I'll say that for him—he couldn't get a cab for several moments—it all happened so fast he was paralyzed. . . .

"When he located a hack he followed, picked up the trail, then lost it in traffic. Picked it up again near 42nd Street and was just in time to see Janney jump out of the cab at Grand Central, pay off his driver, and disappear into the terminal. . . . And that's the last of Janney, blast the luck!"

Ellery looked thoughtful. "Deliberately disobeyed instructions, eh? Skipped town. Of course, it's only one thing. . . ."

"Naturally. He's gone to warn off Swanson." The old man was morose now. "Ritter was caught in a jam around the terminal and by the time he got out and into the station Janney had disappeared. He recruited a squad of cops right away to watch the outgoing trains but it was useless. Like looking for a needle in a haystack."

"Well," muttered Ellery, frowning, "it's practically certain that Janncy went to warn Swanson, and that Swanson therefore lives somewhere in the suburbs."

"Taken care of already. Thomas has a group working on the suburb angle. . . ." The Inspector's eyes brightened momentarily. "There's one ray of light, though. Know what this Fuller lunatic has done?"

"Sarah Fuller!" The name leaped from Ellery's lips. "What?"

"Slipped out of the Doorn house about an hour ago. Hesse was tailing her all day. He followed her to—the home of Dr. Dunning! What do you think of that?"

Ellery stared at his father. "Dr. Dunning, eh?" he said slowly. "Now, that *is* interesting. Anything else from Hesse?"

"Nothing much. The fact alone is enough. She remained in the house for a half-hour. When she came out she took a taxicab directly back to the Doorn place. Hesse reported by 'phone and is still there, working with another man on the job."

"Sarah Fuller and Dr. Lucius Dunning," murmured Ellery. He sat down at the table and, looking into the fire, drumming incessantly on the cloth. "Sarah Fuller and Lucius Dunning. There's a combination for you. . . ." He smiled at his father suddenly. "The prophetess and the healer. A classic *non sequitur.*"

"It's funny, right enough," said the Inspector. He drew his outer robe more closely about him. "We'll have to follow that up in the morning."

"Evidently," said Ellery with a strange satisfaction, "on the Slavic assumption that 'the morning is wiser than the evening.' Well—we'll see."

The old man said nothing. Just as suddenly as it had appeared, the pleasure vanished from Ellery's face. He rose quickly and went into his bedroom.

18

CONDENSATION

THE JOURNALISTIC explosion which later was to reverberate through the press of the entire world did not achieve its full fury until the day after Abigail Doorn's murder.

On Tuesday morning every newspaper in the United States carried blazing headlines, voluble front-page stories, and a pitiful handful of facts. The New York press in particular made up for the dearth of available data by devoting whole pages of stories to Abigail Doorn's astonishing career, her outstanding financial transactions, her enormous list of charities, and the details of her romance with the long-deceased Charles Van der Donk. One syndicate began a hastily assembled series of feature articles titled *The Life Story of Abigail Doorn.*

With the early afternoon editions, peals of editorial thunder began to make themselves heard. Thinly veiled shafts of criticism were hurled at the Police Commissioner, at Inspector Queen, at the Police Department as a whole, and in one case, obviously as a political move, at the Mayor. "Twenty-four precious hours have slipped into eternity," ran one indignant account, "and still not the tiniest shred of fact or clew has been unearthed which might lead to the identity of that foul murderer whose bloody hand yesterday sent the great soul of a great woman weeping into the hereafter, long long before her time." "Is the redoubtable Inspector Queen about to fall down after so many years of successful man-hunting in this, his most important assignment?" queried another. A third stated categorically that the Police Department of the greatest city in the world, for years "notoriously incompetent" in its regulation of the morals of that vastly moral community, would now have the unexampled opportunity of displaying to the sneering world exactly how incompetent it was.

The only newspaper in New York which neither groaned nor flayed the police was the sheet, strangely enough, to which Pete Harper rendered reportorial service.

But it had not required the insinuations and accusations of a vitriolic press to rouse officialdom from its alleged lethargy. The political and social worlds were rocked to their foundations, and the tremors were recorded on the sensitive seismographs of Headquarters. Public figures in all walks of life showered the Mayor with telegraphed, telephoned and personal demands for swift justice. Wall Street, alarmed at the financial unrest and unable to stem the inevitable tide of falling quotations and growing panic, rose in its wrath. The Federal Government evinced an unusual interest in the case. A Senator in whose State Abigail Doorn owned huge properties made a flaming speech from the floor of Congress.

City Hall was a maelstrom of frenzied conferences. Centre Street buzzed like a gigantic bee-hive. Inspector Queen was nowhere to be found; Sergeant Velie flatly refused to talk to reporters. Rumors, feeding on the atmosphere of mystery and doubt, circulated magically all over the City, whispering that an unnamed and "protected" financier of great power had strangled Abigail Doorn with his own hands in revenge for a financial struggle which he had ignominiously lost to the dead woman. The rumor's patent absurdity, it seemed, did not retard its circulation. Within two hours official cognizance was being taken of it. . . .

Late Tuesday afternoon a solemn group gathered secretly in the innermost sanctum of the Mayor's chambers. Seated around the conference table in the thick smoky air were the Mayor himself, the Police Commissioner, District Attorney Sampson and his aides, the Borough President of Manhattan, and a half-dozen secretaries. Inspector Queen was conspicuous by his absence.

Gloom hovered over them, leering. They had discussed the case from every conceivable angle while a mad, chattering horde of reporters besieged the outer offices for interviews. The Mayor held in his hand a great sheaf of reports, all signed by Inspector Queen, which gave in painstaking detail every fact, conversation and finding accumulated in the case up to Tuesday morning. Personalities had been weighed and judged: the Borough President had expressed himself as satisfied that the fine Irish hand of Big Mike Cudahy was somewhere mixed into the murder, possibly employed by a mysterious enemy of Abigail Doorn. Dr. Janney's stubborn silence, the search for Swanson, were the subjects of fruitless debate.

The conference seemed doomed to failure. Nothing new had been discovered; not even a lead toward possible action. A private wire to Police Headquarters stood waiting at the Commissioner's elbow; it rang incessantly, reporting failure in the investigation of the scant hoard of clews.

It was precisely at this critical moment that the Mayor's personal secretary entered the room with a heavily sealed envelope addressed to the Police Commissioner.

He tore it open and eagerly scanned the top sheet of a number of typewritten pages.

"Special report from Inspector Queen," he muttered.

"He says here a full report will come later. Let's see. . . ." He read in silence. Suddenly he handed the papers to a stenographer at his side. "Here, Jake, read these aloud."

The clerk began to read rapidly in a clear flat voice.

"REPORT ON MICHAEL CUDAHY

"At 10:15 A.M. Tuesday Cudahy was physically able, according to medical advice, to give testimony regarding possible connection with Doorn case. Questioned in Room 328 at Dutch Memorial Hospital where he was brought yesterday after operation for appendicitis. Weak, in great pain.

"Cudahy professes no knowledge of the murder. First quizzed in effort to confirm story of Dr. Byers and Grace Obermann, nurse, that masked and gowned figure of unknown passed through Anæsthesia Room and into Anteroom Monday morning while Cudahy was lying in Anæsthesia Room ready to be anæsthetized in preparation for appendectomy. Confirms seeing man in white gown, cap, surgical gag, etc., walk hurriedly through, as above, entering from South Corridor. Did not see him leave because ether-cone was adjusted almost at once and he was put to sleep. Cannot identify man. Seems to recall limp but is not sure. This however may be discounted; testimony of Dr. Byers and Miss Obermann sufficient to establish same.

"Careful quiz about Hendrik Doorn. Protection as promised to Doorn by story that D. was watched, suspicious movements led to search of his private apartment in Doorn house and nothing incriminating found except a memo hinting at dealings with Cudahy. C. seemed to accept this fictitious story absolutely. Questioned about these 'dealings.' C. admitted lending huge sums of money to D. at *6% interest with bonus,* payable when D. came into his share of the Doorn estate. Exhibited bravado, said he himself has nothing to fear or conceal in this matter since it was above-board and in no way criminal. *Q.* by Inspector Queen: 'You were never tempted, eh Mike, to hurry Mrs. Doorn's end a bit in order to collect your money sooner?' *A.* by Cudahy: 'Inspector, is that nice? You know I wouldn't do a thing like that.' Under pressure also said that he has been urging Hendrik Doorn for payment, and that he would not be surprised if D. knew more about murder of his sister than he professes. *Q.* by Inspector Queen: 'How about Little Willie, Snapper and Joe Gecko? Come clean now, Mike!' *A.* by Cudahy: 'You got 'em in the can, ain't you? They didn't have anything to do with this bumpoff, Inspector. They were here to guard me while I couldn't guard myself. You ain't got a thing on them.' *Q.* by Inspector Queen: 'Now you'll be watching out for the health of Doorn, Mike—won't you?' *A.* by Cudahy: 'He's as safe as a newborn babe. Think I want to lose my hundred and ten grand? Nothin' doing!'

"CONCLUSION: Cudahy has perfect alibi. Was under ether while crime was being committed. No evidence on which to base conviction of Joe Gecko, Snapper, Little Willie, except their physical presence in Hospital at time of murder. No case at all in this direction."

The clerk deposited this report carefully on the table and picked up another, clearing his throat.

"A blank again," grumbled the Commissioner. "This bird Cudahy is as slippery as an eel, Mr. Mayor. But if there's anything there, Queen will sweat it out of him."

"Come, come!" interrupted the Mayor. "We're getting nowhere. Who's the next report on?"

The clerk read:

"REPORT ON DR. LUCIUS DUNNING

"Dr. Dunning questioned in his office at Dutch Memorial Hospital, 11:05 A.M. Accused of secret meeting with Sarah Fuller Monday evening. Seemed disturbed, but refused to give reason for Sarah Fuller's call or substance of their talk. Claimed visit concerned purely personal matter in no way connected with crime.

"Neither threat of arrest nor appeal was successful. Was willing to submit to any indignity, he said, but claimed he would file suit for libel and false arrest if drastic action taken. No evidence or reason to hold Dunning. Matter therefore left in abeyance. Unsatisfactory answer when questioned how well he knows Sarah Fuller. 'Not well,' he said, and refused further explanation.

"SUBSEQU. ACTION: Put man on job of questioning other members of Dunning household. Mrs. Dunning saw Fuller woman enter house Monday evening, but took it to be usual professional call. Knows her only slightly through superficial social contact with deceased. Edith Dunning not at home during half-hour Sarah Fuller was in house. Testimony of maid that woman was closeted with Dr. Dunning in private examining-room for half-hour mentioned. Fuller left house to return to Doorn place, as per Report AA7 (Doorn).

"CONCLUSION: No action can be taken except judicious pressure to discover subject of Fuller-Dunning conversation. No reason to doubt irrelevancy of such conversation in connection with case except that secrecy is maintained. Fuller and Dunning both under surveillance. Further developments, if any, to be reported."

"Still nothing," murmured the Mayor with annoyance. "I feel sorry for your Department, Commissioner, if you can't make better progress than you've evinced so far. Is this man Queen competent to handle this case?"

The Borough President twisted in his chair. "Oh, come now," he said irritably. "We can't expect the old warhorse to perform miracles. Blamed case is only thirty hours old anyway. It seems to me he hasn't overlooked one lead. I—"

"And not only that," put in the Police Commissioner stiffly, "but this isn't a mere mob bump-off, Mr. Mayor, where the police can get stool-pigeon information. It's quite out of the usual run of murders. I think—"

The Mayor threw up his hands. "Who's next?"

"Edith Dunning." The clerk crackled the paper in a business-like way and began to real unemotionally:

"REPORT ON EDITH DUNNING

"Nothing of interest. Monday morning movements apparently quite innocent, although no complete check-up is possible because she was in and out of Hospital several times on Monday morning until time of operation. Movements accounted for from then on.

"Miss Dunning can give no explanation for the crime or possible motive (nor can her father, Dr. Dunning). She knows Hulda Doorn well, but cannot explain apparent coolness between her father and Mrs. Doorn other than that they were never particularly friendly.

"Conclusion: Nothing to be gained from further inquiry in this direction."

"Oh, unquestionably," said the Mayor. "Who's on the list after that? Let's have it, quickly!"

The stenographer continued:

"Further Report on Dr. Janney"

He paused as there was a distinct murmur from his intent audience. To a man, they hitched their chairs closer to the table. The clerk picked up the thread of the typewritten report:

"Further Report on Dr. Janney

"Dr. Janney returned Monday night to his residence, the Tareyton, at 9:07, emerging from a taxicab, according to the report of Operative Ritter, on the Janney assignment. Subsequent evidence of the taxicab driver, Morris Cohen (Amalgamated Taxi Corp., License No. 260954),* revealed that he picked up his fare outside Grand Central Terminal and was instructed to take him at once to the Tareyton. J. remained in his rooms for the rest of the evening. Telephone calls numerous, but from friends and professional acquaintances, all on subject of deceased. J. placed no calls.

"This morning (Tuesday, 11:45 A.M.) was questioned about Swanson. J. self-contained, alert, wary; looks ill and harassed. Refused again to discuss Swanson or his where-

---

* It must be borne in mind that the period during which the Doorn investigation took place preceded the current Police Department regulation which makes it obligatory for taxicabs to bear a special police-license number.—The Editor

abouts. Q. by Inspector Queen: 'Dr. Janney, you deliberately disobeyed my order last night. I told you not to leave town. . . . What were you doing in Grand Central at 6 P.M. yesterday?' A. by Dr. Janney: 'I did not leave town. Went to the station to cancel my ticket for Chicago. I told you yesterday I was going and you said not to. So I decided the medical convention could get along without me.' Q. 'Ah, then you merely canceled your reservation? Didn't take a train to any place?' A. 'I've told you. You can check up on me easily enough.'

"NOTE: Immediate check-up at Grand Central Terminal revealed that Dr. Janney's ticket and reservation were actually canceled at approximately the time he testifies they were. Impossible get description of man who canceled ticket—ticket-seller does not remember. Nor can verification be secured of J.'s statement that he did not buy a ticket for another destination.

"Q. 'You left your hotel at 5:30, getting to the station at about 6:00. Yet you didn't get back to your hotel until after 9:00. . . . You don't mean to tell me that it took you three hours to cancel a railroad reservation which could have been done just as easily by telephone!' A. 'It took only a few minutes, naturally. I left Grand Central and took a long walk up Fifth Avenue and in Central Park. I was depressed. Needed air. Wanted to be alone.' Q. 'How is it then that you hailed a cab outside Grand Central to take you home, if you were in Central Park?' A. 'I walked back part of the way, but I felt too tired to continue on foot.' Q. 'In this walk of yours, Doctor, did you meet any one or stop to talk to any one who might verify your story? A. 'No.'

"Q. by Mr. Ellery Queen: 'You're a man of intelligence, Doctor, now, aren't you?' A. 'That's my reputation.' Q. 'Well deserved, Dr. Janney, very well deserved. Now how does the following analysis strike this acute mentality of yours?—You are, let us say, impersonated in the Hospital for a brief period. In order to impersonate you it is essential for the impersonator to remove you temporarily from the scene. Lo and behold! a gentleman named Swanson comes to call on you about five minutes before the great impersonation is scheduled to begin, takes up your time for the entire period during which Abigail Doorn is being eased out of this world, and then releases you when the impersonator presumably has had a chance to escape. . . . I say, how does this strike your intelligence?' A. 'Purely coincidental! Can't be anything more. I told you my visitor had nothing to do with this confounded business!'

"Janney, on being definitely warned that unless he discloses Swanson's identity he will be held in large bail by the police as a material witness, remained silent. Exhibited facial indications of worry, however.

"CONCLUSION: There can be little question of the possibilities. Janney lied when he said he spent the time from 6:00 to 9:00 strolling about the streets. It is fairly certain that he did purchase a ticket to some unknown destination, probably near to New York (at the Lower Level of the station) and that he did entrain for this unknown destination. We are now working on all outgoing trains at approximately the correct hour in an effort to discover a conductor or passenger who can identify Dr. Janney as a traveler on the train during the significant hours. Nothing on this score as yet.

"The holding of Dr. Janney without definite evidence that he has lied (identification on the train would be such evidence) will accomplish nothing. In any event, even with identification the arrest of Janney would be useless unless it leads to the appearance of Swanson. It is not at all unlikely that this entire Swanson incident has assumed, due to Janney's stubbornness and 'principles,' a greater importance than it actually deserves. We have nothing against Janney except his withholding a material witness."

The clerk quietly laid the report on the table. The Mayor and the Police Commissioner regarded each other with deepening gloom. Finally the Mayor sighed and shrugged his shoulders.

"I'm inclined, for one," he said, "to agree with that conclusion of the Inspector's. Despite all this newspaper hullabaloo, I'd rather see you men go easy and make no mistakes than be hasty and pull a nasty boner. What do you think, Sampson?"

"Absolutely in accord."

"I'd follow Queen's advice," remarked the Commissioner.

The clerk picked up another typewritten sheet and read aloud:

"FURTHER REPORT ON SARAH FULLER

"Most unsatisfactory. Refuses to disclose purpose of visit to Dr. Dunning's house Monday night. Woman is half-insane. Replies obscurely and her talk bristles with Biblical references. Questioned in Doorn house at 2 P.M. Tuesday.

"CONCLUSION: No question but that a conspiracy exists between Sarah Fuller and Dr. Dunning to withhold information that may be pertinent. How prove it? Woman under constant watch, as is Dunning."

"Unbelievable, how little these people have revealed," exclaimed the Borough President.

"I've never seen a more stubborn set of witnesses," muttered the Commissioner. "Anything else there, Jake?" he snarled.

There was one report more. It was quite long and the attention of the conferees riveted immediately upon it. The clerk read:

"Report on Philip Morehouse

"Interesting development here. Contact through D.A.'s office brought word from Assistant District Attorney Rabkin that Probate Clerk revealed on query fact hitherto unknown. One of provisions of Abigail Doorn's will, already filed by Attorney Morehouse for probate, authorized said Attorney to destroy certain secret and undescribed documents immediately upon the death of testator. Documents designated in will as being in custody of the Attorney.

"Inquiry immediately of Morehouse, found at Doorn house with Hulda Doorn at late hour this P.M., discloses peculiar situation. Inspector Queen warned Morehouse at once not to destroy said documents, but to turn them over to the police as possibly containing information pertinent to the investigation of the crime. Morehouse replied coolly that he has already destroyed these papers!

"Q. 'When?' A. 'Yesterday afternoon. It was one of my first acts after the death of my client.'

"Inspector Queen demanded information contained in documents. Morehouse disclaimed knowledge of their contents. Averred he followed instructions of will to the letter, destroying papers without breaking seals on the envelope. Claimed never to have known; that documents were in possession of Morehouse firm for years, even while elder Morehouse, now deceased, handled Doorn affairs; that, in taking over father's clientele, he naturally inherited responsibilities and ethical duties of father's high standing, etc., etc.

"Confronted with accusation that under the circumstances—a murder—he had no right to take such action without consulting police, let alone destroy possible evidence, Morehouse maintained he was within his legal right."

"We'll see about that," shouted Sampson.

"Hulda Doorn, present and perturbed during this colloquy, questioned as to destroyed documents. Averred total ignorance of their contents or even their existence, although claims to have handled much of deceased's private correspondence during the old woman's latter years.

"CONCLUSION: Recommend immediate inquiry by District Attorney Sampson's office into legal rights of this matter. If Morehouse exceeded authority vested by State in him as servant of the law recommend further possibility of prosecution or, if prosecution cannot be secured, relegation of entire matter to Association of the Bar. Feeling prevalent, with few dissenters in Department, that these lost documents were in some way crucial to solution of the crime."

"Old Q. is sore, sure enough," said the District Attorney more calmly. "This is the first time since I've known him that he's shown such a streak of vindictiveness. He must be hard hit by this case. I'd hate to be in poor Morehouse's shoes.

The Mayor heaved himself wearily to his feet.

"I guess that's all for to-day, gentlemen," he said. "About all we can do is hope for the best and see what developments to-mor-row will bring. . . . I'm satisfied from these reports that Inspector Queen is conducting the inquiry to the best of his ability—which seems to be considerable. I shall issue a statement to that effect at once for the benefit of these newshounds and to reassure the Governor." He turned to the head of New York's police system. "Is that agreeable to you, Commissioner?"

The Commissioner, wiping his neck heavily with a large damp handkerchief, nodded with a sort of baffled resignation and slouched out of the room. As the Mayor pressed a button on his desk, the District Attorney and his aides followed in depressed silence.

In the following chapter of THE DUTCH SHOE MYSTERY—
*which is properly not a chapter at all but an interlude during
which the Queens discuss various phases of the Doorn case—
extra-wide margins have been provided on each page for the
use of the reader in jotting down his personal notes about the
solution.*

*When the reader comes to page 249, where a formal challenge is made (following a precedent set down in previous
Queen novels), he may perhaps find it helpful to refer to such
notes as he may have written in the forthcoming interlude.*

—THE EDITOR

INTERLUDE

IN WIIICII

The Queens Take Stock

Inspector Queen's head-cold, treated heroically by Ellery, was markedly improved by Tuesday evening; but his nerves were in such a ragged, maudlin state that it had been necessary to adopt coercive measures and put the old man to bed with mingled pleas and threats.

Ellery, aided by Sergeant Velie and Djuna, finally induced the old man to shed his clothes and seek peace among the pillows. But peace would not come; and soon the Inspector was demanding that the door between the bedroom and living-room be opened wide so that he might hear what was being discussed by the assembled company—Ellery, District Attorney Sampson, Sergeant Velie and Pete Harper.

To their astonishment, the doughty old warrior marched into the living-room five minutes later attired in pajamas, robe and slippers, took his favorite chair before the fire in dignified silence, and refused obstinately to hear anything further about retiring.

"It's no use—no earthly use, comrades," said Ellery, softly laughing. "'It is not for a man in authority to sleep a whole night,' Homer being the authority. . . . Well, dad, there's something vital and new on your mind. The usual signs. What is it?"

Quizzical humor crept into the old man's eyes as his grey brows bunched. "Know everything, don't you?" He snapped. Then suddenly he chuckled. "Guess I feel better already. . . . Djuna get out the old coffee-pot!"

Djuna grinned and whisked into his tiny kitchen, from which the rich aroma of liquid coffee soon floated.

"Nothing on Swanson—hey, Thomas?"

The behemoth moved uncomfortably; the chair creaked beneath his weight. "Not a thing. Not a damned thing. Looka here, Chief—it just isn't possible. We've had men all along the line, all through the suburbs, on every train—jabbering with every conductor. Where *is* that guy Swanson?"

"Have you tried to trace his movements from the time he left the Hospital yesterday morning?" asked Sampson.

"Everything's been done, Henry," said the Inspector glumly. "After all, nabbing one ornery-looking man in a city of millions isn't exactly child's play. I'm hoping the suburb lead is right. It will make things simpler."

"Say," drawled Harper, "has it occurred to any of you birds that this Swanson mug may be pure fiction?"

Ellery cocked his head and smiled. "The ever-alert newsmonger," he said. "Yes, Mercury, it has. The good *padre* can tell you something about it—eh, dad?"

"Nothing much to tell," said the Inspector wearily. "Ellery made the same suggestion this morning, although I have the feeling he didn't believe it himself...."

Ellery wagged his head. "I didn't say I didn't."

"I haven't brought you up for nothing," grunted the old man. "At any rate, we got hold of Isaac Cobb, that doorman, and pumped him dry again. Looked up all his antecedents, jobs, private affairs. Absolutely on the level. But since he was the only person in the Hospital besides Janney who claims to have seen Swanson, it was necessary to make sure.

"No," he continued disconsolately, "we've not the slightest reason to doubt Cobb's testimony. The man is straight as a die. Swanson exists, all right."

Velie coughed. "You'll pardon me if I seem to horn in—but I got a feeling in my bones. I been in this business too long. Mark my words, Swanson will turn up when we least expect him."

The Inspector craned his neck and stared in open surprise at his subordinate. A slow smile spread over his careworn features. "By jiminy!" he exclaimed in a soft undertone, "that gives me an idea, a *real* idea, Thomas! Let me think a moment...."

They waited upon him in silence. Djuna kicked open the door from the kitchen and crossed the room majestically bearing a large tray on which were perched a steaming percolator, several cups and saucers, a pitcher of sweet cream and a bowl of sugar. He set it down on the table and ran back, reappearing with a huge platter full of cakes. And still silence, while Djuna poured, the men drew their chairs about the table, and the Inspector sat wrapped in his robe, staring into the leaping flames....

Ellery watched him with curious intentness. The old man suddenly slapped the arms of his chairs and jumped to his feet. "That's what I'll do!" he cried. "It's sure to work!"

He flung himself into a chair by the table and began to drink coffee in gulps.

Sampson seemed worried. "What's that you're going to do, Q.?" he demanded.

The bushy brows contracted; the old man's eyes gleamed above the lifted cup. "To-morrow morning, unless a certain thing happens, *I'm going to arrest Dr. Janney for the murder of Abigail Doorn!*"

The Inspector would not utter another word in explanation until he had finished his coffee and taken a giant's pinch of snuff.

The old man drew his chair up to the fire again and gestured his guests forward to more comfortable seats in the light of the fire.

"I know it sounds crazy," began the Inspector, when they were grouped about to his satisfaction, "but I think I can outline a good circumstantial case against Janney. And besides, there's another reason. . . .

"First let me lay the cards on the table . . . show you the way I figure it. . . get your reaction to it as a courtroom argument. You'll be able to help there, Henry."

He cleared his throat and proceeded in a slightly clogged voice.

"In a certain light, Janney seems guilty as sin. A great many people concerned in this case have darned good motives. But Janney has the strongest, I think, of all.

"It's money. No—wait a minute." He held up his tiny hand for silence as a protest burst from Sampson's lips. "Don't forget that under the terms of Abby's first will, Janney comes in for *two* bequests—a very large one on a personal basis, and a smaller but respectable one for the continuation of the research.

"Now, Janney's motive isn't all money. Don't get me wrong," he said calmly, "for he isn't the type of man who would kill for money alone, as I very well appreciate. In some respects, he's like Kneisel. It seems you can't be a scientist without getting the lord-and-master bug. People just don't mean anything. It's knowledge that counts ... and recognition. Take that metallic alloy, for instance. I'll bet Janney doesn't care a rap how many millions it's worth—but the fame—aha! that's what he wants.

"But to get that fame he needs money. Money to carry his researches to a successful finish. Look at the hole he's in. His own savings are gone, and now his only hope is that the old lady will be willing to see them through financially. And suddenly, just as he and Kneisel see daylight, by a woman's whim Abby withdraws her support and failure stares them in the face.

They were listening in concentrated silence. Ellery watched his father's lips.

"Now, what would be the effect—I mean psychologically," continued the old man rapidly, "on a man like Janney? The only thing that separates him and Kneisel from their precious fame is the life of an old and eccentric woman. And what is the life of one old woman, diabetic and past her usefulness, to a man who deals with death every day? Nevertheless, in spite of Abby's poor health, she could go on living for years, delaying indefinitely the completion of the experiments. But by waiting the whole business might be jeopardized. Especially since a new will is to be signed which will deprive them of one of Janney's legacies, leaving only the personal legacy which wouldn't materialize for years. By acting quickly Janney prevents the signing of the new will, assures immediate funds and much more than he would get if the new will went into effect. Isn't this powerful enough motive to make Janney kill even his former benefactress?"

He stopped and peered slyly at them. Harper's cigarette drooped forgotten from his lips; there was a distinct glint of admiration in his eye. Velie grunted with approval, and Sampson nodded slowly.

"Ingenious enough," murmured Ellery. "Go on, dad."

"Very well!" said the old man briskly. "We've established motive—much stronger than that of any other individual in the case. Now let's take a look at other things."

"Psychology on Janney's side? Perfect! No one would ever dream of accusing Abby Doorn's protégé, personal friend, personal physician and most grateful debtor of her murder. To think that such a man would strangle his benefactress is ridiculous. . . . Maybe Janney, who's certainly shrewd enough, counted on this very psychology to shield him!"

Sampson stirred. "Damned subtle, but it would make a beautiful defense in the mouth of a smart trial lawyer."

"Now look at it from the standpoints of opportunity and accessibility," went on the Inspector. "Abby was strangled in the Hospital. To plan her murder there the murderer must have known a great deal about the institution. Who was in a better position than Janney to be absolutely familiar with the time-schedules, the routine, the physical lay-out, the personnel? No one. As practically head of the Hospital, he could actually make circumstances fit his plans. . . .

"Swanson? An accomplice," continued the Inspector triumphantly. "Why doesn't Janney produce him? Because he's protecting the man, that's why. Maybe he never expected us to harp on Swanson the way we have. Maybe he thought we would take his word and Cobb's that Swanson was just an ordinary visitor who happened to occupy Janney's time while the murder was being committed, thereby giving Janney a perfect alibi without having to produce the witness."

"Weak," came from the depths of Ellery's chair, almost inaudibly.

"What's that?" cried the Inspector sharply, turning toward Ellery.

"I'm sorry, dad," said Ellery in a contrite voice. "Please go on"

Queen sniffed. "At any rate, forgetting Swanson for the moment, let me come to what I feel is the cleverest part of the Janney hypothesis. . . . And that is—that Janney, in killing Abby Doorn, to all intents and purposes *impersonated himself!*"

Sampson looked startled, and Harper slapped his thigh and began to chuckle. The old man grinned. "Well," he said, "I'm glad you cotton to the idea. . . . You see, this Janney is smart. He figured, if I'm right, that the police would say: 'Here's this murderer. He dressed like Janney, looked like Janney, even limped like Janney. He made it appear as if he *wanted* to be taken for Janney. Would a man be such a fool as to leave a trail like that? Not on your life! No, the murderer of Abby Doorn was somebody impersonating janney, not Janney himself.' That's how he must have doped it out, and it's as sound as a dollar because that's exactly what we did say!"

Velie growled, "Damn if that don't sound like the real McCoy, Chief!"

"This is brilliant, dad," said Ellery warmly. "Really brilliant. Go on."

"Well, it all works out logically enough. Impersonating himself, he left the clothes we found as a blind, to make it seem like a *real* impersonation—as if the impostor, having no further use for the clothing, dropped it in the first convenient place and made his getaway.

"He covered his backtrail very well. Let's say he started out from his office, leaving Swanson on guard behind a locked door, did the job, maybe planted the fake clothes beforehand in the telephone-booth, then returned to his office. Simple as eating pie. To make the Swanson story hang together, he actually gave Swanson a check. We've proof of that now. Did you get that photoprint, Thomas?"

"Sure enough," rumbled the giant. "The canceled check came through the Clearing House—we caught it there. Late this afternoon. Endorsed by a *T. Swanson.* We took pictures of it, back and front, and let the check go on through."

"And that means," explained the Inspector, "that

we have his first initial and also a handwriting speci-
men. . . . Well, boys, what do you think?"

"The fact," said Sampson carefully, "that a man so
closely resembling Janney was seen going into that Anteroom, undoubtedly committing the murder, and coming out again is strong evidence. And there's only one
way Janney can break it down. . . ."

"By producing Swanson, of course," drawled Harper. "But tell me—I feel dumb to-night—if Janney killed
Abby Doorn the way you described, Inspector, why in
hell didn't he fall all over himself producing Swanson to
support his alibi rather than make himself a suspect by
withholding Swanson's address?"

"I'll admit that's a fair question," said the old man.
"Strange, all right. It's occurred to me a-plenty—the
only weak point in my argument. . . . But, strong case or
not as far as Janney is concerned, we've just got to find
Swanson. And arresting janney will do it, I think—he'll
make fine bait. . . . Pete, here's where you come into the
picture."

"Who—me?" Harper sat up abruptly. "Don't tell me
you're going to give me a break, Inspector! Tell me
quick!—what do I have to do?"

The old man said dryly, "I'm giving you a scoop,
Pete."

"You mean," cried the reporter, leaping to his feet,
"that you're arresting Janney and giving me the chance
of scooping the town on the story?"

"Exactly. Sit down, Pete, you make me nervous.—It's
not just altruism, feller. There's a mighty good purpose
behind it. I can give the news, by the way, only to one pa-

per because I don't feel like explaining my plan to every city editor in New York. Besides, you're a sort of member of the family, and your sheet's been the only decent one in the City on this case. . . ."

"Here's the idea. You're on a morning paper. I want your paper to run a front-page story—ballyhoo, Pete!—to the effect that Dr. Janney, according to exclusive information, is to be arrested some time to-morrow morning on the charge of murdering Mrs. Doorn. Get the story out now—so that your first editions, appearing late to-night, will carry it. *Because I want Swanson, wherever he is, to read that story!*"

"By George!" roared Sampson. "That's a good stunt, Q.! You think he'll bite?"

The Inspector shrugged his thin shoulders. "Who knows? If he really lives somewhere out of town, he probably works here in the City. So that if he doesn't read the story to-night, he'll catch it in the morning. Oh, I know it's a gamble, but it's a good one, I think.

"You see, I want to draw Swanson into the net before an arrest can be made. Let's look him over and get his spiel. If he's the straight goods and we're convinced both he and Janney are on the level, Harper's paper can promptly retract its announcement—say it was based on a false report. The paper isn't getting into any trouble because I'll back it up; oughtn't to kick—it will have an exclusive story for one edition, anyway.

"Whether Swanson is innocent of complicity or not, he'll walk in on us after that statement. Because if Janney is guilty, he'll need Swanson's alibi fast, and Swanson knows it. Of course, if Swanson bears up under examination, we can't arrest Janney. His alibi will be perfect."

Harper shouted, "Excuse me!" and dashed into the bedroom. His excited voice was heard calling his paper. He reappeared dragging his hat and coat, straggly white hair flying, a grin all over his face. "Told 'em to hold everything," he said. "This is one story I'm not telephoning. On my way, gents. Back me up on this, Inspector, and I'm your friend for life!" And he was gond like the wind.

"You haven't said much," smiled the Inspector. He was scrutinizing Ellery in his bird-like way.

Ellery's lips curled into an amused grimace. "Well, sir, I've been thinking."

"What about?"

"I've been thinking that you don't really believe Janney did the job."

The old man laughed aloud, and Sampson looked from father to son suspiciously. "I'll be switched and tanned," chuckled the Inspector, "if I'm sure of anything. But I want Swanson, and I'll go to any lengths to get him."

Ellery rested luxuriously on the nape of his neck. "You're a bull's-eye in wanting Swanson," he said. "He's a cog. A big cog. Perhaps the biggest in the whole case so far."

"Look here, Ellery," frowned Sampson. "I know you don't come to conclusions without good reasons. Just why don't you believe Janney killed Abby?"

Ellery lifted his eyes peacefully. "If I told you that,"

he said, laughing, "you'd know as much as I do. . . . No, old man, Janney didn't do it, and you'll have to exert your faith in me when I say I can't tell you the reason just now."

"Well," sighed the Inspector, "that's the way he is, Henry. Can't get a thing out of him until he's good and ready."

"Yes, sir," murmured Ellery submissively.

"To-morrow will tell the tale. . . . By thunder, there isn't much grist in our mill. This feller Morehouse—I could wring his neck. He did a darned stupid thing in destroying those papers, and he certainly doesn't appear stupid. Mark my words, Henry, he'll bear watching. What are you going to do with him?"

"Anything you say," replied Sampson promptly. "But he has a good reputation, Q., and maybe it would be better to wait. . . ."

"You'll positively break a certain damsel's cardiac organ," said Ellery, "if you step on the lad. Dad, let young Philip alone for a while. I have an idea about him."

"Oh, all right," growled the Inspector. "But that sort of thing tries my patience. . . . Take the crazy Fuller woman, for instance. What's behind all that gab between Dunning and her? What the deuce did she and Abby quarrel about all the time? There are so many loose ends. . . ."

"Well, I guess I'd better be going," said the District Attorney, rising and stretching. "Tomorrow's going to be a hectic day."

The Inspector laid a restraining hand on his arm. "Just a moment, Henry.—Ellery, you've been unusually close-mouthed so far. For cripe's sake, what's your idea about this mess?"

"I could give you a fairly accurate description of the so-called fiend you're seeking," said Ellery.

"What!"

Inspector Queen sprang from his chair. Velie's jaw fell and Sampson stared at Ellery as at an apparition.

Ellery smiled. "In fact, I can tell you practically everything about your criminal but—the name!"

"But—but," stammered sampson, "who is it?"

Ellery's eyes clouded. "Honestly, I'm not prepared to say. It's too indefinite."

Sampson, Velie and the Inspector gaped at each other. "Well—but," spluttered the Inspector, "how on earth did you arrive at your conclusion?"

Ellery shrugged his shoulders and reached for another cigarette. "It's really very simple. Purely a matter of observation and deduction. . . . You see, I gathered most of my data from—that pair of shoes!"

PART TWO

DISAPPEARANCE OF A CABINET

"Have you ever watched a log-jam? You may see them in the swirling rivers of the forests high on the flanks of the Kjolen. . . . A great mass of freshly cut logs shoots down the river. At broken water one strikes a snag. The mass struggles but cannot go on. It halts, it churns, it crashes. And soon there is a mountain of logs, crushing each other, building with magical rapidity a broken rampart of wood.

"Then the lumberman seeks to discover the log which is causing the jam—the log which is stemming the wooden tide—in a word, the key-log. Aha! he has found it! A tug, a twist, a pull—it snaps out, upends, darts away. And as if Merlin's wand had waved above the spot, the wall of wood collapses and makes a mad rush down the river. . . .

"The investigation of a complex crime, my young friends, is much like a log-jam at times. Our logs—our clews—are racing toward a solution. Suddenly—a jam. To our bewilderment the stubborn clews keep tangling, piling up.

"Then the lumberjacking sleuth finds the key-log and, lo! The recalcitrant clews tumble down, range themselves in swiftly moving rows, open and intelligible, and make for the distant saw-mill—the solution."

—from an address to the recruits of the Stockholm Police Academy on November 2, 1920, by the Swedish criminologist. . . .

DR. GUSTAF GOETEBORG

19

DESTINATION

INSPECTOR QUEEN was at his desk in Police Headquarters at a rare hour Wednesday morning. Propped before him was a morning newspaper—announcing in blatant Gothic headlines the reported impending arrest of Dr. Francis Janney, noted surgeon, on "suspicion of homicide"—a delicate phrase intending to convey the meaning that the surgeon was to be held, charged with the strangling of Abigail Doorn.

The Inspector did not seem too satisfied with himself. His bright little eyes glimmered with worry, and he gnawed his mustache to shreds as he read and reread the story written by Pete Harper. Telephone-bells jangled incessantly in the next room; but the instrument on the old man's desk preserved a discreet silence; he was officially "out" to every one but the Department.

Reporters had camped in the vicinity of the big police building all night. Say, Cap, is it true about Janney being collared for the old lady's killing? No one knew, it seemed; at least no one would discuss the matter.

The Police Commissioner and the Mayor, apprised by the Inspector late Tuesday night of his plan, in their turn refused to talk with the press. In lieu of official confirmation, other sheets picked up Harper's story. At the offices of Harper's newspaper itself over-powering ignorance was expressed by all parties in authority concerning the source of the trouble-making story.

At 9:00 o'clock a special telephone-call from Dr. Janney was reported to Inspector Queen. The surgeon had demanded to be connected with the Inspector and had been switched to the desk Lieutenant instead. He was informed blandly that the Inspector was in conference and could not be disturbed. Janney exploded into curses. He had been pestered all morning, he roared, by reporters seeking to interview him.

"You tell me one thing," he snarled over the telephone. "Is that newspaper report true?"

The Lieutenant was abysmally sorry, to judge from his tone, but he really didn't know. Janney vowed audibly that he would retire to his private office at the Hospital and see no one; he was so angry his voice was blurred and indistinct. The sound of his receiver being replaced on the hook crashed into the Lieutenant's ear.

This conversation was relayed to the Inspector, who smiled grimly and issued orders through Sergeant Velie that no reporters were to be allowed within the walls of the Dutch Memorial Hospital.

He called the District Attorney. "No word yet from Swanson?"

"Not a peep out of him. Well, it's early yet. I'll let you know the moment he calls. You'll want to trace him back anyway, to make sure he gets here."

"We're taking care of that." A pause, and then the Inspector spoke more truculently. "Henry, have you thought over my recommendations about that whipper-snapper Morehouse?"

Sampson coughed. "Now, look here. Q., I'll go the full length of the rope with you, and you know it. But I'm afraid we'll have to let the Morehouse thing go by."

"You've changed your tune, haven't you, Henry?" The old man scowled into the mouthpiece.

"I'm still with you, Q.," said Sampson. "But after the first heat died down, I thought the whole situation over. . . ."

"And?"

"Q., he was absolutely within his legal rights! That clause in Abby's will pertained not to a part of her estate, but to a private trust. As a private trust, Morehouse didn't have to wait until the will passed through probate to destroy the documents. It's a separate thing entirely. You can't show cause why the documents should have been preserved, can you?"

The Inspector sounded weary. "If you mean can I show that the documents contained evidence—no."

"Then I'm sorry, Q. I can't do a thing."

When he had replaced the receiver, the Inspector laid Harper's paper carefully on his desk and rang for Sergeant Velie.

"Thomas, get me that pair of canvas shoes we found in the 'phone booth!"

Velie scratched his huge poll and brought the shoes.

The old man set them down on the glass top of his desk and eyed them longingly. He turned to Velie, frowning. "Do you get anything out of these blamed shoes, Thomas?"

The giant caressed his granite jaw. "All I get," he said at last, "is that the shoelace broke and whoever wore the shoes stuck a piece of adhesive on to hold the broken pieces together."

"Yes, but what that means is beyond me." The Inspector looked unhappy. "Ellery wasn't talking through his hat, Thomas, my boy. There's something in these shoes that tells an important story. Better leave 'em here. I may get a brainstorm."

Velie tramped out of the room, leaving the old man deep in contemplation of two very innocent-looking white canvas oxfords.

Ellery had just crawled out of bed and performed his ablutions when the doorbell rang and Djuna admitted the tall windy figure of Dr. John Minchen.

"Hullo! Don't you ever see a sunrise?"

Ellery wrapped the folds of his dressing-gown more closely about his spare body. "It's only 9:15. I was up half the night thinking."

Minchen dropped into a chair, making a face. "On my way to the Hospital, and I thought I'd drop in to find out firsthand if that newspaper story this morning about Janney is on the level."

"What newspaper story?" asked Ellery blankly, attacking an egg. . . . "Join me, John?"

"Had breakfast—thanks." Minchen stared at him keenly. "So you don't know, eh? Well, the paper this morning has it that Dr. Janney will be arrested to-day for the murder of the old lady."

"No!" Ellery crunched into a piece of toast. "Modern journalism is certainly a wonderful thing."

Minchen shook his head sadly. "No information to-day, I see. But it all seems too silly for words, Ellery. The old man must be boiling mad. Murder his benefactress!" He sat up straight. "Say! I'll be coming in for my share of notoriety too, won't I?"

"How do you mean?"

"Well," said Minchen soberly, "as Janney's colleague in writing our book—*Congenital Allergy*—the press will naturally look me up and just about pester me to death."

"Oh!" Ellery sipped coffee. "I shouldn't worry about that, John.

And forget Janney for the moment—he'll be all right. . . . How long have you two been working on your magnificent opus?"

"Not so long. You see, the actual writing is the least of it. It's the case-records that count. It's taken Janney years to assemble his histories. They're quite valuable, incidentally. If anything should happen to Janney I'll fall heir to them—they wouldn't mean anything to a layman."

Ellery wiped his lips tenderly. "Naturally not. By the way, if I'm not nosing, John—what's your financial arrangement with Janney on this thing? Equal partners?"

Minchen flushed. "He insisted on it, although he's contributed so much more than I that it's a shame. . . . Janney's been very decent to me, Ellery."

"Delighted to hear it." Ellery rose and made for his bedroom. "Give me five minutes to dress, John, and I'll walk down with you. Excuse me."

He disappeared into the next room. Minchen rose and began to amble about the living-room. He stopped curiously at the fireplace and examined a pair of crossed swords above the mantelpiece. There was a swift rustling noise behind him; he turned to find Djuna, grinning up at him in a knowing manner.

"'Lo, son. Where did these swords come from?"

"Dad Queen got 'em from a feller." Djuna stuck out his thin chest proudly. "Feller in Europe. . . ."

"Oh, John!" shouted Ellery from the bedroom. "How long have you known Dr. Dunning?"

"Ever since I've been with the Hospital. Why?"

"Just curious. . . . What do you know that's interesting about Dr. Pennini, our Gallic Amazon?"

"Very little. She's not a friendly person, Ellery. Never mixes with the rest of us if she can help it. I think she has a husband somewhere."

"Really? What's his occupation?"

"Sorry. I've never seen him, or discussed him with Pennini."

Minchen heard Ellery bustling energetically about the bedroom. He sat down again, restlessly.

"Acquainted with Kneisel?" came Ellery's voice.

"Barely. He's a real hound for work. Spends his life in that laboratory of his."

"Were he and Abby Doorn chummy?"

"I think he met her several times through Janney. But I'm sure he didn't know her well."

"How about Edith Dunning? Is she friendly with Gargantua?"

"You mean Hendrik Doorn? That's a queer question, Ellery." Minchen laughed. "I can close my eyes and picture the young and businesslike flapper in the arms of friend Hendrik—yes, I can't!"

"Nothing doing there, eh?"

"If you're looking for a *liaison* between those two, you're simply crazy."

"Well, you know the German *bon mot*," chuckled Ellery, appearing in the doorway fully dressed. "'The stomach is master of all arts. . . .' Let me get my hat, coat and stick and we'll be off."

They strolled down upper Broadway, talking over light matters of mutual recollection. Ellery refused to discuss the Doorn case further.

"By George!" Ellery halted suddenly. "There's a little volume on Viennese crime-methods I meant to get at my bookseller's. Forgot completely that I'd promised to call for it this morning. What time is it?"

Minchen consulted his wrist-watch. "Just 10 o'clock."

"Going directly to the Hospital, are you?"

"Yes. If you're dropping off here, I'll hop a cab."

"All right, John. I'll join you at the Hospital in a half-hour or so. It will take you ten or fifteen minutes to make it anyway. *A rivederci!*"

They parted, Ellery to walk rapidly down a by-street and Minchen to hail a taxicab. He climbed in. It swung around the corner and headed east.

20

CAPITULATION

"HE'S IN!"

The grapevine telegraph of the Police Department had never better lived up to its reputation for speed than on Wednesday morning, shortly after 9:30 A.M., when a slender man, slight and small-boned, and garbed in dark clothes walked down Centre Street, passed Police Headquarters, and proceeded with a trace of nervousness to scan all the building-numbers within range of his vision, as if he did not know precisely the site of his destination. When he came to Number 137, he furtively studied the ten-story structure which housed the official residence of the District Attorney, adjusted the collar of his black overcoat, and walked into the yellow-bricked building.

Mysterious, elusive Swanson!

The word flashed into every nook and cranny of Centre Street. It traveled from a whispering clerk in the District Attorney's office through the bridge to the dingy old brownstone Criminal Courts Building, and from there sped across the Bridge of Sighs into the cavernous Tombs. Every guard in the Tombs, every detective at Headquarters, every traffic officer on duty within a radius of four blocks, every bondsman and hanger-on in the vicinity had heard the news within five minutes of the moment when Swanson stepped off the elevator at the sixth floor of Number 137, flanked by two detectives, and vanished within the private office of District Attorney Sampson.

Ten minutes later, at 9:45, Swanson was perched in the center of a ring of intent faces. Surrounding him were the District Attorney and Timothy Cronin, his assistant, and several aides; a faintly smiling Inspector Queen, who had made a supernaturally rapid appearance; Sergeant Velie, taciturn and dour as ever; and the Police Commissioner himself, who sat a little to one side in watchful silence.

Up to this moment the newcomer had spoken only once. He had said, in a thickish baritone surprising from one of his thin physique, "I'm Thomas Swanson." The District Attorney had courteously inclined his head and indicated a central chair.

Swanson sat quietly enough, surveying the gathering of his inquisitors. He had dull blue eyes and dark lashes, but he was a pronounced blond type, with sandy thinning hair and even, clean-shaven, undistinguished features.

When the company was seated and a detective's shadow wavered and fixed itself beyond the glass pane of the door, the District Attorney said, "Mr. Swanson, why have you come here this morning?"

Swanson seemed surprised. "I thought you wanted to see me."

"Ah, then you've been following the papers?" asked Sampson quickly.

The newcomer smiled. "Oh, yes. . . . I may as well clear up everything at once. But first—look here, gentlemen, I realize that you're all suspicious of me because I kept away despite the newspaper stories that you were looking for me. . . ."

"We're delighted to hear that you realize it." Sampson regarded him coldly. "You have plenty of explaining to do, Mr. Swanson. You've cost the City a pile of money. Well, what's the excuse?"

"Not really an excuse, sir. I've been in trouble and I'm in trouble now. This whole business is something of a tragedy for me. You see, there was a good reason for my not coming forward before to-day. And then I didn't believe Dr. Janney was seriously involved in the murder of Mrs. Doorn. Nothing in the papers even hinted at such a fact. . . ."

"You've still to explain," said Sampson patiently, "what was behind your hideaway stunt."

"I know, I know." Swanson looked down at the carpet thoughtfully. "It's really tough on me," he said. "If not for the fact that Dr. Janney is going to be arrested for a murder which I know positively he didn't commit, I wouldn't have shown up to-day. But I can't let you do a thing like that when he's so plainly innocent."

"Were you in Dr. Janney's office between 10:30 and 10:45 Monday morning?" demanded Inspector Queen.

"Yes. His story was correct in absolutely every particular. I came to borrow a small sum of money. We were in his office together the entire time—neither of us left for a moment."

"Hmm." Sampson looked him over carefully. "Such a simple story, Mr. Swanson, and yet you've allowed us to scour the City for you merely to get an unimportant substantiating piece of testimony."

"What's Janney protecting you from?" said the Inspector suddenly.

Swanson lifted his hands in a gesture of helplessness. "I see it has to come out. Gentlemen, it's quickly told. . . . I'm really not Thomas Swanson at all. I'm Thomas Janney—Dr. Janney's son!"

The story was involved. Thomas Janney was the stepson of Dr. Francis Janney. The surgeon had been a childless widower when he remarried. His second wife was Thomas's mother, and Thomas was two years old when Dr. Janney legally became his father. His mother died eight years after.

There had never been a question, according to Thomas Janney, about the purpose of his thorough education. He was to become a second Janney—a surgeon. He was sent to Johns Hopkins.

In a low and shamed voice, the man for whom the entire Police Department of New York City had searched vainly for two days related how, wild and irresponsible, he had betrayed the trust of his famous step-father.

"I knew it all in those days," he mumbled. "I had a good academic record—stood near the head of my class—but I drank like a fish and gambled away the generous allowance dad gave me."

Janney had been calm about this youthful defection. His steadying hand had guided the young hellion through his preparatory work and medical studies, and upon Thomas's graduation had placed him in the Dutch Memorial Hospital as an interne.

"So that's why Isaac Cobb thought his face looked familiar!" muttered the Inspector to himself. He was listening with a puzzled frown.

His interneship served, and for a long time on good behavior, Thomas Janney became a member of the regular surgical staff of the Dutch Memorial Hospital under his step-father. He did well for a short period.

Swanson paused, licked his lips—continued with a faraway stare above the head of the District Attorney. "Then it happened," he said in a brittle voice. "It was five years ago—just about this time of year. I slipped. Began to drink again. And one morning I operated on a patient while under the influence of liquor. My hand trembled at a critical moment, the knife cut too deeply . . . and the patient died on the operating-table."

No one spoke. The ex-surgeon seemed to be living over that devastating moment when the work, the plans, the dreams of his youth came crashing about his ears. He had been afraid, he said—unnerved and sickened. There had been three witnesses to the tragedy, but the rigid ethical code of the profession kept the story from leaking out of the Hospital at that time. Then Dr. Janney himself informed Mrs. Doorn of the tragedy—and his step-son's culpability. The old lady was inexorable. The young surgeon would have to go. . . .

He was compelled to resign. Quietly, despite all the efforts of his step-father, the news circulated and he found all Hospital doors barred to him. Without fanfare or publicity he lost his medical license. Dr. Thomas Janney became plain Thomas Janney, and in self-protection Thomas Janney changed his name to Thomas Swanson—his mother's maiden name.

He moved out of New York City to Port Chester, New York. And through his step-father's influence and wide acquaintance-ship he was able under cover to go into business as an insurance solicitor. He sobered. The awful experience had shocked him into an abrupt realization of his folly, he said. But it was too late. His career was beyond redemption or atonement. . . .

"Oh, I didn't blame any of them," he said bitterly, in the silence of the District Attorney's office. "The old lady acted according to her lights, and so did my step-father. His profession is the world to him. He could have saved me, I guess, through his personal influence with Mrs. Doorn. But then he has a stern code and besides he realized that I needed a sharp lesson if I was ever to make anything of myself. . . ."

Dr. Janney had never upbraided his wayward step-son despite

the infinite hurt he must have suffered during the collapse of his plans and hopes. Covertly he aided the young man in establishing a new business and a new life. He promised without equivocation that if Thomas led a sober industrious existence there would be no difference in their future relations. The young man would still be the Janney heir; there was and would be no one else.

"It was decent of him," muttered the ex-surgeon, "damned decent. He couldn't have acted whiter if I were his real son. . . ."

He stopped, crumpled his hat-brim nervously between his long powerful fingers—the fingers of a surgeon.

Sampson cleared his throat. "Of course, this puts a different complexion on the affair, Mr.—Mr. Swanson. I see now why Dr. Janney refused to put us on your track. The old scandal. . . ."

"Yes," drearily. "It would have destroyed five years of honest living—ruined my business and held me up publicly as a renegade surgeon who had criminally failed in his trust and could not be relied upon in other things, either. . . ." They had both suffered poignantly, he went on, from the notoriety the incident had aroused in the Hospital during those hectic days. If Dr. Janney had given the police the means of finding Swanson, the old story must inevitably have come out. They were both horribly afraid of that.

"But now," said Swanson, "now that I see dad so terribly involved, I can't let personal considerations stand in the way. . . . I hope I've cleared Dr. Janney of suspicion, gentlemen. It's all been a ghastly tragedy of errors.

"You see, my only purpose in visiting him Monday morning was to secure a small loan—twenty-five dollars—business had been a little slow and I needed the money to tide me over a few days. Dad—he was generous, as usual—he gave me a check for fifty. I cashed it as soon as I'd left the Hospital."

He looked about him. There was an unspoken plea in his eyes. The Inspector was gloomily examining the worn brown surface of his snuff-box. The Police Commissioner had unobtrusively left his chair and slipped out of the room: the expected bomb-shell had proved a dud, and there was no further reason for his presence.

Swanson's voice, as he continued, grew less assured. Were they satisfied? he asked timidly. If they were he would appreciate if they withheld his true identity from the press. He was entirely at their command. If his testimony were required he would be only too happy to present it on the witness-stand, although the less publicity he got the better off he would be, since it was always possible that a reporter would dig up his past history and publish the reeking facts of the old dead scandal.

"You needn't worry on that score, Mr. Swanson." The District Attorney seemed troubled. "Your story to-day of course clears your step-father. We can't arrest him in the face of such a perfect alibi. So it will never reach a public hearing—eh, Q.?"

"Not now, anyway." The Inspector sneezed over a pinch of snuff. "Mr. Swanson, have you seen Dr. Janney since Monday morning?"

The ex-surgeon hesitated, scowled, looked up with a frank expression. "No sense in denying it now," he said. "I *have* seen dad since Monday morning. He came out to Port Chester secretly Monday night. I didn't want to mention it, but . . . He was worried about the search being made for me. He wanted me to leave town, go West or something. But when he told me how angry the police were about his silence—well, I naturally couldn't go and leave him holding the bag. After all, neither of us had anything to conceal as far as the murder was concerned. And flight would be construed as an admission of guilt. So I refused, and he went home. And this morning—well, I had to come into the City early, and there was that newspaper story staring me in the face. . . ."

"Does Dr. Janney know you've come to us with your story?" asked the Inspector.

"Oh, no!"

"Mr. Swanson." The old man stared at the ex-surgeon. "Can you give me any explanation of this crime?"

Swanson shook his head. "It's a complete puzzle to me. I didn't know the old woman too well, anyway. I was a kid when she was helping dad so much, and in my adolescence I was away at school. But it certainly wasn't dad. I—"

"I see, I see." The Inspector picked up one of the telephone instruments on Sampson's desk. "Well, just as a matter of form, young man, I'm going to check up on you. Hold still a moment." He called the number of the Dutch Memorial Hospital. "Hello! Let me speak to Dr. Janney."

"The operator speaking. I—who is this, please?"

"Inspector Queen—headquarters. Hurry."

"Oh! Just a moment, please." The Inspector heard a confusion of clicks, and then a deep male voice said, familiarly, "Hello, dad."

"Ellery! How the devil—Were you—Where are you?"

"In Janney's office."

"How'd you get there?"

"Just dropped in a while ago. Three minutes ago, to be exact. Came down to see Johnnie Minchen. Dad, I've got—"

"Haul up!" growled the old man. "You let me talk. Here's news. Swanson walked in this morning. We just got his story. Very interesting, Ellery—I'll tell you the details, give you a transcript of his testimony when I see you—he's Dr. Janney's son. . . ."

"What!"

"Just what I'm telling you. Where's Dr. Janney? Are you going to stand there all day and—let me speak with Janney a moment, son!"

Deep silence from Ellery. "Well!" exclaimed the Inspector.

Ellery said slowly, "You can't very well speak with Janney, dad."

"Why? Where is he? Isn't he there?"

"I was trying to explain when you stopped me before. . . . He's here, very much here," said Ellery grimly, "but the reason he can't talk to you is—well, he's dead."

"DEAD?"

"Or somewhere in the fourth dimension. . . ." Ellery's tone was one of profound depression, despite the flippancy of his words. "It's 10:35 now—let's see—I got here about 10:30. . . . Dad, he was murdered thirty minutes ago!"

21

DUPLICATION

ABIGAIL DOORN, Dr. Francis Janney. . . .

Two murders now instead of one.

Inspector Queen was sunk in a black slough of reflection as the heavy police car, commandeered outside the District Attorney's office, dashed uptown to the Dutch Memorial Hospital. . . . Janney murdered! It was incredible. . . . On the other hand, this second one might be easier to solve—might lead to a solution of the first, in fact. . . . Or maybe the two killings had nothing to do with each other. . . . But then it's impossible, anyway, for a murder to have been committed in a building full of police and detectives without some trace, some clew, some witness, some. . . . District Attorney Sampson and a thoroughly unnerved Swanson huddled to left and right of the old man.

The Police Commissioner, who had been hastily informed of the new development, was following closely in an official automobile. He was biting his fingernails in desperation—fuming with rage and worry. . . .

The rushing cavalcade ground to a stop with a squeal of brakes. The cars disgorged their impatient occupants, who ran up the stone steps to the front entrance of the Hospital. The Com-

203

missioner panted to the Inspector: "As much as your job and mine are worth, Queen, if this thing isn't settled. Now. To-day. God . . . what a mess!"

A policeman opened the big door.

If the Hospital had been upset after the murder of Abigail Doorn it was now, after the murder of Dr. Janney, completely disrupted. All professional activity seemed to have come to a standstill. No white-garbed nurse, no doctor was in evidence. Even Isaac Cobb, the doorman, was missing from his post. But plainclothesmen and bluecoats overran the corridors; the floor in the vicinity of the entrance especially was alive with them.

The elevator-door gaped wide; it was unattended. The Waiting Room was shut tight. The office-doors were also closed; behind them, segregated by the police, was the numbed office force.

And a buzzing sound of detectives surrounded the dosed door upon which was lettered: DR. FRANCIS JANNEY.

The throng melted away as the Inspector, the Police Commissioner, Sergeant Velie and Sampson strode through. The Inspector entered the dead man's quiet office. Swanson followed with lagging steps, his face pale and working. Velie shut the door softly behind him.

In the bare expanse of that room there was only one object for which their eyes instantly sought, and there it was—the figure of Dr. Janney sprawled in the careless attitude of death over his littered desk. . . . The surgeon had been seated in his swivel-chair when death overtook him; now the upper part of his body lay loosely on the desk-top, grey head resting on a crooked left arm, right arm stretched on the glass, a pen still clutched between the fingers.

Seated on plain varnished chairs at the left side of the office were Ellery, Pete Harper, Dr. Minchen and James Paradise, the

Hospital superintendent. Of the four, only Ellery and Harper faced the dead man; Minchen and Paradise both were half-turned toward the door, and both were visibly trembling.

Dr. Samuel Prouty, Assistant Medical Examiner, was standing near the desk. His black bag lay closed on the floor; he was putting on his overcoat and whistling a cheerless tune.

No one uttered a word of greeting or comment. It was as if, to a man, they found nothing adequate verbally to express their astonishment, their surprise, their horror in the face of this unexpected, inexplicable catastrophe. Swanson leaned weakly against the door; after one quick fascinated look in the direction of the carved cold figure in the corner he kept his head sedulously averted. The Inspector, the Commissioner and Sampson stood shoulder to shoulder and stared about the death-room.

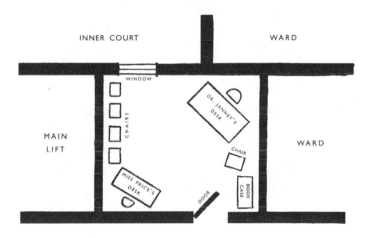

It was square. There was one door, by which they had entered; there was one window. The door led from the South Corridor and was obliquely across from the main entrance. The window, at the rear left of the room, was wide, overlooking a long open-air inner court. To the left of the door stood a small stenographer's desk, with a typewriter upon it. On the left wall were the four chairs on which Ellery and his companions sat. The dead man's big desk was at the right-hand farther corner, set at an angle and facing outward to the front left corner. Except for the swivel-chair in which Janney's body rested there was nothing behind the desk. The right-hand wall served as a background for one large leather chair and a heavily filled bookcase.

And except for four steel-engraved portraits of bewhiskered surgeons on the walls and an imitation-marble linoleum on the floor, the room held nothing else. . . .

"Well, Doc, what's the verdict?" demanded the Commissioner harshly.

Dr. Prouty fumbled with a dead cigar. "It's the same story, Commissioner. Murder by strangulation!"

Ellery bent over, resting his elbow on his knee and grasping his jaw with searching fingers. His eyes were abstracted, almost pained.

"Wire, like in the last one?" asked the Inspector.

"Yep. You can see for yourself."

Queen stepped slowly toward the desk, accompanied by Sampson and the Commissioner. Gazing down at the grey head of the dead man they saw a dark thick clot. Both the Inspector and the Commissioner looked up quickly.

"He was hit on the head before he was strangled," volunteered Dr. Prouty. "By some heavy blunt instrument—it's hard to say what. There's a contusion back there, directly over the cerebellar region."

"Put him to sleep so he wouldn't cry out when he was choked," muttered the Inspector. "That tap is at the back of the head, Doc. How do you figure he was sitting when he was hit? Couldn't have been taking a nap or something, could he, so that the blow might have been struck while the assailant stood in front of the desk? Because if he was sitting up it looks as if whoever hit him stood behind him."

Ellery's eyes glittered, but he said nothing.

"You've got it, Inspector." Prouty's lips writhed comically about his cold cigar. "Whoever hit him did stand behind the desk. You see, he wasn't lying forward this way when we found him. He was sitting *back* in the chair—here, let me show you. . . ." He stepped back and wriggled between the corner of the desk and the wall, to get behind the desk. Gently, but with complete unconcern, he lifted the dead man by the shoulders until the body perched upright in the swivel-chair, head slumped forward on the chest.

"That's the way he was, wasn't it?" demanded Prouty. "Hey, Mr. Queen?"

Ellery started, smiled mechanically. "Oh! Oh, yes. Quite."

"Here. You can see the wire now." Prouty lifted the head carefully. About the neck was a thin bloody line. The wire was so deeply imbedded in the dead flesh as to be almost invisible. Behind the neck the two ends of the wire were twisted into one strand, exactly as in the case of Abigail Doorn.

The Inspector straightened. "This is the way it goes, then. He was sitting here, somebody came in, got behind him, hit him over the head and then strangled him. Right?"

"That's it." Prouty shrugged, picked up the bag. "One thing I'll take my oath on. That smack on the head couldn't have been delivered from anywhere except behind the desk. . . . Well, I'll be off. Photographers have been here already, Inspector, and so have the fingerprint boys. Loads of prints all over the place, especially on this glass-top, I understand, but I guess most of 'em come from the fingers of Janney and that steno or assistant of his."

The Assistant Medical Examiner jammed his hat on his head, took a fresh grip with his teeth on the battered cigar, and stumped out of the office.

They stared down at the dead man again. "Dr. Minchen, this wound on the head couldn't have caused death, could it?"

Minchen gulped. His eyelids were red, his eyes bloodshot. "No," he said in a low voice. "Prouty's right. Just stunned him, that's all. He died—he died of strangulation, Inspector, absolutely."

They bent over the wire. "Looks like the same kind," mused Queen. "Thomas, first chance you get, I want you to check up on that." The giant nodded.

The body was still upright in the chair, as Prouty had left it. The Commissioner muttered something to himself as he carefully studied the face. It was devoid of horror, surprise, or fear. A characteristic blue tinge had crept under the swollen skin, but the features were calm—almost peaceful. The eyes were closed.

"Noticed it too, sir?" said Ellery suddenly, from his chair. "Doesn't appear like the face of a man violently attacked and murdered, does it?"

The Commissioner faced about, regarding Ellery shrewdly. "Just what I was thinking, young man. You're Queen's son, aren't you?—Strange is the word for it."

"Exactly." Ellery sprang from his chair and crossed to the desk to look reflectively at Janney's face. "And the blunt instrument that Prouty talked about—that's gone. Murderer must have taken it away. . . . Notice what Janney was doing when he went West?"

He pointed to the pen in the dead man's fingers, then to a sheet of white paper on the glass directly at the spot where the hand would rest if the body were leaning forward. The paper was half-covered with close, painstaking script; Janney had obviously stopped writing in the middle of a sentence, for the last word on the page ended with a convulsive jerk in a smear of ink.

"Working on his book when the blow came," murmured Ellery. "That's elementary. He and Dr. Minchen here, you know, have been collaborating on a technical work called *Congenital Allergy*."

"What time did he die?" asked Sampson thoughtfully.

"Prouty puts it between 10:00 and 10:05, and John Minchen agrees."

"Well, this isn't getting us anywhere," snapped the Inspector. "Thomas, have the body removed to the morgue downstairs. Don't forget to go through his clothes thoroughly. And then come back—I want you. Sit down, Commissioner. You, too, Henry . . . Swanson!"

The ex-surgeon started. His eyes were staring. "I—can't I go now?" he asked in a hoarse whisper.

"Yes," said the Inspector gently. "We shan't be needing you for a while. Thomas, send some one back to Port Chester with Mr. Swanson."

Velie herded Swanson out of the door. He shuffled from the room without a word or a backward look; he seemed dazed, frightened.

Ellery swiftly roved the room. The Commissioner seated himself with a grunt and commenced a low-voiced conversation with the Inspector and Sampson. Paradise was still huddled in his chair, shaken. Minchen said nothing—merely stared at the bright linoleum.

Ellery stopped before him, looked down quizzically. "What are you looking at—the new linoleum?"

"What?" Minchen licked his dry lips, attempted to smile. "Oh. . . . How do you know it's new?"

"Rather obvious, John. Is it?"

"Yes. All these private offices were recovered just a few weeks ago. . . ."

Ellery resumed his pacing.

The door opened again. Two internes entered with a stretcher. They were both white-faced, brusque in their movements.

As they were lifting the dead body from the chair Ellery paused at the window, frowned, and then looked back at the desk, which was laterally across the room. His eyes narrowed, and he strolled over to stand near the working internes.

As they deposited Janney's limp form on the stretcher, Ellery wheeled and said sharply—every one looked up startled—"Do you know, there really ought to be a window behind this desk!"

They stared. Inspector Queen said, "What's buzzing about inside your head now, son?"

Minchen laughed mirthlessly. "Is it getting you, too? Why, there's never been a window there, Ellery."

Ellery wagged his head. "An architectural omission that bothers me. . . . It's really too bad that poor old Janney didn't remember the motto on Plato's ring. How did it read? 'It is easier to prevent ill habits than to break them. . . .'"

22

ENUMERATION

SEVERAL HOURS later a small tight-lipped company sat in the dead man's office, now murky with bluish-grey smoke-haze. From the set faces, the rigid jaws, the wrinkled foreheads it was evident that realization of failure was upon them, that Dr. Janney's murder was as hopelessly far from explanation as Abigail Doorn's.

Their numbers had dwindled. The Police Commissioner, his face the color of ashes, had gone. A subdued Harper had left an hour before to communicate certain news of importance to his paper. Sampson, his eyes screwed up with worry, had left the Hospital at the same time to return to his office and the inevitable task of facing the press and the public.

Sergeant Velie was still scurrying about in the corridors assembling facts and testimony. The lethal picture-wire had definitely been established as the same type as had been used in the first murder. With little else to go upon, the Sergeant had instituted another search for a possible source—so far without the slightest success.

Only the Inspector, Ellery, Dr. Minchen and Lucille Price, the dead man's nurse-assistant, were left. The girl had been recruited in the emergency to take stenographic dictation from the Inspector.

Of the four, despite Minchen's patently dazed condition, Ellery seemed most affected by the second murder. His face was drawn into long lines of suffering and concentration; his eyes were dull, unhappy, even pained. He was huddled in a chair by the lone window, gazing fixedly at the linoleum. . . .

"All set, Miss Price?" rasped the Inspector.

The nurse, sitting at her small desk in the corner, pad open and pencil poised, looked frightened. She was very pale; her hand trembled; she kept her eyes on the blank stenographic notebook, avoiding the mute desk across the room in which the tragedy had so recently been enacted.

"Take this, then," began the Inspector. He strode up and down before her with bristling brows, his hands clasped tightly behind his back. "Philip Morehouse. Morehouse found the body.

"Details: Morehouse had called at the Hospital, carrying briefcase, to see Dr. Janney concerning his share of the Doorn will, arriving about 9:45. Entrance seen by Isaac Cobb, doorman; time substantiated. Switchboard operator on duty plugged Janney's office, transmitted message that M. wished to see the doctor. Voice, *unquestionably Janney's*—underline that, Miss Price—replied that he was unavoidably busy at the moment; would be free soon; M. was to wait. M. expressed annoyance at the delay, says operator, but decided to wait. Cobb saw him enter Waiting Room from vestibule and sit down. . . . Am I going too fast?"

"No—no, sir."

"Add this note," resumed the Inspector. "In the entire period following, Cobb cannot swear that M. did not leave Waiting Room for a moment. Cobb station in vestibule; another exit from Waiting Room exists off South Corridor, making it possible for occupant of Waiting Room to slip out of said door without being seen if no one is in South Corridor at the time. . . .

"Details, continued: Morehouse claims to have sat in Waiting Room a half-hour, until approximately 10:15. Then approached switchboard operator again, coming through vestibule door into office, impatiently asked operator to ring Janney once more. Operator rang; no answer. M. furious, impulsively crossed South Corridor and knocked on J.'s door. No answer. Cobb, seeing this action, approached M. to protest. Policeman on duty on steps outside also came in. M. said: 'Did you see Dr. Janney leave this office in the last half-hour?' Cobb said: 'No; but I wasn't watching all the time.' M. said: 'Maybe something has happened to him.' Cobb scratched his head; policeman tried the door. Moran (patrolman on duty) found door unlocked. Cobb, Morehouse, Moran went in and found J.'s body. Cobb raised alarm at once, Moran got aid of detectives in Hospital, Dr. Minchen entered building at this moment. Minchen took temporary charge until help came. Ellery Queen entered Hospital several minutes later. . . . Got that, Miss Price?"

"Yes, sir."

Minchen sat with his legs crossed, sucking at his thumb. Bleak uncomprehending horror was in his eyes.

The Inspector prowled about the room, consulting a scrap of paper. He leveled his arm at the nurse. "Add this to the Morehouse data. Observation: M. has no absolute alibi for danger period. . . . Now, start a fresh one on Miss Hulda Doorn.

"Hulda Doorn in Hospital. Arrived 9:30, seen by Cobb and Moran. Purpose was to collect personal effects of Abigail Doorn from room she occupied when she had accident Monday and was to be operated on. No one in room with Miss Doorn. Claimed she became suddenly overwhelmed with grief at sight of dead woman's clothing and did nothing but sit down and think. Was found there weeping on bed at 10:30 by Nurse Obermann. No corroboration of story that she had not left room for even a moment."

The pencil raced over the page. There was no sound in the death-room except the softly harsh scrape of the graphite.

"Dr. Lucius Dunning and Sarah Fuller." The Inspector's lips clamped together over the last syllable; he had fairly crackled the words. "Dunning arrived at Hospital usual early morning hour, attending to routine work. This corroborated by assistants. Sarah Fuller arrived at 9:15 to see Dunning—this brought out by Moran, Cobb, operator. Closeted together for an hour; Sarah Fuller attempted to leave a minute after Dr. Janney's body was discovered.

"Both refused to relate subject of their conversation. Each alibis the other—claims they did not leave Dunning's office. No third party to confirm this statement." The Inspector paused, stared at the ceiling. "On insistence of Police Commissioner, both Dunning and Sarah Fuller were then put under arrest, held as material witnesses. Still refused to talk. Bail later set at $20,000 each by immediate action; both released on payment of bail by Attorney Morehouse's office."

He went on rapidly. "Edith Dunning. On duty in Social Service Department from 9:00 A.M. on. In Hospital entire period. Attended social service cases. No absolute check-up on time or movements. No assistant with her long enough to eliminate her from list of possibilities. . . .

"Michael Cudahy. Still in Room 328, recovering from appendectomy. Guarded by detectives. Impossible for him to have left bed. No communication with outside, as far as detectives know. But this means little, as Cudahy has notoriously effective methods of doing things. . . .

"Dr. Pennini. Did her regular work in Obstetrical Department. She visited some twenty patients, no check-up on exact movements. Not out of building all morning, according to Cobb, Moran. . . .

"Moritz Kneisel. In private laboratory all morning, undisturbed, unsubstantiated. Claims Janney visited lab shortly before 9:00, seemed upset by news story of impending arrest, mentioned going to office, seeing no one and working on his book. Discussed progress of experiments briefly, and left. Kneisel noncommittal on this murder, but seems hard hit. . . . All right, Miss Price?"

"I've got it all, Inspector Queen."

"That's very good. There's one more." The Inspector scanned his scribbled notes and resumed dictation. "Hendrik Doorn. Visited Hospital, arriving at 9:20, as part of regular three-times-weekly ultra-violet ray treatment for nervous condition. Waited in fifth floor ray laboratories until 9:35, finished with treatment 9:50. Lay down to rest in private room on main floor until discovery of body. No corroboration of his being in this room all the time. . . .

"That's all, Miss Price. Please type these off immediately. Make two carbons and give the whole batch to Sergeant Velie—the big fellow outside. He'll be here all afternoon."

The nurse nodded submissively and began to transcribe her notes on the desk typewriter.

Ellery looked up tiredly. "If you've concluded these empty, useless, dithering reports, dad, I vote for home." He stared unseeingly out of the window.

"In a moment, son. Don't take it so hard. You can't hit it all the time." The Inspector leaned against Janney's desk and helped himself to a long pinch of snuff. "It just beats the band," he went on carefully. "I'd have said such a thing was impossible. To think that no one had his eyes on this office-door long enough to see any-thing, and the place infested with men who ought to know bet-ter." He tossed his head sadly. "Janney seems to have conspired his own death. Shuts himself in his office, tells Miss Price he doesn't want her this morning—peeved as the deuce, it seems—and just leaves himself wide open for a murderous attack that, as luck would have it, was unwitnessed. Last seen alive by Cobb when he came back from Kneisel's lab and entered his own office. This was a few minutes after 9:00. And not a soul seems to have spoken to him or seen him except for the time the operator, at 9:45 or so, spoke to him about Morehouse's visit. And the doctors agree that Janney was killed between 10:00 and 10:05, so undoubtedly it was Janney talking at 9:45. . . . Well!"

"It's a fearful muddle," said Ellery slowly, without turning away from the window. "Hulda Doorn, Hendrik Doorn, Dun-ning, Sarah Fuller, Kneisel, Morehouse—all in the Hospital and unaccounted for."

Minchen stirred, smiling vaguely. "The only one who couldn't have done it was this Big Mike Cudahy fellow. And me. You're sure you don't suspect me, Inspector? After this, anything is pos-sible. . . . Oh, God!" He buried his face in his hands.

The typewriter clacked on in the silence.

"Well," said the old man grimly, "if you did it you're a spiri-tualist, Dr. Minchen. Couldn't be in two places at once. . . ." They chuckled together; Minchen's voice held a note of hysteria.

Ellery wrapped his overcoat tightly about him. "Come along," he said in a sharp tone. "Come along before this damned brain of mine bursts from futile thinking."

23

TRIPLICATION ? ? ?

CHAGRIN AND bafflement pursued Ellery Queen from the stricken corridors of the Dutch Memorial Hospital to the interior of his father's office at Police Headquarters.

He had disgustedly expressed the desire to return to the Queen house on West 87th Street and bury his troubles in Marcel Proust. The Inspector, shrewdly appraising, would listen to no such proposal. They would all go down to his office, he had said, and have a quiet talk, and be bawled out *en masse* by the Mayor, and generally make merry. . . .

So they sat, Richard and Ellery Queen and District Attorney Sampson, and two of them chatted pleasantly about everything but the Doorn and Janney murders.

The newspapers of New York City were making Roman holiday. Two murders in three days, and both victims of the utmost journalistic importance! City Hall Park seethed with reporters; the Police Commissioner had disappeared; the Mayor had retired to the privacy of his home "on advice of his physician." Every person whose name had appeared, even briefly, in the case had been haunted by photographers and leg-men. The news about Thomas Swanson had leaked out and a journalistic hegira began with Port

Chester as the goal. Inspector Queen had exerted every ounce of official pressure at his command to keep the true identity of Swanson a secret; thus far he had been successful, but the threat of disclosure hung over them. Swanson was by now under heavy guard.

Sergeant Velie was pursuing a will-o'-the-wisp. It had been his most pressing assignment to trace back the movements of the dead surgeon; and nothing met the eye other than a perfectly innocent series of contacts. Janney's private correspondence at his apartment had been scanned with microscopic suspicion; aside from several letters from Thomas Janney which substantiated the Swanson story, this search too was fruitless.

Everywhere a blank wall. . . .

Ellery's long fingers played with a tiny figurine of the great Bertillon on the Inspector's desk. The old man was, genially enough, relating an anecdote from out of his youth; but there were dark-shadowed pouches beneath his eyes, and his gayety was pitifully forced.

"Let's not delude ourselves." Ellery spoke abruptly and both the Inspector and Sampson turned to regard him with apprehension. "We're like frightened children babbling in the dark. Dad, Sampson—we're licked."

Neither of the older men replied. Sampson hung his head, and the Inspector thoughtfully examined his square boot-toes.

"If it weren't for my Gaelic pride, and the fact that no matter what I do, dad has to carry on," continued Ellery, "I would figuratively fall upon my sword and seek peace in the warrior's heaven. . . ."

"What's the matter with you, Ellery?" The Inspector did not look up. "I've never heard you talk this way before. Why, only yesterday you were saying that you had a pretty good idea who the murderer is."

"Yes," said Sampson eagerly, "if anything this second murder, which unquestionably is linked with the first, should throw light on the original problem. I'm sure something will turn up."

Ellery grunted. "The curse of fatalism is the sublime spinelessness, which it engenders. You see, Sampson, I'm not so sure . . ." He pulled himself out of the chair, looked moodily down at them. "What I said yesterday still stands. I know in a vague way who strangled Abigail Doorn. I could name half a dozen people in the case who, from the nature of the clews, simply couldn't have done for Abby. But—"

"There aren't many more than a half-dozen in the case altogether," said the Inspector challengingly. "So what's worrying you?"

"Things."

"Look here, son," said the old man with energy, "if you're upbraiding yourself because you didn't prevent this second crime, forget it. How could you or any of us have foreseen that Janney, of all people, would follow Abby?"

Ellery waved his hand negligently. "Oh, it's not that. With all my suspicions, I couldn't have foreseen Janney's death, as you say. . . . Sampson, you just said these two crimes are linked. What makes you so certain?"

Sampson looked startled. "Why—I took it for granted. The two crimes came so close together, the two victims were so intimately linked, the location is the same, the methods are identical, everything bears out the—"

"Seems Gospel, eh?" Ellery bent over. "Isn't that just as good an argument for the belief that the two crimes *aren't* linked? Assume two murderers instead of one. Abby Doorn is sent outward bound in a certain way under certain circumstances. Murderer Number Two says: 'Aha! Here's the perfect opportunity to avenge myself on Janney and make the police think Murderer Number One did the job!' Consequently we perceive the similar locale, the similar method and all the rest of it. Refute this with evidence, please."

The Inspector squirmed. "Oh, for goodness' sake, boy, you can't mean that. Why—we'd have to start all over again."

Ellery shrugged. "Mind you, I'm not saying I believe a different person committed the second crime. I'm merely pointing out the possibility. So far one theory is as good as the other."

"But—"

"I confess that the assumption of one criminal pleases me more than the assumption of two. But mark my words," said Ellery earnestly, "if the same person committed both crimes we must look for a reason to explain why such a clever rogue should have taken the dangerous course of deliberately duplicating the method."

"You mean," asked the Inspector in a puzzled way, "that it would be more to the murderer's advantage to avoid strangulation?"

"Of course it would. If Janney had been found shot, or stabbed, or poisoned, we'd have no physical reason at all to believe that the crimes were allied. Observe that in the second case the murderer actually struck Janney over the head before strangling him! Now why didn't he finish the job with his bludgeon? Why merely stun him and then go to the trouble of putting a wire about his neck? . . . No, dad, it seems very likely that the murderer *wanted* us to see that the crimes were linked!"

"By golly, that's right," muttered the old man.

"It's so right, to my mind," replied Ellery, sinking wearily into his chair again, "that if I knew *why* the murderer wants us to believe the two murders part of the same crime, I'd know the whole story. . . . But I'm keeping an open mind on this second homicide. I have still to see *proof* that the two crimes were committed by the same scoundrel."

The inter-office communicator on the Inspector's desk rasped. The Inspector lifted the receiver from the hook.

A muffled voice barked: "Man by the name of Kneisel wants to see you, Inspector. Says it's important."

"Kneisel!" The old man was silent, his eyes gleaming. "Kneisel, hey? Send him up, Bill."

Sampson was leaning forward. "What the devil can Kneisel want?"

"Don't know. Say, Henry . . . that gives me an idea." They looked at each other, mutual comprehension in their crossed glances. Ellery said nothing.

A detective opened the door. The small figure of Moritz Kneisel appeared on the threshold.

The Inspector got to his feet. "Come in, Dr. Kneisel. Come in. All right, Frank."

The detective left and the swarthy little scientist advanced slowly into the room. He was wearing a rusty greenish overcoat with a tawny velvet collar. He carried a green velour hat in his blotched hand.

"Sit down. What's on your mind?"

He seated himself punctiliously on the edge of a chair, placing his hat on his knees. His soft dark eyes restlessly ranged over the office; in an abstracted, automatic way he seemed to be appraising, storing away what he saw.

He spoke suddenly. "When you interrogated me earlier to-day, I was naturally upset by the unfortunate death of my friend and colleague. I had no time to think carefully. Now I have surveyed the facts, Inspector Queen, and I tell you very frankly—I fear for my personal safety!"

"Oh, I see."

The stilted phrases fell idly from the man's lips. The District Attorney winked at the Inspector from behind Kneisel's stiff figure. The Inspector nodded imperceptibly.

"Just what do you mean? Have you found out anything about the murder of Dr. Janney which we ought to know?"

"Not that, no." Kneisel held up his hands and looked at their mangled, bleached skin absently. "But I have a theory. It has been bothering me all afternoon. It is a theory which, if true, makes me—victim number three in a diabolical series of murders!"

Ellery's eyebrows bunched. Interest had crept into his eyes. "A theory, eh?" he murmured. "And a melodramatic one, too." Kneisel looked at him sidewise. "Well, Kneisel, we're a little short of theories to-day. So let's have it in detail. It's bound to prove refreshing."

"Is the imminence of my death a matter of jest, Mr. Queen?" asked the scientist curtly. "I am beginning to alter my first opinion of you. I feel that you are mocking what you cannot understand . . . Inspector!"

He turned squarely away from Ellery, who slipped back on his spine again.

"My theory, summarily, is this: That a fourth party, whom I will call X, has engineered a series of murders beginning with the strangulation of Abigail Doorn, continuing with the strangulation of Dr. Janney—and concluding with the strangulation of Moritz Kneisel."

"A fourth party?" The Inspector knit his brows. "Who?"

"I do not know."

"For what reason, then?"

"Ah, that is another question!" Kneisel tapped the Inspector's knee lightly. "To gain undisputed possession of the secret and profits of my alloy, *doornite!*"

"So that's it. . . ." Sampson looked skeptical. But the Inspector wore a serious frown; his eyes flickered from Ellery to Kneisel. "Murder for a secret worth millions. Not bad. Not bad at all. . . . But why on earth murder Mrs. Doorn and Dr. Janney? It seems to me that your murder alone, after your formulæ were completed, would be enough."

"It would not." The scientist was coldly deliberate; he seemed made of iron. "Let us suppose that this hypothetical fourth party lurks somewhere in the background. And that he is most desirous of securing the results of my labors. And also, in doing so, leave himself sole possessor of the vital knowledge.

"The murder of Abigail Doorn would be to his advantage. He allows her to live just so long as she furnishes funds for the continuation of the experiments. When she threatens to stop, he kills her and achieves two ends in doing so—he insures her financial support even after her death, and he eliminates one of the three holders of the secret."

"Go on."

"Then," continued Kneisel imperturbably, "it is the turn of Dr. Kneisel's partner, Dr. Janney. I am logical, you see. . . . He precedes me in the order of our going for the reason that he is technically not so essential as I to the completion of the work. His usefulness, in providing me with the means of fulfilling my life-work, is past. So he is murdered; and the second of the triumvirate, whose continued existence would prevent the murderer from commercializing his theft without opposition, disappears from the scene. Do you follow me so far, gentlemen?"

"We follow you, all right," said the Inspector harshly. "But I don't quite see why it was necessary for Janney to be killed so soon after the old lady. What was the rush? And then your job is incomplete. Janney might have helped, even in a small way, to perfect the alloy."

"Ah, but we are dealing with a person of subtlety and foresight," said Kneisel. "If he had waited for the work to be done, it would then have been necessary to commit *two* murders at almost the same time. With Janney gone, now only one murder is required in order to eliminate the last of the trio and take undisputed possession of a secret worth millions."

"Clever, but weak," murmured Ellery.

Kneisel ignored him. "To continue. The deaths of Mrs. Doorn and Dr. Janney leave me a clear field, more than sufficient funds to work with, and the scientific ability to bring the experiments to a head. . . . You see the possibilities."

"Yes," said Ellery softly, "we see the possibilities."

Kneisel's womanish eyes sharpened momentarily, but the glint died out and he shrugged his shoulders.

"That's a pretty theory, Dr. Kneisel," said the Inspector, "but after all we need more than guesses. Names, man, names! I'm sure you've some one in mind."

The scientist closed his eyes. "Specifically, I have not. And why you should insist on concrete evidence from me I do not understand. Surely you don't despise theories, Inspector? I believe Mr. Ellery Queen himself works on some such intellectual plan. . . . This theory is solid, sir. It is based on a consideration of all the facts. It is—"

"Not true," said Ellery distinctly.

Kneisel shrugged again. Ellery said, "It's a poor syllogism that doesn't educe an incontrovertible conclusion from its major and minor premises. Come now, Kneisel, you're being cagy. What are you holding back?"

"Your guess is as good as mine, Mr. Queen."

"Who besides Mrs. Doorn, Dr. Janney and yourself knows enough about the exact nature of your work to realize its financial possibilities? Of course we've known it since Mrs. Doorn's death Monday, but weren't there others before?" asked the Inspector.

"You force me to be dogmatic. I can think of one person who might very well have been informed by Mrs. Doorn of the secret. That is the lawyer who drew up her wills—Morehouse."

"Preposterous," said Sampson.

"Oh, no doubt."

"But you know perfectly well," said the Inspector, "that it might have been anybody in the Doorn household or in the circle of the old lady's friends. Why pick on Morehouse?"

"No specific reason." Kneisel looked bored. "He merely appears to me to be the logical person. I am quite sure I'm wrong."

"You just said that Mrs. Doorn must have talked. Are you certain Dr. Janney mightn't have done the same?"

"Positive!" said Kneisel sharply. "Dr. Janney was as zealous in guarding our secret as I have been."

"One little item occurs to me," drawled Ellery. "When you were first examined, Kneisel, you said that you originally met Janney through a mutual colleague who was aware of what you were endeavoring to do. It seems to me that you've overlooked that possibly loquacious gentleman."

"Mr. Queen, I have overlooked nothing." Kneisel actually smiled for an instant. "The man to whom you refer could not be behind these crimes for two excellent reasons: one, he died two years ago; two, despite your statement which is a misstatement of my own of Monday, he knew nothing of the nature of my work, so that he could not have transmitted knowledge of it to any one."

"*Touché*," murmured Ellery.

"What's all this leading to?" demanded the Inspector. "What's your conclusion, Dr. Kneisel?"

"My theory embraces even the eventualities. The man behind these murders will be in a position, after my death, to dispose of and cash in on my metal alloy by dealing with innocent metal interests. That is where the trail will lead, Inspector. So if I should die suddenly—"

Sampson drummed on the arm of his chair. "Disturbing, all right. But there isn't a particle of evidence, of tangibility."

Kneisel smiled frigidly. "I beg your pardon, sir. I hesitate to assume the air of a sleuth—but can you or Inspector Queen or Mr. Ellery Queen offer a better motive for the apparently unrelated murders of Mrs. Doorn and Dr. Janney? Can you offer any motive *at all?*"

"Beside the point!" snapped the Inspector. "You're assuming that there's going to be another funeral, at which you'll be the main attraction. Well, suppose you're disappointed, and the murders of the Dutch Memorial Hospital are now at an end? Where's your theory then?"

"I should grant the error of a mere theory to preserve my scientific skin, Inspector—gladly. If I am not killed, I'm wrong. If I am killed, I'm right—doubtful satisfaction either way. But right or wrong, I am entitled to play—as you say—safe. Inspector, I demand protection!"

"Oh, you'll get that, all right. Twice as much as you've bargained for. We don't want anything happening to you, Dr. Kneisel."

"I suppose you realize," put in Ellery, "that, even if your theory is correct, Mrs. Doorn may have whispered the secret to more than one person? Is that right?"

"Well—yes. Why? What do you mean?"

"I'm simply being logical, Doctor." Ellery folded his hands peacefully behind his head. "If more than one person have been told, it stands to reason that your mysterious Mr. X, party of the fourth part, is aware of the fact. Then you aren't the only character in our melodrama who needs protection. There are others, Dr. Kneisel. I trust you see my point?"

Kneisel bit his lip. "Yes. Yes! There will be other murders, too. . . ."

Ellery laughed. "I scarcely think so. However, let it pass. One moment more, before you leave. I'm in a questioning mood. . . . *Doornite* is not yet perfected, you said?"

"Not completely."

"How near completion is it?"

"A matter of weeks—no more. I am safe for that length of time, in any event."

"I'm not so sure of that," said Ellery dryly.

Kneisel turned slowly in his chair. "What do you mean?"

"Simply this: your experiments are virtually finished. What is to prevent this fictive schemer of yours from killing you now and completing the work himself? Or having it completed for him by a competent metallurgist?"

The scientist looked startled. "True. Very true. It *could* be finished by some one else. That means—that means I'm not safe—no, not even now."

"Unless," said Ellery amiably, "you destroy at once every vestige of your researches."

Kneisel's voice was strained. "A poor consolation. Either way. My life or my work."

"The well-known horns, eh?" murmured Ellery.

Kneisel sat up stiffly. "I may be killed to-day, to-night—"

The Inspector stirred. "I don't think it's as bad as all that, Dr. Kneisel. And you'll be well taken care of. Excuse me." The old man manipulated his inter-office communicator. "Ritter! You've got a new assignment. You're to take care of Dr. Moritz Kneisel from the moment he steps out of my office. . . . Now. Stay with him, Ritter, and get a good relief for the night. . . . No, this isn't a tail— you're a bodyguard from now on. Okay." He turned back to the scientist "It's all fixed."

"Considerate of you, Inspector. I shall be going." Kneisel fumbled with his hat-brim. He rose suddenly and, without glancing at Ellery, said in a rapid way, "Good-day. Goodbye, gentlemen." He slipped out of the room.

"The spalpeen!" The Inspector was on his feet now, his white face brightly colored. "That was slick! God, he's got his nerve!"

"What do you mean, Q.?" asked Sampson.

"It's as plain as day," cried the old man. "This theory of his is pure hogwash. It's a blind, Henry! Didn't it occur to you as he was speaking that *he's* the man left with a clear field, that *he's* the biggest gainer by the death of Abby Doorn and Janney, that *he's* figuratively the 'fourth party' of his theory? In other words that there is no fourth party?"

"By thunder, Q., I think you've hit it!"

The old man turned to Ellery in triumph. "All this pretty talk about X wiping out Abby, Janney, and himself. . . . Why, it's nonsensical! Don't you think I'm on the right track, son?"

Ellery did not speak for a moment; his eyes were haggard. "I haven't a morsel of concrete evidence," he said at last, "to bolster my belief—but I think both you and Kneisel are wrong, I don't think Kneisel did the jobs, nor this fourth and purely hypothetical person Kneisel talked about. . . . Dad, if we ever hit bottom in this investigation, which I seriously doubt, we'll find that it's a much more subtle crime than even Kneisel postulates—and much more impossible, to be thoroughly unrhetorical."

The Inspector scratched his head. "How you can blow hot and cold in the same breath, son! Now, I suppose you'll tell me, after saying Kneisel doesn't figure, to keep my eye on him as if he were the most important suspect in the case. That would be just like you."

"Amazingly enough, that is precisely what I was going to say." Ellery lit another cigarette. "And don't misinterpret my statement. You did just now, you know. . . . Kneisel must be guarded as if he were the Maharajah of Punjab. I want a detailed report of the identity, conversation and subsequent movements of every soul who comes within ten feet of him!"

24

REEXAMINATION

So Wednesday passed, and with every crawling hour the mystery of New York's most sensational murder case retreated farther and farther into the shadowy region of unsolved crimes.

The investigation of Dr. Francis Janney's death, as of the death of Abigail Doorn, had reached its critical stage. It was generally agreed throughout the offices of the law that if a beginning were not made within forty-eight hours toward clearing up the crimes they might be considered beyond the pale of solution.

On Thursday morning Inspector Queen awoke after an uneasy night in a blank, clammish mood. His cough had recurred and his eyes burned with the unhealthy glitter of fever. But he brushed aside the protests of Djuna and Ellery and, shivering in his greatcoat despite the mild winter air, plodded down 87th Street toward the Broadway subway and Headquarters.

Ellery sat at the window and blindly watched him go.

The table was cluttered with breakfast dishes. Djuna grasped a cup and fixed gypsy eyes on the sprawling figure across the room. Not so much as a muscle of his jaw twitched. The boy possessed an uncanny immobility, a gift for noiselessness that was uncivilized, feline.*

Ellery spoke without turning his head. "Djuna."

Djuna was at the window in a flash.

"Djuna, talk to me."

The thin body quivered. "Me—talk to you, Mr. Ellery?"

"Yes."

"But—what?"

"Anything. I want to hear a voice. Your voice, son."

The black eyes sparkled. "You and Dad Queen are worryin'. How'd you like fried chicken for supper? I think that book you made me read about this here big whale, Moby Dick, is swell. It ain't like—"

"*Isn't*, Djuna!"

"It *isn't* like those Horatio Algers and things. I skipped some parts though. Boy, what a nigger that—that Quee—Quee—"

"Queequeg, son. And never say 'nigger.' Negro is the word."

"Oh! . . . Well, now. . . ." The dark satiny skin of the boy's face writhed and wrinkled. "I wish it was baseball season. I want to see Babe Ruth smack 'em. Why don't you make Dad Queen stop coughin'? We need a new electric pad—old one's all wore out. They made me quarterback on the football team at the Club. I got them guys learnin' signals, boy!"

"I have those. . . ." A sudden smile lifted Ellery's lips. His long arm curled and drew the boy down to the window-seat. "Djuna, old son, you do me no end of good. . . . You heard Dad and me discussing the Doorn and Janney cases last night, didn't you?"

Djuna said eagerly, "Yes!"

"Tell me what you think, Djuna."

* For more detailed descriptions of Djuna, his background, and his association with the Queens, see *The Roman Hat Mystery.*—Editor's Note

"What *I* think?" The boy's eyes opened wide.

"Yes."

"I think you'll catch'm." He swelled visibly.

"Really?" Ellery's fingers explored the boy's thin strong ribs. "You need some flesh there, Djuna," he said severely. "Football will do it. . . . So you're convinced I'll catch'm? Confident youth! I suppose you heard me say I was—well, not entirely successful so far?"

Djuna cackled. "You was foolin', wasn't you?"

"Not at all."

A cunning look invaded the bold eyes. "You givin' up?"

"Horrors, no!"

"Y'can't give up, Mr. Ellery," the boy said earnestly. "My team was playin' two days ago an' in the last quarter they had us 14 to 0. *We* didn't give up. We made three touchdowns. They were pretty sore."

"What do you think I ought to do, Djuna? And in telling me I want you to advise me to the best of your ability." Ellery did not smile.

Djuna did not answer at once; his mouth hardened and he gave himself over to deep thought. And after a long and pregnant silence, he said distinctly, "Eggs."

"What?" demanded Ellery in astonishment.

Djuna seemed pleased with himself. "I'm talkin' about eggs. 'Smornin' I was boilin' eggs for Dad Queen. I'm careful about Dad Queen's eggs—he's finicky. I let 'em boil too hard. So I threw 'em out an'—I started all over again. Second time they were just right." He stared at Ellery meaningly.

Ellery chuckled. "Environment's a bad influence in your case, I see. You've robbed me of my allegorical method. . . . Djuna, that's a rich and fruity thought—an excellent thought, forsooth!" He rumpled the boy's black hair. "Start all over again, eh?" He sprang from the chair. "By all your *romani* gods, son, that's sound advice!"

He disappeared into the bedroom with new energy. Djuna began to clear away the breakfast dishes, not without shaking fingers.

"John, I'm going to follow young Djuna's rede and retrace the ground of both crimes."

They were seated in Dr. Minchen's office at the Hospital.

"Do you need me?" The physician's eyes were lusterless and underscored with purple welts; he breathed heavily.

"If you can spare the time. . . ."

"I suppose so."

They left Minchen's chamber.

The Hospital this morning had resumed something of its routine air; bans had been lifted and with the exception of a few *verboten* areas on the main floor the business of life and death proceeded as if nothing out of the way had ever happened. Detectives and uniformed men still prowled about, but they kept out of the way and did not interfere with the activity of the doctors and nurses.

Ellery and Minchen made their way down the East Corridor and turned the corner into the South Corridor, going west. At the door of the Anæsthesia Room, sitting comfortably on a commandeered rocking-chair out of a convalescent ward, sat a dozing bluecoat. The door itself was closed.

He snapped to his feet in a flash as Ellery tried the handle of the door. And until Ellery wearily exhibited a special pass signed by Inspector Queen the policeman stoutly refused to allow the two men to enter the Anæsthesia Room.

The Anæsthesia Room was exactly as they had left it three days before.

At the door leading into the Anteroom sat another policeman. Again the pass brought electric response. He gawped, grinned feebly and mumbled "Yes'r." They passed inside.

Wheel-table, chairs, supply-cabinet, door to the elevator. . . . Nothing had changed.

Ellery said, "Nobody's been allowed in here, I see."

"We wanted to take out some supplies," muttered Minchen, "but your father left strict orders. We haven't been permitted past the outer door."

Ellery looked gloomily about. He tossed his head. "I suppose you think I'm daft for coming back here, John. As a matter of fact, now that the first flush of Djuna's inspiration has faded, I feel a little foolish myself. There *can't* be anything new here."

Minchen did not reply.

They looked into the operating theater and then returned to the Anteroom. Ellery crossed to the door of the lift and opened it. The elevator stood there, barren. He stepped into the elevator and tried the handle of the door on the opposite side. It would not budge.

"Taped on the other side," he murmured. "That's right—it's the one that leads into the East Corridor."

He stepped back into the Anteroom and looked about. Near the elevator was the door leading to the tiny Sterilizing Room. He peered inside. Everything appeared as it had been left on Monday.

"Oh, it's puerile!" cried Ellery. "Let's get out of this appalling place, John."

They left through the Anæsthesia Room and headed down the South Corridor toward the main entrance. "Here!" said Ellery suddenly. "Might as well make a complete fiasco of this ghastly business. Let's peep into Janney's office."

The bluecoat at the door blundered out of the way.

Inside the office Ellery sat down in the dead man's swivel-chair behind the large desk and motioned Minchen into one of the chairs on the west wall. They sat in silence as Ellery cynically examined the bare room through the smoke of his cigarette.

He spoke in a calm drawl. "John, I have a confession to make. It would seem that something has happened which for years I have maintained lies in the realm of the impossible. And that is— the commission of the insoluble crime."

"You mean there's no hope?"

"Hope is the pillar of the world, as the Woloffs of Africa say." Ellery flicked his cigarette and smiled. "My pillar is crashing. A terrific blow to my pride, John. . . . I shouldn't mind it so much if I felt sincerely that I'd met my master—a criminal mind which has concocted a pair of crimes so clever in their execution as to be impossible of solution. I'd admire that quite properly.

"But note that I said 'the insoluble crime'—not 'the perfect crime.' This isn't the perfect crime by a long shot. The criminal has actually left clews clearly comprehensible and, as far as they go, conclusive. No, these crimes don't exhibit the master touch, John. Far from it. Either our gentle fiend has been able to neutralize his errors, or fate has stepped in to accomplish the same end. . . ."

Ellery savagely crushed the butt of his cigarette into an ashtray on the desk. "There's only one thing left for us to do. And that is to go over with a fine-comb the background of every individual we've examined so far. By Christopher, there must be *something* hidden somewhere in the stories of these people! It's our last port-o'-call."

Minchen sat up with sudden eagerness. "I can help you there," he said hopefully. "I've come across a fact that may be useful. . . ."

"Yes?"

"I worked rather late last night trying to catch up on the book Janney and I were doing. Sort of taking up where the old man left off. And I discovered something about two of the people in the case which, strangely enough, I never even suspected before."

Ellery frowned. "You mean a reference in the manuscript? I fail to see—"

"Not in the manuscript. In the records which Janney has been collecting for twenty years. . . . Ellery, this matter is a professional secret, and under ordinary circumstances I wouldn't let even you know about it. . . ."

"Whom does it concern?" asked Ellery, sharply.

"Lucius Dunning and Sarah Fuller."

"Ah!"

"You promise that if it doesn't affect the case you'll not let it get into the records?"

"Yes. Yes. Go on, John; this interests me."

Minchen spoke rapidly. "You know, I suppose, that whenever specific cases are cited in a medical work, only initials are given, or case-numbers. This is done out of consideration for the patient, and also because whatever else about him may be vital to an understanding of his pathology, certainly his name and identity are not.

"In looking over some case-records last night which had not yet been incorporated into the manuscript of *Congenital Allergy,* I came across one—an old one dated about twenty years ago— which bore a special footnote. This note explained that *special care* was to be exercised in citing the facts so that no clew, not even the legitimate initials of the patients involved, was to be left to their identity.

"This was so unusual that I immediately read the case even though I was not yet prepared to put it into the book. The case concerned Dunning and the Fuller woman. Sarah Fuller was described as a patient in a premature confinement—a Cæsarian delivery—and there were certain other circumstances surrounding the confinement and the sex background of the parents which made the case pointed material for our book." Minchen's voice sank. "The child was illegitimate. And she's now known as—Hulda Doorn!"

Ellery gripped the arms of his chair as he stared unseeingly at the physician. A slow humorless smile began to form on his face. "Hulda Doorn a bastard," he repeated distinctly. "Well!" He relaxed and lit another cigarette. "That's information indeed. Clears up most perplexing point. I don't see that it alters the ultimate state of the case's solubility but—go ahead, John. What else?"

"At this time Dr. Dunning was a struggling young practitioner who devoted a few hours a day in the Hospital on a visiting basis. How he met Sarah Fuller I don't know, but they had the clandestine affair and Dunning couldn't marry her because he was already married. In fact, he had a daughter two years old—Edith. I understand that Sarah was far from unattractive as a girl. . . . Of course these items aren't strictly medical; all the cases before they're whipped into shape bear voluminous notes about contributory facts."

"Of course. Proceed!"

"As it turned out, Abby learned of Sarah's condition and because of her interest in Sarah took a lenient view of the affair. She preferred to hush up the Dunning end, even retaining him subsequently on the Hospital staff. And she solved the whole nasty situation by adopting the child as her own."

"Legally, I suppose?"

"Apparently. Sarah had no choice; the record says that she agreed to the arrangement without much argument. She swore never to interfere in the rearing of the child, who was to be known as Abigail's daughter.

"Now, Abby's husband was alive at this time, although she was childless. The matter was kept a dead secret from everybody, including the Hospital personnel, with the exception of Dr. Janney, who delivered Sarah of the child. Abby's powerful influence smothered any contemporary rumors."

"This really goes a long way toward explaining some obscure points," said Ellery. "It explains the quarrels between Abby and Sarah, who no doubt came to regret her enforced bargain. It explains Dunning's eagerness to defend Sarah's innocence of the murder of Abby, since the story of his youthful indiscretion would come out if she were arrested and ruin him domestically, socially and I suppose professionally." He shook his head. "But I still don't see how it helps us to a solution. Granted that it gives Sarah a strong motive for killing Abby and an understandable one in the case of Janney. Perhaps this is one of those paranoiacal crimes induced by a persecution mania. The woman's obviously unbalanced. But . . ."

He sat up abruptly. "John, I'd like to cast my peepers over that case-record, if I may. There may be something there the significance of which has escaped you."

"No reason why I shouldn't show it to you, as long as I've spilled this much," said Minchen in a tired voice.

He dragged himself to his feet and with an absent look began to walk toward the corner of the room behind Dr. Janney's desk.

Ellery chuckled as Minchen tried to squeeze behind Ellery's chair. "Where do you think you're going, professor?"

"Huh?" Minchen looked blank for an instant. Then a grin

stretched his mouth and he scratched his head. He began to re-trace his steps, crossing to the door. "Just goes to show how mud-dle-headed I've become since the old man died. Absolutely forgot that I'd had Janney's files removed from behind his desk there as soon as I got here yesterday and found him murdered. . . ."

"WHAT?"

Years afterward Ellery liked to recall this seemingly innocent scene, at which time, he would say, he experienced "the most dra-matic moment of my nefarious career as a crime-investigator."

In one forgotten incident, in the short space of a single state-ment, the entire Doorn-Janney case assumed a new, a startling complexion.

Minchen remained where he was, dumfounded by the vigor of Ellery's exclamation. He regarded Ellery unbelievingly.

Ellery had flung himself to the floor and was now on his knees behind the swivel-chair, examining the linoleum with minute care. After a moment he rose energetically, smiling even as he wagged his head to say, "Not a trace of the files on the floor. And all because of a new linoleum. Well, that exonerates my powers of observation. . . ."

He rushed across the room and seized Dr. Minchen's shoul-der in an iron grip. "John, you've clinched it! Wait a minute now. . . . Come back in here, man—never mind that blasted case-record!"

Minchen shrugged helplessly and sat down again, watching Ellery with mingled amusement and despair. Ellery strode up and down the room, smoking furiously.

"I gather that here's what happened," he chanted gleefully. "You got here a few moments before I did, found Janney dead, knew the police would be all over the place in no time, and so you decided to spirit away those cherished and valuable records—put 'em where they would be safe. Am I right?"

"Why, yes. But what was wrong in that? I can't see that those files had anything to do—"

"Wrong?" cried Ellery. "You've unwittingly retarded the solution of the case by a full twenty-four hours! You can't see that the filing-cabinet had anything to do with the crimes? Why, John, it's the crux—the crux! Without realizing it, young Sherlock, you nearly wrote 'finis' to my dad's career and my own peace of mind. . . ."

Minchen was gaping. "But—"

"But me no buts, sir. And don't take it to heart. The main thing is that I've discovered the key-clew." Ellery paused in his mad gyrations about the room and regarded Minchen with quizzical brows. He flipped his hand toward the right. "I *told* you there was a window in that corner, John. . . ."

Minchen stupidly followed the line of Ellery's accusing finger.

He saw nothing but the blank wall behind Dr. Janney's desk.

25

SIMPLIFICATION

"GET ME a map of the main floor, John."

Dr. Minchen found himself being carried away by the explosive blast of Ellery's newborn enthusiasm. From a man harassed by sterile speculations, morose, moody, Ellery had become a man transformed—vital, electric, crisp. . . .

Superintendent Paradise himself brought the blueprint plan to the dead surgeon's office. On being pointedly excused, he smiled a sickly smile and backed out of the room, as if Ellery had been royalty.

Ellery paid no attention. Already he had unrolled the map and spread it over the desk; he was tracing with his finger some labyrinthine route which for Dr. Minchen, watching over his companion's shoulder, held nothing but mystery. The physician marveled inwardly at the exclusive concentration of the tall young man. Ellery pored over the blueprint quite as if the world of reality had ceased to exist except in the delineated mazes of the map.

And after long moments, while Dr. Minchen waited patiently, Ellery straightened up not without an expression of peculiar satisfaction, and removed his *pince-nez*.

The blueprint rolled together with a little swirling noise.

Ellery began thoughtfully to stride up and down, tapping his lower lip with the *pince-nez*. He lit a cigarette and his head disappeared in a billow of smoke. "One visit more—one visit more." The words crept out of the cloud. "Ho, John!"

Ellery clapped the physician resoundingly on a shoulder. "If it's possible. . . . If the force of habit—" He stopped and burst into a little chuckle. "If the gods are with us, Jonathan! One morsel of evidence, one tiny scrap. . . . *En avant!*"

He ran out of the office and into the South Corridor, Minchen padding behind. Ellery halted before the door of the Anæsthesia Room and whirled.

"Quick! Let's have the key to the supply cabinet in the Ante-room!" His fingers were impatient.

Minchen produced a bunch of keys. Ellery snatched a proffered key from the physician's hand and hurried into the Anæsthesia Room.

On his way across the room he hastily took a small notebook from his breast pocket and riffled the pages until he found one on which appeared a crude and unrecognizable pencil-drawing. It bore a geometric shape in outline, peculiarly jagged on one edge. This he studied earnestly for a moment, and then he smiled; whereupon without a word he stuffed the notebook back into his pocket, brushed past the policeman at the door, and entered the Anteroom. Minchen followed, wondering.

Ellery made straight for the white supply cabinet He unlocked the glass door with Minchen's key and stood, eyes agleam, scanning the array of narrow drawers before him. Each drawer had a labeled description of its contents in a central metal pocket.

He ran his eye swiftly over the labels. Toward the bottom of the cabinet he read one at which he visibly brightened. He pulled the drawer open and bent over to examine each separate article within. Several times he took something out of the drawer and eyed it closely, but he seemed dissatisfied until he had reached into the shallow receptacle for the fourth time. Then, with a soft exclamation, he retreated from the cabinet, reached into his pocket for the notebook, turned again to the page which bore the strange pencil-drawing, and carefully compared with it the article from the drawer.

He smiled, tucked the notebook back into his pocket, and restored his find to the cabinet. He seemed to think better of this, however, for he again withdrew the article, this time meticulously placing it in a glassine envelope which he put away in his coat.

"I suppose," ventured Dr. Minchen in an exasperated voice, "you've found something important. But it's just so much mumbo-jumbo to me. Why the deuce are you grinning so?"

"It's not a discovery, John—it's a corroboration," replied Ellery soberly. He sat down in one of the Anteroom chairs and swung his legs like a boy. "This is one of the most peculiar cases I've ever encountered.

"Here's a piece of evidence strong enough, I think, to confirm a complicated hypothesis, and yet even if I'd thought of looking for it before this, it wouldn't have done me much good.

"Imagine. It was under my nose all the time, and yet *I had to solve the crime first* before I could suspect the whereabouts of this precious evidence!"

26

EQUATION

EARLY THURSDAY afternoon Ellery Queen might have been observed climbing the steps of the brownstone house on 87th Street, bearing under one arm a bulky package and under the other a long, thin roll of paper. There was a wide smile on his face.

When Djuna heard the rattle of Ellery's key in the lock, he dashed for the apartment door. Flinging it open, he surprised Ellery in the act of thrusting the bulky package behind his back.

"Mr. Ellery! Back so soon? Why'n't you ring?"

"I—ah—" Ellery grinned and leaned against the jamb. "Djuna, tell me. . . . What do you want to be when you grow up?"

Djuna stared. "When I grow up? . . . I wanna be a detective!"

"Know anything about disguising yourself?" asked Ellery in a sharp tone.

The boy's lips fell apart. "No. No, sir. But I c'n learn!"

"That's what I thought," said Ellery, bringing his concealed hand into the light. He thrust the package into the boy's arms. "Here's a little something to start practicing with."

And he strode with dignity into the Queen apartment, leaving behind him a Djuna speechless with stupefaction.

Not two minutes later Djuna came flying into the living-room. "Mr. Ellery!" he cried. "F'r me?"

He deposited the package reverently on the table. He had torn off the paper wrapping; within it was a metal box, its lid raised, displaying a gaudy and most mysterious collection of hair-tufts, chalks, paint-sticks, wigs and numerous other articles of a similar nature.

"For you, young limb." Ellery flung his coat and hat in a corner, leaned over the boy. "For you, Djuna, and it's because you're just about the best detective in the Queen family."

Djuna's face was a canvas of riotous colors.

"If it hadn't been for you," continued Ellery oracularly, pinching the boy's cheek, "and your uncanny suggestion this morning, there would be no solution to the Doorn and Janney cases."

Djuna found his tongue instantly. "Y' got'm?"

"Not yet, but I promise you it won't be long.—Now get out of here with your disguises, and let me think. There's a heap of it before me."

Djuna, trained to the vagaries of the Queen temperaments, disappeared into the kitchen like Aladdin's genie.

Ellery spread the long roll of paper on the table. It was the blueprint which Superintendent Paradise had brought him in the Hospital. Cigarette drooping from his mouth, he studied the map again for a long time.

Occasionally he scribbled his cryptic notes on the margin of the diagram.

Something seemed to perplex him. He began an endless pacing about the room, smoking innumerable cigarettes. The map lay forgotten on the table. His forehead was damp, white-lined, corrugated.

Djuna stole in shyly. He presented a fearsome aspect. On his black curly hair he sported a glaringly crimson wig. A sandy van dyke beard hung from his chin. A ferocious black mustache trailed beneath his nose. To complete the hirsute decoration of his features, his eyebrows spurted heavy grey patches, not unlike those of the Inspector. Rouge reddened his cheeks; black pencil had rimmed his eyes until they resembled the legendary orbs of Svengali.

He stood hopefully by the table, attempting to catch Ellery's eye.

Ellery stopped short, a look of utter amazement spreading over his face. The surprise vanished; his face assumed a grave, even apprehensive, expression.

In a slightly quavering voice he asked, "Who are you? How did you get in here?"

Djuna's eyes popped. "Why—Mr. Ellery—it's me!"

"What!" Ellery retreated a step. "Get out," he whispered hoarsely. "You're fooling me . . . Djuna—that's not really *you?*"

"Sure it's me!" cried Djuna in triumph. He whipped off the mustache and beard.

"I'll be eternally switched!" murmured Ellery, and the laughter which had been lurking in his eyes sparkled clear. "Come here, imp!"

He sat down in the Inspector's big armchair and drew the boy to him. "Djuna," he said solemnly, "the case is quite solved. All but one thing."

"Shucks."

"I echo that delightful sentiment—shucks." Ellery's frown crept back. "I could put my hand on the criminal today—the one and only person who could have committed both murders. I have a perfect, an airtight case. But that one stubborn little point. . . ."

He was talking to himself more than to Djuna. "One little point. Peculiarly enough, it doesn't affect the capture in the slightest, and yet I won't know everything until I learn the answer to . . ." His voice trailed off startlingly as he sat up with half-closed eyes, pushing Djuna from him.

"By heaven," he said quietly. "I've got it."

He leaped from the chair and vanished within the bedroom. Djuna followed him quickly.

Ellery tore the telephone from the night-table and rapped a number into the instrument. . . .

"Pete Harper! . . . Pete. Listen carefully. . . . Don't ask questions. Just listen.

"Pete, if you'll do what I ask now I promise you a bigger story than the one you got the other day. . . . You heard me! Pencil and paper ready? And for the love of your eternal soul, don't breathe a word of this to any one. *Any* one, do you hear? It's not for publication until I say so.

"Now, I want you to go down to the . . ."

CHALLENGE
To the Reader

At this point in the story of THE DUTCH SHOE MYSTERY, *according to a precedent I created in the first of my detective novels several years ago, I inject a* Challenge to the Reader . . . *maintaining with perfect sincerity that the reader is now in possession of* all the pertinent facts *essential to the correct solution of the Doorn and Janney murders. . . .*

By the exercise of strict logic and irrefutable deductions from given data, it should be simple for the reader to name at this point the murderer of Abigail Doorn and Dr. Francis Janney. I say simple advisedly. Actually it is not simple; the deductions are natural, but they require sharp and unflagging thought.

Remember that knowledge of the article which the author extracted from the cabinet in the Anteroom, and of the information which the author gave to Harper over the telephone in the preceding chapter is not necessary to the solution . . . although if you have correctly followed the logic you may deduce what the article was, and with less certainty, what the information was.

To avoid any charge of unfairness I submit the following refutation: that I myself deduced the answer before going to the cabinet and before *telephoning Harper.*

—Ellery Queen

PART THREE

Discovery of a Document

"Every man who has spent his life in the pursuit of criminals has amassed, by the time he has reached his doddering retrospective years, the visible evidences of a phobia. . . . I know a detective whose rooms are heaped with lethal weapons, and another who surrounds himself with fingerprint records. . . . My own weakness has been the collection of paper—*paper of all sizes, shapes, colors and uses—but all, too, bound together by their common source: i.e., their significance in a criminal case. . . .*

"You will find among my treasures, for example, that precious scrap of yellow pasteboard from a study of which I was able to determine that Rezillos, the Brazilian slayer of nineteen people, had headed for Guiana. And the half-burned cigar-band which led to the apprehension of that queer maniac called Peter-Peter, the renegade Englishman of Martinique. . . . I have in my files complete case-histories which revolve upon such innocent-appearing paper-items as a pawnticket, a twenty-year-old insurance notice, a pricetag of a woman's cheap cloth coat, a little packet of cigarette-papers, and an interesting one which is perhaps the prize of my collection. . . .

"When it was found it seemed merely a water-soaked, absolutely blank piece of once heavy paper, with no apparent trace of writing or printing. It was so wet that we barely managed to keep the fibers together. . . . And this innocuous scrap turned out to be the clew which hanged the greatest pirate of the twentieth century.

"It was an old whiskey-label, chemical analysis of which disclosed it to have been immersed in the salty waters of the ocean . . ."

—from A Sleuth's Syllabus
—by Bartholomew Tean
Melbourne, Australia

27

CLARIFICATION

PHILIP MOREHOUSE
Attorney-at-Law

Friday, January —

Inspector Richard Queen
No. — 8/th Street
New York

By messenger

DEAR INSPECTOR QUEEN:

I am writing this at the special request of Mr. Ellery Queen, with whom I conversed this morning over the telephone.

Mr. Queen advised me that he was entirely familiar with certain personal secrets whose facts were not in possession of the police until he learned of them from Dr. John Minchen, of the Dutch Memorial Hospital, yesterday.

Since the secret is out, there is no longer any reason for silence or evasion on my part, and I take this opportunity to clarify such points of the Dunning-Fuller story as may still be unexplained or unclear.

Before I proceed, however, allow me to take the liberty of re-

254 · ELLERY QUEEN

minding you of Mr. Ellery Queen's personal assurance to me this morning. He said that every precaution would be taken to keep the story of Hulda Doorn's true parentage out of the papers and even, if it were possible, out of your police files.

The documents which were ordered destroyed by Mrs. Doorn's will were in substance a personal diary kept by my client during the years surrounding the events herein described, and taken up again some five years ago, from which time it was religiously kept.

Mr. Queen shrewdly guessed that I had exceeded my legal authority on Monday when, instead of destroying the envelope without breaking its seals, as legal ethics demanded, I had opened it and read its contents.

Inspector Queen, I have been practicing law for a long time now and I have faithfully, I think, upheld the integrity of my father's business reputation; especially in the case of Mrs. Doorn, a friend as well as a client, and always to her very best interests. If Mrs. Doorn had died a natural death I should never have breached my legal trust. But her murder, combined with the fact that I was—and am now—engaged to be married to Miss Doorn with the full consent of her deceased foster-mother, so that I am really a member of the Doorn family—forced me to open the envelope and investigate its contents. If I had turned it over to the police before opening it, personal facts absolutely unrelated to the murder would have come out. So I opened it myself, assuming the position of a member of the family rather than its attorney, with the mental reservation that if anything in the documents seemed to relate to the crime I would place them in your hands.

But when, on reading the diary, I discovered the awful facts surrounding Hulda's birth . . . Inspector, can you blame me for withholding the information and destroying the diary? Not for my-self—the shame means nothing to me—but think of what it would mean to such an untainted young girl as Hulda to have the world know that she is the illegitimate child of her own housekeeper.

There is only one other item in this connection . . . which may be verified by consulting the will now filed for probate. That is, that Hulda inherits the major portion of the Doorn estate with no reservations of birth or parentage, but rather as the legal daughter of Abigail Doorn, which she is. Her true parentage can in no way affect the bequest to her. Consequently, my reticence regarding the whole shameful story cannot be construed as having been animated by selfish motives, such as might be ascribed to me if Hulda's inheritance hinged upon her being a blood relation of the deceased. . . .

Mr. Queen was also correct in his surmise that Abigail and Sarah Fuller quarreled incessantly over the secret of Hulda's birth. The diary stated specifically that Sarah had regretted her bargain, and that she was perpetually threatening to disclose her mother-hood unless the girl were returned to her. With the passage of the years Abigail had grown to regard Hulda with genuine maternal love; and it was only her fear that Sarah would tell the story to the world that prevented her from discharging the middle-aged and by now fanatical woman in her employ.

Since the death of Mrs. Doorn I have confidentially spoken with Sarah Fuller and have received her positive assurance, now that Abigail—the object of her hate—is dead, and that I, whom for no reason that I can see she likes, am to marry Hulda—that she will not reveal the secret. Dr. Dunning for selfish reasons may be depended upon to keep his mouth shut; his entire career and reputation depend upon his silence.

It is not difficult to guess, as Mr. Ellery Queen did, that it was this matter of Hulda's parentage and the course they should adopt which caused Sarah Fuller to seek out Dr. Dunning at various times in the past few days. Strangely enough, she bears him no ill will. The crazy whims of a crazy woman! She told me yesterday that they discussed the matter from every angle; and with a shy pride announced that Dunning had persuaded her to let the girl live out her life thinking she was a Doorn.

Another matter disclosed by the diary was important in that it described Dr. Janney's part in the affair. As you may or may not be aware, Dr. Janney was Mrs. Doorn's confidant at all times; particularly since he was one of the handful who knew the real facts of Hulda's birth. Dr. Janney's attitude, the diary stated in one place, toward Dunning was quite unaffected by his knowledge of Dunning's virtual rape; it seems that Dunning got by with the worldly view that a man may be forgiven sowing his wild oats. At any rate, Janney often upbraided Sarah for her trouble-making propensities, her willingness to ruin Hulda's life merely to satisfy her own thwarted maternal instincts. Queer, isn't it? Perhaps his broad-minded attitude toward Dunning was due to his honest admiration of Dunning's ability professionally and his own sophistication.

In every sense of the word, Dr. Janney was a friend of Mrs. Doorn's. He defended her every action; there was never the slightest hint of disaffection or disloyalty between them.

Please pardon me if I renew my plea for your silence. Not for myself; I think you know that. But for the sake of Hulda, who to me is everything worth living for.

Sincerely,

PHILIP MOREHOUSE.

P.S.: I should greatly appreciate your destroying this letter, of which there are no duplicates, as soon as you have read it.

P.M.

The only other incident of that serene Friday which Inspector Queen afterward had reason to recall, was a telephone message for Ellery Queen at 6:30 Friday evening.

Ellery's attitude in the past twenty-four hours had subtly altered. He no longer chafed, nor did he pace the floor with the fierce absent energy which had characterized his movements during the hectic days before.

All day Friday he remained at the living-room window, reading and, for one interval of two hours, typing at his creaky, cranky old machine. Inspector Queen, who flew into the apartment at noon for a hasty luncheon and a telephone consultation with various subordinates at Headquarters, peered over his son's shoulder and saw that Ellery was writing away at a detective novel—one which had been begun long months before but which had been tossed aside and neglected during a fitful period enduring for weeks.*

The old man grunted, but there was a smile beneath his grey mustache. It was a good sign. He had not seen his son wear such an air of detachment and peace in many moons.

The eventful telephone call came just after the Inspector had reappeared in the apartment after another barren afternoon. Lines of discouragement lengthened his face. They dissolved and his features stiffened into an intent mask as he heard Ellery's voice from the bedroom.

It was an excited voice—a fresh and joyous voice—such a voice as Ellery employed only at rare intervals.

---

* The manuscript of *Murder of the Marionettes,* one of the detective stories Ellery wrote under his own name.—J. J. McC.

The Inspector closed the outer door softly and stood listening, scarcely breathing.

"Pete! Where are you?" At first there was a note of anxiety. Then the voice deepened, grew gay. "Marvelous! Marvelous, Pete! Connecticut, eh? Reasonable enough. . . . Hard time? Well, no matter. . . . Good man! Guard it with your life. You got the paper? Great! . . . Well, no. Make a copy and let me have it the moment you return to town—three o'clock in the morning, if necessary. I'll be waiting up for you. . . . Right. Hurry!"

The Inspector heard the crash of the receiver and Ellery's strong voice shouting, "Djuna! It's over!"

"What's over?" demanded the old man as Ellery bounded into the living-room.

"Oh, dad!" Ellery grasped his father's arm and shook it gently. "My case is complete. *Finis.* Pete Harper—"

"Pete Harper, eh?" The Inspector was grim. Lines of fatigue bordered his old mouth. "And if you had work for somebody, why didn't you let my boys take care of it?"

"Now, dad," chuckled Ellery, forcing the old man into the arm-chair, "you should know better than to ask that question. There was a reason—case wasn't complete. And I didn't want the official mark on the work Pete did for me. If it hadn't worked out there would have been a lot of explaining to do. . . .

"It's all over but the shouting. When Pete gets here tonight and delivers to me that very interesting document. . . . A *leetle* more patience, sire."

"All right, son." The old man looked tired. He lay back in the chair and closed his eyes. "I'm due for a rest. . . ." The wise old eyes flew open. "You didn't seem particularly pleased about these murders twenty-four hours ago."

Ellery raised his long arms in mock adoration of an invisible idol. "But I wasn't successful then!" he cried. "And to-day I am. For—to quote the irrepressible Disraeli—'Success is the child of audacity'—and I have been so audacious in my reasoning, good father, as even you would not believe. . . . Hereafter I'll follow as a blessed rule the Gallic precept of *Toujours Audace!*"

28

ARGUMENTATION

ALWAYS, TOWARD the climax of a case, the tension which the Queens inevitably experienced communicated itself to the atmosphere of their apartment. It was something in the air—an effluvium of excitement which they neither controlled nor concealed, revealing itself in the jumpiness of Djuna, the silent irritability of the Inspector, the vigorous certainty of Ellery.

Ellery had summoned his father's cronies to solemn conclave. His plans were shrouded in mist and mystery. If during the darkness of Friday night he had confided to his father something of what was in his mind, neither father nor son revealed the confidence. Nor did either refer to the incident of Pete Harper's nonchalant appearance at their door at 2:30 A.M. Saturday morning. Perhaps the Inspector was unaware of the reporter's nocturnal visit; he had been tossing on his bed when Ellery, in dressing-gown and slippers, admitted Harper to the apartment, gave him a stiff drink of whisky and a handful of cigarettes, took from him a slim crackling document and packed him off, bleary-eyed but imperturbable, to his own rooms.

On Saturday afternoon at 2:00 o'clock Inspector Queen and Ellery Queen entertained two guests at luncheon—District Attorney Sampson and Sergeant Velie. Djuna, lips parted, hovered about them.

Sampson's eyes accused Ellery. "There's something in the wind."

"A veritable tornado," smiled Ellery. "Drink your *café*, Honorable D.A. We are about to embark on a voyage of discovery."

"You mean—it's all over?" Sampson was incredulous.

"Nor more nor less." Ellery turned to Sergeant Velie. "Did you get that report of Kneisel's contacts during the past day or so?"

"Sure, Mike." The giant tossed a sheet of paper across the table. Ellery scanned it with half-closed eyes. Then he tossed it back. "Well, it doesn't matter now."

He slumped in his chair and rested in his favorite position— on the nape of his neck. He regarded the ceiling dreamily. "It's been a fascinating chase," he murmured. "Involved some pretty points—some pretty points indeed. I don't know when I've enjoyed myself more thoroughly—I mean after it was all over." He grinned.

"I shan't tell you the answer yet. . . . Some of my reasoning was complicated, and I want to see what dad, or you, Sampson, or you, Velie, make of it.

"Let's see what we have in the first murder. Well, in the case of Abigail Doorn, there were two extraordinarily fat clews. And so innocent-appearing! Just a pair of white canvas shoes, for one thing, and a pair of white duck trousers, for the other."

"What of them?" grumbled Sampson. "They were both interesting, I'll admit, but to base a whole prosecution on 'em—"

"What of them, indeed?" Ellery closed his eyes completely. "Let's see what you do with them when I bring out some salient items.

"We found a pair of shoes. There were three significant features in these shoes: the broken lace, the adhesive on the lace, and the tongues smoothed up inside to the top of the toe-box.

"On the surface, the explanation seems elementary. The broken lace connotes an accident, the adhesive connotes a repair, and the back-flapped tongues connote—what?"

Sampson fiercely bunched his brows. Gigantic Velie merely seemed bewildered. The Inspector wore a look of concentration. None of the three uttered a sound.

"No answer? You don't see the logical reasoning?" Ellery sighed. "Well, we'll let it go at that. Except to add that it was these three items from the impostor's shoes which gave me the first— and in its way the most important—indication of the truth."

"Say," said Velie hoarsely, "you mean to tell me, Mr. Queen, you knew right then and there who pulled the job?"

"Velie, good and earnest soul," smiled Ellery, "I aver nothing of the kind. But I do say that from analysis of the shoe-points, and from a most illuminating point gleaned from the trousers, my field of speculation narrowed to a gratifying degree. So amazingly so that I could have told you a good deal about the criminal's general description.

"As for the trousers, surely it must have struck you how interesting and informative were those basted stitches above the knees, and the very presence of the trousers at all. . . ."

"Aside from showing that the original owner of the pants, whoever he was," said the Inspector wearily, "was taller than the impostor who stole 'em—thereby making it necessary for the impostor to shorten the legs—I can't see anything eye-opening about the trousers."

Sampson decapitated the head of a cigar, savagely. "I must be the world's prize cluck," he said. "I simply can't see one conclusive theory so far."

"*Miserere,*" murmured Ellery. "And a couple of *Kol Nidres.* To proceed. We reach the second murder, wherein our late and lamented friend the good leech was summarily removed from the ken of men. . . .

"Here again permit me to be categorical. Before a certain eventuality occurred, there was only one point which stood out. And that was—the *condition* in which Janney was found."

"Condition?" Sampson was puzzled.

"Yes. The evidence offered by the simple fact of Janney's post-humous facial appearance. You will recall that he was murdered obviously in the midst of his work—on the *Congenital Aller-gy* manuscript. The expression of his face was as serene as if he had died in his sleep. No surprise, no horror, no apprehension of death.

"Link this with the wound which stunned him and its specific location on his body—and you have a damnably intriguing situation.

"A situation which grew even more intriguing when the second clew presented itself."

"It doesn't intrigue me," said Sampson. He seemed to be in a disagreeable mood.

"Waived, sir." Ellery smiled again. "The second clew. . . . Ah, the second clew! There's fate for you, *messieurs.* Dr. Minchen's removal of the filing-cabinet which contained Janney's case-re-cords—knowledge, light, my case was complete. So beautiful, so snugly mortised! And how closely I came to missing it altogether through Minchen's overdeveloped sense of property value. . . .

"Had the second crime never been committed, the murderer of Mrs. Doorn must have gone scot-free. With all humility I sub-mit the confession that if Janney hadn't met his Maker as he did I should be helpless to-day. Only by solving the mystery of Janney's demise was I able to retrace the astounding story of how Mrs. Doorn was murdered."

Inspector Queen dipped his fingers into his snuff-box. "I'm afraid I'm as dense as friend Henry thinks he is," he said. "As usual when you're 'explaining' a solution without making a darned thing clear, I feel like the feller who's told a joke, doesn't see the point, and laughs anyway to save his face. . . . El, just what is the meaning of that filing-cabinet? From what you say it's almost as important to you as those shoes, although I can't see *that* either. Just how does the cabinet clinch the case?"

Ellery chuckled. "Whereupon we embark upon the voyage of discovery which I predicted a moment ago. The time has come, and so on." He rose and leaned over the table. "I must admit my pulse is far from normal at the prospect. And I can promise all of you a most delightful surprise. . . . Get your things on, boys, while I call the Hospital."

They shook their heads at each other as Ellery strode into the bedroom. They heard him call the number of the Hospital.

"Dr. Minchen. . . . John? This is Ellery Queen. I'm going to conduct a little laboratory experiment, and I require the wherewithal. . . . Yes, a little job for you. . . . Fine! Have Dr. Janney's filing-cabinet restored to his office. And placed in precisely its old and accustomed position. . . . Is that clear? . . . Yes, at once. I'm leaving for your sacred stamping-ground with a small but distinguished party in two shakes of a whisker. Good-bye!"

29

TERMINATION

DR. JOHN Minchen, pale and curious, was waiting at the door of Dr. Janney's office—a policeman on stolid guard at his side—when Ellery, Inspector Queen, the District Attorney, Sergeant Velie and, incredibly, a trembling hot-eyed Djuna walked rapidly into the Dutch Memorial Hospital.

For all of Ellery's vaunted suavity, he was patently the most excited of the group, Djuna not excepted. Two red spots burned in his dark cheeks, and his eyes glittered—liquid and lively.

He herded them into the office impatiently, pushing the muscular policeman out of his way with scant ceremony and, as an afterthought, a clipped apology.

Minchen, quiet, sad, introspective, merely looked at his friend.

Ellery gripped the physician's biceps. "John! I need some one to take a bit of stenographic dictation. Who . . . ? Oh, yes. That nurse. Dr. Janney's assistant. Lucille Price. Get her for me immediately, there's a good fellow."

He dashed into the office as Minchen hurried away.

The Inspector was rooted in the center of the room, hands folded behind his back. "What now, you stage manager?" he asked mildly. There was a rueful gleam far back in his eyes. "I can't see the cabinet's made any difference."

Ellery glanced over at the corner of the room behind the dead surgeon's desk. A single green-steel filing-cabinet now stood directly behind it, across the right-angle made by the meeting walls. In this way it was exactly parallel to the desk.

"Velie," drawled Ellery, "you're the only one of us, to my knowledge, who was in the room *before* the murder of Dr. Janney. Remember? It was during the preliminary examination of Mrs. Doorn's death, and you came here to search Janney's office for his address-book. On the Swanson trail."

"That's right, Mr. Queen."

"Do you recall seeing this cabinet?"

The giant rumbled reproachfully, "Sure do. It's my business, Mr. Queen. Even tried to open the drawers, thinkin' the address-book might be in the cabinet. But it was locked. I didn't mention it, anyway, because these drawers were marked with cards—they're there now, I see—tellin' what's in each one. Didn't look likely that book was there."

"Very naturally." Ellery lit a cigarette with flying fingers. "And was the cabinet in *exactly* the position it's in now?"

"Yep."

"Were the corners of the desk as close to the wall as they are now?"

"That's the ticket, Mr. Queen. I remember the corners were so near the wall over on that side that I could only get behind the desk on the side nearer the window. Even then it was a tight squeeze."

"Excellent! That checks. I might say, Velie," said Ellery with an unoffending grin, "that by omitting to mention the existence and position of the cabinet you missed your great opportunity for undying fame. Of course, you couldn't have known. . . . Ah, come in, John. Come in, Miss Price."

Dr. Minchen stepped aside to allow the trimly uniformed Lucille Price to enter. When they had both stepped over the threshold Ellery crossed the room quickly and closed the door.

"*Nous commençons,*" he said in a cheerful voice. He returned to the center of the room, rubbing his hands. "Miss Price, I want you to sit at your desk and take more notes for us. That's right" The nurse sat down and, unlocking the top drawer of her small desk, extracted a notebook and a pencil; she waited quietly.

Ellery waved at his father. "Dad, I'd be obliged if you will sit in Dr. Janney's swivel-chair." The Inspector obeyed with a faint smile. Ellery clapped the big sergeant's back with vigor, motioning him to take his stand by the door. "Sampson, you might sit— here." Ellery pulled a chair forward from the west wall and the District Attorney seated himself without a word. "Djuna, old son." The boy was breathing hard with excitement. "You're naturally in on this. You stand over by the bookcase, where you'll be close to Sergeant Velie's huge and protective wings." Djuna scuttled across the room and stood in precisely the spot indicated, as if by standing one inch farther to the right he would have completely upset Ellery's plans. "John. You might sit down beside District Attorney Sampson." The physician obeyed. "And now we're ready. The stage is set. Old spider's waiting with figuratively dripping jaws, and if I'm not mistaken we'll have the unsuspecting fly quicker than quick!"

Ellery dragged the large chair on the east wall to a commanding position in the office, sat down, adjusted his *pince-nez* with annoying deliberation, slumped in the chair and with a sigh stretched his legs.

"Ready, Miss Price?"

"Yes, sir."

"Very well. Take a memorandum to the Police Commissioner of the City of New York. Address it 'Dear Commissioner.' Got
that?"

"Yes, sir."

"Sub-head. 'From Inspector Richard Queen *re*'—indicate ital-
icization by underlining that, Miss Price—'*re* Murder of Mrs. Abigail Doorn and Dr. Francis Janney.' Message. 'I have the extreme
honor and pleasure to report—'"

At this moment, when the only sounds in the room were the
slow even words of Ellery, the scratch of the nurse's pencil and the
heavy breathing of Ellery's audience, there came a sharp rap on
the door.

Ellery's head jerked toward Velie. "See who it is."

The sergeant opened the door a few inches and growled,
"Well?"

A male voice said uncertainly, "Is Dr. Minchen in there? Dr.
Dunning wants to see him in his office."

Velie looked at Ellery with a question in his eyes. Ellery turned
to Dr. Minchen and asked mockingly, "Would you like to leave,
John? Dunning evidently needs you badly."

The physician gripped the arms of his chair, half rose. "Well—
do you think I ought to—?"

"Suit yourself. I think there will be a most diverting enter-
tainment enacted here in a moment or so which you shouldn't
miss. . . ."

Minchen muttered, "Tell him I'm busy." He sank back.

Velie shut the door in the man's face.

"Who was it, Velie?" inquired Ellery.

"This guy Cobb, the doorman."

"Oh!" Ellery leaned back again. "To proceed, Miss Price, from the point where we were so rudely interrupted. What did I dictate?"

The girl read in a clear rapid voice, "'Memorandum to the Police Commissioner of the City of New York. From Inspector Richard Queen *re* Murder of Mrs. Abigail Doorn and Dr. Francis Janney. Dear Commissioner: I have the extreme honor and pleasure to report—'"

"'—that both of the abovementioned cases are now solved. Mrs. Doorn and Dr. Francis Janney were murdered by the same assailant. For reasons which I shall explain later, in my regular detailed report—'"

Ellery jumped to his feet as another knock sounded on the door. His face flamed. "Who is that, for the love of heaven?" he cried. "Velie, keep that door closed. I don't want these confounded interruptions!"

Velie opened the door a few inches, thrust his ham-like hand out into the corridor, gestured pointedly and briefly, and withdrawing his hand slammed the door.

"This here Dr. Gold," he said. "To hell with him."

"Verily." Ellery jabbed his finger at the nurse. "Continue, 'For reasons which I shall explain later, in my regular detailed report, I shall not go into the matters of motive and method in this memorandum.' Paragraph, Miss Price. 'The killer of Mrs. Doorn and Dr. Janney is—'"

Again Ellery paused, and this time there was no faintest whisper of sound in the office. "One moment. I forgot. There's a bit of information I must include here—it's on that Fuller-Dunning case-history of Janney's. . . . Miss Price, please get me that report before we continue."

"Certainly, Mr. Queen."

The nurse rustled crisply out of her swivel-chair and, placing her notebook and pencil on her typewriter, crossed the room to Dr. Janney's desk.

"Pardon me—?" she murmured.

Inspector Queen muttered something beneath his breath and hitched his chair forward to allow her to pass behind him, between desk and wall. She brushed past the old man, took a small key from her starched apron-pocket and bent over, inserting the key into the lock of the bottom drawer of the filing-cabinet.

The room was still as death. The Inspector did not turn his head; his fingers were playing with a glass paperweight. Velie, Sampson, Minchen and Djuna watched the girl's businesslike movements with varying expressions of tension and befuddlement

She straightened up with a blue-bound sheaf of papers in her hand and, again brushing past the Inspector, handed the case-history to Ellery. She returned quietly to her seat and poised her pencil over the notebook.

Ellery lay comfortably in his chair, smoke dribbling from his lips. Mechanically his fingers flipped the pages of the blue-bound report, but his shuttered eyes were boring into the eyes of his father, sitting behind the dead man's desk. A communication was born and sparked across the space between them. Something leaped into the Inspector's face—an expression of intelligence, of amazement, of purpose. It died almost instantly, leaving the old man grim-lipped and lined.

Ellery smiled. "I have an idea," he drawled, "that Inspector Richard Queen has just made an important discovery. Leave it to the Queens!" The Inspector shifted restlessly. "Dad, how would you like to complete the dictation of this memorandum to the Police Commissioner?"

"I believe I shall," said the Inspector in a cool placid voice. He rose from the swivel-chair, squeezed by the desk and, crossing the room, set his knuckles on the nurse's typewriter.

"Take this, Miss Price," he said, and his eyes were bright and dangerous. "'The killer of Mrs. Doorn and Dr. Janney is—' grab her, Thomas!—'Lucille Price!'"

30

EXPLANATION

THE LATE afternoon editions of the newspapers shrieked the news that Lucille Price, trained nurse and secretarial assistant to the late Dr. Francis Janney, had been apprehended for the murders of her employer and the mighty Abigail Doorn.

Nothing else.

For there was nothing else to write.

The managing editor of every sheet in New York City had asked his crime-reporters the same question: "Is this on the level, or is it another gag like that Swanson-arrest thing?"

The reply in each case but one was: "Don't know."

The exception was the reply of Pete Harper, who hurled himself into his editor's office and was closeted there for half an hour, talking, talking, talking.

And when he had gone, his managing editor with trembling hands picked up from his desk a thick bundle of typewritten sheets and began to read. His eyes popped. He shouted orders into his battery of telephones.

As for Harper, his precious scoop assured by the knowledge that he, and he only, had the whole story ready to roll off the cylinder-presses the instant he received Ellery Queen's permission—Harper jumped into a taxicab and was borne rapidly away in the direction of Police Headquarters.

His thirty-six hour quest for Ellery Queen had blossomed into golden fruit.

The District Attorney's Office was in an uproar.

After a hurried conference with Timothy Cronin, his assistant, District Attorney Sampson slipped out of his office, eluded a yelling pack of reporters, and clawed his way down the street toward Police Headquarters.

At City Hall hell had broken loose. The Mayor, locked in his office with a squad of secretaries, was pacing the floor like a rampant tiger—dictating, commanding, answering telephone calls from City officials. Beads of sweat dripped from his crimson face.

"Long distance. Governor calling."

"Give me that!" The Mayor ripped the instrument from his desk. "Hello! Hello, Governor. . . ." And presto! his voice calmed, his face assumed its well-publicized Washingtonian air, and he bounced a little on the tips of his toes in that jaunty manner known to millions of movie-going citizens. "Well, it's all over. . . . True enough. The Price woman did it. . . . I know, Governor, I know. She hasn't appeared in the case much. Slickest thing in my experience. . . . Five days—not so bad, eh?—five days to wipe up two of the most sensational murders in the City's history! . . . I'll 'phone the details later. . . . Thank you, Governor!"

Respectful silence as he hung up. And again the beads of sweat dripped, and again the snarled orders came as his feet stopped bouncing and his face lost its dignity. "Damn it! Where's the Commissioner? Try his office again! What's behind all this?

My God, am I the only man in New York City who doesn't know what it's all about?"

"Yes, Mr. Mayor. . . . Sorry I couldn't get to the 'phone sooner. Grilling our catch. Busy—very busy. Ha, ha! . . . No, I can't give you any details now. Everything's all right, though. Nothing to worry about. . . . Price woman hasn't confessed yet. She just won't talk. . . . No, that's just a temporary stubbornness. She's playing safe. Doesn't know how much we know. . . . Oh, yes! Inspector Queen's promised me that she'll talk before the day is out. It's in the bag. . . . What? . . . Certainly! Most interesting case. Has some very *nice* points of interest. . . . Yes. Ha, ha! Good-by."

And the Police Commissioner of New York City replaced the receiver on its hook and subsided like a sack of meal in his chair.

"Hell," he said weakly to an aide, "Queen might have given me *some* idea of what it's all about."

Two minutes later he was in the corridor, mopping his brow with a glare in his eyes and walking furtively toward Inspector Queen's office.

Inspector Queen's office was the calmest official spot in New York that day. The old man sat his chair like a bareback rider, droning quiet orders into his inter-office communicator and in odd moments dictating to a stenographer.

Ellery lounged in a chair by the window, eating an apple. He seemed at peace with the world.

Djuna squatted on the floor at Ellery's feet, engaged in annihilating a bar of chocolate.

A steady stream of detectives passed through the office.

A plainclothesman lurched in. "Hulda Doorn wants to see you, Chief. Shall I let 'er in?"

The Inspector leaned back. "Hulda Doorn, hey? All right. Stick around, Bill. It'll only take a minute."

The detective reëntered almost at once with Hulda Doorn. The girl was dressed in black—an attractive supple figure pink-cheeked with excitement. Her fingers trembled as she grasped the Inspector's coat-sleeve.

"Inspector Queen!"

Djuna dutifully rose and Ellery uncoiled his length from his chair, still munching his apple.

"Sit down, Miss Doorn," said the Inspector kindly. "I'm glad to see you looking so well. . . . What can I do for you?"

Her lips quivered. "I wanted to—I mean I—" She stopped in confusion.

The Inspector smiled. "I suppose you've heard the news?"

"Oh, yes! I think it—it's all so ghastly," she said in her clear girlish voice, "and so wonderful that you've caught that—that awful, terrible woman." She shuddered. "I can hardly believe it yet. Why, she used to come to our house with Dr. Janney sometimes, to help him treat mother. . . ."

"She's guilty, Miss Doorn. Now what . . ."

"Why—I hardly know where to begin." She fumbled with the gloves in her lap. "It's about Philip. Philip Morehouse, my *fiancé.*"

"And what about Philip Morehouse, your *fiancé?*" asked the Inspector gently.

Her lids flew wide, and the large liquid eyes pleaded with the Inspector. "I'm worried about—well, about the way you threatened Philip the other day, Inspector Queen. You know—about those papers he destroyed. You don't really intend, now that you've got the real criminal . . ."

"Hmm! I see." The old man patted the girl's hand. "If that's what's worrying your pretty head, my dear, forget all about it. Mr.

Morehouse acted—let's say injudiciously, and I was very angry. I'm not any more. We'll let it go at that."

"Oh, thank you!" Her face brightened.

The door burst open and the detective called Bill was propelled into the room by a violent shove from without. Philip Morehouse ran in, his eyes searching. On seeing Hulda Doorn, he stepped to her side, put his hand on her shoulder, and glowered fiercely at the Inspector. "What are you doing with Miss Doorn?" Morehouse growled. "Hulda—they told me you'd come here—what are they doing to you?"

"Why, Philip!" She twisted out of the chair and his arms tightened about her waist. They looked into each other's eyes, and suddenly both smiled. The Inspector frowned, Ellery sighed and Djuna's mouth flew open.

"Excuse me if I—" There was no immediate response. The Inspector barked, "Bill, get out of here! Can't you see the young lady's well taken care of?" The detective tramped out, rubbing his shoulder. "And now, Miss Doorn—Mr. Morehouse—as much as we thoroughly enjoy seeing you two young people happy, and all that, please remember that this is a police-office. . . ."

Fifteen minutes later the Inspector's office presented a different picture.

Chairs had been set around the desk, and in them were seated District Attorney Sampson, the Police Commissioner and Pete Harper. Djuna perched on the edge of a chair directly behind the Police Commissioner; surreptitiously he was touching the Commissioner's coat as if it were a talisman.

Ellery and Dr. Minchen stood by the window talking in low tones. "I suppose the Hospital's a good deal of a bedlam, John?"

"It's awful." Minchen seemed dazed. "Nobody knows what to

do, or what to say. The place is thoroughly disorganized. . . . Lucille Price, of all people! It's—why, it's incredible."

"Ah, but that's the unhabitual murderer's greatest psychological defense," murmured Ellery. "Rochefoucauld's epigram: 'Innocence finds not near so much protection as guilt—' was based on a universal truth. . . . By the way, how did our metallurgical friend Kneisel take the news?"

The physician grimaced. "As you might expect. The man's not human. Far from showing elation at the thought that now he's got more than enough to finish his damned experiments, or feeling badly about his co-worker's death, he simply goes about his business, locked up in that laboratory, as if neither murder nor sympathy existed. He's as cold-blooded as a—as a snake."

"Not in the grass, I hope?" chuckled Ellery. "Nevertheless," he continued, half to himself, "I'm willing to wager that he's relieved that a certain theory of his was proved erroneous. I wonder if his alloy theory isn't just as fantastic. . . . Incidentally, I hadn't realized before that the ophidians are cold-blooded. Thanks for the information!"

"I want to go on record," said Ellery a short time later, when Minchen was seated and the Inspector had waived his right to take the floor, "with the blanket-statement that, in all the years in which I've taken a more or less active interest in my father's cases, I've never encountered a more thoroughly planned crime than the murder of Abigail Doorn.

"It's a little difficult to know where to begin. . . . I suppose the same unbelieving thought has crossed all your minds—how it was possible for Lucille Price, whose presence in the Anteroom was attested by a number of reliable witnesses—Dr. Byers, Grace Obermann the nurse, and the doubtful gentleman known as 'Big

Mike'—witnesses who at the same time vouched for the presence of Dr. Janney's impersonator—I say, how it was *possible* for Lucille Price to have been two distinct personalities at apparently the identical moment."

There was a vigorous nodding of heads.

"That she was, you now know," continued Ellery; "how she accomplished this spiritistic feat I'll tell you by analysis.

"Consider the amazing situation. Lucille Price was Lucille Price, the trained nurse, dutifully watching over Abby Doorn's unconscious body in the Anteroom. Yet she was also the seemingly masculine figure of Dr. Janney's impersonator in the same period. Unimpeachable witnesses swore that two people occupied the Anteroom (I mean omitting Mrs. Doorn)—a nurse and a doctor. The nurse was heard talking. The doctor was seen going in and coming out. How could any one dream that both nurse and doctor were one, that Lucille Price's original story concerning herself as the nurse, and the impostor as the doctor, was anything but the absolute truth? Now that it's all over, and we know what actually happened, we can put our finger on the significant feature which makes a seemingly impossible series of circumstances not only possible but plausible—that is, that while the nurse was heard *she was not seen;* and that while the impostor was seen, *he was not heard.*"

Ellery sipped at a glass of water. "But this is beginning the wrong way. Before telling you how Lucille Price accomplished this apparent miracle of duality, let me go back to the inception of the case and describe the deductive steps by which we finally arrived at that blissful state in which *vincit omnia veritas.*

"When the clothing of the impostor was found on the floor of the telephone booth the face-gag, gown and surgical cap proved unproductive of clews. They were ordinary samples of such wear, without interesting characteristics.

"But three items—the trousers and the two shoes—were rather startlingly illuminating.

"Let's dissect—if I may use a laboratory word—the shoes. On one of them a scrap of adhesive had been wrapped about a torn shoelace. What did this mean? We went to work.

"In the first place, it was patent after a little thought that the lace must have broken *during* the crime-period. Why?

"This was a carefully schemed murder. We had ample evidence of that. Now, if the lace had snapped during the *preparatory* period—that is to say, some time before the crime-period, when the clothes were being assembled by the criminal at some place other than the Hospital—would a piece of adhesive have been used to patch up the tear? Hardly. For it would have been more in keeping with the general method of the murderer to procure a new, unbroken lace and insert it in the shoe, in order to *prevent* another breaking during the crime-period to come, when seconds were precious and any delay would be fatal.

"Of course, the natural question arose: Why didn't the criminal *knot* the broken ends instead of using the peculiar method of *pasting* them together? Examination of the lace revealed the reason: If the lace had been knotted, so much of its length would have been consumed that it would have been literally impossible to tie up the ends.

"There was another indication that tended to show that the lace had broken and had been repaired some time during the crime-period: the adhesive was still slightly moist when I removed it from the lace. Obviously it had been applied not long before.

"From the very use of the adhesive, then, and its moist condition, it was virtually a certainty that the lace had broken during the crime-period. Now—*when* during the crime-period had it broken? Before the murder, or after? Reply: Before the murder. And why? Because if the lace had snapped as the impostor was taking the shoe off, he wouldn't have been put to the necessity of repairing it at all! Time was precious; what harm in leaving a broken lace when the shoe had already served its purpose? That's clear, I hope?"

Heads bobbed in unison. Ellery lit a cigarette and sat down on the edge of the Inspector's desk.

"I knew, then, that the lace had torn while the criminal was dressing in his impostor's clothing, just before the murder.

"But where did this lead?" Ellery smiled reminiscently. "Not very far at the time. So I tucked it away in a corner of my brain and tackled the most curious problem of the adhesive tape itself.

"I asked myself this question: What two complementary groups of the most general nature could be said to have committed the murder? Any number of arbitrary *genera* might have been set up." Ellery chuckled. "As for instance—smokers and non-smokers, Wets and Drys, Caucasians and Negroes. Any irrelevant and ludicrous divisions like these.

"Seriously, however. Since we were considering a murder in a hospital, the answer naturally fell into the following elementary, relevant classification: that is, the murder was committed either by an unprofessionally minded person or by a professionally minded person. Surely a pertinent generalization.

"Let me define my terms. By 'professionally minded persons' I meant persons with trained or acquired knowledge of hospitals and medical routine—knowledge in its least detailed sense.

"Very well! I considered the possibilities in the light of the fact that adhesive tape was used to repair the shoelace. I reached a conclusion—that the impostor-murderer was a *professionally* minded person.

"How did I attain this mental resolution? Well, the shoelace break was an accident—an accident that, as I've shown, couldn't have been foreseen. In other words, the impostor had no inkling, in the period before he donned the prepared surgical clothing prior to the murder, that one of his shoelaces was going to snap as he put on the shoes. Therefore he could not have provided against such a contingency. Therefore whatever he did to repair such a break in an emergency was unplanned and quite instinctive under the pressure of haste. But the impostor in this emergency used adhesive to mend his broken lace! I ask you: Would an unprofessionally minded person—in the sense I postulated a moment ago—carry adhesive tape about with him? *No.* Would an unprofessionally minded person even *think* of carrying such a professional article about with him? *No.* Not carrying it about with him, would an unprofessionally minded person think of *looking for* adhesive if he needed something to repair a break? *No.*

"So THAT," and Ellery tapped the desk with his forefinger, "the fact that adhesive *was* thought of, the fact that adhesive *was* used in the emergency, indicated clearly some one on terms of familiarity with such an article. In other words, *a professionally minded person.*

"To digress for the merest moment. This classification must be held to include not only nurses, doctors and internes, but also non-medical persons so accustomed to hospital routine that for all logical purposes they fall into the professionally minded class.

"But if a piece of adhesive tape could have presented itself—thereby suggesting its use—to the impostor at the very instant he discovered his need of an article of repair, all my reasoning would be invalidated. For such accessibility would have permitted *any one,* professionally minded or not, to have taken advantage of the lucky availability of the tape. In other words, if the impostor saw a piece of adhesive lying before his eyes at the moment his lace snapped, his use of the tape to mend the lace would have indicated, not instinct or a professional cast of mind, but merely a taking advantage of a circumstance which *forced itself* on his attention.

"Fortunately for the strict progression of my argument, however," continued Ellery as he puffed at his cigarette steadily, "I had learned from a talk and little inspection tour with Dr. Minchen even before the murder that the Dutch Memorial Hospital has most rigid rules about medical supplies—of which adhesive is necessarily an adjunct. Supplies are kept in special cabinets. They are not scattered about on tables or in easily penetrated supply rooms. They're quite out of sight—and ken—of the uninitiate. Only a Hospital employee or some one accepted in the same sense would know where to lay hands on the adhesive on the split-minute notice necessitated by the murderer's time-schedule. The adhesive wasn't under the impostor's eye; he had to *know* where to get it before he could use it.

"To put it more directly—not only was my conclusion about a professionally minded criminal substantiated, but I was now able to limit my first generalization even further: that is, my criminal was *a professionally minded person connected with the Dutch Memorial Hospital!*

"I had hurdled a high obstacle, therefore. I knew quite a bit from my deductive attack upon the facts about the impostor-murderer. Let me sum up once more, so that my reasoning may be utterly crystal in your minds: The murderer, to have thought of and used the adhesive, must have been professionally minded. The murderer, to have known where to procure the adhesive on a moment's notice, must have been connected in some way with, not just any hospital, but the Dutch Memorial Hospital itself."

Ellery lit another cigarette. "It narrowed the field, but not to the limit of satisfaction. For from these conclusions I could not exclude such people as Edith Dunning, Hulda Doorn, Moritz Kneisel, Sarah Fuller, Gatekeeper Isaac Cobb, Superintendent James Paradise, elevator-men, mop-women—all of whom were regularly on the Hospital premises and knew its layout and regulations, either as employees or as constant visitors with special privileges. So they had to be classed for my purpose with the Dutch Memorial's medical personnel as professionally minded persons.

"But that wasn't all. The shoes were bearers of still another tale. In examining them, we encountered a most unusual phenomenon—the tongues in both were found pressed against the upper insides of the toe-box, quite flatly. What could be the explanation of this?

"The shoes had been used by the impostor—the adhesive showed that. The murderer's feet had been inside. And yet the tongues were—as they were!

"Have you ever put on your shoes when the tongue was pushed back by your toes as you slipped your feet in? It happens to every one occasionally. You knew the difference at once, didn't you? You couldn't help but feel that the tongues were out of position. . . . Well, certainly the impostor didn't put on those shoes, no matter how much of a sweat he was in, and deliberately leave the tongues to crush his toes. Then the impostor was unaware of what happened to the tongues, or was not made uncomfortable as he put the shoes on. . . .

"But how in God's name was this possible? Only by one explanation: the impostor's feet were considerably smaller than the shoes he was putting on—the shoes we later found in the

booth. But the shoes we found were ridiculously small themselves—they were size 6! Do you realize what this means? Size
6 is quite the smallest ordinary man's size in shoes. What sort of
masculine monstrosity in the adult stage could have worn those
shoes? A Chinese whose honored sire had mistaken him for a
girl-child and stunted his infant feet? After all, the man whose
feet could have slipped into those shoes, pushing the tongues
back, without feeling the difference, must have been the user of
much smaller shoes! Size 4 or 5? There's no such size in men's
shoes!

"So the analysis resolved itself into this: the only kind of feet
which would have been so much smaller as to permit the tongues
to be pressed back without discomfort or inconvenience would
be—one, the feet of a child (palpably ridiculous from the testified
height of the impostor); two, the feet of an unnaturally small man
(untenable for the same reason); and three, the feet of a medium-sized woman!"

Ellery pounded the desk. "I said, gentlemen, several times
during the past week's investigation that those shoes told me an
important—an all-important—story. They did. From the adhesive
on the lace I conjured a professionally minded person connected
with the Dutch Memorial Hospital; from the tongues I conjured
a woman.

"It was the first indication that the impersonator was not only
posing as another individual but also as an individual of the opposite sex. *Id est*, a woman made up as a man!"

Some one sighed. Sampson muttered, "Evidence . . ." and
the Police Commissioner's eyes gleamed with appreciation. Dr.
Minchen stared at his friend as if he were viewing him for the first
time. The Inspector said nothing, sunk in reflection.

Ellery shrugged his shoulders. "Before I leave the shoes to tackle another angle of the problem, it might be interesting to point out the lack of discrepancy between the heights of the two heels. Both were worn down to approximately the same degree. If they had been Dr. Janney's shoes one heel would have been worn away considerably more than another—Janney limped heavily on one foot, as you know.

"The shoes, then, weren't Janney's; and while this did not prove that Janney wasn't the murderer, since he could have left some one else's shoes in the telephone booth for us to find, or worn the equal-heeled shoes, still not his own, these equal-heeled shoes made a good corroborative assumption that Dr. Janney was innocent; that is, that he was actually impersonated. For of course the thought crossed more than one mind that Janney might have impersonated himself—pretended that some one else was using his identity, while in reality it was he himself all the time.

"I didn't believe this from the first. Look: If Janney himself was the person we have nominated as the 'impostor,' he could have done the whole bloody job in his own surgical clothes, the ones he wore that morning. That would mean that the clothing we found in the booth was a 'plant'—not used while he committed the crime, merely left to give a false impression. But how about the adhesive and tongues in the shoes? Those shoes were certainly used, as I've proved. And how about the basted trousers—the second essential point about the clothes? I'll take them up in a moment. . . . But as for impersonating himself—why didn't he produce Swanson to substantiate his alibi that he was in his office during the crime-period? That would be the inevitable thing for him to do. But he stubbornly refused to produce Swanson, thereby with his full realization of the results putting his head into the noose of police suspicion. No, his actions as well as the clothes cleared him in my mind of the possibility that he impersonated himself.

"As for the basted trousers—why were they basted?

"If Janney had planted them, he wouldn't have had to wear them—as I said, the clothes he was wearing would have served. Then the basting was another plant? For what purpose? To mislead us as to the murderer's height—to make us think the impostor was two inches shorter than he actually was? But this is sheer nonsense, for the murderer knew he couldn't mislead as to his height; it had to be part of his plan to be *seen* during the impersonation period, thereby establishing his height in the eyes of witnesses. No, the basting was for the legitimate purpose of shortening the trousers that were too long for the murderer. Beyond a doubt, these trousers were literally on the legs of the murderer during the impersonation."

Ellery smiled. "I subdivided my possibilities, as before, into complementary classifications; this time into four all-inclusive ones. The impostor could have been: one, a man connected with the Hospital; two, a man not connected with the Hospital; three, a woman not connected with the Hospital; four, a woman connected with the Hospital.

"See how three of these were quickly weeded.

"The impostor couldn't have been a man connected with the Hospital. Every man so connected by rigid rule had to wear, and did wear at all times on the premises, a white uniform of which white trousers were a necessary part. If a man connected with the Hospital was the impersonator, therefore, he was already wearing white trousers before the crime. Why then should he divest himself of these whites (which fit him), put on the telephone-booth whites (which didn't fit him), and then proceed to commit the crime? It's inane. If such a man wanted to impersonate Janney, he would commit the crime wearing his own white trousers, leaving no other trousers to be found. But trousers *were* found, and we've shown that they weren't a plant; that is to say, that they were actually worn by the impersonator. However, if the trousers were actually worn by the impersonator it was only because he was not *already* wearing regulation pants.

"If he were not already wearing regulation pants, the impostor could not have been a man connected with the Hospital. *Quod erat demonstrandum.*

"*Secundus.* It could not have been a man *not* connected with the Hospital. For by our reasoning from the use of the adhesive we had already eliminated all people *not* connected with the Hospital.

"In this connection, you might say: Well, how about men like Philip Morehouse and Hendrik Doorn, and Cudahy's thugs? They didn't wear the hospital uniform.

"The reply to this is: While Morehouse, Doorn and the thugs would have to wear a uniform to impersonate Janney, none of them was well enough acquainted with the Hospital to know exactly where to get the tape. Doorn might have known, to stretch a point; but then his physical make-up was against the possibility— too gross and huge. The impostor seen going into the Anteroom was very near to Janney's physique—and Janney was a small, slender man. As for Morehouse, there was nothing to indicate that he knew where supplies were kept; and this applies also to Cudahy's little army. Cudahy himself wasn't the remotest possibility; he was being anæsthetized while Mrs. Doorn was being strangled. And all the other men in the case with a professional background were eliminated because, as I have shown, it would not have been necessary for them to change trousers—Dunning, Janney, Dr.

Minchen, the internes, Cobb, the elevator-men—the whole kit and boodle of 'em wore the regulation white uniform.

"Then it wasn't a man, either connected or unconnected with the Hospital. Corroboration!

"Women? Let's see. It couldn't have been a woman *not* connected with the Hospital because while she would have to wear trousers for the impersonation, since she normally wears skirts, the adhesive reasoning again removes such a person, for by definition such a person is unconnected with the Hospital.

"The only other possibility, then, from this complex system of cross-checks, was that the impostor-murderer was a woman connected with the Hospital. Under this head came Hulda Doorn and Sarah Fuller, who were naturally as familiar with the Hospital as Mrs. Doorn herself; Edith Dunning, who worked there; Dr. Pennini, the woman-obstetrician; and all other females, like nurses and mopwomen, on the premises.

"Can we re-check?

"Yes! A woman connected with the Hospital of the impostor's approximate size would have needed white trousers for the impersonation and would have been forced to leave them somewhere in order to return to her identity as a female. Being a medium-sized woman she would have had to shorten the long trousers by basting. The small physical size would also account for the tongues being caught in the shoes, since most women's feet are much smaller and slimmer than men's, and it was men's shoes she had to wear. And, finally, a woman connected with the Hospital would instinctively think of adhesive and know where to get it without a moment's delay.

"Gentlemen, it checked in every particular!"

They looked at each other, each mind probing, analyzing, weighing what it had heard.

The Police Commissioner crossed his legs suddenly. "Go on," he said. "This is the—the . . ." He stopped and scratched his blue-stubbled jaw. "I'll be damned if I can give a name to it. Go on, Mr. Queen."

Ellery plunged ahead. "The second crime," he said, staring thoughtfully at the smoldering tip of his cigarette, "was quite a different matter. In attempting to apply the same methods I had used in the first crime, I discovered that success had fled. Whatever I was able to conclude—and it was little enough—led to no specific end.

"In another generalization, it was evident that the two crimes might have been committed by the same criminal or by different ones.

"The first thing I became puzzled about was the unanswerability of the question: if this professionally minded woman I postulated as the murderess of Abigail Doorn had killed Janney also, why did she deliberately duplicate her weapon? That is, why did she kill both by strangling them with the same kind of wire? The murderess was not dull; it would seem to be more to her advantage to use a different weapon in the second crime so that the police would be seeking two murderers. In this way, obscuring the trail. Yet, if she killed both, she *purposely* made no effort to hide the linking of the crimes. Why? I could find no reason.

"On the other hand, if Janney were killed by a different murderer, the duplication of method would indicate that Janney's murderer was cleverly attempting to make it appear as if Abby's murderer were also Janney's murderer. This was a very pointed possibility.

"I kept an open mind on the problem. Either speculation could be true.

"Besides the seemingly deliberate duplication of method,

there were other disturbing factors about the second crime, to not one of which was there a plausible explanation.

"Until the time Dr. Minchen told me about his removal of the filing-cabinet from behind Dr. Janney's desk—before I reached the Hospital that morning—I was absolutely at sea about the second murder.

"But my knowledge of the filing-cabinet's very existence, and its original location in Janney's office, altered everything. It was as significant to the explanation of Janney's death as the shoes and trousers had been to the explanation of Mrs. Doorn's death.

"Consider the facts. Janney's dead face was surprisingly placid, showing a natural expression, unmarked by astonishment, fear, horror—any of the unusual signs of violent death. Yet the position of the blow which first stunned him showed that the murderer must have stood *behind* him in order to hit him over the cerebellar region of the head! How did the murderer get behind Janney without arousing his suspicions, or at least his apprehension? There was no window behind Janney's desk to permit the murderer to hit Janney from the outside while leaning over the window-sill; the absence of a window behind Janney's desk also removed the possibility of a person standing behind Janney with the excuse of looking outside. There is a window on the north wall, looking out over the inner court, but a person standing here could not possibly have delivered the blow.

"As it was, the desk and chair formed the hypotenuse of a triangle, the converging north and east walls being the other two sides. There was hardly room to squeeze behind the desk, let alone get there without the knowledge of the desk's occupant. And Janney was sitting at his desk when he was killed—no question about that. He had been writing at his manuscript when he was stunned. The ink had trailed off in the middle of a word. Then his murderer not only got behind Janney but got behind Janney with Janney's knowledge and consent!"

Ellery grinned. "An appalling situation. I was quite put out. There was *nothing* behind the desk to account for a person's being there, and being *accepted* as being there. Yet that the murderer had been there without arousing the slightest responsive emotion on Janney's part was evident.

"There were two conclusions, however: one, Janney knew the murderer well; two, Janney was aware of the murderer's presence behind him, and accepted this circumstance without either suspicion or fear.

"Now, until I learned that a filing-cabinet had stood behind the desk, I was so stumped that it made me intellectually ill. But when John Minchen told me . . . For what reason would explain Janney's acceptance of the murderer and the murderer's position? The only object in the corner, I now knew, was the filing-cabinet. It followed incontrovertibly that the filing-cabinet accounted for the murderer's position behind Janney. Logical?"

"Oh, quite!" burst out Dr. Minchen. Sampson glared at him and he subsided a little sheepishly.

"Thanks, John," said Ellery dryly, "The next step was inevitable. Fortunately for me, the filing-cabinet was not an ordinary one filled with the usual Hospital data. It was a special, privately owned cabinet which housed perhaps Janney's most precious and personal documentary possession. The records were case-histories pertinent to the book which Janney was writing with Dr. Minchen. It was only too well-known how passionately Janney guarded these case-histories from those whom he considered outsiders. They were kept under lock and key; no one was allowed to see them. No one, that is to say," interjected Ellery in a stronger voice, and his eyes burned, "but three people.

"The first was Janney himself. Out for obvious reasons.

"The second was Dr. Minchen, Janney's co-worker. But Minchen couldn't have killed Janney because he was not in the Hospital at the time of the murder. He had been with me for part of that morning, and just a few moments before the murder—far too short a time to get to the Hospital and kill his collaborator— he had been with me on Broadway, near 86th Street, talking.

"But was that all?" Ellery took off his *pince-nez* and began to scrub its lenses. "Not by a long shot, it wasn't. Even before the murder of Mrs. Doorn I knew that there was some one besides Janney and Minchen who could visit that cabinet with impunity. That some one was not only Dr. Janney's secretarial assistant and clerical helper on Hospital matters and in his literary activities, she was also a rightful occupant of Janney's office, having a desk there. Helping Janney continuously on the manuscript, she inevi- tably had access to that precious file behind Janney. Her presence in that corner, where she undoubtedly came many times during the day, even while Janney was at work, was normal and taken for granted by Janney! . . . I am referring, of course, to my third possibility, Lucille Price."

"Good work," said Sampson in a surprised voice. The Inspec- tor was regarding Ellery with affection.

"It fitted beautifully!" cried Ellery. "No other person in the Hospital, or outside the Hospital for that matter, could have got behind Dr. Janney under those peculiar circumstances without arousing some expression of suspicion, fear or anger. Janney was unusually jealous of those records, had refused on many occa- sions to let any one touch them. Dr. Minchen and Lucille Price were the exceptions. Minchen was eliminated. Then Lucille Price was left!"

Ellery agitated his *pince-nez*. "Conclusion: She was the only possible murderer of Dr. Janney.

"Lucille Price. . . . I chewed that name in my mind with a sudden inspiration. Why, what are Lucille Price's characteristics? She is a woman, she is professionally connected with the Dutch Memorial Hospital!

"BUT THIS IS EXACTLY THE SORT OF PERSON WHOM I WAS SEEKING AS THE MURDERESS OF ABIGAIL DOORN! Was it conceivable that this innocent-looking and efficient nurse was also the murderess of Mrs. Doorn?"

Ellery gulped down a mouthful of water. The room was still as death.

"From that moment the entire story was spread before my eyes. I asked for a map of the main floor, and sought to retrace the route by which she might possibly have engineered that daring crime in such a way that she was apparently her own self as a nurse, and the impostor of Dr. Janney at the same time.

"By study and careful piecing together of old elements I was able to work out a time-schedule such as Lucille Price must have used to accomplish this seeming miracle. Let me read it to you."

Ellery dug into his breast-pocket and took out a tattered notebook. Harper became unusually busy with a pencil and a scrap of paper. Ellery read rapidly:

"10:29—The real Dr. Janney called away.
"10:30—Lucille Price opens door from Anteroom, slips into Anteroom lift, closes door, fastens East Corridor door to prevent interruptions, dons shoes, white duck trousers, gown, cap and gag previously planted there or somewhere in the Anteroom, leaves her own shoes in elevator,

her own clothes being covered by the new. Slips into East Corridor via lift door, turns corner into South Corridor, goes along South Corridor until she reaches Anæsthesia Room. Limping all the time, in imitation of Janney, with gag concealing her features and cap her hair, she passes rapidly through the Anæsthesia Room, being seen by Dr. Byers, Miss Obermann and Cudahy, and enters Anteroom, closing door behind her.

"10:34—Approaches comatose Mrs. Doorn, strangles her with wire concealed under her clothes; calls out in her own voice at appropriate time, 'I'll be out in a moment, Dr. Janney!' or words to that effect. (Of course, she did not go into the Sterilizing Room as she claimed in her testimony.) When Dr. Gold stuck his head into the Anteroom he saw Miss Price in surgical robes bending over the body, her back to him. Naturally Gold did not see a nurse; there was none, as such, there.

"10:38—Leaves Anteroom through Anæsthesia Room, retraces steps along South and East Corridors, slips into lift, removes male garments, puts on own shoes, hurries out again to deposit male clothes in telephone booth just outside lift door, and returns to Anteroom via lift door as before.

"10:43—Is back in Anteroom in her own personality as Lucille Price.

"The entire process consumed no more than twelve minutes."

Ellery smiled and put away his notebook. "The shoestring broke as she put on the men's canvas shoes in the lift before committing the murder. All she had to do was to return to the Anteroom through the lift door, open the supply cabinet next to it, snip off a piece of adhesive tape with her pocket-scissors from a roll in the drawer, and go back to the lift. Any one could do this in twenty seconds if he knew, as she did, just where to look for the adhesive. Incidentally, it was the roll of adhesive from which the shoe piece had been cut, that I looked for after outlining the schedule roughly. It was not absolute certainty that the tape was taken from the Anteroom cabinet, but it was surely the logical place. And so I found, having compared the jagged edge left on the roll with the piece we found in the shoe. They jibed exactly. That's evidence, Mr. District Attorney?"

"Yes."

"Miss Price could have put the adhesive-roll in her own pocket after she used it, thereby disposing of it. But she didn't think of it. Or if she did, she may have decided to risk a few extra seconds in order to avoid having the dangerous roll on her person.

"Remember that the Anteroom had been unused from the time the investigation started—and under guard. However, even if she had taken the roll away, this wouldn't have affected the solution. Please bear in mind that I solved the crime *before* I thought of looking for the roll. And so I say—to sum up—the shoes and the trousers told me everything but the name of the murderess; the cabinet told me the name. And it was all over."

He stopped and regarded them with a weary smile.

Puzzled looks were breaking out on the faces of his audience. Harper was quivering with excitement; he sat on the edge of his chair strained and tense.

Sampson said uneasily, "There's something loose somewhere. It isn't all. . . . How about Kneisel?"

"Oh, I'm sorry," said Ellery at once. "I should have explained that the guilt of Lucille Price didn't eliminate the possibility of an accomplice. She might have been the instrument, with a male brain directing her from the background. Kneisel might have been the owner of that brain. He had motive—with the deaths of Mrs. Doorn and Dr. Janney, he made certain of plenty of funds to carry on his work and absolutely sole possession of its proceeds. And all his pretty theories might have been so much sand thrown into our eyes. But—"

"Accomplice . . ." muttered the Police Commissioner. "So that's why Swanson was nabbed this afternoon. . . ."

"What!" exclaimed the District Attorney. "Swanson?"

Inspector Queen smiled faintly. "It was rush, Henry, and we didn't get a chance to notify you. Swanson was arrested this afternoon as the accomplice of Lucille Price. Just a moment, please."

He telephoned to Sergeant Velie. "Thomas, I want you to get those two together. . . . Swanson and the Price woman. . . . Nothing out of her yet? . . . See if that does it." He hung up. "We'll know very shortly."

"Why Swanson?" objected Dr. Minchen mildly. "He certainly couldn't have done either job himself: Janney alibied him for the first murder, and you yourselves alibi him for the second. I don't see—"

Ellery said: "Swanson was my *bête noire* from the beginning. I simply couldn't believe that pure coincidence made him claim Dr. Janney's attention at precisely the time when Janney was being impersonated. Don't forget that Lucille Price's plan absolutely depended on getting Janney out of sight while she was posing as him. Then, getting Janney out of sight at the right time wasn't coincidence, but planned. Swanson was the instrument, therefore. Was he innocently involved—did she get him to call on Janney without knowledge of what the call signified—or was he a guilty accomplice?

"But when Mr. Swanson visited the District Attorney's office, giving himself a clear alibi from the most unimpeachable source in the city just as Dr. Janney was being murdered, I knew that he was a guilty accomplice. And I remembered that Swanson was the greatest gainer from the deaths of both Janney and Abby! Abby's legacy to Janney; Janney's death, leaving the money to Swanson— it fitted perfectly."

The telephone rang and Inspector Queen snatched it from the desk. He listened with reddening face. Then he banged the receiver on its hook, shouting, "It's all over! The minute Swanson and Lucille Price were brought together Swanson broke down and confessed! We've got 'em, by God!"

Harper leaped from his chair. His eyes pleaded wildly, beseeching Ellery. "Can I beat it now—or better, can I 'phone the office from here?"

"I think so, Pete," smiled Ellery. "I keep my bargains." Harper grabbed the telephone. "Shoot!" he cried when he had received his connection. And that was all. He sat back, grinning like an ape.

The Police Commissioner without a word rose and departed.

"Y'know," said Harper thoughtfully, "I've wondered all along how it was possible for the murderer to have arranged such a complicated scheme of action in less than two hours after an accident which could not have been foreseen. And even aside from that, it seemed to me that the whole murder was sort of unnecessary. After all, Mrs. Doorn might have died as a result of the operation, and it sure would have saved a load of trouble for the murderer."

"Excellent, Pete." Ellery looked pleased. "Two very excellent doubt-stimuli. But there's an even more excellent answer to each of them.

"Mrs. Doorn was scheduled to be operated on for appendicitis about a month from now; it was common Hospital gossip.

Undoubtedly the crime was planned for this time, with perhaps some variations in method. For example, an anæsthetist would have been present in the Anteroom, since the old lady would not then be in a coma; and the presence of the anæsthetist would have made it difficult for Lucille Price to commit the murder *before* the operation. I suppose she planned to kill Mrs. Doorn after the operation, in the old lady's private room in the Hospital, when she could enter as Dr. Janney just as she entered the Anteroom in the actual crime-period. I'm positive that she would again have been the nurse in charge of Mrs. Doorn, due to her affiliation with Janney; so that substantially every detail of the crime was prepared even before the accident occurred—that is, clothes secreted somewhere on the premises, arrangements for Swanson to get Janney out of the way, and so forth. So that when the accident occurred, it merely required a slight readjustment under even more favorable conditions than she had hoped for—no anæsthetist chiefly—to set in motion the murder plan. A hasty telephone call to Swanson informing him of the new development, and the thing was done."

Ellery felt his throat tenderly. "Dry as dust. . . . As for your point that a murder might not have been necessary at all, it's not tenable for this reason: Both Minchen and Janney were perfectly confident that Janney would pull the old lady through. Now certainly Lucille Price, so close to the surgeon, would be bound to accept his confident attitude. And consider that if Mrs. Doorn recovered, and the appendix operation were delayed indefinitely, Lucille Price would have had to *wait* indefinitely, and all her plans would have been up in the air. No, Pete, the accident merely hastened the commission of the crime; it certainly did not inspire the commission of the crime."

Sampson sat still as stone, thinking. Ellery was watching him with amusement; Harper was chuckling to himself. Sampson said: "But Lucille Price's *motive*? I don't get it. What connection can there be between her and Swanson? There's never been a hint— Why should she do the dirty work for him, if he's the gainer by the double murder?"

Inspector Queen took his hat and coat from a clothes-tree, mumbling an apology. There was work to do. Before he left, he said in a mild voice, "Let Ellery tell you, Henry. It's his story, no matter what he says . . . Djuna, be a good boy."

As the door closed, Ellery relaxed in his father's chair and crossed his feet on his father's desk. "Very good question, Sampson," he drawled. "I asked myself that one whole afternoon. What connection *could* there be between two apparently unrelated people? Swanson, nursing his hate of the old woman for having smashed his career by evicting him from the Hospital; a warped mentality, criminally scheming the death of his step-father for sanctioning the smash-up of his career, and also for financial reasons, since he was his stepfather's heir despite everything. . . . And Lucille Price, a quiet trained nurse—Yes, what connection was there?"

In the silence that followed Ellery extracted from his pocket the mysterious document which he had commissioned Harper to find on Thursday afternoon. He waved it in the air.

"This was the laconic answer. It explains why Lucille Price did the dirty work for Swanson, since it makes her heir with him to Janney's estate.

"It conceals the story of several years of planning, criminal deliberation and hellish skill.

"It shows how and where Lucille Price was able to secure men's surgical clothing without leaving a trail—from Swanson, the ex-surgeon, accounting by the way, for her use of trousers too long for her. The shoes are probably his, too; he is about five feet nine, but he's small-boned.

"It points to their close and secret cooperation; such things as dangerously discussing, perhaps by telephone—for they must have been too canny to meet or live together—the premature killing of Janney. For Swanson was forced by the newspaper ruse the other day to visit your office, inadvertently and fortunately giving him a perfect alibi while Janney was being murdered.

"It explains why the same method was used to kill both people: for if Swanson were suspected and even arrested for Mrs. Doorn's murder—a possibility in their minds—and Janney was then murdered in such a way as to make it seem the work of the same criminal, Swanson's alibi for the second murder would automatically clear him of suspicion for the first.

"It implies that not even Janney knew that his step-son, Thomas Janney, alias Swanson, and Lucille Price were inextricably linked. . . .

"Yes, what *could* be that link, I asked myself?"

Ellery tossed the document across the Inspector's desk, so that District Attorney Sampson, Dr. Minchen and Djuna could lean over and inspect it. Harper merely grinned.

It was a photostatic copy of a marriage certificate.

AMERICAN
MYSTERY *from*
CLASSICS

*Available now
in hardcover and paperback:*

Charlotte Armstrong . . . . *The Unsuspected*

Erle Stanley Gardner . . . . . . *The Case of the Careless Kitten*

H.F. Heard . . . . *A Taste for Honey*

Dorothy B. Hughes. . . . . *The So Blue Marble*

Frances & Richard Lockridge . . . . *Death on the Aisle*

Stuart Palmer . . . . *The Puzzle of the Happy Hooligan*

Ellery Queen . . . . *The Chinese Orange Mystery*

Patrick Quentin . . . . *A Puzzle for Fools*

Clayton Rawson . . . . *Death From a Top Hat*

Craig Rice . . . . *Home Sweet Homicide*

Mary Roberts Rinehart . . . . *The Red Lamp*

Join Ellery Queen for another puzzling tale of detection, *The Chinese Orange Mystery*, out now in the American Mystery Classics series!

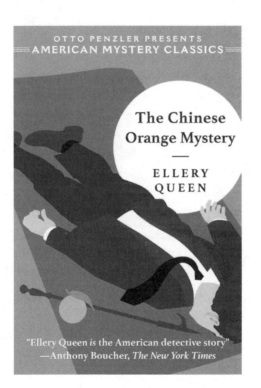

Read on for the first chapter of the book *Publishers Weekly* calls "one of the most bizarre puzzles in crime fiction" . . .

1

THE IDYLL OF MISS DIVERSEY

MISS DIVERSEY fled Dr. Kirk's study followed by a blistering mouthful of ogrish growls. She stood still in the corridor outside the old gentleman's door, her cheeks burning and one of her square washed-out hands pressed to the outraged starch of her bosom. She could hear the angry septuagenarian scuttling about the study in his wheel chair like a Galapagos turtle, muttering anathemas upon her white-capped head in a fantastic potpourri of ancient Hebrew, classic Greek, French, and English.

"The old fossil," thought Miss Diversey fiercely. "It's—it's like living with a human encyclopedia!"

Dr. Kirk made Jovian thunder from behind the door: "And don't come back, do you hear me?" He thundered other things, too, in the argot of strange tongues which filled his scholar's brain; things which, had Miss Diversey been possessed of the dubious advantages of higher culture, would have made her very indignant indeed.

"Slush," she said defiantly, glaring at the door. There was no reply; at least, no reply of a satisfactory nature. There's nothing, she thought with dismal consternation, you can say to a ghostly chuckle and the slam of a dusty book dug out of somebody's grave. He *was* the most exasperating old— She almost said it. For a moment, in fact, it trembled upon the brink of utterance. But her better nature triumphed and she closed her pale lips sternly. Let him dress himself if he wanted to. She had always hated dressing old people, anyway. . . . She stood irresolute for a moment; and then, her color still high, clumped down the corridor with the firm unhurried steps of the professional nurse.

The twenty-second floor of the Hotel Chancellor was pervaded, by inflexible regulation, with the silent peace of the cloister. The quiet soothed Miss Diversey's ruffled soul. There were two compensations, she thought, to playing nurse to a creaking, decrepit, malicious old devil afflicted—thank heaven there was justice!—with chronic rheumatism and gout. One was the handsome salary young Donald Kirk paid her for the difficult task of taking care of his father; the other was that the Kirk *ménage* was situated in a respectable hotel in the heart of New York City. The money and the geography, she thought with morbid satisfaction, made up for a lot of disadvantages. Macy's, Gimbel's, the other department stores were only minutes away, movies and theatres and all sorts of exciting things at one's doorstep. . . . Yes, she would stick it out. Life was hard, but it had its compensations.

Not that they weren't a trying lot at times. Lord knows she had crawled to the whims of plenty of nasty people in her day. And that old Dr. Kirk *was* nasty; there was no pleasing him. You'd think a body would be pleasant and human and grateful *sometimes*; give a person a "please" here or a "thank you" there. But not old Beelzebub. A tyrant, if ever there was one. He had eyes that gave a person the shivers; and his white hair stood on end as if it were trying to get as far away from him as it possibly could. He wouldn't eat when you wanted him to. He refused massages and threw shoes about. He would totter around the suite when Dr.

Angini said he mustn't walk and refuse to budge when Dr. Angini said he must exercise. About the only good thing about him was that when his purple old nose was buried in a book he was quiet.

And then there was Marcella. Marcella! Snippy little fluff *she* was; in fifty years she'd be the feminine counterpart of her father. Oh, she had her good points, reflected Miss Diversey grudgingly; but then so have criminals. Adding her up, good and bad, you wouldn't have much. Of course, conceded Miss Diversey, who had a strong sense of justice, she couldn't really be as worthless as all that; not with that nice tall pink-cheeked Mr. Macgowan so crazy about her. It certainly did take all kinds of people to make a world! Now, Miss Diversey was sure that if Mr. Macgowan had not happened to be Mr. Donald Kirk's best friend there never would have been an engagement between Mr. Macgowan and Mr. Kirk's young sister. That's what comes of having a brother *and* pots of money, thought Miss Diversey darkly. You go out and snare just about the best catch—Miss Diversey read the society-gossip columns critically—in the social whirl. Well, maybe when they were married he'd find out. They generally do, thought Miss Diversey, who possessed among other admirable qualities a decided strain of cynicism. The stories she could tell about these society people! . . . As for Donald Kirk, he was all right in his way; but his way was not Miss Diversey's way. He was a snob. That is, he treated people like Miss Diversey with a certain good-humored, absent tolerance.

It did seem, reflected Miss Diversey as she trudged down the corridor, that the easiest way to bury the woman part of a person was to become a trained nurse. Here she was, thirty-two—no, one must be honest with oneself; it was closer to thirty-three—and what were her prospects? That is to say, her romantic prospects? Nothing, simply nothing. The men she met in the travails of her profession were roughly of two kinds, she thought bitterly: those who paid no attention to her at all, and those who paid far too much. In the first category were doctors and male relatives of rich patients; in the second were internes and male employees of rich patients. The first class didn't recognize her as a woman at all, just a machine; Donald Kirk belonged to *that* class. The second kind wanted to—to take her apart with their grubby fingers to see what made her tick. That groveling little Hubbell, now, she thought with a curl of her lip—Mr. Kirk's butler and valet and Lord knows what else. When he was with his betters he was the soul of self-effacement and rectitude; but still and all she'd had to slap that pasty face of his only this morning. Patients, of course, didn't count. You could hardly get goo-goo about a person when you fetched bedpans and that sort of thing. Now, Mr. Osborne was different. . . .

A gentle vagueness settled upon Miss Diversey's hard features; almost a girlish smile. Thoughts of Mr. Osborne were—there was no denying it—pleasant. First of all, he was a gentleman; none of Hubbell's low tricks for *him*. Come to think of it, he was in a third class, sort of in a class by himself. Not rich, and yet not a servant. As Mr. Kirk's confidential assistant he was in between. Like one of the family and yet not like one of the family, as you might say; he worked on a salary like herself. That made it—somehow—very, very satisfying to Miss Diversey. . . . She wondered if she really hadn't overstepped the bounds of propriety weeks and weeks ago, when she'd only just met Mr. Osborne. How *had* the talk drifted around to—she blushed faintly—marriage? Oh, nothing personal, of course; she'd merely said that *she* would never marry a man who couldn't provide a good—a more than good—living. Oh, no. She'd seen too many marriages break up because of money; that is, lack of it. And Mr. Osborne had seemed so distressed, as if she'd hurt him; now, could that mean anything? Surely he wasn't thinking . . .

Miss Diversey took a firm grip on her errant thoughts. Her amble had brought her to a door on the opposite side of the corridor from the Kirk suite. It was the last door on the wall, the door nearest the other corridor that led from the elevators to the Kirk apartment. A plain door, really an undistinguished member of the family of doors; and yet sight of it brought a slight flush to Miss Diversey's cheeks, a flush subtly different from the angry red response to Dr. Kirk's brimstone blasphemies. She tried the handle; it gave.

It wouldn't hurt to peep in, she thought. If there were some one waiting in the anteroom it would mean that he—that Mr. Osborne was probably very busy. If the anteroom was empty, surely there wouldn't be any harm in . . . under the circumstances . . . The old fossil couldn't talk to *her* that way! . . . A person was human, wasn't she?

She opened the door. The anteroom was—happy chance—empty. Directly opposite her was the only other door of the room, and it was closed. On the other side lay . . . She sighed and turned to go. But then she brightened and hurried in. A bowl of fresh fruit on the reading table against the wall between the windows beckoned. It was nice of Mr. Kirk to be so thoughtful of other people, even strangers; and the Lord knew enough of *them* came to see him and sat in the little anteroom, with its nice English oak furniture and its books and lamps and rug and flowers and things.

She pecked among the fruits, making up her mind. One of those huge sugar-pears, now? Hothouse, most likely. But no, it was too close to dinner. Possibly an apple. . . . Ah, tangerines! Now that she came to think of it, tangerines were her favorites. Better than oranges, because they were easier to peel. And they came apart so nicely!

She stripped the rind from the tangerine with the industry of a squirrel and proceeded to chew the damp, sweet morsels of orange with her strong teeth. The pips she spat daintily into the palm of her hand.

When she had finished she looked about, decided the room and the table were too trim and neat and clean to be defiled with pips and orange-peel, and cheerfully hurled the handful of remains out one of the windows into the court made by the setback of the building four stories below. On passing the table, she hesitated. Another? There were two very alluring fat tangerines left in the bowl. . . . But she shook her head sternly and went out by the corridor door, shutting it behind her.

Feeling a little better, she sauntered around the bend into the main corridor. What to do? The old devil would kick her out if she went back now, and she didn't feel much like going to her own room. . . . She brightened once more. A stout middle-aged woman dressed in black, with severe gray hair, was sitting at a desk farther up the corridor, directly opposite the elevators. It was Mrs. Shane, clerk on duty on the twenty-second floor.

Miss Diversey shut her eyes when she passed a door on her right; the door which—she blushed again—opened into the office of Mr. Donald Kirk, the office adjoining the anteroom. It was in this office that the gallant Mr. Osborne was to be f— She sighed and passed on.

"Hullo, Mrs. Shane," she said cheerily to the stout woman. "How's the back this afternoon?"

Mrs. Shane grinned. She peered with caution up and down the corridor, kept an eye cocked on the elevators facing her, and said: "Why, it's Miss Diversey! I declare, Miss Diversey, I never see you any more! Is the old scoundrel keepin' you that busy?"

"Damn his soul," said Miss Diversey without rancor. "He's Satan himself, Mrs. Shane. Just now he chased me out of his room. Imagine!" Mrs. Shane clucked with horror. "Mr. Kirk's partner came back from Europe or some place today—that's Mr. Berne—and Mr. Kirk is giving a dinner-party for him. Naturally, he would have to go. So what do you think? He has to dress for dinner, so—"

"Dress?" echoed Mrs. Shane blankly. "Is he nekkid?"

Miss Diversey laughed. "I mean a tuxedo and things. Well *he* can't dress himself. He can hardly stand on his feet, with his joints all twisted up with rheumatiz. Why, he's seventy-five if he's a day! But what do you think? He wouldn't let me dress him. *Chased* me out!"

"Imagine," said Mrs. Shane. "Men-folks are funny that way. I remember once my Danny—God rest his soul—was taken bad with lumbago and I had to—" She stopped abruptly and stiffened as the elevator evacuated a passenger. The lady, however, was not on the alert for possible defections of hotel employees. She exuded a faint odor of alcohol as she staggered by the desk bound up the corridor toward the other side of the floor. "See that hussy?" hissed Mrs. Shane, leaning forward. Miss Diversey nodded. "The things I could tell you about her, dearie! Why, my girls who clean up on this floor told me the *awfullest* things they've found in her room. Only last week they picked up from her floor a—"

"I've got to go," said Miss Diversey hastily. "Uh—is Mr. Kirk's office—I mean, has Mr. Kirk—?"

Mrs. Shane relaxed to fix Miss Diversey with a shrewd suspicious eye. "You mean is Mr. *Osborne* alone?"

Miss Diversey colored. "I didn't ask that—"

"I know, honey. He is that. There's been not a soul near that blessed office for an hour or more."

"You're sure?" breathed Miss Diversey, beginning to poke her square-tipped fingers in the reddish hair beneath her cap.

"Of course I'm sure! I haven't stirred from this spot all the afternoon, and nobody could 'a' gone into that office without me seeing him."

"Well," said Miss Diversey carelessly. "I think, since I'm here, I'll stop in for a minute. I've nothing to do, anyway. It gets so boring, Mrs. Shane. And then I do feel sorry for poor Mr. Osborne, cooped up in that office all day with not a living soul to talk to."

"Oh, I wouldn't say that," said Mrs. Shane with demoniac subtlety. "Only this morning there was a perfectly *stunning* young lady. Something to do with Mr. Kirk's book publishing—an author, I do think. She was in there with Mr. Osborne for the longest time—"

"Well, and why shouldn't she be?" murmured Miss Diversey. "I'm sure *I* don't care, Mrs. Shane. And anyway it's his work, isn't it? Besides, Mr. Osborne isn't the kind . . . Well, so long."

"So long," said Mrs. Shane warmly.

Miss Diversey strolled back the way she had come, her strides growing smaller and smaller as she approached the enchanted area before the closed door of Donald Kirk's office. Finally, and by some miracle of chance precisely opposite the door, she came to a stop. Her cheeks tingling, she darted a glance over her shoulder at Mrs. Shane. That worthy dame, basking in the glow of acting a stout middle-aged Eros, was grinning broadly. So Miss Diversey smiled rather foolishly and put off all further pretense and knocked on the door.

James Osborne called: "Come in," in an absent tone and did not raise his pale face as Miss Diversey slipped with high-beating heart into the office. He was seated on a swivel-chair before a desk, working with silent concentration over a curious loose-leaf album with thick leaves faintly quadrilled and holding tiny rectangles of colored paper. He was a faded-looking man of forty-five, with nondescript sandy hair grizzled at the temples, a sharp beaten nose, and eyes imbedded in tired wrinkles. He worked over the bits of colored papers with unwavering attention, handling them with a small nickel tongs and the dexterity of long practice.

Miss Diversey coughed.

Osborne swung about, startled. "Why, Miss Diversey!" he exclaimed, dropping the tongs and scrambling to his feet. "Come in, come in. I'm dreadfully sorry—I was so absorbed . . ." A redness had come over his flat lined cheeks.

"You go right back to work," directed Miss Diversey. "I thought I'd look in, but since you're busy—"

"No. No, no, Miss Diversey, really. Sit down. I haven't seen you for two days. I suppose Dr. Kirk has been keeping you busy?"

Miss Diversey sat down, arranging her starched skirts primly. "Oh, we're used to that, Mr. Osborne. He's a little fussy, but he's really a grand old man."

"I quite agree. Quite," said Osborne. "A great scholar, Miss Diversey. He's contributed a good deal, you know, to philology in his day. A great scholar."

Miss Diversey murmured something. Osborne stood in an eager, sloped attitude. The room was very quiet and warm. It was more like a den than an office, fitted out by some sensitive hand. Soft glass curtains and brown velvet drapes shrouded the windows overlooking the setback court. Donald Kirk's desk was in a corner, heaped with books and albums. They both felt suddenly a sense of being alone with each other.

"Working on those old stamps again, I see," said Miss Diversey in a strained voice.

"Yes. Yes, indeed."

"Whatever you men see in collecting postage stamps! Don't you feel silly sometimes, Mr. Osborne? Grown men! Why, I've always thought only boys went in for that sort of thing."

"Oh, really no," protested Osborne. "Most laymen think that about philately. And yet it absorbs the attention of millions of people all over the world. It's a universal hobby, Miss Diversey. Do you know there's one stamp in existence which is catalogued at fifty thousand dollars?"

Miss Diversey's eyes grew round. "No!"

"I mean it. A bit of paper so messy you wouldn't give it another look. I've seen photographs of it." Osborne's faded eyes glowed. "From British Guiana. It's the only one of its kind in the world, you know. It's in the collection of the late Arthur Hind, of Rochester. King George needs it to complete his collection of British colonies—"

"You mean," gasped Miss Diversey, "King George is a *stamp-collector*?"

"Yes, indeed. Many great men are. Mr. Roosevelt, the Agha Khan—"

"Imagine that!"

"Now, you take Mr. Kirk. Donald Kirk, I mean. Now, he has one of the finest collections of Chinese stamps in the world. Specializes, you know. Mr. Macgowan collects locals—local posts, you know; stamps which were issued by states or communities for local postage before there was a national postage system."

Miss Diversey sighed. "It's certainly very interesting. Mr. Kirk collects other things, too, doesn't he?"

"Oh, yes. Precious stones. I haven't much to do with that, you see. He keeps that collection in a bank-vault. I devote most of my time to keeping the stamp collection in apple-pie order, and doing confidential work for Mr. Kirk in connection with The Mandarin Press."

"Isn't that interesting, now!"

"Isn't it?"

"It's certainly very interesting," said Miss Diversey again. How on earth, she thought fiercely, did we ever get to talk about *these* things? "I read a book once published by The Mandarin."

"Did you, really?"

"*Death of a Rebel*, by some outlandish name."

"Oh! Merejinski. He was one of Felix Berne's discoveries—a Russian. He's always scouting around in Europe, you know, looking for foreign authors—Mr. Berne, I mean. Well." Osborne fell silent.

"Well," said Miss Diversey. And she fell silent.

Osborne fingered his chin. Miss Diversey fingered her hair.

"Well," said Miss Diversey a little nervously. "They do publish the artiest books, don't they?"

"Indeed they do!" cried Osborne. "I don't doubt Mr. Berne's come back with a trunkful of new manuscripts. He always does."

"Does he, now." Miss Diversey sighed; it was getting worse, much worse. Osborne regarded her crisp cleanness with admiring eyes—admiring and respectful. Then Miss Diversey brightened. "I don't suppose Mr. Berne knows about Miss Temple, does he?"

"Eh?" Osborne started. "Oh, Miss Temple. Well, I suppose Mr. Kirk's written him about her new book. Very nice, Miss Temple is."

"Do you think so? I think so, too." Miss Diversey's broad shoulders quivered. "Well!"

"You're not going so soon?" asked Osborne in a dashed voice.

"Well, really," murmured Miss Diversey, rising, "I must. Dr. Kirk's probably in a fit by now. All that exertion! Well . . . It's been very pleasant talking to you, Mr. Osborne." She moved toward the door.

Osborne swallowed. "Uh—Miss Diversey." He took a timid step toward her and, in alarm, she retreated, breathing very fast.

"Why, Mr. Osborne! What—what—?"

"Could you—would you—I mean, are you—"

"What, Mr. Osborne?" murmured Miss Diversey archly.

"Are you doing anything tonight?"

"Oh," said Miss Diversey. "Why, I guess not, Mr. Osborne."

"Then would you—go to the movies with me tonight?"

"Oh," said Miss Diversey again. "I'd love to."

"The new Barrymore picture's playing at Radio City," said Osborne eagerly. "I hear it's very good. It got four stars."

"John or Lionel?" demanded Miss Diversey, frowning.

Osborne looked surprised. "John."

"Well, I should say I'd love to!" exclaimed Miss Diversey. "I've always said John's my favorite. I like Lionel, too, but John . . ." She raised her eyes ceiling-ward in a sort of ecstasy.

"I don't know," muttered Osborne. "It seems to me in his last few pictures he's looked rather old. Time will tell, you know, Miss Diversey."

"Why, *Mr.* Osborne!" said Miss Diversey. "I do believe you're jealous!"

"Jealous? Me? Pshaw—"

"Well, I think he's simply divine," said Miss Diversey with cunning. "And it's wonderful of you to take me to see him, Mr. Osborne. I know I'll have the most thrilling time."

"Thank you," said Osborne glumly. "I meant to ask you . . .

Well, that's fine, that's fine, Miss Diversey. It's about a quarter to six now—"

"Five-forty-three," said Miss Diversey mechanically, consulting her wrist-watch with professional swiftness. "Shall we say," her voice lowered and became intimate, "a quarter to eight?"

"That's fine," breathed Osborne. Their eyes touched, and both quickly looked away. Miss Diversey felt a sudden surge of warmth beneath the starched apron. Her blunt fingers began to search her hair mechanically.

Mr. Ellery Queen was wont to point out in confidentially retrospective moments that not the least remarkable feature of the affair was the subtle manner in which the dead man's very lack of existence impinged upon the unexciting little lives of little people. At one moment all was commonplace. Miss Diversey trifled with herself and Mr. Osborne's heart in Kirk's hide-away office. Donald Kirk was off somewhere. Jo Temple was dressing in a new black gown in one of the guest-rooms of the Kirk suite. Dr. Kirk's thorny nose was buried in a Fourteenth Century rabbinical manuscript. Hubbell was in Kirk's room laying out his master's evening kit. Glenn Macgowan was striding fast up Broadway. Felix Berne was kissing a foreign-looking woman in his bachelor apartment in the East Sixties. Irene Llewes was regarding her very admirable nude figure in her bedroom mirror in the Chancellor.

And Mrs. Shane, who a few moments before had played Cupid, was suddenly called upon to play a new role—Prologue in The Tragedy of the Chinese Orange.

Continued in *The Chinese Orange Mystery*...